Gallantry in Action
(Book 1 of the Jonah Halberd Series)

John J. Spearman

DEDICATION

For Alicia, who has made my life so great in every way.

OTHER BOOKS BY THIS AUTHOR

Halberd Series

In Harm's Way
True Allegiance
Surrender Demand

Pike Series
Pike's Potential
Pike's Passage

FitzDuncan Series
FitzDuncan
FitzDuncan's Alchemy

ACKNOWLEDGMENTS

I'd like to acknowledge my readers. They are the whole reason to do this.

1

"Captain, we have detected hyperspace emergence approximately 8.7 light minutes aft and 37 degrees above the elliptical," Petty Officer Sanchez, manning the sensors, barked.

Captain Jonah Halberd turned to the ship's second officer, Lieutenant Commander Alexandra Volkov, and ordered, "Sound general quarters."

Immediately, warning klaxons began blaring and red lights flashing.

"Sensors, report," the captain asked.

"Computer has identified mass and emission profile as consistent with a *Putin*-class cruiser, sir. It's accelerating on an intercept course."

"Mr. Volkov," the captain inquired, "how long until he reaches missile range at present course and acceleration?"

"Um, one moment, captain," Volkov replied as she struggled to pull her ship suit over her uniform. Part of coming to general quarters was the necessity of everyone putting on ship suits with the hoods in place. The hoods on the suits would automatically extend a clear membrane to cover the face in the event of a hull breach and the exposure to the vacuum of space that would result. Equipped with a rebreather and heating element, the suits could keep the wearer alive for a time but were rated to last only 30 minutes.

"Uh, I've got it now, sir. Approximately an hour and twenty-six minutes if he maintains current course and acceleration and we do not change our course."

"Comms," the captain ordered, "open a channel on standard hailing frequencies."

"Channel open, captain," the communications officer responded.

The captain turned to the camera on his console. "Attention, unidentified vessel. You have entered an area claimed by the Commonwealth of His Majesty Edward XII. Please state your intention and activate your IFF beacon. If you fail to do this, we will consider you a hostile intruder and respond accordingly."

That finished, Captain Halberd glanced at the running timer on his console, started when general quarters had been sounded. It had just passed the four-minute mark. He looked at Lieutenant Commander Volkov expectantly.

She noticed the captain's attention, and a look of despair flickered on her face. She was well aware of how much time had passed, and yet all stations had not yet reported manned and ready. Until that happened, the klaxons and warning lights would continue.

"Does there seem to be a problem, Mr. Volkov?" the captain asked calmly.

"Sir, the ship reports manned and ready except for the dorsal rail guns and starboard tube six," she responded.

"Is there a problem?" the captain asked again calmly.

"I don't know, sir. They haven't reported in," she answered.

"Why don't you ask them?" the captain inquired.

"Aye, aye, sir. Right away, sir."

"Starboard tube six, respond," she barked on the comm.

"Jeezus Volkov," came a slurred voice, "don't get your panties in a twist. It's just another fuckin' drill."

Volkov responded, more calmly than she felt, "Petty Officer Smyth, is starboard tube 6 at general quarters?"

"Fuck general quarters," came the obviously drunk response, "and fuck you too, you tight-ass bitch."

Two red spots grew on Lieutenant Commander Volkov's cheeks, but she calmly keyed another button on the comm and stated, "Security, send two men to starboard tube six, take Petty Officer Smyth into custody and escort him to the brig. Confirm when this is done."

Keying another button on the comm, she asked, "Dorsal railguns, report."

Hearing no answer, she keyed the comm again. "Fire control, dorsal rail guns have not responded to general quarters. Determine their status."

She then cocked her head slightly, a nervous tic many people had when receiving messages via earbud. She looked to the captain. "Sir, security has PO Smyth in custody. I'm putting Gunner's Mate DiPerna in charge of Starboard 6."

Without waiting for any reaction from the captain, she keyed the comm. "Gunner's Mate DiPerna?"

"Aye, aye, Lieutenant Commander Volkov," he responded briskly.

"DiPerna, you are in charge of Starboard Six until further notice. Carry on."

"Aye, aye, sir."

Again, she cocked her head slightly. Reporting to the captain, she relayed,

"Dorsal railguns are down, captain. Engineering pulled the computer drive for maintenance. They estimate they can have them back up in 40 minutes."

With that, she pressed a button, and the flashing red lights and klaxons stopped. Wincing inwardly, she glanced to see if there was any reaction on the captain's face. Seeing none, she asked, "Sensors—any change in bogey's course or acceleration?"

"Negative, sir."

"Comms, any response to our hail?"

"Negative, sir. None expected for another 12 to 15 minutes."

Turning to the captain, she stated, "Sir, the ship reports manned and ready at general quarters with the exception of the dorsal rail guns, which are down for engineering maintenance. We have an unidentified bogey on an intercept course with an estimated one hour and seventeen minutes to missile range. Mass and emissions profile fit the description of a *Putin*-class cruiser. They have not yet responded to our hail."

"Very well, Mr. Volkov. Cancel the drill and have the men stand down from general quarters. I want all officers to meet in the wardroom at 14:00."

"Aye, aye, sir," she responded glumly. This drill had been a disaster, and she knew it. The seven others they had conducted since departing Southhampton Station less than two days earlier had not been any better. She tried reading the captain's expression, but it did not show anger or frustration. She was both angry and frustrated with the poor response of the crew to these drills and knew she was not doing as good a job of masking it as the captain.

Captain Halberd rose from the command chair and returned to his quarters. Once inside, he looked at his tablet, summarizing the results of the eight drills they had conducted over the last 48 hours. None of them had been acceptable. He found this aspect of taking over a new command to be the most strenuous but knew that hard work and high standards now would pay huge dividends in the future.

He shook his head. It was only five days ago that he was sitting in an outer office at the Admiralty, waiting for the meeting to which he had been summoned early in the new year. He had arrived five minutes early, as he had been taught eleven years before at the naval academy. His appointment was for 15:00 local, and precisely on the hour, the yeoman turned to Jonah and told him, "Vice Admiral von Geisler will see you now."

Jonah nodded his thanks to the yeoman, opened the door, and strode inside. Stopping three paces in front of the desk, he came to attention and snapped a salute.

"Commander Halberd reporting as ordered, sir," he stated formally. The gray-haired man behind the desk returned the salute.

"At ease," he responded, standing up with arm outstretched in greeting. "It's good to see you again, Jonah," he remarked.

Shaking his hand, Jonah replied, "It's good to see you again too, sir."

The admiral waved him over to the sitting area. "I'm sorry we could only give you three weeks' leave, Jonah. God knows you deserve more of a break, but there *is* a war on," he said, sitting down.

Jonah replied noncommittally, "I understand, sir."

"Good," the admiral smiled. "You had quite an exciting tour on the *Essex* last time out. Your report was one of the more interesting I've had the pleasure of reading recently."

"Thank you, sir. I had a good crew and my fair share of good fortune," Jonah replied modestly.

"Good captains make good crews and make their own luck to a certain extent, Jonah. Unfortunately, no good deed goes unpunished, and your success has earned you an even bigger challenge."

"Sir?"

"You won't be returning to *Essex*, Jonah. She'll be another ten weeks in the yard, fixing all the holes you put in her. We can't afford to have good officers and crew sit idle that long, so you've all been reassigned."

Jonah felt his heart sink. He had been hoping to return to HMS *Essex* and her crew. They had developed into a great team, and he had loved being captain of the frigate. She was a yar ship, quick, nimble, responsive. Though he tried to remain impassive, Admiral von Geisler noticed his disappointment.

Smiling ruefully, the admiral continued softly, "I remember my time commanding a frigate, too, Jonah. When I was given a new ship, I thought I would never be able to love a ship as much as I did the *Hebrus*. Fortunately," he chuckled, "I was wrong. You'll find you have a special place in your heart for all your commands. Perhaps this might help soften the blow."

The admiral handed over a small box of navy blue with gold trim. Jonah opened it and looked down at the two gold stars inside.

"Congratulations, *captain*," said the admiral.

Stunned, Jonah had difficulty getting his mouth to work. "Thank you, sir," he blurted out finally.

"You've earned them, Jonah. Now, as I was saying, Captain Halberd, I hope you find a special place in your heart for all your commands. And it's time you started to get to know your new ship."

At that moment, Jonah received notification of new files arriving on his comm unit. In a message from the Admiralty entitled HMS *Cumberland*, he was being sent encrypted files containing the ship specifications, high-level schematics, command codes, and personnel data. Though intensely curious, Jonah ignored his comm and turned his attention back to the admiral.

The admiral nodded to the wall, which had shifted to a view screen mode. It now displayed a large picture of the ship at the Southhampton Orbital Station. Jonah looked at it, puzzled.

"It's not one of ours, sir," he uttered doubtfully.

"No, it's not," the admiral replied easily. "It's German-built. It was only days away from being commissioned when the Rodinans captured the New Bremen system three years ago. We captured it from them nine months ago after the Battle at New Delhi. An old friend of yours, Commander Delhomme, managed to sneak a shot up her skirt and blow her EM drives. She was dead in the water and surrendered once the rest of the Rodinan fleet jumped out. Other than the blown drives, she didn't have a scratch on her. Her captain was bloody upset, let me tell you."

Jonah chuckled. "Well, Pierre always did have a knack of upsetting people he didn't like. How is he doing?"

"Commander, er, Captain Delhomme is doing well," the admiral answered. "Nearly as well as you, and like you, was given a well-deserved promotion and a larger command. He didn't like leaving *Iphigenia* any more than you like leaving *Essex*. He's now in Roosevelt, in Third Fleet under Admiral Lord Johannsen."

"Well, if he can do it—" Jonah offered.

"That's the spirit," von Geisler responded. "Let me tell you a little more about the *Cumberland*. While it's only a little bit larger than our *County*-class heavy cruiser, it has about fifteen percent greater mass. This is due to a thicker layer of the new AT-38 alloy armor which is both reflective and ablative. Its EM drives are larger than our standard *County* class and more than compensate for the larger mass. Its acceleration curve is better than any other heavy cruiser in the fleet."

"That sounds good, sir, but I sense a 'but' coming," Jonah said.

"Well, it does seem a little less maneuverable, according to what the trials showed," the admiral admitted. "That's due to the extra mass. It has two more missile tubes directly forward than a *County* and the same number of broadside tubes. It has the same number of photon cannons in roughly the same locations, and point defense is similar, with one exception."

"Am I going to like this exception?" Jonah asked.

"Well, the boffins at Advanced Warfare think so," the admiral grinned. "The Germans included rail guns in the design, something we haven't done for nearly 100 years."

"The development of effective shielding made rail guns obsolete," Jonah chimed in. "I don't see how they'll be much use."

"Yes, for ship-to-ship combat," the admiral explained, "but nevertheless, the Germans put four twin-rail batteries in, two above and two below. The spods at AW learned that the Germans planned to tie them into the point defense network—something the Rodinans never figured out in the time they had her. AW developed flak cartridges for them based on the original German design. Imagine a barrel of ball-bearings, which explode on a signal from your point defense system."

Jonah immediately grasped the concept. "That's brilliant!" he exclaimed. "And you could also use them to launch chaff cartridges."

"Chaff cartridges," the admiral smiled, "are also part of their capability. Jonah, you've shown an ability to improvise and find unique solutions. It's why I pushed for you to be given command of the *Cumberland*. I think you will show us some things she can do that no one has thought of yet."

"What about my crew, sir?"

"Sorry to say that's another of the 'buts'," the admiral admitted. "Your mates from *Essex* have been reassigned already, so you'll be starting with a new crew, 75 of whom just came out of basic training. You have a mostly solid group of petty officers to help get them up to snuff. Your officers are a mixed lot, I'm afraid. Some with potential, but some who were available because they were no longer wanted on their previous ships. One or two of the petty officers also fall into this group.

"One last piece of bad news," the admiral continued. "You're now assigned to Second Fleet. You'll be reporting to Rear Admiral Rodriguez at Hercules Station for your duty assignment as part of her task force. I hate to lose you from Fifth Fleet but think you will enjoy working with Sonia Rodriguez. She's sharp, and I've always enjoyed my interaction with her."

Pulling his mind back to the present, Jonah thought to himself that at least Petty Officer Smyth had shown his true colors quickly. He'd be busted down to Able Seaman and spend a few weeks in the brig unless Jonah found a way to get him off the ship at their next stop. They were due in at Hercules Station in another eleven days.

Jonah considered the actions of Lieutenant Commander Volkov. While she had been rattled early on, she had recovered quickly and had dealt with Smyth decisively. He could read the disappointment on her face that the ship had not responded better while she was the officer of the deck. He much preferred disappointment to shoulder-shrugging complacency.

One thing that was handicapping them was that they had sailed without a master chief petty officer. Apparently, their master chief would be waiting for them at Hercules Station, but BuPers had not released his or her name yet. From experience, Jonah knew the value of a good MCPO. He had been blessed on his last two commands with one he trusted completely, but Master Chief Bradshaw had been reassigned when they broke up the crew from *Essex*.

He sighed and looked at his notes on the tablet. It had taken over nine minutes to secure general quarters. The navy standard was two minutes, but every ship he had been on, even as an ensign, had been able to come to general quarters in 90 seconds. The attitude displayed by Petty Officer Smyth was present in quite a bit of the crew and some of the officers. Pulling experienced crew from other ships was supposed to be a way of giving opportunities to promising personnel, but many captains used it as an easy way of getting rid of underperforming people. It was easier to "pass the trash" than to go through the navy's formal process of progressive discipline.

The Smyth incident had slowed the response, as did the railguns being offline. He knew he would have to dig into Smyth's behavior and find out if his insubordination was general or he targeted Volkov specifically. Volkov had come through the ROTC conduit and had earned positive marks since but had served entirely in staff positions. This was her first line assignment, and it showed. There was a certain hesitancy to her interactions with her subordinates that came from her unfamiliarity.

The railguns being offline was no surprise to him. Engineering had asked his permission to work on them, and he had agreed, even though he knew it would interfere with the drill he had planned. Parts of the ship being offline due to repairs and maintenance was a fact of life. It did not always happen at convenient times.

A bigger problem was that the lieutenant in charge of the starboard missile tubes had not dealt with the problem on Tube 6 and their delay in reporting ready. It should not have been left to Volkov to deal with Smyth. In the same vein, engineering should have informed Volkov about the railguns instead of making her track down the information.

Fortunately, Jonah suspected he knew the answer why those things happened, as well as other problems he had observed in earlier drills. With a new crew that didn't know each other and a captain and officers who were also unknown, the easiest thing is to do nothing and let someone higher up make decisions. He also knew that it was no way to run a ship, and he intended to lead his officers to the same conclusion. By forcing responsibility down the chain of command, response time and efficiency improved in every situation.

Volkov was probably expecting a tongue lashing in the upcoming meeting, but Jonah had no intention of that. He thought this was an opportunity, a "teachable moment" as he had learned at the academy, and he intended to use it to show his officers how much more quickly and easily the problems would have been dealt with at the lowest possible level. Once they understood he was serious about this, he knew results would improve dramatically.

2

The soft chimes of the hyperspace transition warning sounded. "Thirty seconds to hyperspace emergence, captain," Lieutenant Kelley announced.

The captain sat in his command chair and nodded. This was the third jump they had made on the way to Hercules Station during their thirteen-day trip from Southhampton. His message to the officers after the incident with Petty Officer Smyth had helped. Knowing that their superiors were supposed to back them up, most of the lower-level officers had made good progress in smoothing things out. The crew had begun to start working together, but there was still an important piece missing.

At Hercules Station, they were supposed to pick up their master chief petty officer, who would be the highest-ranking enlisted man in the crew. Good master chiefs were worth their weight in gold. As of yet, Jonah had not heard from BuPers who they were taking on, which he thought was unusual. They were also going to be leaving Able Seaman Smyth, busted from petty officer, on the station for reassignment. Jonah had convinced BuPers that with one-third of his crew fresh out of training, keeping someone as troubled as Smyth on board would be a problem.

The hyperspace transition warning sounded again; the transition was imminent. Jonah felt the flip in his stomach that signaled they had crossed back into normal space and that the Alcubierre warp bubble had disappeared. As soon as he felt the transition, he ordered, "Shields up. Sensors hot. Comms raise Hercules on the kewpie."

The kewpie was the Quantum Particle Communications System, a way of transmitting signals instantaneously over infinite distances. As often happens, it had almost immediately been given a nickname based on its acronym. For generations, the system had been known as the kewpie. It enabled instantaneous communications regardless of distance but, like all other communications systems, would not operate in hyperspace, only in 'normal' space.

"Hercules Station acknowledges, captain, and welcomes us to the system. Traffic Control is monitoring our approach."

"Navigation," the captain asked, "ETA at Hercules?"

"A little over seventeen hours, captain. Flip point is eight hours and forty-one minutes out."

The HMS *Cumberland* was traveling at $0.23c$ or 23 percent of the speed of light. This was the speed at which it had entered hyperspace, and there was no loss of normal velocity due to hyperspace transition. The maximum speed that men had been able to reach in normal space was $0.3c$. Beyond that speed, the mass compensators would overload. If that happened, the relativistic mass of the ship would increase instantly with catastrophic results.

In hyperspace, surrounded by a warp bubble produced by the Alcubierre drives, the *Cumberland* traveled at many times the speed of light. Hyperspace travel was only possible in corridors of space that were free from dark matter. There were many star systems that had been bypassed during human settlement of space because there were no hyperspace corridors to them. Even so, 79 worlds had been colonized in the last 900 years. There were hundreds of times more planets that had been discovered, but the 79 planets colonized were those considered in the "Goldilocks zone." The "Goldilocks zone" was where gravity and atmosphere were similar to Earth and where there had been a relative absence of native flora and fauna. These planets were surrounded by heavy Van Allen belts, which prevented solar radiation from reaching them. Most had only simple single-cell organisms when they were found. Planets with more evolved life were usually passed over and kept under ecological observation.

At the point halfway to the station, they would "flip" or begin decelerating by firing the EM drive so that their speed when they arrived would be zero. The inertial dampeners would prevent the huge change in g-forces from turning his crew into smears of flesh on the bulkheads. Without the dampeners, the forces of gravity due to deceleration would be hundreds of times higher.

With contact established with Hercules Station, Jonah was not surprised when his console registered that new orders had been transmitted to him. He waited until the change of watch, then surrendered the bridge to his executive officer, Commander Renee Fung. Fung had impressed him during the brief time they had worked together. He had looked at her files, and her credentials were solid. She had started on an engineering track and switched to command after graduating from the academy. While she had apparently been a brilliant engineer, her personality did not match the introverted stereotype that most engineers either had by nature or developed as a result of the job. She was tall, just under 180 centimeters, and strikingly attractive, a blend of Chinese and European ancestry. She just came from a tour commanding a patrol boat, and her command experience showed in her bearing. Like Jonah, she projected a personality of approachable authority without encouraging too much familiarity. From what little Jonah had seen, she belonged in the command track.

When Jonah returned to his quarters, he accessed the secure files from the ship's system that had been sent over the kewpie when they contacted Hercules Station. He was to report to Rear Admiral Rodriguez when they arrived to receive detailed orders concerning their assignment in the sector.

Though they could have tied the systems of the *Cumberland* to Hercules Station's traffic control system, Jonah wanted his officers to gain necessary experience in ship handling. The officer on deck was again Lieutenant Commander Volkov, and Jonah wanted to see how she would do. It was a perfectly safe trial, as traffic control would override the ship's systems if there were any danger, but that was something Volkov would do her best to avoid. He watched as Volkov brought the ship in carefully, over-correcting slightly at one point but immediately noticing the error and adjusting. When she was finished, the ship had come to a dead stop opposite their assigned berth, just 1.3 meters off from the specified (but rarely attained) 100-meter distance at which the station's tractor beams would pull the ship in. When Jonah complimented her on a good job, she smiled, and he could see the tension leave her shoulders.

A few minutes later, the ship had been pulled in, gangways extended, and conduits for power, water, and air established. Jonah texted the admiral's office, notifying them of their arrival, and was instructed to bring his XO and report to the admiral for a briefing on their new orders.

Jonah commed Commander Fung and told her, "Commander, the pleasure of our company is requested by the admiral."

He stood and turned to Volkov, saying, "You have the ship, lieutenant commander. The XO and I have been invited to meet with the admiral. I do not know how long we will be at the station, so do not allow liberty until you hear back from the XO or me."

"Aye, aye, sir," she responded.

The captain turned and left the bridge, heading for the lift. He dropped three levels and turned down the corridor to the gangway hatch. Commander Fung was waiting for him. He nodded and they continued to the hatch. He had taken only two strides when he stopped abruptly. A gray-haired block of a man, wearing master chief's stripes, was handing his data card to the marine sentry and asking for permission to come aboard. When the master chief saw the captain, he straightened instantly and snapped a salute. "Master Chief Bradshaw reporting for duty. Permission to come aboard, Captain Halberd?"

"Permission granted. And may I say you're a sight for sore eyes, master chief."

"Well, sir," the master chief responded with a smile, "I heard about your promotion and this new ship of yours and figured you're probably in over your head again. So BuPers sent me here to save your butt again."

The two men clasped hands, warm smiles on both their faces. Jonah turned to his executive officer and introduced her. "Commander Fung, Master Chief Bradshaw."

He turned back to Bradshaw. "Tom, I am delighted to see you, but we have an appointment with the admiral. The three of us should meet when we return."

"Aye, aye, sir," Bradshaw answered.

Jonah and Fung walked down the gangway towards the station. Along the way, Fung asked, "Have you known the master chief long, sir?"

"Yes, I have, commander. A little over ten years."

"How did you meet? Did you serve together?"

"Not at first. The master chief was then just an engineering mate on a civilian freighter that had been captured by brigands. They had killed everyone else on his ship but kept him alive and brought him to their ship because they wanted him to tune their drives. He had been on their ship for weeks, waiting for an opportunity. They finally left him alone, and he sabotaged the engines—right out of hyperspace. I was a freshly-minted lieutenant only two years out of the academy on board the light cruiser *Dauntless*, and this ship dropped out of hyper right under our guns. It was a fairly small fast freighter, with beefed-up drives and more armament than you've ever seen on such a little ship.

"They were at a dead stop, well within range of our photon cannons. Our captain was drunk in his cabin, but the XO called for them to surrender, and they did. It was a small crew, a dozen men, and we took them on board *Dauntless*. We found Bradshaw locked in the head, looking worse for the wear. We asked him if he would help us repair the drive since the equipment had been heavily modified and our engineers would have taken forever to sort it out. He agreed. I was sent over in command of the prize crew to fix the drives and get the ship back to port. There were only six of us, plus Bradshaw.

"Without waiting to see if we could actually fix the drive, *Dauntless* pulled out."

"You're kidding," Fung stated. "That's totally against regs."

"Hell, even a wet-behind-the-ears lieutenant knew that, but it's a part of a longer and less interesting story," the captain explained.

"Anyway, a couple of hours later, Bradshaw fixed the drive. We started off on what should have been a three-jump, eight-day trip back to Aries Station. Next thing I know, I wake up with a massive headache, locked in the head with him. Two of the bad guys had hidden in a special compartment that spoofed our sensors and came back out when we were underway. They killed the other crewmen on board. They kept me alive because I was an officer, to use as a bargaining chip in case they needed it, but they were going to space me as soon as we cleared the Commonwealth. They kept Bradshaw alive in case the engines had more trouble, not realizing he had sabotaged them in the first place.

"Bradshaw and I knew we had to do something fast. I shouted for help and told them Bradshaw had passed out, and I was afraid it was a skull fracture—that he might die. When they unlocked the door, we rushed them. Bradshaw killed one by stabbing him in the eye with a pair of scissors from the first aid kit, and I bashed the other one in the head with the toilet seat. We managed to get back to Aries Station without further difficulty. When we arrived, Bradshaw enlisted in the service. He didn't have any family and he said he'd better enlist if only to keep my sorry ass alive.

"My next ship was HMS *Surprise*. I was the sixth officer on the ship. It was sort of a step back, which is related to the *Dauntless'* captain, but again—a story for another time. I hadn't seen Bradshaw for months since he'd enlisted. About three months after I joined the ship, there he was in engineering.

"I have no idea how he does it—there must be some secret cabal for enlisted at BuPers—but he has followed me on every posting since. We keep moving up in rank together, though he's been a little ahead of me. When I made commander, I was given *Essex*, but he showed up within days already a master chief. After two tours on *Essex*, they just promoted me to captain and gave me *Cumberland*. When I reported to *Cumberland*, and he wasn't on board, I figured that he had finally run out of juice with BuPers. When they told me that we would pick up our new master chief here, I gave up hope since I'd last seen him back at Southhampton."

"That's a pretty amazing story, captain," Fung remarked.

Jonah chuckled. "You don't know the half of it. I've learned an awful lot from that man."

3

Jonah's story had taken them from the gangway to the doors of the Admiralty. They walked inside and were directed to the lifts. They went up five floors and down the hall to Rear Admiral Rodriguez' office. They presented themselves to the yeoman outside her door and sat down to wait. After a few minutes, the yeoman nodded, receiving a message on his screen, and told them to enter.

Fung and Jonah strode into the room, stopped in front of the admiral's desk, and saluted. The admiral rose from her chair and returned the salute, and asked them to sit. She clicked a button on her desk, and the wall to their right changed appearance and now showed a three-dimensional map of this sector of space.

"As you know, the last large-scale action in the ongoing war with the Rodinan Federation was nine months ago, at the Battle of New Delhi. Since then, other than some raids initiated by plucky frigate commanders," she said, staring meaningfully at Jonah, "things have been pretty quiet. The diplomats have made some efforts to iron things out but haven't made much progress. Out here, we continue to try to enforce the blockade and keep an eye on them.

"Your assignment is going to be here, in an unsettled system known by the romantic name of H2813." As she spoke, she manipulated the map on the wall. "H2813 has a K-class star with a couple of rocky planets and an asteroid belt. The inner planet is too close and the outer too far to support human life. The asteroid belt is in between, and there are a handful of rock rats trying to make a living. The primary importance of H2813 is that it has a hyperspace corridor to the Rodinan Venera system and a corridor here to Hercules, although the transit time from here to H2813 is just over three days making it the longest corridor in the sector. It has two other corridors: one back into Rodinan space and the other into Chinese space.

"This is really an assignment more suitable for a frigate," the admiral stated, "but you know what they say in the Royal Navy—"

"Never enough frigates," Fung and Jonah replied in unison with the admiral.

The admiral smiled. "So, I don't have enough frigates. The frigates I do have are watching other corridors to other Rodinan systems. What I do have is a heavy cruiser that just arrived out of the blue. I don't really need a heavy cruiser, but one just landed in my lap. Turns out this ship has an acceleration curve almost as nice as a frigate and a captain who probably remembers what it was like to command a frigate since he was doing it until a few weeks ago.

"So, Captain Halberd," she summed up, "that's your assignment. Oh, and I need you there yesterday."

"If you can give us some help with supply," Jonah said. "We need to stock the pantry since my recollection of blockade duty is that it always lasts longer than planned. We'll need to load out on missiles since we were ordered to travel light. We'll do the usual horse-trading for spare parts and top off the fuel tanks. We should be ready to pull out in—" he looked to Commander Fung since most of these were her responsibility as executive officer.

"Twenty-four hours," Fung answered confidently. "Less if your supply people don't engage in the usual nonsense."

"I'll send my flag lieutenant down to look over their shoulders," Rodriguez offered. "That should guarantee that the monkey business will be kept to a minimum."

"Thank you, sir," Fung said. "That will help a lot."

With that, the meeting ended. The officers exchanged pleasantries, and Jonah and Fung withdrew, heading back to the ship. On the way, Fung contacted the admiral's flag lieutenant, only to find that he had already contacted supply and was planning on meeting her there. She contacted the ship's supply officer and ordered him to meet them. Jonah watched her, coolly efficient as she addressed the task. Halfway back to the ship, she peeled off to head to supply, and he continued back to *Cumberland*.

Master Chief Bradshaw wasted no time in asserting himself once he arrived. As soon as he dropped his gear in his bunk, he called a meeting of all the petty officers on *Cumberland*. He had already studied their files while waiting for the ship to arrive and had a good idea of what to expect. He had checked up particularly on those he thought would be trouble. He was not at all surprised that Smyth had already shown his true colors. There were a couple of others who had earned less-than-stellar reputations that he would be keeping a close eye on.

When the group assembled, he introduced himself and asked them to do the same. He then explained, "I've had the privilege of serving under Captain Halberd on my last two tours and have known him for longer than that. His expectations, and mine, are simple: we want this ship and this crew to meet and then exceed their potential. The only way that can happen is for us, in this room, to make it happen. I've read all your files.

"What happened a couple of days ago with Smyth is unacceptable," he continued. "How many stills are currently operating on board?"

No one answered. Illegal alcohol distilling took place on every ship in the navy, but no one liked to admit it. Bradshaw scanned the group, all studiously avoiding his gaze.

"Bullshit," he thundered. "When I ask a question, I want a straight answer. How many stills?"

Petty Officer Gardella cleared his throat nervously. "I think there are three, master chief."

"'I think?' Or 'I know'?" Bradshaw demanded.

Gardella gulped. "I know of three, master chief. One in engineering, one in the shuttle bay and one in food service."

"Anyone else know of others?" Bradshaw asked.

Most members of the group shook their heads. Two glared at Bradshaw. Bradshaw glared right back.

"Fine," Bradshaw continued. "Shut down the ones in the shuttle bay and engineering. Keep the one in food service. They usually do the best job anyway."

Some of the group looked mildly surprised at his instruction. Bradshaw explained, "There's going to be one, no matter what regulations say. It's a fact of life in the navy. So, let's have it run by people who know what they're doing. But along with that, we need to make sure that every single member of this crew understands that being drunk on duty will land them in the brig, and if we're called to general quarters, they'd better swallow a sober pill before they pull on their ship suit. Got that?"

Murmurs came from the group along with nods.

"Next," Bradshaw added, "let's talk illegal substances. When we're done here, you will inform the crew that we will have a ship-wide inspection at 23:00 this evening. They have until then to dispose of anything. The inspection will be conducted by Fleet, and they have detailed schematics of the ship. There isn't a hiding place they won't find. If we have any addicts on board, they have until then to turn themselves in to medical personnel for the appropriate treatment. If they do not turn themselves in and we catch them, they will be put in the brig until we can get them to a navy treatment center. If any of you tries to cover up for any of them, you will be put in the cell right next to them.

"Third," Bradshaw said, "is bullying. I will not tolerate bullying or harassment on my ship. If I find that any of you is using your rank or position to threaten, intimidate or otherwise influence members of this crew, you will face the most serious consequences the regulations will allow. None of you are to tolerate it either. Is that understood?"

Most of the group mumbled in acquiescence, but again, two looked defiantly at Bradshaw. "Sumner and Jadovich," Bradshaw noted to himself, "as expected."

"Finally," Bradshaw stated, "be on the lookout for better ways to get things done. We won't cut corners, but if you or one of your people come up with a better, faster, cheaper way of getting something done, air it out. This is a German-built ship, so some things might not be in familiar places. What worked on your last ship might not be the best way to do it on *Cumberland*. Any questions? No? Fine, report back here at 22:50 prior to the inspection."

4

The inspection of the ship had uncovered two caches of illegal drugs, and two crewmen were left behind to be sent to a rehab center. They made the trip to H2813 without incident. Once there, they settled in on blockade duty. Jonah and other veterans of blockade duty knew that it consisted of days and weeks of boredom, occasionally spiced with some excitement if an attempt was made to break out. Upon entering the system, they did a full scan, looking for any sign of Rodinan presence, but so far, the only inhabitants of the entire system were five small asteroid mining operations.

Cumberland contacted the asteroid miners, commonly known as rockrats, as a courtesy, but Jonah's experience with asteroid miners told him that asking if they'd seen any Rodinan presence in the system would be a waste of time. Miners typically didn't spend money on long-range scanners, so wouldn't have seen anything worth reporting. Like old earth moles, he thought, focused on the digging right in front of them.

A day after entering the system, Jonah summoned the junior officers to the wardroom. In addition to Lieutenant Volkov were Lieutenants Kelley, Dietrich, and Blutarsky and Ensigns Lee and Sieber. Kelley had been the one who had failed to deal with Smyth when they shipped out and hadn't improved much since. He was almost 30—if he didn't make the promotion list this year, they'd muster him out of the service. Though he had seniority over the other lieutenants, Commander Fung had moved him lower and lower in the duty roster until only the ensigns were below him. Blutarsky was a maverick—a former enlisted man who had been sent to Officer Candidate School and commissioned. He'd been made available to *Cumberland*, Jonah suspected because he was too blunt for his previous CO. Jonah appreciated bluntness. He believed he would get along with Blutarsky just fine.

Jonah had them all sit and then outlined a question for them. When he had been an ensign, fresh from the academy, his first captain, now admiral,

Von Geisler had conducted sessions like this. Jonah had learned a great deal from those sessions and had instituted them when he took his first command, the *Essex*.

"Gentlemen," Jonah began, "can you tell me why we are here in lovely system H2813, the garden spot of the sector?"

Ensign Sieber's hand shot up. "To enforce our blockade of the Rodinan Federation, sir."

"Just so, ensign," the captain affirmed. "Now, more important, how do we do our duty?"

Sieber was puzzled.

Jonah helped him out. "To enforce a blockade, we need to think first in terms of how we would try to elude a blockade?"

The group was quiet for a moment, then Volkov offered, "The only hyper corridor worthwhile for the Rodinans would be the one to Chinese space."

"True," the captain agreed. "So how would you try to run the blockade? What sort of ship would you use, what route would you take, what sort of countermeasures might you employ? I will leave you here for the duration of the shift. I would like you to develop at least two different possible solutions for how you would try to escape interdiction and reach the Chinese corridor or for a ship to leave the Chinese corridor and get to Venera. If you don't develop at least two solutions by the end of the shift, we will meet again tomorrow and continue working on this problem. If you develop your solutions before the end of the shift, buzz my comm and I'll return. Understood?"

The group nodded and murmured. As the captain was leaving, their conversation was already beginning as five of the six of them started to tackle the problem. He noticed Kelley just sort of sitting there. He returned to the bridge. Commander Fung was in the command chair. With all the junior officers in the wardroom, she was the only officer on the bridge. All the consoles were manned by enlisted personnel.

"Captain, may I ask what the 'exercise' is that you have all the junior officers working on? I shifted the watch schedules as you asked, but you didn't tell me why you needed them."

"Number one," Jonah said, "I'm glad you asked. I gave them a little problem to solve. I'm going to ask you and the ratings here," he nodded over his shoulder at the other two men and three women manning the bridge, "to work on the same problem."

He looked and noticed all the people on the bridge now looking at him intently. "This is not a race, not a contest," he explained. He then outlined the problem for them as he had for the officers and returned to his quarters.

Jonah had already puzzled over the problem himself and had developed two answers, one more likely to succeed than the other. He was open to the possibility that one of his crew might think of something he did not, but even if they didn't, they would have the chance to work together in solving the problem, and he felt that made the exercise valuable. He knew that under Fung's guidance that the solutions the ratings on the bridge developed would be as workable as those of the junior officers, and that would teach both groups an important lesson.

One of the most productive parts of being on blockade duty was the chance to continue to work the crew into shape. Master Chief Bradshaw made an immediate positive difference, sorting through matters on the lower decks. He had a knack for being present to observe the snarls and snags in the different departments. His debriefs with the officers and noncoms helped them sort out the problems they were having. For the most part, he worked with Commander Fung, adjusting watch schedules and assignments and implementing vigorous cross-training of the enlisted men. Though Bradshaw had only been aboard three days, the results were already starting to show. The last drill had the entire ship at general quarters in just over two minutes—a marked improvement.

A little bit more than three hours later, Jonah's comm buzzed, summoning him to the wardroom. Just before he reached it, Commander Fung called him and told him that the bridge crew had developed some solutions. Jonah entered the wardroom and saw the officers engaged in eager discussion. When they noticed him, they jumped to their feet and saluted. He returned their salute and said, "At ease."

He asked if they were ready to share their ideas with him, and they looked to Lieutenant Commander Volkov. She nodded and said, "Affirmative, sir."

"Let's go to the bridge then," Jonah asked. "I gave Commander Fung and the ratings the same problem, and they're ready too. You can use the tactical display on the bridge to help illustrate your ideas."

"Sir," Volkov asked, "who will go first?"

"How about we flip a coin for the honor?" Jonah suggested.

When they entered the bridge, Jonah saw the petty officers gathered in a group around the command chair, engaged in a lively discussion similar to what he had interrupted in the wardroom. They did not salute, as navy protocol did not require it on the bridge. Immediately they quieted and looked at the junior officers with a wary, competitive glance as they returned to their stations.

"Both groups finished at about the same time," Jonah explained, "so I thought we could use the bridge to go over their ideas. You can use the tactical display to illustrate your ideas if you want. Lieutenant Commander Volkov asked which group would go first, and I thought a coin toss would work. Is that acceptable?"

Seeing nods of agreement, Jonah produced a one-pound coin, with the picture of King Edward XII on one side and a griffin on the other. He indicated that Commander Fung should call it. He flipped it with his thumb, and Fung called, "Tails!" Jonah caught the coin and slapped it down on the back of his left hand, and showed it to everyone. "Tails it is. Commander, your group will show us their first solution, then the officers will have a turn."

Renee Fung nodded and began explaining. "The difficulty for a blockade runner is that the hyper corridor to Chinese space is on an arc 55 degrees from the Venera corridor, center to center. That's also a problem for *Cumberland*. Petty Officer Sanchez came up with our first idea." She nodded at Sanchez.

Sanchez began, shuffling his feet nervously at first. "We felt," he began, "that one approach to consider would be to rely on stealth as much as possible. The fusion cores on a normal freighter could, just barely, supply enough power to maintain a stealth envelope. They'd have to sacrifice all their shielding except navigational protection and wouldn't have the juice for much in the way of point defense either.

"The arc to get to or from the Chinese corridor is another problem. To maintain stealth, they'd have to use a ballistic approach because lighting up the drives can't be hidden. But the angle rules that out—unless they slingshot all the way around H2813." Sanchez used the tactical display to generate a holographic image of what he was describing. "If they waited until they were in the asteroid belt to do their course corrections, they'd have a good chance of masking their emissions, especially if they could keep their corrections to thrusters only. Of course, they might run into a rock, which would mean a more severe course correction that would be detectable, but their chances of that are less than 1 percent."

Jonah nodded in agreement. Looking at the junior officers, he noted, "Judging by the glum expressions on your faces, this is similar to one of your ideas?"

They looked at one another before Volkov replied, "Yes, sir."

"Great minds think alike, then," Jonah said affably. "Tell me then, what would this look like to us on *Cumberland*?"

The officers conferred briefly. This time Blutarsky responded, "We'd detect their emergence from hyperspace if they came out close to the normal exit. But if they were quick to get their stealth envelope up, like immediately upon transition, all we might see would be a sensor ghost if we were close enough to pick it up. If they exited the corridor a couple of light-hours early, we might not even get a sensor ghost, but the extra distance probably would require them to make a bigger course adjustment once they were in-system."

Jonah nodded in agreement. Turning back to the ratings, he asked, "If, before we had discussed this, you were on sensors and had a hyperspace detection alert with nothing more than a sensor ghost, what would you think?"

The ratings looked to Sanchez again. He shrugged his shoulders. "Before we talked about this here, if I'd had that happen, I'd just have figured the system got wonky, and I'd shut it down and reboot it."

Several of the ratings and junior officers nodded slightly at this.

"Officers, anything to add?"

Jonah was quite pleased when Volkov looked over at the ratings to see if they had a response before she answered. When Sanchez shook his head slightly, she replied, "Yes, sir. We had an additional thought on this approach."

"The asteroid belt is both a help and a danger for them, sir. While they would use it to mask detection of their course corrections, they'd have to be aware that the belt provides the ideal place for us to lay in wait. The reason is that they could leave the exit corridor at any time, giving us a huge area to try to cover if we tried to patrol the corridor mouth. The good news for *Cumberland* is that if they use a ballistic approach," she continued, "their vectors narrow as they approach H2813 if they want to hit the escape corridor safely.

"If we were trying to run the blockade, we'd probably send a stealthed recon drone into the system to see where a warship was. If the drone showed a warship patrolling the exit to the corridor, we'd just exit early, go to stealth and coast in from further out and take the chance on a bigger course adjustment later. It might take a little longer, but it would be almost impossible for a warship to detect. If we saw the warship entering the asteroid belt on our approach vector, we'd have to use a different approach."

Jonah saw the enlisted men nodding at this. "I see you agree," he remarked. "What do you think the chances are that the Rodinans already have that probe in place?"

Sanchez didn't wait for his comrades but blurted out, "One hundred percent. We figure it's already here."

The captain grinned. "I agree. So, officers, suppose I decide to take *Cumberland* and hide in the asteroid belt along the probable vector of a stealthed ship. Your probe alerts you to my presence there, though it can't pinpoint my location. What solution do you have for that?"

"Well, sir, we made a big assumption on this because we don't know how good the Rodinan probes are. We figured that they're probably no better than ours and maybe a little worse. Is that okay?" she asked.

Jonah considered it. "Fair enough," he agreed.

Volkov breathed, relieved. "Our recon probes don't work as well when they're in a stealth envelope. They don't last as long either, but that's a different problem. We're guessing that a stealthed probe would be able to tell them generally where our ship was and approximately how big it was. It wouldn't be able to read emissions signatures enough to identify which ship."

"Sounds like a fair assumption," Jonah admitted.

"Then our solution would be to use a fast freighter with beefed-up engines like pirates use, sir," Volkov stated, "especially if our drone told us that the ship in-system down in the asteroid belt was a cruiser, heavy or light, doesn't matter. We might even give it a try if it's a frigate."

"Probably would," murmured one of the enlisted men. The other ratings were nodding their heads at this remark, and Jonah knew both groups had come to the same conclusion.

"Explain your reasoning," Jonah requested.

"If *Cumberland* is lying in wait along the probable approach vector, tucked in behind a nice rock, it's going to have to climb all the way out of the gravity well to come get us. If we came out of the corridor at $0.23c$ and then accelerated as fast as we could—" Volkov explained.

"Balls to the wall," Blutarsky agreed.

Volkov picked up on the comment, "Balls to the wall, from one corridor to the other, it would take about 40 hours to traverse that chord. We'd get there with enough time to slam on the brakes and get back down to $0.23c$ before a heavy cruiser got within missile range, which we estimate would take about 44 hours at max acceleration. A frigate's max acceleration is quicker, right around 40 hours. We wouldn't have a chance to slow down and would have to enter the corridor at $0.3c$, but we'd be in missile range for at most a couple of minutes if the frigate moved as fast as it could. Entering a corridor hot like that is a little risky—"

"Yeah," Sanchez interrupted, "but if I'm a blockade runner, I'm already used to living a little risky."

"Exactly," Volkov agreed.

"Excellent," Jonah remarked. "You mentioned a frigate might cause you to reconsider. Any other ships?"

Sanchez and Volkov looked at one another for a moment, and both ended up shaking their heads. Sanchez offered, "Maybe a corvette, sir. A corvette would be able to climb out of the gravity well and catch a fast freighter, but the Commonwealth doesn't have any corvettes. One of our patrol boats could catch it, too. Anything bigger than a frigate would never catch it."

Nodding, Captain Halberd summed up, "The stealthed approach and the fast approach are the two best I came up with as well," Jonah admitted. "For tomorrow, I want your groups to come up with a way for us to catch them no matter what."

Sanchez and Volkov looked at each other inquiringly, then turned and whispered to their groups briefly. Then they turned back to one another and with a slight nod, Volkov indicated Sanchez should speak.

"Sir," he requested, "would you mind if we all worked on it together, and right now? I mean, we're all here already, and the juices are flowing."

"That's fine by me," Jonah agreed. "Though some of you are scheduled to go off watch here in a few minutes. If you don't mind staying past the end of your shift to work on this, I think that's a great idea."

Sanchez and Volkov looked at their people and got a couple of shrugs in response with slight smiles. Volkov answered, "Everyone wants to stay, sir."

"Then go ahead. If you don't mind, I'll take Commander Fung with me for a while," he asked. "Buzz me on the comm if you come up with something before the end of the next watch."

With Volkov's nod, Fung said, "Very well, you have the conn, Mr. Volkov," and left the bridge with the captain.

Once the hatch had shut behind them, Renee commented, "Interesting, captain. Would I be correct in guessing that what we just left behind was the result you hoped for?"

"You would," he chuckled. "Sometimes though, the enlisted men don't want to work with the officers if they think they can 'win.' If any of the officers don't want to work together, that's pretty obvious, too, and a sign that someone needs an attitude adjustment. But you're right; having them want to work together is what I hoped for."

"And having it be their own idea instead of being told to do it—" she added, raising her eyebrows.

"An extra added benefit," he grinned.

"Is this something you came up with on your own?" she asked.

"Heck, no," he admitted. "I was a lowly ensign, the ink on my diploma from the academy still drying. My first posting was to the frigate *Hebrus*, Commander Karl von Geisler."

"Vice Admiral von Geisler?" she asked.

"The very same," he affirmed. "This was what he did. As an ensign, I have to tell you I was thrilled and terrified to be included in those discussions. Boy, did I learn from those sessions! It was a good group of officers and men," he reminisced.

"I enjoyed it," Renee allowed. "The ratings didn't really need my help. At first, they kept turning to me for validation that they were on the right track, but then I started to pretend I was really busy with something, so they forged right ahead without 'interrupting' me."

"Perfect," Jonah said. By now, they had reached the officers' mess. "I'm getting a cup of coffee. Want anything?" he asked.

When she shook her head, he said, "I'll buzz you when they're done, and we can go see what they come up with. I'll be interested to see if it matches what you develop on your own."

5

Renee returned to her quarters, mulling over their discussion and Captain Halberd's approach. Though she had only met him a few days before, she had already observed he had a deft way of involving his subordinates. Though he was only slightly older than she was, he reminded her of some of her favorite instructors at the academy. She found herself looking forward to learning more from working with him.

Her last three postings had not given her much opportunity to learn from a mentor. Before *Cumberland,* she had commanded a patrol boat for ten months. While she had learned a lot from the experience, much of it had been trial and error as there had been no one to "show her the ropes." Before that, she had served under two captains who had been domineering in their manner—unimaginative micro-managers who gave their people no opportunity to think for themselves. Her performance had been satisfactory enough that she continued to be promoted, but she felt the only things she had learned were things to avoid.

The second of micro-managing captains had also subjected her to an unending stream of sexual innuendo and hints that Renee's performance review would be enhanced only by sleeping with her. Fortunately, Admiral von Geisler had plucked her from Third Fleet, despite the mediocre performance reviews she had been given, promoted her to lieutenant commander, and put her in command of the patrol boat.

For months, she had wondered how or why Admiral von Geisler had selected her. While on leave just before being assigned to *Cumberland,* she ran into a former shipmate under whom she had served when she was a lieutenant. He told her that Admiral von Geisler made a practice of asking his subordinates to identify for him any promising young officers. Someone had likely given her name to the admiral.

So far, she had seen that Captain Halberd made sure his expectations were clearly understood and performance was tracked and recorded. He left it to his officers to determine how to achieve those expectations. In debriefs of the many drills they had conducted, he led his people to figure out for themselves what went wrong and how to correct it, rather than dictating a specific solution. He held his people accountable but did not peer over their shoulders.

She had seen the same approach from Master Chief Bradshaw since he had joined the ship and had asked him about it. Bradshaw had shrugged. "If you treat folks like grown-ups, they tend to act like grown-ups. If you treat 'em like little kids, then they'll act like little kids."

Renee had never heard a management philosophy expressed so succinctly. For those members of the crew who were used to a more autocratic command structure, this was new. It would take some time to train them to think and act on their own initiative, but she could see the process beginning. She found it refreshing.

It was nearly the end of the next four-hour watch by the time the group on the bridge contacted the captain. He buzzed Renee, and the two of them went to the bridge. When they entered, he noticed that the group was mingled together with no clear separation between the enlisted men and the officers, though Lieutenant Kelley seemed to be just a bit outside the rest of the group's periphery. Jonah shrugged it off, attributing it to his being a little too critical of Kelley.

"Okay," Jonah said, "What have you come up with?"

Expecting either Volkov or Sanchez to be the spokesperson, Jonah was mildly surprised when Blutarsky began to speak. "Cap'n," he began, "we came up with the basic ideas right away, but we needed to get some input from other folks to see if our ideas could work. Lieutenant Commander Patel in engineering and Master Chief Bradshaw helped us a lot, sir."

"Go on."

"Well, it starts out real simple, sir, but then it gets complicated right quick. If we position *Cumberland* to catch the stealthed freighter, down in the asteroid belt, then we give 'em an opening to get a fast 'un through. If we station *Cumberland* to be able to cut off the fast 'un, that gives 'em a chance to slip a stealthed ship through. And then Marie, uh, Petty Officer Delnicki, said that if she were running the show for 'em, she'd do both."

"Both?"

"Yessir," Blutarsky continued, "She said what's to stop the Rodinans from sending a fast 'un from their corridor to pull us away while the Chinese send a stealthy 'un through. The fast 'un would come in hot like we talked about until *Cumberland* pulled up to missile range, then they'd probably surrender an empty ship. Meanwhile, old stealthy would just slip on by. It's no risk to the Chinese, sir. They're just out a little bit of fuel. If we wait for 'em in the belt, soon as we light 'em up with the sensors, they'll turn on their

IFF and make a diplomatic incident out of it. We couldn't take it as a prize because the Interstellar Court would make the Commonwealth give it back to 'em. All we could do is remove any cargo on the contraband list.

"They could try the same thing in reverse, too, Cap'n. The Rodinans could send a stealthy one and delay just a smidgen in pulling up the stealth envelope, so we'd see it, and then either chase it if we were out in the system or wait for it if we were hiding in the belt, then send a fast 'un through from the Chinese side once we were committed." As he was describing these scenarios, he was expertly manipulating the tactical display to illustrate what he was saying.

"I think Petty Officer Delnicki identified pretty accurately what we'll be facing," Jonah acknowledged. "What did you come up with to solve this dilemma?"

"The problem is that *Cumberland* can't be in two places at the same time," Blutarsky explained. "But then Ensign Sieber figured out a way that maybe we could."

Jonah turned to the ensign. The young man's face was flushed with nervous energy. Jonah knew his palms were probably sweating, and his mouth had probably never felt so dry as it did for him now.

Sieber began, "When Petty Officer Delnicki was explaining how she'd use the one ship as a decoy to pull us out of position and then get the other past us, it gave me an idea that we could try the same thing on them. Which tactic they use will be due to where they think we are. The stealthed recon drone we think they've already put in place can tell them that, but its performance is degraded due to being in the stealth envelope. I thought that maybe we could spoof the drone, sir."

Jonah was intrigued. "Go on," he said.

"We contacted Lieutenant Commander Patel down in engineering to see if he could tune the EM drive on the Marine Assault Shuttle to make it look like a bigger ship. Petty Officer Wallis and Lieutenant Dietrich were pretty sure they could reprogram an ECM transmitter to fool the drone into thinking the MAS was much bigger. It took a while to see if it would work, and it does, almost."

"Almost?" Jonah asked.

"Lieutenant Commander Patel was able to figure out a way to make the shuttle engines throw off enough emission to make it seem pretty close to what a *County*-class cruiser throws off, sir. And Petty Officer Wallis and Lieutenant Dietrich were able to reprogram a transmitter to make a much larger mass shadow, but not quite as much as a *County*-class cruiser. But since the drone is operating inside the stealth envelope, we think it might be enough to fool them, sir. With the ECM transmitters and the altered drive signature, we would send the MAS out in a good position to intercept a fast freighter and bait them into sending a stealthy one instead, which

Cumberland would be waiting for; tucked in the asteroid belt."

"But me and CPO Sanchez," Blutarsky picked up, "worried that Rodinans might still be able to figure out that the MAS is a decoy and run right past it, or even worse, try to take it out."

"Because the MAS doesn't have any launch tubes," Sanchez chimed in.

"And because they've been watching the system, they know that whatever it is had to be small enough to fit in *Cumberland*, so it's probably a shuttle and not a patrol boat. But then we figured out," Blutarsky jumped in, "how to make the MAS into sort of a patrol boat. It doesn't have launch tubes, but it does have a big f—, uh, ramp, and we thought maybe we could just roll a missile out the ramp and light it up outside the boat. So, we asked the master chief if he thought he could rig up some kinda cradle to hold a missile—"

"With wheels on it and maybe some compressed air nozzles to help us shove the missile out. Fire control here on *Cumberland* would have to light the missile up, but once that's done, the missile runs on its own. We figure we can put at least a pair and maybe three in the shuttle. Master chief says he can make the cradles in less than a day if you give us the go-ahead," Sanchez concluded.

"This way," Blutarsky added, "even if they figure out that it's just a MAS we're using as a decoy, they'll find out the hard way that even our decoys are lethal."

"I like it," Jonah grinned. "Anything else?"

"We need to launch recon drones to cover the corridor entrances, sir. If we're parked down in the asteroid belt, we'd be too far away to pick up even a sensor ghost from a stealthed ship if they exited the corridor early," Sanchez explained. "We figured one near the hyper limit, which is the end of the corridor, and one further out to try to catch them."

"One other problem is the MAS doesn't have long-range tactical," Blutarsky said. "But the missiles have enough sensor range that they should be able to lock in on target without it. We just need to figure out a way to activate the missiles' targeting systems without actually firing the birds. Their sensors will know when they've been kissed by the targeting system, and they'll probably give up without us needing to actually launch."

6

It took a little bit more than a day to pull everything together, the chief obstacle being configuring the MAS engines to produce a signature much more like the massive drives of the *Cumberland*. The recon probes had been launched and would be in place shortly. The *Cumberland* had flown into the asteroid belt and tucked itself next to a big rock. Commander Fung took command of the shuttle. The whole group of officers and ratings had volunteered to join her (with the exception of Lieutenant Kelley, Jonah noted). Fung chose Petty Officer Delnicki to come along. She took two other crew members and a squad of a dozen royal marines in case they needed to board an intercepted ship.

In the rear of the shuttle sat three Vulcan anti-ship missiles tipped with laser warheads. The bomb-pumped lasers on each missile would slice through any freighter that didn't heave-to and follow orders. The master chief made three cradles on electromagnetic rails to get the missiles out of the shuttle. Once the loading hatch was open, the targeting systems on one of the missiles would be activated. The missiles took up a lot of room, and quarters for sailors and marines were tight. There was only room for eight sleeping berths, so everyone had to "hot bunk" with another member of the team, including Commander Fung.

There were no cooking facilities, so they would be eating ration packs the entire time they were away. There were no shower facilities, and with the necessity of wearing ship suits at all times on the shuttle, the atmosphere was going to get rather ripe quickly. In spite of these discomforts, Commander Renee Fung was excited to be commanding the shuttle. Up until a few weeks before joining *Cumberland*, she had been commanding a patrol boat based on the Aries Station. She had only been a lieutenant commander, but she had been captain of her little boat. As cramped and smelly as it was, it was hers. Patrol boats in the Royal Navy were not given names, and hers was officially known as PB-336, but she had always referred to it as 'Nellie.'

Renee guided the shuttle out of the *Cumberland* and set a course for the intercept point they had plotted along the chord between the corridors to Venera and Chinese space. The adjusted drives and EW transmitters were working as planned. They had enough food, fuel, and water to last a month, but they were only going to be out there for two weeks. After two weeks, Captain Halberd thought it would be wise to rotate the crew (and air the shuttle out!). It would take them just over two days to reach their station, climbing up the gravity well.

From the briefing she and Halberd had received from Rear Admiral Rodriguez, this system had been uncovered by the Commonwealth blockade before *Cumberland* arrived. She guessed there had been regular traffic between Venera and the Chinese that only stopped when they showed up. Renee thought that if the plan of deception worked, they might know as early as tomorrow since if the Rodinans believed her little shuttle was the *Cumberland*, they would probably try to send a stealthed freighter through.

It didn't happen immediately. The shuttle had departed four days before and had been on station for two days when Lieutenant Blutarsky commed the captain in the middle of the night.

"Sir, the drones picked up a hyperspace emergence from the Chinese corridor, followed by a sensor ghost," he announced.

"Did we get a fix on the 'ghost'?" Jonah asked.

"Yessir, we did," Blutarsky confirmed. "We've estimated time to perihelion as 72 hours if they're making $0.23c$ as we figured. I've also sent a message to Commander Fung."

"Good, lieutenant," Jonah replied. "Nothing to do but wait now. Halberd out."

Over the next two and a half days, they waited. Based on the very brief sensor reading they obtained, they had been able to fix the position of the target's entry and plot its probable course. Blutarsky had even started a 'countdown' clock based on his estimate of when the target would enter scanning range.

Stealth technology enabled a spaceship to blend in with the background and make it nearly impossible to find, given the vast expanse of space. What stealth technology could *not* do, however, is provide concealment when an enemy knew approximately where you were or mask emissions from drive engines. In a few minutes, *Cumberland* would ease out from behind the rock it had been using for cover and focus its powerful though short-range LIDAR systems on the vector they had plotted. If their assumptions proved correct, they would light up the incoming freighter like a Christmas tree.

When Blutarsky's countdown reached thirty minutes, Jonah went to the bridge. Lieutenant Commander Volkov was the OOD, and he asked her to sound general quarters. She did. The ship now responded quickly and efficiently. She turned to the captain.

"Sir, the ship reports manned and ready at general quarters," she stated. Under her breath, she added, "Eighty-seven seconds."

Jonah stage-whispered back to her, "Not bad."

Resuming his normal voice, he called, "Navigation, ease us into the middle of the plotted vector. Thrusters only."

When Blutarsky's clock reached zero, Jonah commanded, "Sensors, full power sweep forward. Tactical, I want missile lock immediately."

Almost as soon as he issued the commands, sensors, manned by the aptly named Petty Officer Warner, called out, "Target, dead ahead and closing. Speed is $0.25c$ now, and distance is now just under 1.2 light minutes."

While she was saying that, the missile lock tone began from tactical. As she finished, Lieutenant Dietrich confirmed with a grin, "We have missile lock, captain."

Jonah saw everyone on the bridge smiling at their success.

"Comms," Jonah requested, "Let's hail them."

"Attention, unidentified vessel. You have entered an area subject to the blockade established by the Commonwealth of His Majesty Edward XII against the Rodinan Federation. Please turn off your stealth systems, activate your IFF beacon and begin immediate deceleration to a stable orbit of H2813 and prepare to be boarded for inspection. Any items you are carrying which are on the list of contraband registered with the Interstellar Court will be confiscated. Any attempt at evasion or resistance will be construed as an act of war, and we will respond with lethal force. You have 30 seconds to comply."

The seconds ticked by. Jonah found himself clenching the arm of the command chair. These few minutes and the boarding process were the times of highest tension. Jonah was beginning to wonder if the ship would comply when Warner on sensors announced, "He's flipping, sir. And he lit his IFF beacon and dropped his stealth envelope. Identified as a Federation-flagged freighter, the *Vasilek*. Computer confirms match between IFF and emissions signature."

"They're hailing us, sir," Ensign Lee on comms reported.

"On screen," Jonah responded.

"Captain Dmitri Lelikov, MV *Vasilek*," the man said. "We surrender."

"Captain Jonah Halberd, HMS *Cumberland*. As long as you and your people comply with our orders, you will have nothing to fear. Your rights as a prisoner of war are guaranteed by the Interstellar Concordat of 3009. Once you achieve stable orbit, our marines will board and take possession of your ship."

"Understood, Captain Halberd," the man replied flatly. "Lelikov out."

Since it would likely be another couple of hours until the boarding operation, Jonah decided to go visit marine country. The *Cumberland* carried a platoon of royal marines. Jonah had not had much interaction outside of normal staff meetings and briefings with their commander, Lieutenant Guglielmo, a short, energetic young man with flaming red hair. Jonah turned the ship over to Lieutenant Commander Volkov and headed toward the shuttle bays, where the marine barracks were.

As soon as he appeared in the hatch, the nearest marine shouted, "Captain on deck!" He jumped to attention and saluted. The rest of the marines were no more than a half-second behind him in acknowledging the captain's presence. Jonah returned the salute and commanded, "As you were, men."

He saw Lieutenant Guglielmo making his way forward. When Guglielmo reached him, he said, "Welcome to marine country, captain. Shall we go to my office?"

Jonah followed the marine into his small office, where they discussed what was likely to take place. Jonah had no reason to suspect any trickery on the part of the Rodinans, but neither would he put it past them. He knew the marines would treat the prisoners with respect but a firm hand. He asked the lieutenant to bring Captain Lelikov on board *Cumberland* for a meeting. After the marines had inspected the *Vasilek* thoroughly and accounted for its crew, he would meet with Guglielmo again and decide how to deal with the ship and its cargo—now a prize of war—and its crew.

7

Captain Lelikov had offered no resistance and his crew, made up primarily of members of his immediate family, seemed to pose no threat. His hold was stuffed with military tech, and both the ship and cargo would be sold at the Royal Navy's prize court. That news cheered the crew. Military tech of the sort *Vasilek* had been carrying usually fetched a good price at auction, plus freighters were always in demand. Each crew member's share would be thousands of pounds. Jonah realized, somewhat dispassionately, that he had become quite a wealthy man in the service of his king. His share of the prizes he had taken while commanding *Essex* had been over ten million pounds. This latest capture would add to that by a noticeable amount. But like every successful captain he knew, he never really thought about prize money.

Captain Halberd had sent the *Vasilek* away, with a prize crew of six led by Lieutenant Dietrich and a couple of Lieutenant Guglielmo's marines. Before he left, Jonah had spoken with Lelikov, who confirmed Jonah's suspicions. Lelikov had admitted that he had been making the run through the system with impunity every couple of weeks until *Cumberland* had appeared. He had purchased the stealth system when the Rodinan drone reported *Cumberland's* presence and was disappointed to have spent all that money and still been caught. Beyond that, Lelikov was evasive and did not provide further information.

Jonah suspected that, after being surprised by *Cumberland* in the asteroid belt, he had sent word back about its location. It meant that the decoy they had devised had worked but that the Rodinans were now aware that it was a decoy. He had contacted Commander Fung and warned her that the next attempt would likely come her way.

Renee Fung had been on station for eight days and away from *Cumberland* for ten when they were alerted that another ship had dropped in at the end of the corridor to Chinese space. In spite of how cramped the Marine Assault Shuttle was, in spite of having only ration bars to eat, in spite of the boredom of waiting, in spite of the smell, she was still happy to be there. The excitement of the next hours would more than compensate for any unpleasantness, she thought.

It would be about 22 hours before the blockade runner came close enough for one of the missiles to paint it with its targeting systems if it stayed on its current course and continued to accelerate to $0.3c$. The runner was probably expecting Renee's ship to be no more than a shuttle—nothing to be concerned about. When the Vulcan missile's LIDAR lit them up, they'd be unpleasantly surprised.

Twenty-two hours later, Renee had rotated the MAS, so the rear faced in the direction of the oncoming blockade runner. She commed *Cumberland* via the kewpie to get them to activate the first missile's targeting systems. She couldn't do that herself because the MAS didn't have the tactical net to control the missiles. Within seconds *Cumberland* reported back that the missile's targeting system was up and had achieved target lock.

Renee then broadcast a hail following standard Royal Navy protocol. "Attention, unidentified vessel. You have entered an area subject to the blockade established by the Commonwealth of His Majesty Edward XII against the Rodinan Federation. Please activate your IFF beacon and begin immediate deceleration and prepare to be boarded for inspection. Any items you are carrying which are on the list of contraband registered with the Interstellar Court will be confiscated. Any attempt at evasion or resistance will be construed as an act of war, and we will respond with lethal force. You have 30 seconds to comply."

The IFF signal came on quickly, identifying the vessel as Chinese, the *Wang Luo*. Renee received a hail at almost the same time. "This is Shao Xiao Xie Qiang. You have no right to stop this vessel. I demand you turn off the targeting radar and stop harassing us."

Renee's console informed her that *shao xiao* meant lieutenant commander. She responded curtly. "Lieutenant Commander, our right to inspect your vessel for contraband is established under the Interstellar Concordat of 3009. The Commonwealth of His Majesty Edward XII declared a blockade on the Rodinan Federation and published a list of proscribed materials with the Interstellar Court as is spelled out in the concordat. Interstellar law states that failure to comply with our request for inspection or any attempt at evasion may be taken as a hostile act, and I am allowed to use lethal force in response. You have 30 seconds to begin deceleration. Our sensors indicate your vessel is of a type capable of a max deceleration at 500 gravities. Deceleration at a rate lower than 500 gravities will be seen as an attempt at evasion, and I will fire. I have a Vulcan anti-ship missile locked on you, and its laser will cut your ship in half. Acknowledge."

The Chinese commander replied, "We will comply under protest. Your government will hear about this outrage. *Wang Luo* out."

Renee smiled. It would take the *Wang Luo* five hours to come to a stop. It would take her about the same amount of time to reach the same point in space. She instructed *Cumberland* to shut the missile down, then commed the marine sergeant in charge of the squad on board to let her know what was going on. She engaged the drives and set off.

Once on course, she contacted *Cumberland* and was connected to the captain. "Congratulations, commander," Halberd offered.

"Thank you, sir," she replied. "I feel a little bit like the python that swallowed the pig. I'm guessing from how the Chinese responded that one hundred percent of the cargo will be contraband. With the missiles on board, we won't really have room in the shuttle for it. What would you like me to do?"

Halberd replied, "We just received a change of orders, so we just lit up the drives to come pick you up. We should be there in two days and a bit. That doesn't eliminate your problem, but it does put a time limit on it.

"Until you have a chance to see exactly what it is, we won't know for sure, but I think we can assume it's of high value. They used a fast freighter and a Chinese-registered one at that, so they knew they would be facing risk. That means it's a small volume, high-value cargo. If it's tech components in properly sealed containers, it should be able to survive a couple of days in space. If it's something biological, space it and destroy it."

"Aye, aye, captain," Renee confirmed.

"I'll be able to tell you more about our new orders when we reach you," he added. "*Cumberland* out."

Renee wondered what the new orders might be but was more concerned with the upcoming confrontation with the *Wang Luo*. Their limited sensor suite on board the shuttle confirmed that the Chinese ship was continuing to decelerate at 500 Gs. She knew she would have to handle the commander but planned to have Petty Officer Delnicki conduct the inspection. The petty officer had spent the bulk of her career in patrol boats and had inspected hundreds of ships in her time.

The hours passed uneventfully, and the shuttle was able to dock with the *Wang Luo* while both ships were decelerating to a stop. Since Renee did not have the composite armor the marines did, safety protocols dictated that she have the marines bring Xie Qiang on board the shuttle to meet with her. She suspected that would further irritate the Chinese commander.

Even though the cockpit door was closed, Renee could hear her querulous voice. A soft rap on the door indicated she had arrived. "Enter," Renee called.

The marine escort opened the door, announcing, "Xie Qiang, sir." He withdrew with a smirk on his face.

The Chinese commander was a short woman, no more than 155 centimeters. She opened her mouth to speak, but Renee held up her hand to cut her off.

"Before you start, shao xiao, let me make myself clear. The only argument you can make is that this is international space, and your government has stated its neutrality in regard to the conflict between the Commonwealth and the Rodinan Federation. To counter that, you were on a direct course to the hyper corridor leading to Rodinan space at $0.3c$. There is no one within this system anywhere close to your heading and no one in this system with whom to do business regardless. Interstellar law gives me the right to stop you and inspect your cargo for contraband. We are permitted to make a *full* inspection, shao xiao, and will open every container in your hold if we have to. Further, if we suspect there is contraband hidden elsewhere in your ship, we have the right to confiscate your entire vessel. You and your government are free to take the matter up with the Interstellar Court, but you will be unsuccessful. Now you may speak."

The diminutive Chinese commander opened and closed her mouth twice. She stood silent with her lips pursed for a few moments, then blurted, "Your ship stinks."

Renee could not repress her chuckle. "I suppose it does. I don't really smell it so much now, but I imagine it's pretty bad."

"It's awful," Xie Qiang confirmed. "With your permission, I'd prefer to go back to my ship."

"Permission granted," Renee said.

As the Chinese commander stepped through the cockpit door, she turned and asked, "Do you really have a Vulcan missile on board? I have to ask."

Renee just pointed to the command console and brought up the video feed from the rear bay, showing the three missiles in their cradles. "Goodbye, shao xiao," she said.

About twenty minutes later, the comm buzzed. "Yes, Delnicki," Renee answered.

"Commander, there are 24 containers on board," the petty officer replied. "The contents of the containers and the information on the manifest do not match. The manifest describes components for industrial robots, but the containers hold what appears to be the command-and-control system for an orbital defense platform. Furthermore, they made an attempt to shield the containers to spoof our scanners, but it wasn't good enough. In addition, we opened a fourth of the containers to make sure the contents matched our scans. They do, but they do *not* match the information on the manifest."

"Very good, Petty Officer Delnicki," Renee answered. "What about the rest of the ship? Anything stashed away in the bulkheads?"

"We're just finishing our scans now," Delnicki continued. "There are a few items, but they appear to be luxury goods brought by members of the crew for their own personal transactions."

"Carry on," Renee said. "When you complete your search, ask the shao xiao whether she intends to continue to Venera or return home. Make sure the containers you opened have a good seal, then have the marines shove all those containers out of the hold with a nav beacon. Make sure they stay clear of the drives. *Cumberland* will be here in a couple of days to pick them, and us, up."

"Aye, aye, sir. Delnicki out."

An hour later, the job was done. All 24 containers floated in space near the shuttle. The *Wang Luo* had left, heading back to the Chinese corridor. All they had to do now was wait for *Cumberland*.

8

Jonah was sitting in his cabin, pondering the orders he had received when he was interrupted by his steward. Having a steward was still something he was not used to. The steward, Ginepri, tried to be quiet and unobtrusive but was so successful at it that he often startled his Captain when Jonah was deep in thought as he had been just now. The steward was unremarkable in build or appearance except for one thing. Ginepri was mostly bald, with only a fringe of black hair growing on the sides of his head. He had let that hair grow long on the left side and combed it all the way over the top. The effect was somewhat ridiculous as it called attention to his baldness rather than disguised it. Even more ridiculous were the times when Jonah had seen him rousted from sleep during a drill when his carefully placed hair had gone askew and stood up in the air or out to the side.

Ginepri was confirming that the coffee was made and that he had brought a selection of breakfast pastry from the officers' mess for the meeting Jonah would be having shortly. Jonah would be sharing the new orders. In addition to the command staff, he also included the engineering heads, Marine Lieutenant Guglielmo and Master Chief Bradshaw. They would also have a visitor join them, Lieutenant Commander Fred MacMurray, who had just arrived in command of PB 410.

MacMurray had served as second officer during Jonah's first tour in command of the frigate *Essex*. MacMurray had come from a part of the Commonwealth settled by North Americans. He spoke English with an accent Jonah had never heard before and used expressions that made no sense. When Jonah had finally asked him about his accent and his unusual expressions, MacMurray had explained that both were normal where he was raised, that he and his family considered themselves something called 'Texans.' MacMurray had gone on to say that it was important among his people that one knows how to ride a horse and be able to fire ancient explosive projectile weapons accurately and quickly. Despite his odd way of speaking and unusual background, nevertheless, he had been bright and capable, and Jonah had recommended him for promotion. MacMurray had been given command of a patrol boat, where he had been for just under a year. Jonah was pleased to be able to work with him again.

At 14:00, Ginepri confirmed that everyone assembled, and Jonah went into his ready room, where they were all standing. After formalities of saluting and introducing MacMurray had been completed, Jonah had everyone sit while he stood next to the viewscreen. He cleared his throat and began.

"We've been given new orders that will involve our taking the war to Rodinan space. As soon as we can make ready, we are to enter the Venera System with the primary goal of destroying the orbital station there on a 'hit and run' mission. While not primarily a military target, the Admiralty feels that damaging infrastructure will help strain the Rodinan economy and war effort. We have a small window of opportunity to achieve a measure of surprise.

"Naval Intelligence confirmed that, as we thought, the Rodinans had placed a stealth drone near the end of their corridor into this system. They have also given us technical information on how we might find the drone, doing emissions scans on a wavelength outside the usual spectrum. Lieutenant Commander MacMurray and sensors will be receiving that information at the conclusion of this meeting, along with a kewpie comm to link with us. Once we account for the drone, we can enter the system at any time without them being forewarned. Intelligence estimates it would be at least five days before they could position another drone of this type. We will task PB 410 with destroying the drone while we appear to be on course back to Hercules Station.

"Once the drone is destroyed, PB 410 will take the corridor to the Venera system, but make an early exit, and engage its stealth envelope immediately upon transition. This is far enough away from the normal corridor exit that their emergence should escape detection. Once there, PB 410 will set a ballistic course for the planet Venera. PB 410 will use passive scans to determine enemy presence in the system and inform us on the kewpie what we'll be running into. According to Naval Intelligence, there were two frigates and a light cruiser in the system, but that could change by the time we arrive.

"If those ships are still there, we will still have an advantage, but it will probably turn into a running battle. I'd like us to come up with ideas to shorten the timetable and knock their ships out early. *Cumberland's* primary goal is to destroy the orbital station and do as much damage to the warships as possible. We will be playing by the rules on this. The Admiralty insists we give the station the thirty-minute evacuation warning spelled out in the Interstellar Concordat before we blow it up. While *Cumberland* is wreaking havoc, PB 410 has an entirely different mission.

"As you recall, a little over nine months ago, the Commonwealth was able to prevent the Rodinan Federation from taking over the New Delhi system even though New Delhi had declared its neutrality in our conflict. Before we were able to respond, the Rodinans captured a passenger liner, the *Calpurnia*, and took the passengers prisoner. Among the passengers were a number of high-profile folks who are being held in different places throughout the Federation. One of those high-profile passengers was Lady Julia Hawthorne, daughter of the leader of the loyal opposition and the fiancée of First Space Lord Chesterfield. Intelligence reports that Lady Julia is being held at the planetary governor's residence on Venera. Rear Admiral Rodriguez has passed along that the king would consider it a great favor if we would try to bring Lady Julia back to the Commonwealth safely.

"Lieutenant Commander MacMurray, you will be taking Lieutenant Guglielmo and his marines in the MAS on board your boat. My hope is that you can take advantage of the chaos caused by our attack on the orbital station to find and rescue Lady Julia. We will assist you as much as possible in eliminating any orbital defense platforms we can, but once we engage in battle with the Rodinan ships, it is unlikely we will be able to offer further support. If we are able to destroy all the orbital defense platforms, you might have a chance at a rescue op. Otherwise, it would be futile. Should you succeed in rescuing her, you are to exit the system with all possible speed and get her to safety."

Pressing a button on his comm unit, Halberd said, "I just sent you the particulars on your comms. Does anyone have any questions about the overall objective of the mission before we begin discussing specifics?"

No one had any questions, so Jonah continued. "By the time *Cumberland* exits the corridor to the Venera system, PB 410 will have to be in orbit around the planet and undetected. I will leave it to you, Fred, to figure that out. Once *Cumberland* exits the corridor, I intend to accelerate to 0.3*c* as fast as possible. Rodinan standard doctrine would be for all their ships to be in-system between the hyper corridor and the orbital station. I expect whatever ships are in-system to join formation before climbing up the gravity well after us. Point defense will be coordinated between all their ships and, if it's close enough, the orbital station as well. *Cumberland's* part of the mission will be like a "smash and grab" jewelry store robbery.

"Our Vulcans have an 800,000 kilometer greater range than their Sokols, but that will be only a two-minute advantage. At the same time as we launch, I intend to flip and decelerate at 500Gs for the next 45 minutes as we approach the primary, so navigation will need to plot our slingshot course, taking that into account.

"The main reason for slowing down is to prolong the chaos and give PB 410 and the marines a chance to accomplish their part of the mission. I am confident we will be able to achieve our primary objective and destroy the orbital station. Decelerating will also allow us to fulfill the 30-minute warning evacuation requirement. Even though they outnumber us, I don't believe they'll be able to hurt us too badly. We're looking at a running battle, folks. Their point defense net concerns me. I am worried that they will be able to pick off all the Vulcans we can launch. Any ideas on how to degrade their point defense would be most welcome since I doubt they'll be dumb enough to stay in cannon range for long," he concluded.

MacMurray and Guglielmo, realizing their set of problems was different, withdrew to one end of the table to go over their options, reviewing the information which intelligence had provided on the layout and defenses of the governor's residence as well as locations of ground-based fighters and land troops on the planet. MacMurray was making notes on his tablet as they conferred. At the other end of the table, there was an embarrassing silence until Master Chief Bradshaw cleared his throat.

"Yes, Master Chief Bradshaw?" Jonah inquired.

"Well, I don't know how we put their point defense on the fritz but seems to me the problem is that we don't have help: it's just us. We fire all the broadside tubes and the bow chasers, and we're throwing 20 at a time. Twenty missiles against three targets, and we'd be lucky to get a single one through. Twenty missiles against one ship, even with the other two helping, odds are better, but not enough to make me happy.

"And it got me thinking, how do you normally beat a point defense system? You throw so many damn missiles at it that they can't get 'em all. And we're just us. And then I started thinking about Mr. Blutarsky's idea, puttin' the Vulcans in the MAS." He stopped. "How many we got?"

"How many what?" Jonah wanted to know.

"How many missiles do we have on board, captain?"

"We have a full load, master chief," Commander Fung answered. "One hundred and twenty laser warheads and 10 anti-matter warheads."

"That's what I thought. What's he got?" Bradshaw asked, jabbing his thumb over at Lieutenant Commander MacMurray.

"He'd have eight and two," Fung replied.

"Not enough to make a difference," Bradshaw replied. "He isn't gonna need lasers or anti-matter warheads, though. He's likely only gonna need kinetics. But back to what I was thinking. If we somehow threw 60 missiles at 'em in the first salvo, I'm thinkin' that we might swamp 'em. Coupla problems with that, though. We'd shoot ourselves dry real quick, and someone who knows more about the tac system needs to figure out if it could handle 60 at once."

"How would you launch an extra 40 missiles in that first salvo?" Jonah asked. "You can only put one missile in a tube."

"Yessir," Bradshaw confirmed, "one missile in a tube. But we didn't have any tubes on the MAS, and we had three Vulcans on it. What I'm thinkin' now is similar but different. I could build some racks, using cradles like the ones I built for the MAS, arranged like this," he held his hands up, making the shape of an X. "I'm thinking four missiles in each rack, ten racks. We tractor the racks out of the shuttle bay just before we engage—there are too many to tow. That'd add 40 to our first salvo. But that'd leave us only three shots each from the tubes for the rest of the fight, so we'd likely shoot ourselves dry. And if we're in a running battle, then that's a problem."

"True," Jonah agreed.

"Sir," Blutarsky interrupted, "I think our chances of doing some damage with 60 missiles are a lot better. That makes our first salvo the equivalent of three heavy cruisers against the point defense of a light cruiser and two frigates. I have to think we'd tag 'em pretty good, sir. And some of the damage we'd cause would be to their point defense, so the remaining salvos would be more effective. Shooting the tubes dry makes me nervous, but we're not planning on staying around, are we?"

"And if we sting them hard enough," Volkov added, "they might not be so eager to pursue us."

"Captain," Commander Fung chimed in, "the tac system can handle it; the coding isn't too tricky. With a salvo weight of 60, we can throw 20 birds at every target, or we can throw more at the cruiser and less at the frigates, maybe 30 and 15."

"Master chief," Lieutenant Commander Volkov asked, "how do you figure Lieutenant Commander MacMurray will need kinetic warheads without talking with him? I'm not second-guessing you, just curious about how you figured that out."

"Sure, lieutenant commander," Bradshaw explained, "well, they're down there looking at a bunch of ground targets."

Volkov considered his answer, then a look of recognition crossed her face. "Right," she said. "Got it."

Ensign Sieber raised his hand timidly. When the captain nodded to him, he asked, "I'm sorry, lieutenant commander, I don't understand."

Volkov smiled. "Laser warheads are ineffective against ground targets, and it's against interstellar law to use anti-matter warheads against ground targets. That leaves kinetic."

Blutarsky added, "You launch a rock from high orbit, boost it to $0.3c$, and it makes a pretty satisfying hole in the ground when it lands. Plus, the shock wave will take out any ground-based fighters that are in the air nearby."

Ensign Sieber sighed, "Oh."

"Master chief," Jonah inquired, "how long will you need to build these racks?"

"They're not complicated," he shrugged his shoulders. "Less than a day."

"Go ahead and make them," Jonah confirmed. "We'll wait and see what we're facing before I commit to using them. But someone once told me,

'Better to have 'em and not need 'em'—"

"'Than need 'em and not have 'em'," the master chief finished. "Aye, aye, Cap'n. I'll get on it as soon as we're dismissed."

Jonah looked to the end of the table where MacMurray and Guglielmo were still hunched together.

MacMurray noticed his glance, held up his hand to quiet Guglielmo, and said, "Done with the big stuff here, captain. Just rounding up the last few strays."

"Do you need anything from us?" the captain inquired.

"We're going to need kinetic warheads," he said. "I'll keep one of each kind of active warhead, but kin I please put in a requisition for eight big rocks? Why are y'all smiling?" he asked.

"Master chief is already working on it," Jonah replied with a grin. "Fred, let me know when you and Lieutenant Guglielmo are finished, and I'll go over how to find that stealthed drone on your way."

9

A few hours later, the master chief confirmed that the fabricator had finished producing the kinetic warheads the patrol boat requested. It was a simple matter of tractoring them over and retrieving the active warheads. Immediately after, Lieutenant Guglielmo and his platoon of marines went aboard the MAS. They left *Cumberland* and attached to the patrol boat. Without the three missiles occupying the bay of the MAS, there was room for the marines and their equipment, but just barely.

Lieutenant Commander MacMurray signaled his departure shortly after and headed for the hyper corridor that led to the Venera system. With the information gleaned from Naval Intelligence, PB 410 had no difficulty in finding the stealthed Rodinan drone a day later and destroying it with a quick pulse from one of its photon cannons. They then accelerated up to 0.23*c* and entered the hyper corridor. After activating their Alcubierre drive, they began the transit to the Venera system.

Under normal circumstances, it made sense to travel to the end of a hyper corridor to lessen the distance that had to be covered at sub-light speeds. In PB 410's situation, traveling to the end of the corridor would allow the Rodinans to detect their emergence from hyperspace, so MacMurray exited three light-hours early. Upon exit, he immediately activated the boat's stealth envelope and adjusted his course for a ballistic entry to the system. His course would take him into the very edge of the sun's corona, where he would engage in a braking deceleration that should allow them to circle the sun and emerge from the far side at a reduced velocity that would enable him to engage in a high orbit of the planet. The interference from the corona would mask the use of the EM drives.

When PB 410 had departed, *Cumberland* had engaged its EM drives and had begun accelerating to the entrance to the Hercules corridor. This was to give the Rodinans the impression that *Cumberland* was returning to

Commonwealth space. Once MacMurray confirmed that he had destroyed the Rodinan drone, *Cumberland* flipped and went to a full deceleration burn. It reversed course and headed for the Venera corridor. Their deceptive move put *Cumberland* roughly three days behind PB 410. By the time *Cumberland* emerged into the Venera system, PB 410 should be tucked in orbit around the planet, undetected.

Shortly after MacMurray entered the Venera system, he was able to confirm via the kewpie that the Rodinan ships were still in the area and that there were still two frigates and a light cruiser. Captain Halberd gave the master chief the green light to load 40 missiles with laser warheads on the racks he just fabricated. Just before engaging in battle, they would shove the missile racks out. The racks would float behind the ship, masked by the wake of the EM drives, and would be difficult, if not impossible, for the Rodinans to detect.

The *Cumberland* entered the hyper corridor, engaged the Alcubierre drive, and started the just under 20-hour journey to the end of the corridor in the Venera system. Jonah made sure to visit every department on the ship during the hyper transit. This, too, was something he had seen his captain do back when he was a young ensign. Jonah had seen that space warfare involved long hours of waiting, followed by intense spasms of action, with flurries of missiles and barrages by photon artillery exchanged in a few frenzied minutes.

The long, slow anticipation of battle could build into a feeling of dread in a crew. With roughly a third of the crew having come straight from recruit training, Jonah knew nerves would be on edge. He had seen that the appearance of the ship's captain, calm and confident, worked wonders in buoying the crew's spirits. Even better was when the captain knew the names of his crew. With only 225 people on board, this was not difficult, and Jonah had taken the trouble to learn all of them. While visiting one compartment on the lower decks, Jonah noticed one of the more cynical veteran members of the crew making a comment to his neighbor. From the expression on the man's face, Halberd suspected he harbored a somewhat skeptical attitude.

Approaching him, Jonah asked, "Seaman Bosco, did I ever tell you the story about the captain in the wet navy back on old earth?"

Realizing the captain must have noticed him commenting to his buddy, Bosco stuck out his chin, preparing himself for what he suspected would be a tongue-lashing. "No, sir," he answered.

"Oh good," Jonah replied with a smile. "Well, a long time ago, way back when, there was this captain. And as they were sailing into battle, he would call down from the bridge to his steward, 'Steward, bring me my red shirt.' Before every battle, the same thing: 'Steward, bring me my red shirt.' After a few months, one of the crew got up the nerve to ask his captain why he did this. The captain answered, 'I do it for my crew. If I am wounded in battle, by wearing a red shirt, the crew won't see me bleed.'"

Bosco thought to himself, "Typical officer." He would have rolled his eyes if he thought he could get away with it.

Jonah continued. "One day, they were sailing into battle against more ships than any of the crew had ever seen, with more guns than they could count. What do you think the captain said that day, Bosco?"

Bosco answered somewhat snarkily, "'Bring me my red shirt,' right?"

"No," Jonah answered with a straight face, "that day he said, 'Steward, bring me my brown pants.'"

It took Bosco a split second to understand. When he did, he couldn't help himself and laughed out loud. Jonah smiled too and told him, "Seaman Bosco, I promise that if we ever head into a 'brown pants' situation, I'll be honest with you."

Bosco looked his captain in the eye and stuck his hand out, smiling. "I'd appreciate that, sir."

A few hours later, *Cumberland* exited the hyper corridor and arrived in the Venera system. Immediately they raised their shields and began a scan of the system. They confirmed Lieutenant Commander MacMurray was in position and began their run into the system, accelerating to $0.3c$. To run into the system would normally take just over 48 hours, but since the Rodinans would be climbing out of the gravity well to come to meet them, that time would be cut almost in half.

The lag on their sensors, which were limited to light speed, was two hours. The Rodinans did not face the same limitation, as they undoubtedly had sensors near the corridor exit with kewpie links. Fortunately for *Cumberland*, MacMurray and PB 410 were much closer. Within a matter of minutes, MacMurray commed and informed them on the kewpie that the Rodinans had mobilized and formed into a standard tactical formation, with a frigate front and rear and the light cruiser in the center. Jonah was unsurprised; it was what he expected.

He went over the watch schedules one final time with Commander Fung. Once they had decided on their plan several days before, they had shifted the schedules to ensure that their best people were on the bridge and fresh for the battle to come. Jonah reminded everyone to make sure they slept and ate normally. He did the same, knowing that sleeping and eating after the battle might be postponed depending on the outcome.

The time crept by as the distances slowly narrowed. When *Cumberland* reached a range of 180 million kilometers from the orbital station, it began broadcasting a message warning that the station was going to be attacked and that all personnel should evacuate for their own safety. This meant the Cumberland was only 30 minutes from attacking the station.

Following the lengthy approach, the battle would be decided in less than ten minutes of furious activity. The action would take place so quickly that human control and intervention of the systems would be impossibly slow. The tactical computers were programmed with primary and alternate attack plans and a wide variety of defensive options. The tactical computer would make decisions and change responses based on the input it received. Jonah would not have to give the order to commence, as the computer would begin when it reached the pre-programmed distance at which they had decided to start the attack.

Renee Fung was excited and, she admitted to herself, a bit apprehensive. The closest she had come to being in a real battle, under live fire, was when her patrol boat had intercepted some smugglers. The ship she had caught had not been equipped with anti-ship missiles, so the danger had been minimal. This time she would be facing fire that could damage or, if the Rodinans were extremely lucky, even destroy the ship.

In her regular meeting with Master Chief Bradshaw, he noticed she seemed a bit tense and commented on it. She immediately thought of denying it but instead nodded once. Bradshaw tried to give her a smile of reassurance. "It's okay to be a little scared. Once the missiles start flying, anything could happen."

"How do you deal with it?" she asked. "How does the captain? He seems so calm."

"Well, I'd say that those feelings go away over time," Bradshaw began, "but that would be a lie. We've just gotten better at not showing it. It helps to have confidence in your ship and your crew, and even your captain. *Cumberland* is a sturdy ship, and the crew has been gelling pretty nicely. That's why the captain drills the crew so much. Of course, anytime your enemy is shooting back at you, there's a risk, but as far as this particular mission, you also have to trust that the folks at the Admiralty believe there's a high probability we should be able to destroy a non-military orbital station and return safely or they wouldn't have issued the orders."

Renee nodded. "I do understand that, and I do have confidence in the crew, so why—?"

"Are you still feeling nervous?" Bradshaw interrupted. "Because the Rodinans will be shooting back at us and hope to do to us what we hope to do to them. Like I said, the feelings don't go away. For what it's worth, commander, I like our chances a lot better now. Being able to throw triple the number of missiles in the first salvo is going to give us a heck of an edge, but we would have been okay even without that. Even so, we'll take some damage and likely have some casualties. You can't do anything about it until it happens—all you can do is be ready when it does."

Renee was still a bit apprehensive but less tense after talking with Bradshaw. Shortly after *Cumberland* had closed to within 4,500,000 kilometers, a chime sounded from the computer, warning the bridge that 100 seconds remained until the commencement of action. It also signaled that the missile frames were being positioned outside the ship. Jonah was confident. He felt that Master Chief Bradshaw's idea of the extra missile racks would be successful. He was hoping that the extra defensive element of the railguns shooting flak and chaff cartridges would be effective but was a bit more skeptical.

He looked around the bridge. Everyone had his ship suit on. The change of watch had taken place a half-hour before, so everyone should be fresh and rested. The waiting was almost over, and hell was about to be unleashed.

10

Second-rank Captain Aleksandr Kaun, Sasha to his friends, commanded the *Kuznetsov*-class light cruiser *Murmansk*. The ship had just been commissioned, and he and his crew had been assigned to the Venera system for their shakedown period. The Rodinan High Command felt it was unlikely that there would be any action in the system, based on their knowledge of the positioning of Commonwealth forces. Accompanying *Murmansk* were two frigates, the *Admiral Essen* and the *Krivak*, though the *Krivak* was due to rotate out in two days for refit at the naval yard in the Demeter system.

Kaun had been second in command of an old destroyer, the *Severomorsk*, in the Battle of New Delhi. He had distinguished himself during the Rodinan retreat from the system after his captain had panicked following the arrival of the Commonwealth fleet. With the backing of the political commissar, he had assumed command and kept the ship fighting in the rearguard as the Rodinans pulled out.

The captain, who had owed his position to his political connections, committed suicide before they reached Rodinan space. Kaun did not think less of the man for that. The captain would have been found guilty of cowardice by the military tribunal and shot. Worse, the captain's family would have been harassed and possibly imprisoned or killed as well. The government listed the former captain as killed in action, allowing his family to collect his pension. Privately, the former captain's political patrons were rebuked.

Sasha was not a political creature himself. He accepted the presence of appointees like his former captain and the political commissars as something that was an integral part of the system. As long as the career navy officers were in charge, the screw-ups of the politicals would be kept to a minimum.

Kaun had just come off watch when his second officer commed him. "Captain Kaun, we have hyperspace emergence from the H2813 corridor.

The emissions signature indicates that it is the former RUS *Esmeralda*."

Acknowledging, Sasha buttoned his jacket and returned to the bridge. Once there, he pulled up a hologram of the system showing the positions of his ship and the two frigates and the '*Esmeralda.*' The schematic showed the three Rodinan ships orbiting Venera. They were almost perfectly positioned to use their orbital velocity to sling-shot toward the intruder.

"Astrogation," he called out, "least time course to our visitor?"

"Already computed, captain."

Kaun checked his console. The course was there and showed that they would need to initiate an acceleration burn in just over two minutes. Perfect, he thought. He contacted the frigate commanders and instructed them to synch with his course, then tapped the console to commit to the course laid out. The time to intercept was just over 24 hours. He turned to his second officer, Commander Dimitrov, and ordered, "Readjust the watch rosters so that we have the alpha crew rested and in place when we engage, then invite the frigate commanders and their seconds to join us in a comm meeting in my ready room in fifteen minutes. Invite the commissar too. You have the bridge."

Without waiting, Sasha strode off the bridge and to his quarters. He was already thinking about why the '*Esmeralda*' would be paying them a visit and the tactical match-up as well. When he reached his ready room, he used a tablet to activate the holographic display over the conference table and brought up the specs on the '*Esmeralda.*'

A few minutes later, Dimitrov knocked on the door, accompanied by the political commissar, a prematurely balding, thin-faced man with a weak chin. Commissar Verenich was the watchdog of the Rodinan Politburo, assigned to the ship by the Federal Security Service, the FSB. He had no naval training, but his authority was second only to the captain. His job was to make sure that no one on board the ship took any action that would be against the interests of the state. Sasha, like most in the navy, despised these watchdogs. At best, one would be assigned a commissar who did his job in an inconspicuous way, but more commonly, he had observed that they stuck their noses into everything. He felt that the former were useless, but it seemed Verenich was tending towards the latter, making him an obstacle to the smooth operation of his ship.

At the appointed time, Sasha's tablet buzzed. He pressed a button, and the two captains and their executive officers appeared in holographic form, seeming to occupy seats at the conference table. Through the interactive displays, they would be able to see the conference room as though they were present, and any materials Sasha projected would also appear in their quarters.

Appearing to all of them was the 3D grid schematic of '*Esmeralda*' suspended over the conference table. "Gentlemen," Kaun began, "here is the ship we will face. We called her *'Esmeralda,'* but the Commonwealth has renamed her *'Cumberland.'* I suggest we call her *'Cumberland'* since she does not belong to us at the present time. The ship was originally built by the Germans, and we captured it when we took over the New Bremen system. It is a sound ship, captained by a certain Jonah Halberd, who was until recently a frigate captain.

"Her armor is thicker than ours and is made of AT-38 alloy. She is able to launch 20 missiles per salvo, so two more than our *Putin*-class and equal to the weight of the salvo of our three ships combined. Where we have the advantage is that our point defense datanet will be more effective due to our numbers. That does not mean we will escape without damage. It means it makes more than equally likely we will cause some damage to her in return. The odds are slightly in our favor in an engagement. Now, the question I would like to ask is, why is she here? Your thoughts?"

11

Jonah sensed the ship shudder the slightest bit when his console informed him that the initial salvo of missiles had launched. Eight flew out from each side of the ship and four more from the bow. At the same time, the racks just ejected from the ship launched their 40 missiles, which ignited their drives and set off in search of their prey. Upon the launch, the ship flipped and immediately began a hard deceleration burn. At the same time, the automatic loaders slid new missiles into each tube for another salvo.

Within 75 seconds, the second salvo launched, of only 20 Vulcan missiles this time. While the reloaders were cycling again, the point defense network on *Cumberland* sprang into action. Each of the Rodinan frigates had fired 4 missiles and the Rodinan light cruiser twelve, so 20 Sokol missiles were bearing down on *Cumberland*. The missiles of both sides carried electronic countermeasures designed to confuse the point defense targeting systems. In addition, once the missiles reached a distance of two light seconds from the target, the guidance systems began to jerk them in rapid random course changes called "drunk walking," as long ago. some wag had compared the maneuvers to the random staggering of a late-night drunk.

No sooner had the second salvo launched than the rail guns on the top and bottom of *Cumberland* began to fire in patterns along the approach vector from the Rodinan ships that the sensors had felt would give the best probability of success. The anti-missile canisters exploded, sending ball bearings shooting out, creating a cloud of flying metal. Every fifth canister was full of electronic countermeasures and reflective chaff designed to give false readings to the missiles' sensors.

The point defense lasers on *Cumberland* also reached out to destroy the missiles. *Cumberland's* sensors tried to track the incoming missiles, sorting out the false images generated by the missiles' ECM and attempting to counter the random course changes. At the same time, the guidance systems on *Cumberland* itself began to initiate "drunk walking" course changes.

Within seconds the larger and more powerful photon cannons fired, stabbing out into space, aiming for the Rodinan ships. The Rodinan photon cannons also fired, seeking to hit *Cumberland*. The lighter Rodinan cannons were at the limit of their range and largely ineffective. The missile reloaders had cycled again, and *Cumberland* was about to launch its third salvo, just as some of the first salvo of Rodinan missiles pressed home their attack. *Cumberland's* third salvo was not directed at the Rodinan ships but at the defense platforms surrounding the orbital station and the planet.

Cumberland's initial salvo had been effective. As Master Chief Bradshaw had hoped, the large number of missiles had overwhelmed the defenses of the Rodinans. Of the 60 missiles fired, *Cumberland* aimed 30 at the Rodinan light cruiser and 15 at each frigate. Though the Rodinan ships were able to coordinate their defense by linking their tactical nets, there were just too many missiles. In addition, the ECM generated by *Cumberland's* missiles was effective, especially when they were used in such a large grouping.

Of the thirty missiles targeting the Rodinan cruiser, five survived to reach their detonation range of 50,000 kilometers. When each of the missiles detonated, a controlled nuclear explosion was set off, generating an extremely powerful, bomb-pumped x-ray laser. Bracketed by five of these, the Rodinan cruiser did not have a chance. The bomb-pumped lasers overwhelmed the ship's protective plasma field in milliseconds, stabbed right through the lightly armored side of the ship, and dug deep into it. One of the shots eliminated the ship's EM drive nodes. Another sliced the nose of the ship off. A third stabbed into the bridge. The fourth and fifth delivered more glancing blows, but the *Murmansk* was already a powerless hulk, drifting in space.

The nearest of the two Rodinan frigates suffered a similar fate. Though only three missiles survived to attack it, the weaker shielding and thinner armor of the frigate were not much of a deterrent to the powerful x-ray lasers. It blew up when one of the lasers breached its fusion reactor core. The other Rodinan ship fared better for a time. The remaining frigate faced the final attack of only a single missile from *Cumberland's* first salvo. The powerful bomb-pumped laser weakened her shields and scorched her armor but was not able to penetrate.

The Rodinan ship was not safe, though, as the second salvo of missiles arrived 75 seconds afterward, and the *Cumberland's* photon cannons delivered their blasts at almost the same time. The tactical computer on *Cumberland* had adjusted targeting instantly based on the results of the first salvo and sent all twenty missiles against the frigate.

With the Rodinan point defense dramatically reduced due to the loss of two ships, six of *Cumberland's* missiles survived to detonate within range of the nearer frigate. The bomb-pumped lasers chewed deep into the hull, finding the fusion cores and setting off a cataclysmic explosion.

The *Murmansk* was heavily damaged. It could not move under its own power with its drive destroyed and its reactors offline. Any life support functions were dependent on the batteries. There were few unbreached compartments regardless, and over three-quarters of the crew had died in the initial assault. It continued to coast away from *Cumberland*. No life pods ejected.

Cumberland did not escape without damage. Of the 20 Sokol missiles, the anti-missile ordnance thrown by the railguns took out 12—far more than Jonah had dared hope. Electronic countermeasures generated by the tactical system and from the chaff cartridges launched by the rail guns managed to lead 4 of the remaining missiles astray, chasing false targets. That left 4 for *Cumberland's* point defense lasers. The Sokol missile had its own ECM and *Cumberland* was able to shoot down 3. The remaining Rodinan missile detonated just as *Cumberland* launched its third salvo of missiles. Vulcan missiles had just emerged from the starboard tubes when the Rodinan missile generated its bomb-pumped laser.

The Rodinan laser hit the missile just launched from starboard tube 5. The laser hit the fusion bottle core, and it exploded, creating an explosion like a tiny sun. That explosion caused the cores of the neighboring missiles from tubes 4 and 6 to explode. The resulting blast overwhelmed the plasma shielding on the entire center portion of the starboard side of the ship. The nuclear fireball boiled away the ceramic alloy AT -38 armor on the side of *Cumberland*, and the pressure of the blast created a smooth round dent on the side of the ship. Tubes 4, 5, and 6 were completely destroyed—no trace they ever existed could be seen in the smooth round scar on the side of the ship. Somehow, the hull was not punctured, though later repairs would show that what remained was paper thin in spots.

Other than the shudders felt when the ship launched its first three salvos of missiles, there was no sign of the intense battle taking place in space until that explosion on the starboard side. The force of the explosion overwhelmed the ability of the ship's inertial dampeners to compensate for it, and those on the ship who were not strapped in were thrown against bulkheads. Seventeen crewmen were killed by their impacts from fractured skulls and broken necks. Another 65 suffered broken bones or sprains. Almost everyone received some bruises.

Jonah was strapped in the command chair when the ship lurched. The force of it tossed him in the chair against his restraints like a rag doll. It caused him some slight disorientation, but he regained focus quickly. As he did, Petty Officer Sanchez on damage control read his console and shouted, "Unknown damage on starboard side center. Tubes 4, 5, and 6 are offline. Starboard shields midships are gone and not regenerating."

Commander Fung read her console and reported, "Three missiles from third salvo are offline." She checked the missile status and added, "They were launched from starboard 4, 5, and 6."

Halberd barked, "Roll the ship!" Given that his shields were gone on the starboard side, he wanted to present the intact shields of the port side to the enemy.

Lieutenant Commander Volkov from sensors then made her report, detailing the damage to the Rodinan ships from the first salvo and then updating quickly as results of the second salvo were known. "The two frigates are destroyed, captain. The cruiser has taken severe damage. Reactors are offline, shields are down, multiple hull breaches—there can't be many survivors, sir."

The Rodinan automated orbital defense platforms orbiting the planet Venera each launched three missiles. Because the missiles were separated, their ECM was less effective. *Cumberland's* anti-missile rail gun ordnance and point defense lasers had no difficulty in eliminating them as a threat.

Captain Halberd then asked, "Status of orbital defense platforms?"

Volkov responded, "Updating, sir. Wait one."

A few seconds later, she was able to report, "Sensors show platforms designated 1, 2, and 4 destroyed. Platforms 3 and 5 appear undamaged. Orbital station appears undamaged." She activated the holographic display to show the remaining platforms and the station.

Jonah asked, "Number one, what do we have left to throw at them?"

At this point, the second salvo of twenty Rodinan missiles arrived. Two of them survived *Cumberland's* defenses. The Rodinan missiles detonated and expended themselves against *Cumberland's* plasma shielding on the port side forward, seconds apart from one another. The second missile took advantage of the resulting shield weakness on the port side, and its x-ray laser broke through. It hit a soft spot, the hatch covering port tube 1. The last emission of the laser breached the hull. The movement of *Cumberland* and the missile caused the laser the slice forward, where it hit thicker armor. The thick armor absorbed the remainder of the laser blast, though it was gouged deeply. Still, it had exposed five compartments on two decks to the harsh vacuum of space. Twenty-three of *Cumberland's* crew were destroyed by the laser or sucked out into space in an explosive decompression.

Fung quickly updated, "Hull breach on decks 3 and 4. Port tube 1 is offline. Port 2 still shows nominal. All four bow chasers are nominal. Starboard 4, 5, and 6 are gone, and so is port 1. Starboard 3 and 7 are reporting their hatches are blown, and they can't load or fire. We have a total of fourteen tubes loaded and ready to fire. The missiles from starboard 3 and 7 would have to be swung to starboard 2 and 8 to fire, and I have no estimate of how long that will take."

"Commander," Jonah replied, thinking quickly, "fire four missiles at each of the platforms. We need to knock those orbital platforms down. Make sure you use starboard 2 and 8 so those tubes are clear and begin swinging the missiles across from 3 and 7 immediately. Hold the other six loaded missiles for now, and let's hope we can get the other missiles in play soon. We'll launch as many of those as we can at the station as soon as we can."

12

Second-rank Captain Kaun watched the approach of *Cumberland*. He knew the Vulcan missiles she carried had a slightly longer range than his Sokols, but he hoped the seconds of delay would prove to be unimportant. When *Murmansk* was still 30 seconds out of range, his tactical officer cursed.

"Sir!" he yelped. "Sensors show 60 missiles inbound!"

"60?" Kaun asked. "Are you sure it's not some new form of ECM?"

"Sir," the petty officer replied, "sensors show launch signatures for 60 missiles. I've never encountered any ECM that can mimic a launch signature."

Kaun did not answer. He had never heard of such a thing either. Despite tying the defense networks of all three ships together, a salvo of 60 missiles would be more than they could handle.

The time rapidly arrived for their own missile launch. As soon as the Rodinan ships were in range, their computers fired the missiles. As soon as he felt the slight vibration indicating the missiles had launched, Captain Kaun asked, "Time to impact?"

"Two minutes, twenty seconds, sir."

Kaun realized he would be able to launch his second salvo of missiles, but only seconds before *Cumberland's* missiles hit him. "Sensors, report," he asked, "how many missiles on the plot now?"

His sensors officer answered in a thin voice, "Enemy missiles have employed ECM. Sensors now show over 100 missiles. Time to impact two minutes."

Kaun wracked his brain, trying to think of anything he knew that might help his ships avoid the oncoming storm. Nothing came to mind. He sat in silence, waiting. He felt his second salvo launch and checked his console. Less than 30 seconds remained before impact.

"Make sure you're buckled in," he reminded the bridge crew. "This is going to be unpleasant."

The impact when it hit was far worse than anything he'd ever imagined. The ship lurched backward as, at the same time, a laser burned into the bridge, obliterating crewmen and equipment and causing explosive decompression. Kaun's suit membrane covered his head instantly, though the force of the ship's sudden movement had banged his head against the back of the command chair hard enough to knock him unconscious briefly.

When he came to, he noticed the normal lights on the bridge were out, replaced by a few of the red emergency lanterns. From what he could see in the dim light, the bridge looked as though a tornado had hit it. None of the consoles were lit, and he could see no other crewmen. His console still had power, so he tabbed the ship comm and ordered, "All personnel, all sections, report."

He noticed he could not feel his legs below the knee. He looked down. An entire section of the deck, including the tactical and sensor stations, had peeled up like a wood shaving and curled into his legs. He tried to move his legs experimentally, but they would not budge. He felt no pain, which meant the medical nanites were doing their job, and his ship suit still had pressure, so it had not been pierced, but he knew his injuries were likely severe.

He turned his attention back to the ship. The schematic on his console showed massive damage. Nothing forward of the bridge was showing as operational. The drives were blinking red, and the reactor showed offline. Worried about the possibility of losing containment on the reactor fusion cores, he immediately tabbed the button to jettison them. Only three compartments on the port side of the ship indicated they still had atmosphere. Over the comm link in his suit, only five people had reported in, though two had indicated they had wounded with them who were unable to respond.

Thinking as quickly as he could in his stunned condition, he tabbed the external comm and said, "Attention, HMS *Cumberland*. This is second-rank Captain Aleksandr Kaun of RUS *Murmansk*. We surrender unconditionally and require immediate assistance."

13

"Attention HMS *Cumberland*. This is second-rank Captain Aleksandr Kaun of RUS *Murmansk*. We surrender unconditionally and require immediate assistance."

Halberd heard the announcement, weak and full of static. He could hardly believe that anyone had been able to survive. At the same time, Lieutenant Commander Volkov reported, "*Murmansk* has jettisoned her reactor cores, captain."

He commed the sickbay and ordered, "Two corpsmen with full medical kit to report to shuttle bay immediately."

The ship surgeon, Dr. Johnson, asked, "How quickly?"

Halberd responded, "Five minutes ago."

He then commed Ensign Lee. "Ensign, report to the shuttle bay at once. You'll meet up with two medical corpsmen. You need to launch immediately. There are survivors on the Rodinan ship. They've surrendered and requested immediate assistance. We'll give you further instructions once you're on your way. You need to launch within the next two minutes if you have any hope of reaching them."

Ensign Lee acknowledged and took off at a dead run for the shuttle bay. Fortunately for him, the corridors were empty due to everyone being at battle stations, and he reached the shuttle bay just as the two corpsmen arrived, each pulling a cart of medical supplies.

Captain Halberd had already contacted Petty Officer Wallis in charge of the shuttle bay, and shuttle Number 2 was waiting. Wallis jogged alongside Ensign Lee to the hatch of the shuttle.

"You have a full load of fuel and life support for 30 people for at least a week, including rat bars. As soon as you strap in, we'll launch."

Ensign Lee nodded and entered the shuttle, quickly strapping into the pilot's chair and pressing the button to shut the hatch. He waited briefly for the corpsmen to stow their supplies and strap in, then spoke on the shuttle's comm, "We're good to go, Petty Officer Wallis."

No sooner did he finish speaking than the shuttle catapulted out into space. With no time to do a pre-flight inspection, he quickly began to scan the read-outs on the console. Commander Fung contacted him before he was through.

"Ensign Lee," she began, "I've pre-programmed your course to take you to what's left of *Murmansk* to rescue any survivors. Because of our velocity, I've set your engines to run at a full emergency 150 percent burn the whole way, with only a slight burn at the end to match the drift of *Murmansk*. It's going to be tight. Rodinan ship suits are only rated for a half-hour in vacuum, just like ours. If they've lost all atmosphere, as we suspect, then you'll barely make it in time. Don't worry about trying to dock with them. Have one of the corpsmen put on an EVA suit with a static line and bring any survivors aboard that way. There's a possibility that keeping your engines on emergency burn for so long will damage them, but don't worry. If worse comes to worst, we'll pick you up on our way back through the system. Any questions at this time?"

"No, sir," Lee responded, "not at this time."

"Good luck then," Fung responded. She then activated the open channel and said, "Attention Captain Kaun and RUS *Murmansk*. We have launched a shuttle with two medical corpsmen that is proceeding at full emergency burn to you. ETA is in 25 minutes. We realize that leaves no margin for error. If at all possible, try to gather your people in one location. If you have a way of telling us where your people are, that will help us get the shuttle close so we can get them on board as quickly as possible. *Cumberland* out."

"Thank you, *Cumberland*," Kaun replied, "we're still assessing but will do as you ask. *Murmansk* out."

Kaun contacted the highest-ranking of the five survivors who had reported in, a Petty Officer named Vasechkin. "Petty Officer Vasechkin," he began, "based on those who reported in, all survivors are on the port side, deck three, between compartments 23A and 36B. The sections between 24 and 32 still show atmosphere. I have you in 32A. Can you retrieve the survivors who are not in atmosphere? A rescue shuttle is on the way, and we should gather everyone near the external hatch at 28A."

Vasechkin replied, "Aye, captain. I've got a seaman with a broken arm who is conscious and five others who are still out cold. Our ship suits seem to be okay. If I open the hatch to find the others, we lose the atmosphere, and I don't think we'll be able to get it back. Where are the others?"

"One person reported in 29B. You should be able to reach him without venting atmosphere. There are two, one in 23A and one in 36B, who are on ship suits. Neither of them reported any other wounded, but there are three other wounded in 29B. I don't know if they're conscious. ETA for the shuttle is less than 25 minutes, so it will be really tight for the guys in ship suits. I'm sending you the comm links for the ones who reported in."

"Yes, sir," Vasechkin answered. "Where are you, sir?"

"On the bridge," Kaun replied.

"When will you be joining us?" the petty officer asked.

"Don't worry about me, petty officer. A section of the deck has peeled up and has my legs trapped. I won't be able to join you."

"Pardon me, sir, but that's bullshit," Vasechkin responded. "We'll figure a way to get you out."

"Negative, petty officer. I'm two decks above you and at least a dozen sections away. Use the time and air you have to save the others. There's nothing you can do for me in the time we have left."

14

Lieutenant Commander Fred MacMurray and PB 410 had been spinning around the planet Venera, waiting for the Rodinans' automated orbital defense platforms to be taken out. Until the orbital platforms were eliminated, he needed to maintain his stealth envelope and remain hidden, or else the powerful lasers on the platforms would carve his little ship into small pieces. He watched the fierce, brief battle between *Cumberland* and the Rodinan force on his sensors. He saw the two Rodinan ships blow up and the fireball along the side of *Cumberland*. He was concerned when *Cumberland* failed to eliminate two of the orbital platforms on the first attempt and crossed his fingers that they would get them. Unless the orbital platforms were taken out, there was no point in uncloaking. As far as the Rodinan ships, he had hoped only that *Cumberland* would lead them far enough away to give him a window in which to accomplish his mission. Having two destroyed and one apparently dead in space was far better than he had expected.

The marines were loaded in the Marine Assault Shuttle. Too big to fit in the patrol boat's snug shuttle bay, the MAS had been attached like a limpet to the patrol boat. This had been done before in the Commonwealth Navy, and there were even pre-positioned connection points and clamps for an MAS. He would release the shuttle when he entered the planet's troposphere. The missiles armed with kinetic warheads were lined up and ready to launch. As soon as his sensors confirmed the orbital platforms were eradicated, he would drop his stealth envelope, fire his EM drives and dive for the planet from his current high orbital position. He would immediately begin launching the missiles. It would take ten minutes to launch all eight.

About the time the missiles began hitting their targets, he would be firing his cannons on ground targets also. The marines would follow him down. Patrol boats were the only warships in the Royal Navy that were capable of atmospheric insertion. Though his photon cannons were pea shooters compared to that of a ship like *Cumberland* (and completely insignificant compared to an even larger battlecruiser), it was much heavier than anything on the MAS. He would then hover overhead to provide air support if the marines needed it.

He watched on the sensors as the two remaining Rodinan orbital platforms disappeared. Keying his comm, he said, "Lieutenant Guglielmo, it's time to put the spurs to 'er.''

"Roger that," the marine lieutenant confirmed.

MacMurray then set everything in motion. The stealth envelope fell away. He lit the EM drives and started the missile launch sequence. The Vulcan missiles exited the tube one at a time, and their powerful drives pushed them forward at nearly 1,000 G toward their targets. He glanced at the two petty officers and the lieutenant and ensign who were his bridge crew and gave them a big grin. "Yippee ki yay, boys!"

The patrol boat streaked downward. When they reached the edge of the atmosphere, he released the clamps attaching the MAS. The patrol boat's plasma shielding enabled it to withstand higher temperatures on re-entry, so it nosed over in a power dive to the surface. The MAS used its EM drive to slow its rate of descent since its shielding was less robust, necessitating a more gradual re-entry.

While still at 10,000 meters in altitude, MacMurray's photon cannons began to fire, targeting defensive installations near the target, the governor's mansion for the planet. Within seconds, the guard barracks were destroyed, and defensive hardpoints like the watchtowers and sentry stations were reduced to smoldering piles of rubble. He swung away from the mansion towards the city, targeting the nearest bridge, then returned over the mansion just as the MAS landed in the courtyard of the building.

The kinetic warheads they had launched had destroyed the nearest airfields and military installations. There were airfields further away, but it would take time for the Rodinans to scramble from the greater distance. MacMurray and Guglielmo had planned to spend no more than 20 minutes on the ground, and ideally much less than that. If the operation took more than 20 minutes, they ran the risk of needing to fight their way off the planet.

As the MAS dropped down to the courtyard, it swung around the building. Marines rappelled from the MAS down onto the roof of the mansion, immediately running to preset objectives. When the MAS touched down, the rest of the platoon boiled down the open ramp, heading to different targets as small arms fire erupted. Naval Intelligence had given them an idea as to which room held Lady Hawthorne. Lieutenant Guglielmo led a small squad there. The marines encountered sporadic fléchette fire from the guards who survived the patrol boat's attack on the barracks and defensive positions, but the guards were disorganized. The marines quickly established control of the building and dispatched the guards they met.

When Guglielmo's squad reached the identified location, they found that the door, though covered with a thin veneer of wood trim, was solid steel. He motioned quickly, and a lance corporal came forward and placed shaped charges on the door. Yelling, "Fire in the hole!" he set them off after the other men stepped to the side. The door fell inward from the top, though still attached by the lowest hinge piece on the right. This caused it to twist as it fell inward.

The room inside was a nicely decorated parlor. It looked appropriate for a governor's mansion, though the solid steel door and the bars on the windows gave a hint that it was still the residence of a prisoner, no matter how nicely appointed. The marines squirted into the room, covering each other and checking for guards. There were four doors leading off from the parlor. Marines burst through each one, moments later calling, "Clear!" except for the door on the right side. From that room, the marine called, "Sir?"

Lieutenant Guglielmo jogged over. Standing with her hands on her hips was a petite woman with short curly black hair. Guglielmo recognized her immediately from the pictures he had been sent. She was wearing a sweater and a pair of trousers. "Lady Hawthorne," he said, "we're here to take you back to the Commonwealth."

"Of course, you are," she answered. "Do I have time to bring anything?" she asked. Noticing the pained expression on the lieutenant's face, she immediately answered herself, "No? That's fine, let's go."

"If you'd come with me, ma'am," Guglielmo requested.

She came into the parlor, and immediately, four marines in combat armor formed up to surround her. They immediately jogged away, heading for the MAS. Lady Hawthorne jogged along with them. The other marines waited until they were aboard and quickly followed. Lieutenant Guglielmo made sure Lady Hawthorne was strapped into her seat, and all his men were aboard, then told the pilot, "Go, go, go!"

With a whine, the engines of the MAS came to life, and the shuttle began to lift from the courtyard even as the access ramp was still closing. The shuttle began to vibrate slightly as it picked up speed, heading to the upper atmosphere. From the moment the MAS had touched down to when it lifted off again was just under thirteen minutes. PB 410 continued to circuit the area, on the lookout for any missiles or ground fire that might target the MAS. It was only after the MAS cleared 25,000 meters that the patrol boat broke off and began to climb.

After Lady Hawthorne was strapped in, she turned to Guglielmo and, after reading his nameplate, said, "Lieutenant Guglielmo?" speaking his name carefully to pronounce it correctly. When he nodded that she did it right, she continued, "Thank you for getting me out of that place. When I woke up this morning, I thought it would just be another long boring day. You guys," she looked around at the rest of the platoon, "sure know how to add a little excitement to a girl's life!"

A couple of the men nearest to her who heard her comment chuckled softly. She continued, "What do we do now? Where are we going? This little ship doesn't seem big enough to get us back to the Commonwealth."

Lieutenant Guglielmo explained that they would be meeting the patrol boat soon, but that would not provide her much of a chance to stretch her legs, and it did not have much room inside. He told her he hoped they would be able to transfer back to *Cumberland* soon, as he and his men had been cooped up for almost a week.

She smiled. "Cabin fever? I can understand. I'd been stuck in those rooms for nearly nine months. How big is *Cumberland*, and what is she doing here? I can't believe the Commonwealth did this all for me. I'm not that important."

Guglielmo answered, "*Cumberland* is a heavy cruiser, ma'am. Only battlecruisers and superdreadnoughts are bigger. You'll have to pardon me, but I'm not at liberty to discuss our orders, but perhaps Captain Halberd might when we reach *Cumberland*."

That answer seemed to content her, and she spent the rest of the trip quietly. At the edge of the atmosphere, the two ships rendezvoused, and the MAS clamped itself onto the patrol boat. Lieutenant Guglielmo excused himself, unbuckled, and headed to the hatch. Lady Hawthorne started to unbuckle herself, but Guglielmo told her, "I'm sorry, ma'am, but please stay where you are for a little while. I need to meet with Lieutenant Commander MacMurray, but I will return soon."

Guglielmo exited the MAS and went through the hatch to the interior of the patrol boat. He went inside, followed the narrow corridor, and arrived at the bridge. He knocked on the door and then entered.

"Lieutenant commander," he began, "how we doin'?"

MacMurray grinned and pointed to a jump seat. "Hey, lieutenant. A whole mess a' stuff done happened. Ole *Cumberland*, she like to kicked the crap outta them Roddies an' that's no lie."

MacMurray proceeded to tell the lieutenant about the encounter between *Cumberland* and the Rodinan ships and updated the current situation by bringing it up on the heads-up display in the front of the bridge. *Cumberland* was currently emerging from the far side of the sun and returning their way. He broke off as the kewpie interrupted.

"*Cumberland* to PB 410, report," came Commander Fung's voice.

MacMurray, adopting a more formal manner, replied, "PB 410, commander. We have secured our objective and are climbing out of the gravity well. We are planning on heading out-system to the coordinates discussed."

"Slight change of plans, lieutenant commander," she replied. "Cycle your antimatter warhead into your launcher. We have eight laser warheads remaining, and we will be firing them at the station. The lasers should knock down their shielding, and I'm going to fire yours just after to make sure we bring it down."

"Affirmative, commander," MacMurray acknowledged. "Cycling missile now."

Ninety seconds later, he confirmed, "Commander, cycling complete, antimatter warhead is in the tube."

Fung then commanded, "Slave your fire control to me."

MacMurray entered the codes on his command console and confirmed. "Done."

As she said, "Mark," the remaining eight missiles launched from *Cumberland* and streaked towards the station orbiting Venera. Though the station was non-military, Halberd wanted to make sure they were able to burn through its shields and destroy it. He hoped two or more of the missiles would survive the station's point defense and that the bomb-pumped lasers would do more than break through the shielding but wanted to make sure. For that reason, *Cumberland* would also be firing an antimatter warhead remotely from PB 410.

The station's point defense eliminated five of *Cumberland's* missiles, but because of the size and relative immobility of such a large structure, ECM was ineffective, and it certainly could not make random shifts in course like warships could. The three x-ray lasers stabbed out, overwhelming the station's shielding, but it took nearly their entire burst to accomplish that. The damage they caused to the station was superficial.

Less than three seconds later, however, PB 410's antimatter missile arrived, heading for the station hub. If the station's plasma shielding had been intact, an antimatter missile striking it would have had no effect at all. With the shielding depleted and not yet regenerated, the missile struck the center of the station, creating a huge explosion. The remainder of the station broke into pieces.

15

While the assault on the governor's mansion was taking place, Ensign Lee had heard from Captain Kaun. Kaun had sent him a schematic diagram of the *Murmansk*, showing where Petty Officer Vasechkin would be waiting with the survivors. Ensign Lee had a little more than ten minutes before he would match the velocity of what was left of the Rodinan ship when he would have to maneuver to bring the shuttle as close as he could. He instructed one of the corpsmen to put on an EVA suit and attach a static line and for the other to ready the cabin for decompression. Shuttles were not equipped with airlocks, so bringing people across would require them to open the cabin to space.

Captain Kaun had communicated with the approaching shuttle. He was about to comm Petty Officer Vasechkin when he heard from Seaman Petryagin, who reported that the survivors had been collected from 23A and 36B. Kaun was about to ask why Petryagin was reporting and not Vasechkin when he saw a flashlight stab into the darkness of the bridge and settle on him.

"Ah, there you are, captain," Vasechkin said.

"Petty officer," Kaun said sternly, "I ordered you not to—"

"Yeah, so bust me down to seaman second class," Vasechkin answered. "I'm not letting you stay here."

"You won't make it back in time," Kaun snarled. "I've only got a few minutes of air left."

"It will only take five minutes to get you to the hatch, captain," Vasechkin said, "I promise. The reason it took me so long is I had to find something to help me get you out."

"Unless you have a laser cutter," Kaun retorted, "you won't be able to cut this wreckage away."

"Sorry, captain," Vasechkin shrugged apologetically, "no laser cutter.

66

Besides, there isn't anything to power one. So, I can't cut through the wreckage. But I can save your life."

Vasechkin held up a RUS marine survival knife. The edge of its blade was a single molecule in thickness. Even that incredible degree of sharpness wouldn't be able to cut through the wreckage of the deck in time. Immediately drenched in a cold sweat, Kaun realized what Vasechkin was going to do.

"Oh, God," he murmured, then thankfully lost consciousness.

Vasechkin quickly cinched cord around the captain's lower thighs so the captain's ship suit would not lose pressure when he was finished. The deck had peeled up to just below the captain's knee, but he could not fit the cord that low. He hoped a few minutes' exposure to vacuum would not prevent surgeons from being able to save the captain's knees. Whether the captain chose prosthetic replacements or to have his lower legs regenerated, it would be easier if they could save the knees.

With the cords in place, Vasechkin quickly sawed through each leg below the knee. There was a small amount of blood loss, but between the cold of vacuum and the medical nanites in the captain's bloodstream, it stopped almost immediately. Vasechkin cut the restraining straps holding the captain in the command chair. He lifted the captain's body and quickly taped the captain's hands together, putting the captain's arms around his neck. He then returned as quickly as he could to the hatch where the rest of the survivors were waiting. "At least," he thought, "the captain passing out might buy him another minute or two of air."

When he returned to the hatch, Seaman Petryagin was the last one remaining. A man in a Commonwealth EVA suit then appeared. Sizing up the situation immediately, the corpsman gestured to Vasechkin to pass him the captain. As soon as he did, the EVA-suited corpsman pushed off and covered the ten-meter gap to the shuttle's hatch and handed the captain to his partner. He then returned and indicated that both the Rodinans should grab his arm. When they did, he pushed off again and deposited them inside the shuttle.

He followed them in and quickly hit the hatch control. The hatch closed, and Vasechkin could feel atmosphere returning to the cabin. After about 90 seconds, a green light appeared above the hatch, and a chime sounded. No sooner did that happen when the one quickly unfastened his helmet and began stripping off the EVA suit. His counterpart had already lifted the captain onto a gurney and began slicing away the clothing near where his legs had been severed. Pausing only briefly to scan the tissue, he unwrapped two containers shaped like flower pots. He quickly fitted each of them over the stumps of the captain's legs.

The corpsman, now stripped of the EVA suit, placed a scanner on the captain's neck. The corpsman then keyed some information onto a pad, then grabbed a hypo injector, and pressed it to the captain's neck. It hissed briefly. He took a thin blanket and covered the captain with it, entering some more information on the tablet after he did. He turned back to Vasechkin.

"You understand English?"

Vasechkin nodded.

"Good. Your officer is in shock. Did he pass out before or after you cut his legs off?"

"Before."

The corpsman smiled grimly. "Lucky him. Why did you cut them off?"

Vasechkin explained the captain's predicament.

The corpsman nodded. "Well, you saved his life. In the time you had... Anyway, he'll be out for a few hours. Our sensors show some damage to the stumps from the cold, so it's too soon to tell if they'll be able to save the knees. We put regen stasis caps on the stumps. Between those and his nanites, that's all we can do for now. The rest of your crewmen seem okay. Bumps, bruises, and a couple of broken bones, but nothing serious. We got here just in time. The ship suits were pretty much done."

"Are there any other survivors?"

"No," the corpsman replied. "We did a scan and saw no life signs anywhere else on the ship. You fifteen are all that made it. If you'll excuse me, I need to report."

The corpsman turned away and knocked on the door of the command cabin. The latch clicked open, and he entered.

"Ensign Lee," he said, "Corpsman Heitmann reporting."

"Go ahead, Heitmann."

The corpsman explained about the more minor injuries before bringing up the captain. He explained what Vasechkin had done. "Unfortunately, sir, we don't have the tech on Cumberland to save his knees, if they can be saved. It makes a big difference no matter whether he gets prosthetics or gets regen on his lower legs. The closest place on our side would be Hercules Station, but we would never get there in time to help him."

"What about planetside?" he asked.

"If we could get him down to Venera within five days, they would probably be able to save them. Sooner would be better."

"Thank you, Heitmann," he answered, "Is he conscious?"

"No, he'll be knocked out for another hour."

"Thank you. I'll call it in."

Corpsman Heitmann returned to the shuttle main cabin and began tending to the other survivors. Ensign Lee commed *Cumberland*, currently swinging around the sun at the heart of the Venera system. He explained the situation to Commander Fung.

Renee Fung then spoke to Captain Halberd. After her explanation, he mused, "There's really only one thing to do. We have to send him down to

Venera. His condition is stable enough that we could leave him alone for a day or so?"

Fung said she would need to speak with the corpsman but then asked, "Won't there be trouble for letting a prisoner like him go? Won't intelligence be angry to lose the opportunity to interrogate him?"

Halberd snorted. "He's a second-rank captain of a light cruiser. His value to intelligence is minimal. Other than information about codes which will change in a few days anyway, he's got no more strategic value than either you or me. No, we'll send him to Venera. Can we use one of his shuttles?"

"No," Fung responded. "We blasted their shuttle bay to oblivion."

"Can we scrub the system on the shuttle in a way to allow them to pilot it back but not give them any sensitive information?" Jonah asked.

Fung thought for a moment. "Not really," she replied. "The best alternative I can think of would be to wipe the shuttle's system completely, then guide it into orbit remotely. They would have to go up and get them from there. I can then fry what's left of the system once they reach orbit."

Two hours later, Fung confirmed that Captain Kaun could be left alone for at least 24 hours as long as the other survivors kept him hydrated and sedated. Halberd then ordered her to rendezvous with the shuttle.

The shuttle docked just under sixteen hours later. Halberd surprised her by asking to meet the Rodinan captain. Kaun was lying on the gurney, pale and drawn.

"Captain Kaun?" Jonah saluted. "Captain Halberd, HMS *Cumberland.*"

Kaun returned the salute and replied guardedly, "Sir."

"Captain, my medical corpsman tells me that we do not have the facilities you will need in order to save your legs below the knee if we were to take you on board."

"He has explained the same to me." Kaun grimaced. "I understand."

"That is why," Halberd continued, "we will be making some adjustments to the computer systems in the shuttle for security reasons, then will pilot it remotely to a stable orbit of Venera. We will set the comm on the shuttle to broadcast in the clear that you and your men are aboard. Once the shuttle has achieved a stable orbit, we will then destroy what is left of the computer system, so your people will need to come get you from there."

Kaun was surprised. "What?" he exclaimed.

Halberd shrugged. "It's the right thing to do."

"It is very gracious of you," Kaun said. "I can never re—"

"Perhaps," Halberd interrupted, "when this war ends someday, you can look me up and buy me a drink." Halberd offered his hand to the Rodinan.

Captain Kaun took his hand and shook it. The two men looked one another in the eye, then with a small nod of his head, Halberd released Kaun's hand, stepped back, saluted, and turned for the hatch.

16

Two days later, the Marine Assault Shuttle was able to return to its berth aboard *Cumberland*. There were no further threats in the system. The remains of the *Murmansk* had drifted out of the system. As the MAS landed in *Cumberland's* shuttle bay, Lieutenant Guglielmo was relieved that he and his men would get the chance to stretch their legs at last, but a bit sad that he would not be sharing Lady Hawthorne's company. She had proven to be a friendly companion for the last two days, never complaining about the cramped conditions or the other hardships and cracking risqué jokes with the marines. He had never met anyone with a title before, and he had been expecting her to be a snob. When he found out she was not, it had been a pleasant surprise. She had also spent time on the bridge of the patrol boat, where Lieutenant Commander MacMurray had entertained her with stories of his adventures with Captain Halberd on *Essex*.

They had to wait briefly as atmosphere was restored, then the ramp at the rear of the MAS lowered, and they exited. Waiting for them were Captain Halberd and Commander Fung. Lieutenant Guglielmo approached, stopped three paces away, and snapped a sharp salute. "Permission to come aboard, sir."

They returned his salute, and Jonah said, "Permission granted. Welcome back, lieutenant."

The lieutenant then added, "Captain, commander? May I present Lady Hawthorne? Lady Hawthorne, Captain Halberd, and Commander Fung."

Instead of merely offering the tips of her fingers as Jonah expected a Lady to do, Lady Hawthorne shook hands just like anyone else. She gave a firm grip and looked each of them in the eye as she repeated their names, first Commander Fung and then Jonah. Jonah asked, "If you'd come with me, ma'am. We've prepared a cabin for you to use. The Admiralty has ordered us not to stop at Hercules Station since they have no shipyard facilities to repair our damage but to continue all the way through to the Aries system. Aries is a regular stop for passenger traffic, so you should be able to go anywhere from there."

"Whose cabin will I be staying in, captain?" she asked. "I know that ships in the Royal Navy usually don't have spare accommodations for unexpected passengers like me."

"You'll be staying in my cabin, ma'am," Jonah admitted.

"And where will you be?" she asked.

"My steward, Ginepri, has made up a cot for me in my ready room," he answered. "It is connected to the cabin, of course, but has a separate hatch to the corridor, so I will not be disturbing you, ma'am."

"Thank you, captain," she said, "but since I will be sleeping in your bed," and she winked at him as she said this, "I must insist that you stop with the ma'am-ing and Lady Hawthorne-ing. My name is Julia."

"Yes, ma'..., er, Julia," Jonah stuttered.

"And your name is?" she inquired, "or did your parents predict your future career and name you 'Captain'?"

"It's Jonah," he answered, a little surprised at her informality.

"Good," she said, linking her arm through his, "then we shall be Julia and Jonah until we reach Aries Station."

They reached his cabin. He opened the door for her and waited for her to enter. It was not spacious. There was his bunk, an armchair, and a desk and chair. The head was a very small nook attached. He shrugged his shoulders as if to apologize.

She caught his look. "It's not the Plaza," she teased, "but it's certainly cozy. I appreciate it very much."

He cleared his throat nervously and said, "My steward is Ginepri, and he will bring you anything you need. You reach him by pushing this button. If you give him your sizes, he will be able to bring you fresh clothing. Commander Fung told him what toiletries to lay in, and you'll find them in the head. I must ask that you not wander the ship without an escort, simply so you don't get lost or get in someone's way. Again, if you ask Ginepri, he will make sure someone can come get you and take you wherever you would like to go. Feel free to use the computer on the desk. You'll find a guest account is ready for you to set up. Keep in mind that any communication with the rest of the world is subject to military censorship. That should be everything," he said, "except one request."

"What is it?" she asked.

"Would you please do us the honor of joining us in the officer's mess this evening at 18:30?"

"I'd be delighted to if someone could show me the way."

"I'll stop by at 18:30 and lead you there," he said. "That gives you a bit more than four hours to relax."

Shortly afterward, the ship accelerated toward the hyper corridor back to H2813. Shortly before reaching the entrance, *Cumberland* slowed to 0.23*c*, the maximum safe speed to enter hyperspace, and then engaged its Alcubierre drives. Jonah felt the small flip in his stomach that happened every time he entered or exited hyperspace.

Jonah showed up at 18:30 and knocked on the door of his cabin. Lady Hawthorne opened it. She was wearing a navy-blue uniform blouse and trousers. She had on a little bit of makeup, but Jonah could only tell because he had seen her before without any. She linked her arm through his again once they were in the corridor, smiled up at him, and said, "Lead on."

Jonah considered her as they walked the short distance to the officers' mess. She could hardly have been more than 155 centimeters tall. Her hair was black and curly, cut somewhat short. She had a thin face with deep-set eyes. He hadn't looked at them closely enough to determine the color yet. She appeared to be about his age, possibly a couple of years younger. She was not 'pretty,' but Jonah decided she was attractive. There was something about the way her personality showed through her facial expressions that intrigued him. Already he realized he had never met anyone like her before, and he was drawn to get to know her.

They entered the officers' mess, and everyone was already at his place at the table. The seat at the end and the one to its right were empty. Jonah escorted Lady Hawthorne to her seat and cleared his throat. "Lady Hawthorne, may I introduce the officers of HMS *Cumberland*?"

He began, pointing to each, "Commander Renee Fung, Lieutenant Commander Alexandra Volkov, Lieutenant John Blutarsky, Lieutenant Commander Shirish Patel, Lieutenant Cyrus Kelley, Lieutenant Amanda Leen, Ensign Glenn Sieber, and Ensign Hannibal Lee. You already know Lieutenant Guglielmo. Lieutenant Michael Dietrich has not yet rejoined us."

Introductions finished, Jonah looked down the table at Ensign Lee. The young man picked up his water glass and said, "Ladies and gentlemen, the king!"

Everyone murmured, "the king," after him and then began to sit. Jonah helped Lady Hawthorne into her seat as his mother had taught him years before. She smiled at him as though to say it wasn't necessary.

She teasingly asked Ensign Sieber if he liked her outfit. The young man was stunned at her question and fumbling for an answer when she laughed out loud. She said, "When Lieutenant Guglielmo invited me to join you on your journey, I had no time to pack. Mr. Ginepri was kind enough to get me some new clothes today. He told me I could have whatever I wanted…as long as it was a uniform blouse or trousers in khaki or navy blue. So tonight, I am wearing my navy-blue ensemble, and tomorrow I think I shall try the khaki, and after that…who knows?"

Picking up on her sense of humor, Commander Fung interjected, "So many choices, so little time."

Delighted, Lady Hawthorne smiled widely. "Exactly!"

Two mess hands entered with plates of salad. Jonah knew Ginepri was behind the scene, supervising dinner, and Jonah was glad of it. He then realized this was only the second formal dinner he had hosted on the ship, the first being the night they left Southhampton. Though only a few weeks before, he and the crew had done quite a bit in that short time.

Lady Hawthorne was a delightful dinner guest. She involved everyone in conversation and even drew Ensign Lee out. She managed to learn from him that his unusual name of Hannibal was not because his parents studied ancient earth history, but a result of his parents hoping for a girl, whom they had planned to name Annabel, from a poem by an author on old earth. As a result of her conversational skill, Jonah learned more about his officers' personal lives in a single dinner than he had in the weeks they had been aboard. He watched her through the dinner. The more he saw of her, the more curious he became.

He had not expected Lady Hawthorne to be so friendly and unpretentious. True, he had never met a lord or lady before, but he was expecting her to be stiff and aloof. She was neither. As a result of her presence, the dinner was full of smiles and laughter, and it ended too soon for everyone.

Jonah was about to escort her back to her cabin when she said, "We're in hyperspace right now, aren't we?"

Jonah nodded.

"I've always found the colors playing on the warp bubbles fascinating. Is there somewhere on the ship I could see them?"

Jonah smiled ruefully. "We don't have an observation deck, Julia. But I can show them to you right here." He used his comm unit to change the wall of the mess into a view screen and selected the video feed from outside the ship. Instantly they saw the aurora of colors that ebbed and flowed on the surface of the warp bubble.

"Oh!" she said softly. The effect was a bit mesmerizing. It reminded Jonah of watching the flames in the fireplace as a young boy in his parents' house on York. The two of them sat at the table for a few minutes, watching.

After a bit, she asked, "Did you notice I didn't ask you any questions about yourself tonight?"

Jonah had not stopped to think about it, but it was true. She had drawn information out of everyone at the table but had not asked him anything. He shook his head slightly.

She reached out and patted his hand. "That's because Fred told me all about you," she giggled. "We had two days in his tiny little ship and, once I got him going, he just wouldn't stop. He quite worships you."

Jonah felt his face grow hot with embarrassment. The sudden realization that she might be flirting with him flustered him. After all, she was a member of the nobility, and he was only the son of a marketing executive at a breakfast cereal company who had been lucky enough to win an appointment to the naval academy. He pulled his hand off the table and cleared his throat.

"Ha-hm. Julia, I'm afraid I must return to my duty now." He keyed his comm unit, and the display disappeared. "May I escort you to your cabin?"

"Certainly," she answered pleasantly, though she noted his sudden mood change.

They walked back to her cabin. When they reached the door, Jonah had recovered his wits a bit. "Thank you for joining us for dinner this evening," he said. "You made it a very pleasant evening, and I learned more about my officers tonight than I had in the previous month."

"You're welcome," she replied. "May I ask you for a small favor? Would you please show me around your ship tomorrow?"

"Ha-hm. I would be delighted to," Jonah answered.

She opened the door to the cabin and went inside. "Until then," she said and closed the door.

Jonah stood outside the closed door for a moment, thoughts racing through his head. He shook himself, a bit like a dog coming in from the rain, and went to the bridge. He sat heavily in the command chair when he reached the bridge. He wrestled in his mind, trying to figure out if she had been flirting with him. He couldn't imagine why she would. After all, she was a member of the nobility, and he was just a captain in the Royal Navy. She was engaged to be married—to the First Space Lord, no less. She couldn't possibly be interested in him in that way, he decided, she must be simply toying with him. Her flirting, if it was flirting, was being done just to tease him, he reckoned, or because she felt the need to practice. Jonah didn't really think about his looks, but women seemed to find him attractive enough, he guessed. He was 188 centimeters tall and just under 90 kilograms, with copper-colored hair and slate-blue eyes.

Especially troubling to Jonah was that he enjoyed her flirting. Even after he decided it meant nothing to her, he couldn't deny that he found her incredibly interesting. He enjoyed watching her at dinner. He thought her perspective on things was refreshingly different. Most of all, he was curious to know more about her.

It bothered him that he was fascinated by this woman he had just met, though she was so far above him socially and already spoken for on top of that. His last relationship had ended quite badly and made him sure that Julia was just toying with him. They were from such different worlds. Further, he thought, if he caused her to break her engagement to Lord Chesterfield, he would be ruined.

These thoughts raced through his brain, filling his head during watch. When his watch ended and he was relieved on the bridge by Lieutenant

Commander Volkov, he was no closer to having things figured out than when he started. If anything, he was more confused. He went to his ready room to sleep on the cot Ginepri had made up for him. Knowing that she was just on the other side of the door prevented him from being able to put this out of his mind, and he spent a restless night.

17

Over the next week, Lady Hawthorne, or Julia, as Jonah now thought of her, found an excuse to spend time with him every day. She didn't pine away when he was unavailable, though. He had seen her with Commander Fung. She had made Renee laugh in a way that he had never seen before. Lieutenant Blutarsky's normally rumpled appearance improved while she was aboard. The two ensigns seemed to be in awe of her. He had even seen her thick in conversation with Master Chief Bradshaw more than once.

Jonah kept telling himself that she was only playing with him, but in spite of that, he looked forward to her company tremendously. When she spoke to him, she had a way of reaching out and touching his hand or his sleeve to help make a point, and those touches thrilled him. He also noticed when she was with others, she kept her hands to herself. That realization gladdened him but also filled him with a sense of doom.

He realized he knew very little about her. He had tried to learn more about her life, but she was skilled in deflecting the conversation onto other topics. He had learned she had grown up on Caledonia, where her father's holdings were substantial. She had attended boarding school and university on Caerleon, the capital planet of the Commonwealth, and that she was the younger of her father's two daughters. Most of that he had learned from researching the computer database, though. Unlike many sons and daughters of the nobility, she had stayed out of the spotlight and the tabloids.

Despite her skill at deflecting his questions, he thoroughly enjoyed spending time with her, even though he knew the relationship could never progress. She looked at things in a way different from what he was used to. Julia's world was the people who controlled the Commonwealth. She was refreshingly direct and outspoken. There was something about her that had stirred his curiosity, and even though he didn't feel he was making much progress towards satisfying it, he found it energizing and not frustrating. He could not predict her behavior. She was appetizingly independent.

As the week wore on, Julia began to reveal more information. Some of it was her explanation of the responsibilities she and her sister had as members of the nobility. She had managed to remain unmarried to this point only because her older sister had already been married. Her time had finally come, though, and her father had arranged for her to marry Lord Chesterfield. She explained that women of her level were rarely allowed to marry for love, that most marriages were de facto political arrangements meant to bind two families together, "like hostages for good behavior," she joked.

She clarified that women in these political marriages were ideally supposed to remain silent and out of the spotlight. He joked that perhaps her directness was the reason she had been able to remain single for so long. She threw her head back and laughed at his quip.

She did not inquire why Jonah was still single, and he did not volunteer any information. He had been involved a few years before with a woman who had hurt him badly. Since then, he had not become romantically involved, and the very idea of a relationship made him intensely uncomfortable. Still, there was something about Julia that drew him in.

Julia's father was the head of the loyal opposition, the political party currently out of power, but who would take over as prime minister if the next election would bring his party, the Liberal Democrats, a majority. Though the Liberal Democrats had lost power, getting trounced in the elections immediately following the beginning of the war with the Rodinan Federation seven years earlier, in the last two elections they had been regaining strength as the war dragged on. The Conservative party still held an outright majority of the seats, but just barely.

They discussed how her rescue might affect the political landscape, almost as though they were talking about someone else. Jonah argued that the navy's ability to bring her back showed that the war was being conducted competently. Julia did not dispute that. Left unspoken was her role in the political chess game as a way of binding the loyal opposition to one of the most influential people in charge of prosecuting the Commonwealth's war effort.

On the second to last night of the voyage to Aries, she suggested that they have another dinner with all the officers present. Jonah had Ginepri arrange things again. Once again, the evening was a success. Julia (everyone now called her Julia) again drew everyone out. At one point, she convinced the normally-reserved engineer Patel to sing a rugby song from his days at university. Hearing the bawdy lyrics sung in his warbling tenor voice amused them all, and that she had somehow convinced the usually shy and quiet lieutenant commander into doing so made it even funnier to everyone.

Everyone stayed at the table long after dinner had been cleared away. When Commander Fung announced that it was time for the change of watch and that some of them had to leave, there were sighs of sadness from many that the evening had come to an end. When Jonah started to rise from his seat, Julia reached over and put her hand on his.

"Can we stay and see the lights again, please?" she asked.

Jonah activated the wall screen and brought up the video feed. Julia asked him if he could lower the lights in the room so she could see better. Jonah fumbled with his comm unit to dim the lights. When he had finished and put it in his pocket, he left his right hand on the table. Almost immediately, she covered his hand with hers. After half a minute, she gave his hand a squeeze. He looked at her in response to this and noticed she was gazing at him, giving him the peculiar look women give men when they want to be kissed.

Jonah hesitated, his mind whirling. She leaned over and pressed her lips to his. Her hand reached behind his head and pulled him closer. Her mouth opened under his, and her tongue traced his lower lip. He brought his hand up to the side of her face and touched his tongue to hers. They kissed hungrily for a few minutes, finally breaking to gasp for breath. She stood and pulled him up from his seat. She reached her arms around his neck and molded her body to his. She pulled his head down to hers to kiss again. Lips sliding, tongues dueling, they kissed. She reached down and grasped his left hand and brought it up to her breast. No sooner had he touched it when he suddenly broke off and stepped back.

A horrified expression on his face, he stammered, "Julia, I'm sorry. I can't!" He looked grief-stricken. His voice grew hoarse as he was overwhelmed with emotion. "I'm sorry. Please forgive me."

He left the room quickly. When he opened the door, the viewscreen disappeared, and the lights came back up. Julia stood in silence for a time, then returned to her cabin. She was not mad at Jonah. His desire for her had been evident. Damn politics! she thought angrily.

She had not been toying with him. She had heard about him in great detail from MacMurray, who considered Jonah a hero. She had seen the way he conducted himself on the ship. She had learned even more about him from the master chief. Through all of this, even though it had been a short time and she was engaged to another, she had felt herself falling for the man. She sensed he felt the same, but she realized that she had allowed herself to indulge in a fantasy. It was selfish of her—she knew this—and might have ruined Jonah. She was frustrated because she wanted him and could not have him, and was sad because she knew, due to her family's position, that she would not be allowed to marry for love.

Jonah was trembling when he returned to his cot. He had wanted Julia. He still wanted her. If she knocked on the door right now, he would not have the strength to say no a second time. But Julia came from a different world, a world of wealth and politics and power, and he felt those differences keenly. They had discussed the fact that her marriage was being dictated by political expediency, not by romantic attachment. He had not felt this way about a woman in years. His memories of his last love and how he had been betrayed seemed fresh and raw. He spent the hours until his next watch fully clothed, lying on his cot, staring at the ceiling.

When he relieved Commander Fung, she noticed the ashen look on his face. She suspected what happened. Everyone on board had seen him with Julia and the way they acted together. It was obvious the two were attracted to one another and equally obvious at the moment that Jonah would not allow himself to act on his feelings. Renee wished she could say something to help him, but it would be inappropriate for her to do so.

They had entered the Aries system and had little more than a day left before they arrived. For the next two watches, Renee saw that Jonah was still shaken. His mind was clearly elsewhere, and his interaction with people was stilted and almost awkward. By his third turn on watch a day later, when they were approaching Aries Station, he looked much better. The circles under his eyes were still present, but he seemed back to normal in every other way.

Renee had seen Julia during this time, and she had seemed little affected by whatever had happened between her and the captain. She noticed that Julia had not been alone with the captain since. Renee wanted to think she saw a trace of sadness underneath Julia's normally positive and pleasant personality but also realized it was probably wishful thinking on her part.

When they docked at the station, it was time to say goodbye to Julia, and many of the officers and crew lined the corridor leading to the hatch to see her off. She stopped along the way to say goodbye to certain people and shared a quiet whisper with Master Chief Bradshaw. When she reached the officers, she gave Ensigns Lee and Sieber a kiss on the cheek. Both young men turned bright red. She shook hands with the rest and finally reached the captain at the end.

She looked up at him. "Farewell, Jonah," she said.

Jonah gave a slight bow of his head. "Goodbye, Lady Hawthorne," he murmured.

She cocked an eyebrow at this. After a moment, she gave an almost imperceptible nod of her head and walked through the hatch and down the gangway. With her departure, the crowd lining the corridor broke up.

Jonah requested that Commander Fung and Lieutenant Commander Volkov stay behind. "Commander," he said, "once again, our presence is requested. We have a meeting with Vice Admiral Antonelli in twenty minutes. Mr. Volkov, a pilot from the yard will be arriving shortly to take *Cumberland* to a slip where they can begin repairs. After our meeting, we will have a better idea of how long we will be on station and will post liberty schedules at that time. Mr. Volkov, you have the ship."

They exchanged salutes, and Lieutenant Commander Volkov acknowledged, "Aye, aye, sir."

Jonah and Renee traveled to the Admiralty in silence. Renee asked Jonah if he knew what the meeting was about. "No idea," he confessed. "I hope just debrief and new orders. There's a chance, though, that he'll rip me a new one for letting Captain Kaun and the prisoners go."

After a brief period, they were ushered in the vice admiral's office. Vice Admiral Giuseppe Antonelli was tall and thin. His head was shaved, and his features were dominated by an aquiline nose and dark, piercing eyes under bushy black eyebrows. Neither Renee nor Jonah had ever met the vice admiral before, but both had certainly heard of him. He had an excellent reputation in the fleet as a decisive leader and as a commander who had engendered an intense loyalty from his officers and crew. After exchanging salutes, he indicated they should sit.

"It's a pleasure to meet you both," the vice admiral said. "Congratulations on an extremely successful mission. Your idea of towing racks of missiles behind you to launch a large opening salvo captured the attention of many. The fleet is about to issue a directive instructing commanders to adopt your tactics wherever possible. In addition, the folks at Advanced Warfare have already seized upon it and have developed self-contained frames of missiles based on the design of the racks you constructed and to simplify the interface with the tactical net onboard."

Jonah raised his hand to interrupt. "I wish I could take credit for the idea, but Master Chief Bradshaw is the one who came up with it."

"We know," Antonelli confirmed, "it was clearly stated in your report. BuPers has already sent a form to the master chief for him to sign. He will be receiving royalties from the sale of these missile frames. He could end up a very wealthy man.

"As I was saying, your mission was a success, marred only by your decision to release the prisoners you picked up. Naval Intelligence is furious with you. I note from your report that you did not contact Rear Admiral Rodriguez before deciding to release them. Would you please tell me why?"

Jonah's face reddened with embarrassment. "Sir, I did not contact the rear admiral because I was afraid she would not agree with my decision. Treatment of Captain Kaun's injuries was time-sensitive, and I believed he and his men would be of limited value to—"

Antonelli stood up and interrupted. "You don't know whether Admiral Rodriguez would have agreed with you because you never asked!" he thundered. He sat back down, muttering, "Better to ask forgiveness—"

Antonelli leaned forward earnestly. "Jonah," he stated calmly, "I know you haven't worked with the rear admiral before or with me. I can tell you, flat out, that given a chance to hear your assessment, both Sonia and I would have agreed with your decision to return Captain Kaun to Venera. I understand why you did what you did, but you were wrong. Neither Sonia nor I will formally censure you for this, but you are never to act on your own initiative in matters like this in the future. Understood?"

"Yes, sir," Jonah replied, abashed.

"One thing you will find as you rise through the ranks, Jonah," the admiral advised, "is that it becomes more and more about politics. No matter how blamelessly you try to live your life, there will be increasing numbers of people looking to second-guess every decision you have ever made. Don't give them any ammunition."

"Yes, sir."

"Jonah, you are a captain of daring and ingenuity. You and your crew certainly proved that on this last mission. As a result, you and your crew have been awarded a Royal Unit Citation by the Crown. You destroyed three ships and an orbital station. You carried off a daring rescue of a high-profile prisoner. Were it not for that unlucky explosion of the missile just outside your ship, you would have escaped almost completely unscathed. You caused just over a trillion pounds of damage to the enemy at minimal cost to the Commonwealth. Suffice it to say," he smiled, "your name is now well-known in all the best circles."

Following right on the heels of his chewing out, Jonah was a bit embarrassed by the praise and did not know what to say, so settled for, "Thank you, sir."

"*Cumberland* has been given first priority in the yard," Antonelli continued. "We plan to have external repairs on the ship complete in ten days, at which point you must depart for Hercules Station. If all repairs are not complete when you have to depart, you will be taking yard personnel along with you to finish in transit. You have also been given priority in resupply and will be receiving ten of the new missile frames, in addition to a normal loadout. We would love to give you more, but *Cumberland* only has space for ten.

"The reason we are rushing you back into the line so quickly is that your success has convinced the Admiralty that the time is right for us to make a significant attack on Rodinan space. The hope is that we can cause enough damage and destruction to break the current deadlock, put a huge dent in their economy and make them sue for peace. The main reason we have not made an attack before now is that our political masters are scared to death of the possibility of having any of our capital ships damaged or destroyed. None of them want to have to defend such a loss to their constituents. For that reason, our offensive actions have been limited to small-scale actions, primarily by frigates.

"The Admiralty has been able to convince the government that we should be able to cause more damage than we receive and that our ability to replace any losses is far greater than the Rodinans. We hope to cause enough damage to put the Rodinans in an economic bind and force them to negotiate. So, as part of a multi-pronged attack, Second Fleet will be sending Rear Admiral Rodriguez with her task force from Hercules Station through H2813 and

Venera and from there into the Rodinan Demeter system. The Demeter system has a number of high-value targets: a shipyard with four battlecruisers nearing completion, cloud scoops on the two gas giants in the system and a large number of orbital industrial nodes. At the same time, Admiral Lord Johanssen's Third Fleet will be making an attack on the New Moscow system itself." Antonelli's lips tightened as he shared that information. "The balance of Second Fleet, here in Aries under my command, is designated as the ready reserve to be sent to exploit whatever gains we make.

"Your departure in ten days will get you back to Hercules in time to join Rodriguez when she jumps off. Understood?"

"Aye, aye, sir," Jonah replied.

"Good. One last thing," Antonelli added. "First Space Lord Chesterfield will be visiting Aries Station in a few days. One week from tonight, he will be hosting a formal dinner at which he will present you with the Royal Unit Citation that *Cumberland* earned. Your invitations should be waiting for you when you return to *Cumberland*.

"If you have no further questions?" Antonelli asked, raising his formidable eyebrows.

Jonah looked at Renee, and she gave a slight shake of her head. "No, sir," he replied.

"In that case," he said, rising from his chair, "you are dismissed."

Jonah and Renee rose from their chairs and saluted. Returning their salute, the vice admiral said, "Captain? Commander?" He stuck out his hand. As Jonah and Renee shook it, Antonelli continued, "That was a damn fine job in Venera. I look forward to hearing more about it over drinks sometime."

Jonah smiled too. "I'd love to swap stories with you sometime, sir."

18

As they headed to the shipyard to return to *Cumberland*, standing on a moving walkway, Renee asked Jonah, "Wow! Did he tear a strip off you or what?"

"Eh," Jonah replied, chagrined. "I deserved it. He's right. I should have given Rear Admiral Rodriguez a chance."

"But if she would have made the same decision, why is it such a big deal?" she inquired.

"Well," Jonah sighed, "she might have agreed, but Antonelli's point is that I didn't give her the opportunity to say yes or no. He's not saying our decision to return Kaun to Venera was wrong—"

"I would hope not," Renee spluttered. "It was the decent thing to do!"

"Yeah, but there's a war on."

"I noticed."

"As I was saying, he wasn't saying our decision was wrong. He was saying that I should have requested approval, if only just to cover my ass and follow proper procedure."

"But—"

"For the same reason I felt Captain Kaun would have little value to intelligence because his rank isn't high enough to know what's going on in the larger picture, my rank isn't high enough to know what's going on in the big picture either," he explained. "Does that make sense?"

"You mean," she clarified, "that there might have been things going on that we didn't know about, where someone would have wanted to keep those prisoners in custody?"

"Exactly," Jonah replied. "This time there wasn't, as far as Antonelli and Rodriguez know, but if there had been, I could have really hurt my career. As it is, it gives people ammunition to use against me, should anyone find the need."

"But who would use that against you?" she asked.

"Well, I don't know right now," he admitted. "But the Liberal Democrats could spin it against the government, I suppose, or if someday I am considered for higher rank, then it could be used."

"That's kind of cynical, isn't it?" Renee asked.

"I wish it were just cynicism," Jonah answered. "Unfortunately, I've seen that the higher one climbs in rank, the more politics matter."

They continued in silence for a time. Eventually, Commander Fung spoke again. "Did you see the admiral grimace when he mentioned Admiral Lord Johannsen's name?"

Jonah glanced around quickly to see if anyone was in earshot. He answered quietly, almost whispering, "I did, and there's a reason for it. And it directly relates to what I was just saying."

Renee's eyebrows shot up. "Really! What?"

Jonah looked around to see if anyone were nearby, then pitched his voice low. "Lord Johannsen rose to his position because of politics and patronage. And politics and patronage are still important in the Commonwealth, though less so than they used to be. That was one of the things that Admiral Antonelli was reminding me. Anyway, about eight years ago, Johanssen was brought before a tribunal on charges of cowardly conduct, willfully failing to do his utmost to encounter the enemy and failing to afford relief and resistance," Jonah explained. "From the scuttlebutt, during the Battle of Canberra, he left the battle claiming his tac net had crashed. Though we won the battle, we took heavy losses. The commodore in charge of the task force was killed in battle, but his adjutant, when he came out of a medically-induced coma, brought Lord Johannsen up on charges several months later.

"The court cleared Lord Johannsen of all charges. The adjutant, who according to testimony by surviving crew should have been awarded at least the Navy Cross, was transferred to Oxbow Station and put in charge of environmental systems."

"You're kidding!" Renee exclaimed.

"I wish I were," Jonah said with a shrug. "Everyone who has crossed him has ended up ruined."

"Have you ever—?" she asked.

"No," Jonah answered. "But I served under his brother once. The younger Lord Johannsen was my captain aboard *Dauntless*."

"The one you said was drunk?" she inquired, "and who later left you and the master chief on the bandit ship?"

"The same," Jonah said rather glumly. "After we returned, I was down planet on liberty and was mugged by two men on a dark street. They took me from behind. They didn't rob me. After beating me up in a thorough and methodical way, one of them told me that there was worse waiting for me if I decided to file charges against my captain. The next day I was summoned to the Admiralty and given my assignment as sixth officer on *Surprise*, which was embarking in less than two hours. It was their way of showing me how much power they had."

"What did you do? Surely—" she trailed off.

"As it turned out, I didn't have to do anything," Jonah said. "Within a week, he resigned to sit the family seat in the House of Lords. He's been there ever since."

She was incredulous, "Really?"

Again, Jonah shrugged his shoulders. "Rumor was that the family decided he was *too* much of an embarrassment—even more than his older brother. He sits in Parliament. His father still runs everything, and young Lord Johannsen votes exactly the way he's told. In return, he gets to indulge himself in whatever he fancies, as long as he is discrete. He occasionally ends up in the gossip columns, but not enough to cross whatever line his father drew."

"Back to the admiral," she reminded, "so the reason Vice Admiral Antonelli sort of grimaced was because Admiral Johannsen is leading the Third Fleet attack?"

"That would be my guess," Jonah confirmed. "But if he's learned to let his subordinates run things, everything should work out fine."

"Let's hope so," Renee said uncertainly.

They arrived at the shipyard and were directed to the slip where *Cumberland* was moored. At the observation port near the gangway, they could see scaffolding already erected over the smooth round dent in the ship's hull centered on where starboard tubes 4, 5, and 6 had been.

"You realize," Jonah commented while they stood looking at the damage, "a split second earlier, and..." He trailed off.

They entered the gangway. Almost immediately, Jonah's comm started to buzz. Master Chief Bradshaw wanted him. He answered the comm and said, "Right away. I'm just coming up the gangway now."

He put his comm away and asked Renee, "Number one, please organize liberty for the crew and officers. Everyone should have three days. Also, get with BuPers to get the replacements we need. If possible, try to get recruits rather than someone's hand-me-downs. The new people we started with are already pretty salty even though it's only been a month or so, so we can take on more. The master chief wants me down where they're going to begin work on starboard tubes 4, 5, and 6."

"Aye, aye, sir," she acknowledged.

Jonah turned left upon entering the ship, found a lift tube, and dropped to the level where Master Chief Bradshaw was waiting. When Bradshaw saw him, he turned, stuck two fingers in his mouth, and whistled piercingly. He then yelled, "Doug! C'mere!"

.   As Jonah approached from one side, he saw a man coming from the other. The man was thick-set, with broad shoulders that sloped up into his head and a barrel chest. He wore a uniform shirt with no insignia. Below his rolled-up sleeves, his arms were covered with tattoos, and he was wiping his hands on a rag. As Jonah arrived, Bradshaw said, "Cap'n, I'd like you to meet an old mate a'mine, Doug Allroyd. Doug, this here's Cap'n Halberd."

Jonah stuck out his hand in greeting, and Allroyd shook it. Bradshaw continued, "Doug's in charge of our repairs."

"Ah," Jonah said, thinking quickly, "then it's probably Master Chief Allroyd?"

"Command Master Chief, sir," Allroyd replied, "but I don't much stand on ceremony."

"I noticed," Jonah said with a smile, flicking his eyes to the places on Allroyd's shirt where his insignia would normally be.

Allroyd shrugged his shoulders. "Cap'n, I've ruined so many uniforms in this job, crawling around in tight spaces and such, I just don't bother anymore. Around here, everyone knows who I am anyway."

"Fair enough," Jonah replied. "How do you and Tom know each other?"

"Well," Allroyd ran his fingers over the close-cut blond hair on his scalp, "it goes back to when he was in petty officer school. I was an instructor. After that first day, I reckoned he was either going to make a damn good petty officer, or I was going to have to beat the crap outta him. We've stayed in touch since."

"Have you figured it out yet?" Jonah asked with a grin.

"Just between you and me, sir," Allroyd leaned in conspiratorially, "I might still have to beat the crap outta him."

They all laughed. Jonah then asked, "How can I help you?"

"We wanted to go over the schedule with you," Bradshaw explained, "and I got something strange from BuPers."

"Schedule first then," Jonah said.

"Cap'n," Allroyd began, "you've only got ten days in the slip before they want you out. *Cumberland* is the number one priority in the whole yard right now. We reckon we'll be able to get the heavy work done by then, replacing the armor and rebuilding the compartments that got hit. But we'll need to keep a work crew on board at least to Hercules and maybe longer to get the mechanics inside sorted out, especially to rebuild the autoloaders in the tubes that got hit. We're gonna need to keep at least 30 of my men on board, maybe more depending."

"I'll get someone working on where your people can bunk," Jonah replied. "What else?"

Bradshaw looked a little sheepish. "I got this thing over the comm from BuPers," he began. "I don't know what to make of it."

Jonah looked at it on Bradshaw's datapad and grinned. "It's a royalty form," he said. "The navy liked what you did with the missile racks you came up with and is going to be using them throughout the fleet, though they decided 'frames' is a better name for them. They've taken your rack design and are going to be including pre-loaded 'frames' of four missiles each on all the ships now. Because the internal structure of these 'frames' is copied from your design, you'll get a royalty payment for each one they make. Vice Admiral Antonelli mentioned it to me, and he thinks you might become a wealthy man."

"You're kidding, right, sir?" asked Bradshaw.

Jonah shook his head. Allroyd punched Bradshaw in the shoulder. "Next round's on you," he chirped. "Hell," he added, strolling away, "all the rounds are gonna be on you!"

19

The week flew by. The rest of the crew took advantage of the chance to get off the ship. Some, like Commander Fung, traveled down to the planet. When she returned to the ship, her skin had darkened a bit. When Jonah saw her, he asked, "Get some sun, commander?"

Renee grinned. "I went to the beach," she explained. "Aries is famous for its white-sand beaches. It was heavenly. I spent two days lolling in the sun and being pampered. What about you? Are you getting off the ship?"

Jonah had been throwing himself into the mundane aspects of being a captain of a starship. He was afraid of having too much free time just then. "No," he answered, "too much to do."

Renee thought about pressing the issue with him but suspected he would not budge, so held her tongue. Though she did not know exactly what had happened between her captain and Lady Julia, she had a pretty good general idea. She understood that him burying himself in work was how he was getting through this.

"Do you have your uniform for the dinner?" she asked. She had not owned a set of the formal evening dress uniform and so had bought one while on liberty. Since she knew he had just been promoted to captain before boarding *Cumberland*, she suspected he did not have the correct formal dress either.

"Oh, for heaven's sake," he said with exasperation, "I completely forgot."

Tonight, they were invited to the formal dinner Vice Admiral Antonelli had told them about. They had received hand-written invitations on heavy cream-colored paper requesting their attendance. It would be a terrible faux pas for the captain to be incorrectly attired.

"There's an outfitter on the station," she told him. "If you hurry, they'll be able to take your measurements, run it through the fabricator and get it here in time."

"Right," he said. "What's the name of the place, and where is it?"

"I'll send it to your comm," she replied. "Better get going."

"Thanks, number one. Uh, you have the ship," he said distractedly as he hurried off.

Later that evening, just before they left for the dinner, they checked one another to make sure their uniforms were perfect. Renee's consisted of a white blouse with a black tie, a navy-blue floor-length skirt, a white cummerbund, and a navy-blue mess jacket with her commander's stripes and epaulets. Her service ribbons were displayed on the left breast of the jacket. Jonah's uniform was a navy-blue tailcoat with navy blue trousers, a white waistcoat, white shirt, and black bow tie, with his captain's stripes and epaulet on the coat and his service ribbons also on his left breast. Neither of them found any egregious lint or loose threads on the other, so they set off.

The event was being held at the officers' mess at the Admiralty. When they reached the door, they surrendered their invitations to the herald who announced them as they entered. There was a small receiving line consisting of Vice Admiral Antonelli, and a woman they presumed was his wife, First Space Lord Chesterfield, and Julia, Lady Hawthorne, his fiancée. Renee knew immediately when Jonah noticed because his facial expression tightened.

Still, they joined the others filing past to be introduced to the First Space Lord. Chesterfield had held the position since before Jonah had entered the academy, and his appearance had not changed in that time—testament to the medical nanites that high-ranking public servants, the upper echelons of the military, and members of the royal household were given. The nanites protected against diseases and poisons and could save the recipient from dying from many types of severe wounds. They also delayed the aging process for a time. The nanites would halt the appearance of further aging from the time they were administered but would only prolong a recipient's life by at most two decades. Jonah knew Chesterfield was at least eighty years old, but he looked as though he were in his late forties.

When they reached the head of the line, Jonah and Renee were introduced to Vice Admiral Antonelli's wife Rebecca and the First Space Lord. Chesterfield then remarked, "I would introduce you to Lady Hawthorne, but you already know one another. I would like to thank you for bringing my fiancée back safe and sound."

Jonah replied with an ease he did not feel, "It was my pleasure, sir."

He turned to Julia and said, "Good evening, Lady Hawthorne. It's a pleasure to see you again."

"Thank you," she replied, "and you as well, captain."

Jonah left. Seeing her here was an unexpected stab in his heart. He thought he had been prepared for her being at the dinner, but he felt the control over his feelings he had worked hard to establish in the last week had just evaporated. Renee, following him in the line, greeted Julia and was slightly surprised when Julia pulled her in close and whispered in her ear. "Please take care of him," she said softly.

Renee raised her eyebrow in inquiry at this, and Julia shook her head, indicating that she couldn't answer at the moment. Renee took her leave and went to find Jonah, standing alone. She crossed over to him, a look of concern on her face.

"That was a bit uncomfortable for you, wasn't it?" she said.

"Ha-hm. Yes, well," he began.

"Oh, never mind," Renee quickly retorted. "We're earning a Royal Citation tonight, and that doesn't happen too damn often. C'mon sailor, buy a girl a drink."

She took him by the elbow and steered him towards the bar. While waiting for the bartender, they ran into a fellow captain who recognized Jonah. He wanted to know more about how the missile racks had worked. It was a pleasant diversion that involved both of them, and before they knew it, a small bell tinkled, summoning them to dinner.

They found their place cards just below the head table. Renee noticed that Julia was sitting at the head table at Chesterfield's right. Everyone stood at their place, waiting for Vice Admiral Antonelli. When he reached his seat, he gestured to his flag lieutenant, who made the ceremonial first toast, "Ladies and gentlemen, the king!"

Just as everyone sat down, Vice Admiral Antonelli stood and rapped his knife against his wine glass. When everyone grew quiet, Antonelli said, "Welcome all, and welcome especially to Lord Chesterfield and his fiancée, Lady Hawthorne."

While everyone else in the room was applauding, Renee worried about her captain. She glanced at him. He betrayed no visible reaction except a tight set to his lips. She looked at Julia at the head table, but Julia was looking at her fiancé as the crowd applauded.

Renee whispered to Jonah, "Are you okay?"

Jonah looked at her oddly. He gave the briefest of nods. Finally, he said, "She comes from a different world."

After a few moments of uncomfortable silence, the officer seated next to her asked her a question. She engaged in conversation and soon learned they had a number of mutual acquaintances. She looked out the corner of her eye a few minutes later and was relieved to see Jonah in an animated discussion with his neighbors.

Finally, dinner was cleared away. The First Space Lord rose, and everyone grew quiet. He began to speak: "Let me say I appreciate your warm welcome and all your good wishes. What Vice Admiral Antonelli did not say in his introduction was that there is an important reason I am here visiting the Aries system at this time."

At this, the crowd laughed. He held up his hand for quiet. "As First Space

Lord, much of my time is spent on politics and budgets and many other unglamorous and unpleasant duties. Once in a while, however, His Majesty calls upon me to do something far more to my liking. Tonight, we are here to recognize the courage, daring, innovation, and excellence of one of the ships in the fleet and its leaders.

"Please allow me to read the following Royal Proclamation.

> For extraordinary heroism and outstanding performance of duty in action against enemy forces in the H2813 and Venera systems from 30 April 3417 to 17 May 3417. During this crucial period, HMS *Cumberland* intercepted and captured two enemy freighters and then carried out devastating attacks against enemy warships and installations and rescued a peer of the Commonwealth from captivity in the face of extremely heavy opposition. Displaying boldness, ingenuity, superb ship handling, innovation, and unwavering courage, HMS *Cumberland* caused over one trillion pounds' worth of damage to the enemy. By their excellent teamwork, dedication, and sustained superior performance, the officers and crew of *Cumberland* and reflect great credit upon themselves and uphold the highest traditions of the Royal Navy. Signed King Edward XII.

"Captain Halberd, Commander Fung; Lady Hawthorne would not be here tonight if it were not for your actions. I owe you a personal debt of gratitude, and I am instructed to tell you His Majesty feels likewise. I am pleased—no, delighted—to award you the Royal Unit Citation. All members of your crew are entitled to wear this ribbon," he said, holding up a military decoration, "and *Cumberland* is entitled to fly this banner." He held up a banner, neatly folded.

"This banner is being painted on the hull of *Cumberland* even as we speak here tonight. Captain Halberd, Commander Fung, please step forward."

Jonah and Renee rose and went to face the First Space Lord. He shook their hands and thanked them, then pinned the decorations on their jackets. When he finished, he indicated they should turn to face everyone.

"Ladies and gentlemen," he called out, "Three cheers for HMS *Cumberland!*"

The crowd stood and yelled lustily, "Hip, Hip, Hurray" three times. When they finished, Jonah and Renee returned to their seats. When they sat, Vice Admiral Antonelli stood.

"Ladies and gentlemen, if you would join me in one final toast before we depart this evening," he asked. He raised his glass in the air and waited for everyone to follow suit. "Confusion to the enemy," he cried.

"Confusion to the enemy," the crowd answered.

20

With only two days before its departure, *Cumberland* was a busy place. Already the damage to the outer hull had been repaired. The outside of the ship looked much as it had a few weeks ago, except for a slight color difference between the repaired section and the older, original sections. The Royal Unit Citation banner had been painted on the hull. Point defense lasers, plasma shield generators, and sensor pods that had been damaged or destroyed had already been replaced. From the outside, things appeared calm.

Inside, the ship was different. The work of rebuilding the compartments smashed by the exploding missiles or slashed by enemy lasers still had a way to go. The repairs to the launch tubes on both sides of the ship were the biggest priority, and there was still a great deal to accomplish to bring them online. Magazines needed to be rebuilt, the autoloaders needed to be installed and tested thoroughly, and the complicated electronics needed to control all of this hooked up properly. After the launch tubes were fully functional, then the repair crews could worry about rebuilding the bulkheads and hatches.

Removing the damaged material had created a large open space. The surviving bulkheads would protect the ship in the event of a hull breach, but it left an area of structural weakness in the ship. Until the interior bulkheads were restored, this would be *Cumberland's* Achilles' heel. Command Master Chief Allroyd had stayed on schedule, and it was indeed miraculous what his men had been able to do in such a brief time. He planned to have the launch tubes functional before they embarked and would be keeping 30 men aboard to begin interior repairs while they were in transit.

Allroyd was true to his word, and *Cumberland* departed on schedule. They began the journey back to Hercules Station to meet up with the other elements in Rear Admiral Rodriquez's task force. They had a four-day journey back, with most of that time spent getting to and from the hyper corridor. The actual time in hyperspace was less than a day.

When they arrived at Hercules Station, Rear Admiral Rodriguez summoned Captain Halberd and Commander Fung to a meeting of all the captains to go over her plans for the upcoming attack. Jonah and Renee arrived and were ushered into the rear admiral's conference room. Waiting for them were the captains and executive officers of the other eleven ships that made up the attack force. Rodriguez would fly her flag on the battlecruiser *Montana*, one of the new *Dakota*-class battlecruisers. Also in the task force were the battlecruiser *Inflexible*, the heavy cruisers *Wessex* and *Norfolk*, the light cruisers *Dido* and *Hermione* and the frigates *Saintes*, *Finisterre*, *Shiloh*, *Guadalcanal,* and *Hampton Roads*.

Jonah knew three of the commanders from the academy and one of the XOs. He knew two others slightly from being stationed in the same sector earlier. Renee knew four of the XOs from the academy and had served with one of the others. They all introduced themselves and waited for Rear Admiral Rodriguez. When she entered, they snapped to attention and saluted. She returned their salutes and asked them to sit.

She brought a holographic display of a star system up, which rotated slowly above the conference table. "This," she explained, "is our objective— the Demeter system. We reach it by traveling from here, through the H2813 and Venera systems. PB 410 has remained on station in the Venera system and has confirmed that the only Rodinan ship in the system is an older destroyer that arrived after your last visit, Captain Halberd. Naval Intelligence has reported that the Demeter system is protected by the *Kirillov*-class battlecruiser *Dzerzhinsky*, two *Putin*-class heavy cruisers, two *Kuznetsov*-class light cruisers, and generally five *Ovechkin*-class frigates, though the frigates come and go.

"Demeter is one of the more heavily industrialized systems in the Rodinan Federation. There are a great number of industrial nodes surrounding the planet Demeter and scattered throughout the asteroid belt. The system has two gas giants, and cloud scoops working both. Most important to us, though, is the shipyard."

She replaced the system map in the display with a holograph of the shipyard. "Naval Intelligence confirms that there are four of the new *Makarov*-class battlecruisers that are nearing completion. According to the information, the ships are still weeks away from being commissioned. Hitting them now, before they are battle-ready, will set the Federation back years.

"Though they will have advance warning we are coming from the Venera system, we do not think they will be able to prevent us from destroying the four ships under construction and causing damage to the other economic assets in the Demeter system. The hyper corridor from Venera to Demeter takes just under 11 hours to traverse, but we are confident they will not be able to reinforce the system before our arrival. That is because our attack is being made in concert with a larger attack being launched by Third Fleet on the New Moscow system.

She returned the display to show the Demeter system again. "Our first objective upon entering the system will be to take out their ships. They will have had enough warning from Venera that they should be close to the corridor when we exit. I do not anticipate they will be waiting for us but do believe they will be farther up the gravity well than their normal position, so we might not have more than a couple of hours before we engage.

"After we destroy their defensive capability, *Montana*, *Inflexible*, and *Norfolk* will target the shipyard and any orbital defense platforms. *Finisterre* and *Hampton Roads* will destroy the cloud scoops, *Wessex* will hit the industrial nodes near the planet, and *Saintes*, *Shiloh*, and *Guadalcanal* will hit the industrial nodes in the asteroid belt. A set of more detailed orders is on your comms. Any questions at this time?"

"Sir," Jonah asked, "you have not discussed the role *Cumberland* will play in this attack."

"Captain Halberd," Rodriguez replied, "since your ship is still undergoing repair, I decided to keep you out of the initial assault as a ready reserve. I plan to leave you behind here while you finish your structural repairs. Depending on the progress you make, you may advance to Venera. If we take heavier damage than expected in our initial assault in the Demeter system, you will then come and help us complete the mission. The fitness of the captain and crew is beyond question, but your ship could use a few more days while the bulkheads on the starboard side are rebuilt. Believe me, I would rather have *Cumberland* with us, but it is more prudent to leave you as a reserve."

"Aye, aye, sir," Jonah responded. Though disappointed, he understood Rear Admiral Rodriguez's logic.

"If there are no further questions," Rodriguez stated, "you are dismissed. We depart for H2813 in less than two hours."

She stood, ending the meeting. The other officers stood and saluted, then waited for her to leave the room.

The captain of *Wessex*, Kyle Glenn, commiserated with Jonah. They had been classmates at the academy and though not close friends, had always gotten along. "It doesn't seem quite right, Halberd," he commented. "It was your success that got this whole operation going. I wish you were coming into Demeter with us."

"Well," Jonah said, "I would like to be there too, but the admiral wants us where she wants us, so we'll bide our time. Probably have to come clean up the mess you make, Kyle," he said with a wink.

Captain Glenn chuckled, "Jonah, I plan on making a *big* mess. But don't worry, the Federation will have to do the clean up this time."

Jonah laughed in response and took his leave. He and Commander Fung returned to *Cumberland*. Along the way, she asked, "Captain, I don't understand. If they aren't going to let us be part of the attack, why rush us out of the yard as quickly as they did?"

"I think Rear Admiral Rodriguez is confident that she'll be able to overcome the ships in the Demeter system without us," he replied. "She's decided one heavy cruiser won't make a difference. Even so, I wish we were going with them," he admitted. "But orders are orders. 'Ours is not to reason why,' commander."

21

The task force under Rear Admiral Rodriguez moved out on schedule. They jumped into the long corridor to H2813. After arriving in H2813, two days later, they began the jump into the Venera system. *Cumberland* remained behind and continued working on repairs. After four more days of round-the-clock work, CMDMC Allroyd informed Jonah that he and his men would be able to finish by the time *Cumberland* made the Venera system if they left now. Captain Halberd sent a message to Rear Admiral Rodriguez and was given the order to advance.

Cumberland uncoupled from Hercules Station and headed to the hyper corridor leading to H2813. Twenty-seven hours later, they activated the Alcubierre generators and entered hyperspace for the slightly more than a three-day journey to the H2813 system. One of the difficulties of such a long hyper corridor was the communications blackout of hyperspace. Not even the kewpie, the Quantum Particle Communications System, would work in hyper.

Upon exiting the warp bubble in H2813, Lieutenant Blutarsky on communications alerted Jonah that there was a priority comm for him on the kewpie. Priority comms such as these were sent with special encryption that only the captain and XO could open. Jonah left the bridge and went to his cabin. Opening the encrypted signal, he found highest priority orders from Vice Admiral Antonelli with a message to establish a video link immediately.

When he did, Vice Admiral Antonelli's face filled his screen. "Captain Halberd," Antonelli began, "you have arrived in system H2813?"

"Yes, sir."

Nodding his head, Antonelli continued. "Rear Admiral Rodriguez has not been heard from in more than a day. Shortly after her arrival in the Demeter system, we received an interrupted message from *Montana*. Then an hour ago, PB 410, which has remained in the Venera system, reported that a Rodinan task force composed of one of the new *Makarov* battlecruisers, a *Putin* heavy cruiser, and two *Kuznetsov*-class light cruisers emerged from hyper and is heading to the H2813 corridor."

"Yes, sir," Jonah acknowledged. "Should we fall back to Hercules Station to wait for reinforcements?"

Antonelli grimaced. "No, captain," he said quietly. "There are no reinforcements. My portion of Second Fleet, except for the frigates on blockade duty, was pulled out of Aries a week ago to support Third Fleet's attack on New Moscow." Antonelli's expression was one of furious disgust. "PB 410 is still in the Venera system, stealthed. They will be notifying us when the Rodinans enter the hyper corridor to H2813. Based on the information we have now, we estimate you have under 48 hours until they enter H2813. *Cumberland* is the only thing standing between the Rodinans and Hercules Station. And if you can't slow them down, they'll make it to Aries before we can."

The full impact of Antonelli's words hit Jonah. He and *Cumberland* had just been given a suicide mission. He swallowed reflexively. "Understood, sir. We will do our best, sir."

"I know you will, captain," Antonelli said sadly. "I wish you and your crew all the luck in the world. I'm sorry to have—"

Interrupting, Jonah held up his hand and said, "Sir, 'England expects that every man will do his duty.'"

"Quite right, captain," Antonelli answered, "quite right. You have your orders. Antonelli out."

The connection was cut. Jonah sat, thinking, but not for long. He commed his executive officer. "Commander," he said, "schedule a meeting for the officers and the master chief at the top of the hour. When you've finished that, come to my ready room."

He stood and crossed into the ready room. When he entered, Ginepri poked his head through the door. "Anything I can get you, sir?"

"Yes, thank you. Some coffee, please."

A few minutes later, Renee entered. Jonah brought her up to speed on their situation. She exhaled sharply when she realized how dire it was. They sat in silence for a few moments, then she raised her head and asked, "What are you thinking, sir?"

Jonah sighed. "I'm thinking of how we can cause as much chaos as we can while we can. I'm pretty sure we can take out the *Kuznetsovs* and damage the *Putin*, but I'm out of ideas for the *Makarov*."

They sat in silence for a few minutes, both lost in thought. Soon the other officers began to arrive. Ginepri scuttled in with a large coffee urn and mugs. Master Chief Bradshaw came, accompanied by Allroyd. Jonah hadn't thought to invite Allroyd but was glad Bradshaw had.

When everyone was settled, Jonah gave them the news. Rather than let them think about it, he brought up a holographic display of the H2813 system. Using his tablet, he manipulated the information to show the position of *Cumberland* and the expected arrival of the Rodinan ships. He began to speak.

"Approximately 28 hours ago, Rear Admiral Rodriguez entered the Demeter system. Fleet received a brief, interrupted message from *Montana*, but there has been no further contact. A little more than an hour ago, PB 410, still hiding in the Venera system, reported to Fleet that a task force of four ships, a *Makarov*, a *Putin*, and two *Kuznetsovs*, had transitioned in from Demeter and were on a least time course for the corridor to this system. They are expected to arrive in approximately 47 hours, based on the last course and heading reported by PB 410. Since he has not updated that information, the Rodinan ships are still on that course.

"Vice Admiral Antonelli has informed me that *Cumberland* is the only Royal Navy ship that stands in the way of preventing the Rodinans from reaching Hercules Station and then the Aries system. Vice Admiral Antonelli and the balance of Second Fleet were transferred to reinforce Third Fleet's invasion of New Moscow. Even if his ships were to start now, they would not reach the Aries system before the Rodinans unless *Cumberland* can slow them down." He paused to let them absorb what he had just told them.

"It is up to us, to *Cumberland*, to slow them down. Tens of thousands of lives depend on us, ladies and gentlemen. I do not think it is an exaggeration to say that what we do here affects the well-being of our entire Commonwealth. Our failure to prevent a Rodinan assault on Aries would be a disaster for our war effort. So now we need to determine how we can do our duty in the most effective way we can.

"We are here," and he pressed a button on his tablet that made the icon showing *Cumberland's* position begin to blink, "and it will take us 21 hours to reach the normal entrance to the hyper corridor if we use a one hundred and ten percent decel burn.

"That will give us less than a full day there to prepare whatever sort of welcome we can for our guests. We have a full missile load of 120 laser warheads, plus ten of the new missile frames that contain four missiles each. Against us, the Rodinans can throw a salvo of 72 missiles: 30 from the *Makarov*, 18 from the *Putin*, and 12 each from the *Kuznetsovs*."

That was a grim number. Facing a salvo of 20 missiles in the Venera system, *Cumberland* had taken some significant damage. She had proven to be a tough ship, but a salvo of 72 missiles would overwhelm their point defense capability. Separately, many at the table reached the same conclusion: that the first blow they struck might be the only one they'd get.

There was a long silence. Lieutenant Blutarsky spoke first. "XO," he said, "how many missiles can the tac system handle at once?"

Renee answered quickly, "The tac system can handle launch and targeting for 72 missiles at a time."

Blutarsky's face fell. For the idea he had come up with, he needed the number to be higher. Though he hadn't told everyone what he was thinking about, it was obvious he was disappointed.

Down at the corner of the table, Allroyd and Bradshaw murmured back and forth briefly. Jonah quickly glanced at them and asked if they had anything to offer. Bradshaw looked at Allroyd and shrugged his shoulders, indicating that Allroyd should speak.

"What if," Allroyd asked, "you were able to send identical targeting and launch information to, say, four missiles at a time? Maybe give four missiles the same system ID?"

Renee thought quickly and responded while puzzling out loud. "If you 'cloned' the system ID for four missiles, so the system would think it's only one, I suppose you could. All four would be targeted and launched identically." She paused, then resumed, "But you wouldn't be able to track them. The tac system would try to track all four as one, and it would probably crash the system."

"Um," Allroyd was fumbling for the right words. "No disrespect, ma'am, but I'm not too worried about tracking. Once the missiles launch, they are hands-free, right?"

"Right," Renee said slowly, trying to think through what Allroyd was suggesting. "But again, all four missiles would have the same target—the same point on the targeted ship. They might approach from slightly different vectors, but they would all attack the same area of the hull at which the tac system pointed them. It might make it easy for their point defense to pick them off too. And that's if I can figure out a way to keep the system from trying to track them."

Allroyd was undeterred. "So, if you can figure how to shut off tracking, we could theoretically launch as many as 35 sets of four missiles each, in addition to our normal weight of 20, with the drawback being that some sets of four missiles would have the same exact target?"

Flustered, Renee answered quizzically, "Yes?"

Seeing that some in the room had not figured out why he was asking these questions, Allroyd spelled it out. "What the master chief and I were thinking, if we could get the system issues ironed out, was that we try to launch all 160 of our missiles in the initial salvo. We'd use the ten missile frames we have and have the fabricator crank out another 25."

Blutarsky, seeing how this idea was similar to what he had been thinking originally, jumped in. "We could pre-position the frames before the Rodinans arrive. Once we detect their emergence from the corridor, we launch everything."

Jonah asked, "How would we pre-position them? We won't have time to drop them all off."

Blutarsky had the answer ready. "We use the shuttles and the MAS to tractor them along different headings, then release them and let them float ballistic. We'll know from PB 410 when the Rodinans enter hyper, so we'll have a pretty good idea of when they'll arrive if they make a normal exit."

"What if they exit early?" Jonah asked.

"Let's think about that," Renee said. "We have to assume that they have some sort of Naval Intelligence outfit of their own, right?"

Jonah shrugged his shoulders.

Renee continued. "If they do, and if they wiped Rear Admiral Rodriguez' force out, which we suspect, then they probably know that the only thing between them and Hercules and Aries is *Cumberland* and maybe a couple of frigates. They probably also know that Vice Admiral Antonelli has been pulled away to Third Fleet. Aries is the high-value target. Hercules is like Venera—other than the station, there's not much. Aries, with the shipyard, industrial nodes, and cloud scoops, has to be their objective. Their only chance to get to Aries before Vice Admiral Antonelli comes back is if they make a least-time journey. That means they'll enter the corridor from Venera as soon as they can, and they'll stay in hyper until the end of the corridor here."

"We'll have to have PB 410 confirm their position, course and speed," she added, "but even if we can't pinpoint their location and precise arrival time, we can plot it close enough that Lieutenant Blutarsky's idea could work."

"Sir," Lieutenant Commander Volkov asked, "I'd like to offer a suggestion, piggy-backing on what Lieutenant Blutarsky and the command master chief offered."

"Sure," Jonah said, "go ahead."

"The weakest area for any point defense system is the rear of the ship because emissions from the EM drive interfere with sensors of all types. It's also where the shields are weakest for the same reason. But the problem is that you're rarely in position to shoot right up someone's tailpipe, and trying to swing them around from the side makes them easy pickings for point defense."

"Yes," Jonah confirmed. This was pretty basic information, but he remembered Volkov didn't have experience in the field; she had spent her career until now in staff positions.

"After the shuttles and the MAS are done sending the other frames on the various courses, could we send them straight up the corridor entrance? The shuttles can carry one frame each, and the MAS should be able to hold two. If we could somehow get them situated behind where a normal corridor exit would happen, we could launch sixteen birds right up their skirts." She added hastily, "Sir."

"Why not release them early and let them coast in ballistically, like the remainder of the missiles?" Jonah asked.

"Because they would be fighting that ballistic trajectory, captain," Volkov responded quickly. "They would need to decelerate to a full stop and then reverse course. That would cut their range by more than half and make them easier for the Rodinans to see and pick off. If we have the shuttles carry them, we can let the shuttles bring them to a stop before the Rodinans exit the corridor.

When no one brought up any new ideas, he concluded the meeting. "Commander," he asked, "find out if you can solve the problem with the tac system and tracking. Master Chief Bradshaw and Command Master Chief Allroyd, please get the fabricator started on making the additional 25 frames we'll need. Lieutenant Blutarsky, come up with how you would propose to deploy the missiles. Lieutenant Commander Volkov, confirm that the MAS can hold two missile frames or racks and work with Lieutenant Blutarsky on the timing of when he will need to use the shuttles and MAS for his positioning and what course and speed *Cumberland* will need to be on when you will need them to depart to be in position. Lieutenant Dietrich, please plot a course that would have us within cannon range at the most likely emergence point, based on normal corridor transit time, after we make any course or speed adjustments Lieutenant Blutarsky needs for his deployment. As far as that course is concerned, we'll have to work backward from when we hear from PB 410 about the Rodinans position, course, and speed. Any questions?"

There were no questions. Jonah then said, "I will be announcing our situation to the crew shortly. Otherwise, they will figure it out soon enough, and I would rather have them hear it from me. Keep your eyes open for any morale or discipline problems. We'll make the kewpie available to anyone who wants to send a text message home. Remind the crew that any message will have to be cleared by the censors."

With that, he closed the meeting. The officers left. Jonah stood and began to pace the length of the room, thinking of how to tell the crew. After a few laps, he looked at the clock. Less than 45 hours remained before the Rodinan ships entered the system.

Jonah sat at the console in his ready room and addressed the crew via the ship's comm. "Attention, crew of the *Cumberland*," he began. "I apologize for interrupting whatever you are doing, but I would appreciate a few moments of your attention.

"In less than two days, we will be facing a Rodinan task force here in system H2813. A Rodinan battlecruiser, a heavy cruiser, and two light cruisers are on their way here right now. *Cumberland* is the only thing the Royal Navy has between those ships and the Aries system. Rear Admiral Rodriguez and her task group have not been heard from since they entered the Demeter system, and Vice Admiral Antonelli's portion of Second Fleet was pulled away to assist with the attack on the New Moscow system. They cannot return to Aries in time.

"It is up to us, *Cumberland*, to slow down or stop the Rodinans. Thousands of lives in the Hercules and Aries systems depend on us. Our ability to stop the Rodinans here will have a huge impact on the war. Though we will be outnumbered and outgunned, *Cumberland* has proven to be a stout ship, and this crew just earned a Royal Unit Citation. We have much to do in a short time to prepare for the battle that is coming. I am confident we will acquit ourselves well.

"God save the king!" he concluded, "and confusion to our enemies!"

He closed the comm channel and sat back. Not his best speech, he thought, but far from his worst. He now needed to determine who would man the two shuttles and the MAS. He believed they might be the only survivors from the Commonwealth after this battle but would likely spend years in a Rodinan POW camp afterward. Deciding who might live, only to face incredible hardship, was not a pleasant choice.

By the time of his next watch on the bridge, Commander Fung had informed him that she believed there was a programming workaround for the tac system. She and Petty Officer Sanchez had begun working on it and would let him know when they had success. Lieutenant Blutarsky had confirmed that PB 410 had updated Fleet quite recently on the position, course, and speed of the Rodinan ships. Based on that, he had drawn up a schedule of deceleration burns to slow *Cumberland* down to the proper velocity for releasing missile frames so that they would arrive on target at the right time. He also had a table of the precise trajectories each frame had to follow. Bradshaw and Allroyd confirmed that the fabricator was already manufacturing the missile frames they would need.

As the frames came out of the fabricator, they were pulling missiles from the magazines and slotting them in. They already had six finished. Once Commander Fung finished the system changes, they would need to change the programming on the missiles so that some sets of four missiles had the same system ID. Blutarsky had added the wrinkle of splitting the matched groupings of four missiles between different frames so that their approach vectors would be as different as possible until they closed within range. Jonah had an inkling that nothing like this had ever been done in the centuries of interstellar combat. He had informed Vice Admiral Antonelli of the broad outlines of what they were trying to do.

Antonelli had remarked that it was an awfully complicated plan and that the system changes they were making would not be sustainable in even the brief nature of a typical combat. He also acknowledged that *Cumberland* did not have many good options, facing the salvo weight of the Rodinan ships as well as the difficulty of piercing their point defense. By the end of the conversation, he had warmed to the idea, realizing that *Cumberland* would likely only get the one shot.

He gave Jonah a brief update on the progress of the attack on New Moscow. Though he tried to keep his voice neutral and the information general, Jonah sensed the vice admiral was angry and frustrated. Jonah knew he should not try to read between the lines, but sometimes the temptation was overwhelming. Antonelli let slip that Third Fleet had not damaged any of the economic assets targeted in the New Moscow system. They had apparently withdrawn to the outer part of the system after receiving some minor damage in their initial encounter with the enemy. This incomplete withdrawal from action also served to freeze Antonelli and Second Fleet in place outside the system. It was appearing as though the only option would be for Antonelli to force an entrance in order to open an escape route for Third Fleet.

It was clear to Jonah that Antonelli knew how hopeless *Cumberland's* position was but that Antonelli did not enjoy ordering good men and women to their likely destruction. The strain of it showed on his face. Jonah recognized it because lately, he was seeing the same signs of stress in himself. Before they signed off, the vice admiral promised to have his systems people consult with Commander Fung on the systems changes.

The next morning, Jonah checked the status of the various elements of their plan. With the help of Second Fleet, Commander Fung had developed a workaround for the system and a protocol for changing the system ID on the missiles. Nearly all the frames had been created and missiles loaded. In less than an hour, Lieutenant Blutarsky would begin releasing them. After that, *Cumberland* would accelerate back to $0.3c$, then release the shuttles and MAS, which would continue at that speed until they began decelerating to come to rest just past where the Rodinans were projected to exit.

Jonah had been wrestling with the problem of which his people to assign to the shuttles and MAS. Ordinarily, he was a decisive man. He weighed the facts, estimated probable outcomes, considered alternatives and contingencies, and made his decision. In this case, he struggled. He called Commander Fung and Master Chief Bradshaw to the ready room.

When they arrived, he explained his difficulty, that assigning a crew member to one of the shuttles would save his life but also would condemn him to what could be years of brutality as a Rodinan prisoner. He then explained, "Whomever I choose will need to be tough and resilient in order to survive. Both of you meet those criteria, so I'm planning on asking you to do it and then pick the crew members you want to have with you."

Bradshaw looked at him with keen eyes. "Are you asking me, Jonah? Or are you ordering me, captain?"

"What do you mean?"

"If you're asking me, as Jonah Halberd, the man I've known these last ten years and who I've entrusted with my life so many times, then I'm going to have to decline," Bradshaw explained. "Because my place is here with you. If you're ordering me, as Captain Halberd, then I'll follow orders reluctantly and may risk insubordination trying to talk you out of it."

Renee looked up, a determined set to her mouth. "I haven't known you that long, so my decision doesn't have the personal basis as the master chief's. In the short time we've worked together, you've earned my trust, respect, and friendship. But more important than that, I know my duty is on this ship."

He looked at them both closely. "You do realize the odds we face?" he asked.

Bradshaw chuckled softly. "A battlecruiser, heavy cruiser, and two light cruisers against us?" he asked rhetorically. "No, we know what the odds are. So does the crew. But we also know about duty and about the thousands of people at risk if we can't stop them and the potential for this to swing the war the wrong way."

Jonah looked at him. "I think that's why I asked you both to help me with this. Whatever decision I make as captain, my private feelings also play a part. When I make decisions as captain, I am thinking of the ship and the crew, of which I am also a part. But in this case, I am making choices for individuals, choices where I will not share the consequences of my orders. But if I don't pick someone, I'm sentencing them to almost certain death. I've never faced this before."

Bradshaw nodded. "Who of the officers and ratings do you feel would best be able to survive the Rodinans?"

"Blutarsky, Guglielmo, Allroyd, Sanchez, you and Renee," Jonah answered.

"I think you'll need to find two more," Renee said. "Who else?"

"Patel and Dietrich," Bradshaw added.

Jonah sat in silence. He nodded his head after a minute, coming to a decision. "Very well," he said.

22

A short time after his meeting with Fung and Bradshaw, Jonah issued the orders to those who would man the shuttles and MAS. They received confirmation from PB 410 that the Rodinan force had entered the hyper corridor on a least-time transit course. Jonah had Fung start a countdown for the estimated arrival time of the Rodinans. They had stationed a recon drone with a kewpie connection near where they expected the Rodinans to exit hyper.

The holographic display in the ready room showed where all the components of their strategy were and where they would be when the Rodinans appeared at the end of the corridor. The shuttles and MAS had already begun braking to get into their positions. According to the display, when the Rodinans exited the hyper corridor, they would find themselves in the middle of a sphere of 160 missiles tipped with powerful x-ray lasers. Renee had already loaded targeting instructions to the tactical computer, so the missiles would launch as soon as the recon drone identified the Rodinan ships.

Jonah was confident that they would be able to deal a heavy blow to the Rodinans but had no way of knowing if it would be heavy enough. He knew he would likely never find out since he expected *Cumberland* to be destroyed shortly afterward. The Rodinans would be able to launch at least one salvo at *Cumberland*, and those 72 missiles would overwhelm *Cumberland's* ability to defend itself.

When the timer reached the ten-hour mark, Jonah decided to take a walk around the ship. He had done this regularly since assuming command but more frequently in the last two days. When he reached the lower decks, he asked where he would find Seaman Bosco. A petty officer told him where Bosco was on duty, and Jonah went to see him.

When he entered the engineering station where Bosco was on duty, he quickly called, "As you were," so he would not disturb the routine more than necessary. He saw Bosco sitting at his station, monitoring the second fusion core.

"Fireman Bosco," he said, "I recall that I promised you I would tell you if we were ever heading into a 'brown pants' situation."

"Aye, sir," Bosco replied, smiling, "but if it's all the same to you, sir, we're all planning on wearing our red shirts."

"Then I'll do the same," Jonah answered with a grin. He reached out his hand, and Bosco shook it firmly.

Jonah left the compartment, pausing outside after he closed the hatch. The courage of the men and women with whom he served amazed him. During his walks through the ship in the last two days, the positive attitude and mental toughness of his crew were apparent. He felt truly honored to serve with them.

With the few hours left, he returned to his quarters, hoping to sleep. Sleep did not come. He tried to compose a message to his mother but could not find the words. While sitting at his console, stumped, he realized he would have no difficulty in composing a letter to Julia. Remembering conversations with her, discussing the responsibility for others each of them had to bear— she would understand what he was feeling. He also knew it would be highly inappropriate for him to write her.

He understood her engagement to the First Space Lord was not necessarily a choice she made. There was nothing in her behavior while she had been on the *Cumberland* that showed she had any inkling that an engagement was in her near-term future. She likely had received orders from her father of what she was expected to do and, like him, would follow those orders to the best of her ability.

He stumbled through writing his mother. Wrapping up this message, he realized sleep was an impossibility. He headed to the mess to get a bite to eat before heading to the bridge.

Reaching the bridge, he relieved Renee, who moved into the tactical chair. She spun to face him. "Couldn't find anything else to do?" she asked with a smile. Jonah merely shook his head.

Renee had also given up on trying to sleep. She had sent messages to her parents and her sister. She had found it difficult to come up with the right words, so just told them she loved them. She found it strange that the nervousness and apprehension she had felt before the battle in Venera was completely absent. She knew that it was likely that she would not survive this battle and that the ship was likely to be destroyed. She pondered all the things in life she had not yet had the chance to do. Though it gave her feelings of regret, she had a feeling of calm acceptance, and her mood was wistful rather than sad. With only a few hours left, there was nothing more to prepare, nothing more to distract her. She found that staying in her quarters made her feel lonely, so she had gone to the bridge. She was not surprised when Jonah appeared a few minutes later.

They waited in companionable silence as the minutes ticked away.

23

When the timer indicated that the Rodinans were estimated to emerge from hyper in 45 minutes, the bridge crew rotated. Lieutenant Commander Volkov took her position on sensors. Petty Officer Delnicki was manning damage control. Commander Fung activated the holographic display showing where the shuttles and MAS were, along with the missile frames they had released earlier, in relation to a small yellow sphere indicating where they expected the Rodinan task force to appear.

The timer hit zero, and the Rodinans did not appear. Seconds ticked by, and Jonah realized he was holding his breath. No sooner did he exhale when an alert tone sounded. Commander Fung confirmed moments later, "We have four ships emerging from hyper, right where we expected."

"Fire!" Jonah exclaimed. Within moments all 160 of *Cumberland's* missiles ignited and set off after their prey. Twenty-five missiles had been sent to attack each light cruiser. Forty missiles targeted the heavy cruiser, and the remaining seventy streaked after the *Makarov*-class battlecruiser.

"Estimated time to cannon range?" he asked.

"Eighty seconds at current course and speed," Fung replied.

Halberd had slowed *Cumberland* as they approached the target area. Rather than having the two groups vectoring towards one another at a combined rate of half the speed of light, he wanted to keep *Cumberland* in cannon range as long as possible. With the missiles expended, the photon cannons were all he had left, and he hoped to do as much damage as he could.

"Estimated time to target?" Halberd asked.

"Fifteen seconds," Fung answered, then added, "Rodinan missile launch, captain. All four ships got their birds away."

"Estimated time to impact?"

"Ninety-five seconds or less," she said with a calm she did not feel.

"Set the computer to fire all photon cannons at the *Makarov* as soon as she's in range," Jonah ordered.

"Aye, aye, sir."

"Sensors, keep us updated," Jonah requested. "We'll have less than a minute to enjoy our success."

Surprisingly, a couple of members of the bridge crew chuckled at that. Jonah shook his head. He felt the slight shimmy as the railguns launched flak and chaff cartridges in rapid succession.

The missiles surrounding the Rodinan emergence point came streaking in. The Rodinan task force had barely had any time to react, but their datanet was up, coordinating defense of their ships. Independent of human interaction, the ships launched counter missiles, and point defense lasers reached out to stop *Cumberland's* attack.

Three missiles reached the first light cruiser. One of the powerful lasers hit the mass compensator, and the ship imploded. Two missiles hit the other light cruiser, but one of the powerful x-ray lasers breached the core of the ship's fusion reactor, and it exploded like a miniature sun. Five missiles survived to hit the heavy cruiser, but three of those expended their blasts on the shields of the ship, causing little damage. The remaining two hit her from behind, though, and destroyed her EM drive. Though intact, the cruiser could not maneuver except on thrusters.

Seventy missiles were aimed at the *Makarov*-class battlecruiser. Only nine survived to hit it. Five of them expended themselves on the tough ship's plasma shielding, weakening it but not penetrating. Three followed immediately and punched through the weakened shield, gouging deep into the hull of the ship. Compartments were breached, dozens of crewmen were killed, three-quarters of the Alcubierre field generators were destroyed, but the damage they caused was not catastrophic. The last missile, coming in from the rear, targeted the big ship's EM drives. The *Makarov* had four huge EM drives. This last missile obliterated one of the four and damaged another, but the battlecruiser could still move.

Lieutenant Commander Volkov updated Halberd and the crew with a running tally of the damage they caused. When she reported the damage to the battlecruiser's EM drives, Jonah felt a strange sense of satisfaction. *Cumberland* had caused enough damage to slow the Rodinan attack: perhaps to force them to turn back or enough that Second Fleet would be able to return to protect the Aries system. The photon cannons had just begun firing, taking advantage of the weakened shielding on the *Makarov* and flaying its hull.

His satisfaction was short-lived. The tactical display showed the estimated time to impact for the Rodinan missiles, less than ten seconds. He had enough time to glance at Commander Fung and nod his head.

The Rodinans launched 72 missiles. The flak cartridges had destroyed 23 of them. The chaff they had launched, and other electronic countermeasures had led another 13 missiles astray. Counter missiles and point defense lasers had eliminated another 25. That left eleven missiles untouched that reached their designated range and sent their bomb-pumped lasers at *Cumberland*. Seven of them erupted moments earlier than the other four. The combined attacks of the first seven overwhelmed the plasma shields, and their beams made the tough AT-38 armor boil where they hit. They caused damage to the outer compartments, but one of them hit close enough to engineering to trigger an automatic ejection of the fusion cores.

In microseconds, the cores ejected, opening the engineering compartment to space. In addition to the cores, all 38 people in the department were vented into space with the explosive decompression. None survived.

The four missiles that hit after the plasma shields dropped caused severe damage. One destroyed the EM drives, useless anyway, with the powerplant ejected. Another struck the middle of the ship and penetrated into the bridge. In the blink of an eye, Commander Fung saw Lieutenant Commander Volkov and Petty Officer Delnicki simply vanish in the blink of an eye, vaporized by the laser. The decompression sucked some other crew members into space in an instant, despite being strapped into their chairs. Debris chewed up by the laser swirled through the compartment on its way out to space. One missile blasted into the empty shuttle bay, slicing all the way through the ship, almost completely separating the rear third of the ship from the front. The remaining missile struck on the front quarter of the ship, angled almost directly down the axis of the ship. It opened a huge hole nearly the length of the ship, exposing compartment after compartment to cold space.

Despite the shock of the decompression of the bridge, Fung clung to consciousness by a thread. She glanced over to see if Captain Halberd were still there. A six-inch shard of metal from one of the consoles was sticking through the membrane of his ship suit, plunged into his right eye. Her heart sank but realizing it was a miracle she was alive, with trembling fingers, she activated an external comm channel. "Attention, Rodinan ships. HMS *Cumberland* surrenders." Then blackness took her.

24

Jonah Halberd awoke, disoriented. He could only see from his left eye, and he had a pounding headache. He was lying in a bunk. He started to lift his right hand to see what was wrong with his eye, but a voice from his right shushed, "Nyet, nyet," and his hand was prevented from moving. He turned his head slowly to the right to see who had spoken and saw a young blonde woman dressed in the black uniform of the Rodinan navy holding his forearm down.

He heard a door hiss open. A moment later, a tall bald man, also dressed in black, appeared. He wore the caduceus symbol of a medical officer on his collar. "Captain Halberd," he said with a slight Russian accent, "welcome back to the land of the living."

Halberd's disorientation did not clear. The last he could remember was nodding at Commander Fung shortly before they expected the Rodinan missiles to hit. The confusion showed on his face.

The bald man noticed and offered, "You are currently on board the battlecruiser *Pyotr Velikiy*. I am Flight Surgeon Nikolai Pavlishchev. We were able to rescue 25 people from what was left of your ship, but sadly, two have since died from their injuries, and another two might not last much longer. Oh, and there were six we pulled from your shuttles."

"Wha—" Halberd started to croak.

Pavlischev murmured a couple of words in Russian, and then the blonde woman tapped his arm. He turned his head slowly to face her and saw she had a cup of water with a straw. She offered it to him, and he took a sip, only realizing then how dry his mouth had been. He took two more sips, then hmm-ed that he was finished for the moment. He looked back at ·Pavlishchev.

The flight surgeon continued, "Please do not touch your right eye. It is covered in bandages since we pulled a 20-centimeter shard of metal from it.

We were not able to save the eye; I am sad to say. The metal also penetrated about eight centimeters into your skull. To stop the bleeding and repair as much damage as we could, we injected you with medical nanites and have kept you under sedation."

Halberd tried to process this information. Rodinan medical nanites were less effective than those the Commonwealth had developed but still exceedingly expensive. Given that the Rodinans had to have suffered serious casualties themselves, supplying a prisoner with medical nanites was quite unusual.

"Thank you," Halberd managed to say. "How long—" he started.

Pavlishchev stopped him. "You've been unconscious for nine days since we brought you aboard. I apologize if you're feeling a bit 'hungover' right now. An unpleasant side effect from the sedatives. Now, I'm sure you will have many questions but now is not the time. Please rest. The captain has been waiting for you to recover consciousness and will be in to see you later. For now, sleep is best."

Pavlishchev left the cabin. Halberd lay quietly, trying to process what he had been told. It was hard to think with his head pounding as it was. The *Cumberland* was obviously destroyed if there were only 25 survivors (now 23, he remembered, plus the six). He wondered where in space they were, whether they were still in the H2813 system or had managed to make repairs enough to return to a Rodinan system. He guessed from the damage he had inflicted on the Rodinans that their attack on the Commonwealth had been thwarted and imagined the Rodinan captain might not be terribly willing to exchange Christmas cards with him right now. He wondered who of his crew had survived. Finally, he realized that the Rodinans would probably be delivering all of them to a prisoner-of-war camp, which would certainly be unpleasant. As captain, though, he wondered if the Politburo and Rodinan FSB might want to conduct a show trial, find him guilty and shoot him. On this happy thought, he dozed off.

When he awoke next, he found himself in the same cabin. His head still hurt, though he thought perhaps a bit less than it had. He turned slowly to his right. A different Rodinan was there, a young man with short black hair. Halberd asked for water, and the man held the cup and the straw up to him. After drinking a few sips, the door hissed open. Words were exchanged in Russian, and the young man got up and left. As the newcomer pulled the stool towards the foot of the bed, Halberd noticed his sleeve carried the broad stripe and single star of a first-rank captain.

The newcomer sat down and began to unbutton his uniform jacket. As he did, he said, "First-rank Captain Maxim Belyaev, at your service."

Halberd noticed his English was almost without a trace of accent. "Captain Jonah Halberd," he offered in return.

"I'm pleased to make your acquaintance," the Rodinan said, and with a trace of a smile added, "Believe it or not. I wanted to meet a man of such ingenuity and courage," he continued, "and honor. Second-rank Captain Kaun sends his regards."

"Is Captain Kaun on the ship?" Jonah asked incredulously.

"No," Belyaev responded, "he is my nephew."

"Oh—"

"Yes," Belyaev continued. "He and I appreciate what you did for him. Your act of kindness made it possible for them to save the nerve endings in his legs and his knees. He is currently wearing some cybernetic replacements but will be able to regen his lower legs in the future."

Jonah shrugged. "It was the right thing to do."

"It was the act of an honorable man, captain."

"Captain Belyaev, if you don't mind my asking," Jonah responded, "I don't seem to be in the sickbay. Am I in one of your officer's cabins?"

"Yes," Belyaev said with a smile. "Mine."

Stunned by such a kind gesture, Jonah was at a temporary loss for words. Finally, he managed to blurt, "Thank you."

"You're probably thinking that I should be furious with you," Belyaev mused, "and I am, so it would make no sense for me to give up my cabin for a wounded prisoner. But on a certain level, as one professional to another, I must confess to some admiration. We have pieced together what you did from the tactical logs, and it was a desperate, brilliant move. It was perhaps the only way you had to prevent us from penetrating deep into Commonwealth space, and it worked." He shook his head with a smile. "You are a hard man to kill, captain. Or lucky. Or both. Plus, you treated my nephew with great kindness in a time of war. Such an unusual gesture demands a response, no?"

"Captain Kaun?"

Belyaev nodded.

Jonah did not know how to respond, so changed the topic of conversation and asked, "Where are we?"

"We are still in what your people call system H2813. We are nearly finished making the repairs we need to make in order to return to the Venera system."

"But the doctor said it has been nine days?" Jonah asked.

"Hm, yes," Belyaev responded. "Well, you shot off my Alcubierre generators, and one of your lasers hit the ship's stores and damaged the replacements. We had to put one together from the damaged parts and then cannibalize the three from the *Kronstadt*—the heavy cruiser whose EM nodes you destroyed. We managed to jury-rig things, but it has been difficult to align the Alcubierre generators properly as they are not designed for this ship. These things cannot be hurried, as you know. We have all the personnel from *Kronstadt* aboard right now as we were forced to scuttle her. A fleet supply ship will meet us at Venera in a few days with more replacement parts so we can make more trustworthy repairs to the Alcubierre generators and EM drives before returning to the shipyard in Demeter to patch all the other holes you put in my ship. It was 'brand new' as they say. You should be ashamed of yourself, captain," he said with a hint of a smile.

Jonah thought for a moment, then asked, "What happened…before? In Demeter?"

"Ah," Belyaev explained, "your forces did not have such a good time of it. You were perhaps expecting the new battlecruisers to still be in the slips?"

Jonah nodded slightly.

"They weren't," Belyaev chuckled. "My *Pyotr Velikiy* and her sister ships had been commissioned in secret a couple of weeks ago. One at a time, they had been taken out for 'yard trials,' which were really shake-downs. We knew you would think they were a tempting target. We learned of your attack plans weeks ago."

"How? I only learned of the plan myself just before we stepped off," Jonah was curious.

Belyaev put his finger aside his nose and smiled. "I do not know for sure," he said, "but if I were you, I'd look at your Third Fleet. But that is telling tales out of school, I think. For once, those stooges at FSB got something right.

"Regardless, with so much time to prepare, our fleet supply was able to erect three automated defense platforms near the emergence point from Venera. Your successful attack against Captain Kaun confirmed what we knew about your admiralty's intention of attacking Demeter. When your Admiral Rodriguez appeared, she had no chance. Your people did well under the circumstances," he allowed. "They managed to destroy the *Dzerzhinsky* and the heavy cruiser *Sverdlov*, as well as a couple of frigates and caused some minor damage to my sister ships, but my *Pyotr Velikiy*, the *Kronstadt*, and the two light cruisers didn't get a scratch. That's why we were sent through to target the Aries system."

"All the ships were destroyed?" Jonah asked.

"Yes," Belyaev answered, nodding. "There were fewer than 100 survivors. Admiral Rodriguez was killed."

"What about," Jonah's throat tightened, and he swallowed. "What about New Moscow?"

"I think we share the same problem in both our fleets," Belyaev said. "Your Admiral Johannsen is an idiot, but he was matched against our Admiral Titov, who is an incompetent boob. Both are political hacks who have achieved their ranks on family connections rather than ability. Some ships were destroyed on both sides, with the Commonwealth gaining perhaps a slight advantage. Your Admiral Antonelli fought a clever rearguard action that allowed Johannsen's fleet to escape the system. However, the slight advantage in ships the Commonwealth gained in New Moscow was more than offset by your losses in Demeter." He shrugged. "If we had managed to reach the Aries system, we would have dealt the Commonwealth a painful blow. As it is, neither side is much stronger or weaker than they were before—except…" He trailed off in thought.

"Except what?" Jonah asked.

"Except for you, captain." Belyaev now had a cold and somewhat distant look to his eyes. "Except for you." Belyaev shook his head as though to dismiss certain thoughts.

"I have a problem, captain," Belyaev confessed. "I don't know what to do with you. If my political commissar were alive, he would know exactly what to do."

"What would that be?" Jonah asked.

"Oh, he would take you back to New Moscow. After the FSB extracted every bit of information out of you, there would be a highly-publicized trial for war crimes, and then you would be shot."

"I see," Jonah said glumly.

"Sadly," Belyaev said with mock sincerity, "the political commissar on board *Pyotr Velikiy* was killed during your attack." He winked. "Any time one of our ships suffers a hull breach in battle, it is amazing, but our political commissars always seem to have a knack for being in the thick of the action and always get killed.

"Regardless, what he would do does not sit well with me, especially since I am sitting face-to-face with the man who did the honorable thing by sending my nephew back to Venera for medical attention."

Jonah's breath caught. He did not dare to hope.

"I am waiting to hear from my, ah—what is the right word, my mentor? My patron? My," he chuckled, "my fairy godmother? Releasing you and your people in a shuttle is the honorable thing for me to do, but I need to make sure that that I would survive such a thing. My mentor agrees with me about what I want to do. He is trying to enlist enough support from his friends to counter the inevitable backlash."

Jonah thought quickly. "What about the rest of my people?" he asked. "Would it be possible to—"

Belyaev laughed, slapping his thigh. "Ha! I win!"

Jonah gave him a puzzled look.

"I bet myself," the Rodinan explained, "that you would ask that. Rest easy, captain. Your people are already loaded on the shuttle."

Jonah took a deep breath. "Thank you," he said quietly. "That is enough for me."

"I win another bet with myself," Belyaev stated. "Unfortunately, we will be leaving for Venera soon. If I do not hear anything, I will have to keep you with me, even though I would be sorry to. We—you and I—we are men of honor. I love my people. Rodina means 'motherland' in Russian. I could never betray my motherland. But the politicians and their toadies who are in charge, I do not wish to sacrifice my honor for them."

"When do you expect—" Jonah began, but Belyaev held up his hand.

"I've been waiting for a couple of days. My mentor will contact me when he has the support lined up that he feels I need. I must leave you now, as duty calls. I will return in an hour or so and let you know. In the meantime, it would be helpful if you would devise a message that I can send in the clear to let your pesky patrol boat know to come looking for a shuttle."

25

After an hour and twenty minutes had passed, Jonah had begun to give up hope. He consoled himself that 28 of his crew would be set free. He had decided on a message which Lieutenant Commander MacMurray would be able to understand but would be meaningless to anyone else.

Captain Belyaev appeared.

"Did you hear?" Jonah asked.

"Yes," Belyaev replied with a sigh, "and no. My mentor and I exchanged messages. He does not yet have all the support he feels I need to survive letting you go."

Jonah's expression fell. "I underst—"

Belyaev interrupted. "But he feels confident he will have it by the time we exit the corridor to Venera. I am pleased to say that I will be able to act as a man of honor."

Jonah, prepared for disappointment, stared at him with his one eye. "Thank you, Captain Belyaev," he said after struggling for words.

"It is my pleasure," Belyaev responded. "And it would please me even more if you would call me Max."

Jonah pointed to himself and said, "Jonah. Thank you, Max."

Belyaev sighed, "Someday, when this war is over, I hope to meet you again, Jonah."

"I think I'd like that too."

Flight Surgeon Pavlishchev then entered the room. "Captain," he said, "I need to ask you to stand up and get in this hoverchair."

Jonah nodded and began to rise from his bed slowly. He was surprised at how weak he felt. As he got settled into the chair, Belyaev stopped him and held out his comm. "What is the message for your patrol boat?"

When Jonah had finished recording the message, he handed the comm back. He kept his hand out, and Belyaev shook it. "Goodbye, Max."

"Goodbye, Jonah."

Pavlishchev then had an aide push Jonah in the chair out of the room. The aide bustled Jonah quickly through the ship, finally reaching the shuttle bays. Waiting for him outside the shuttle was Commander Fung. The relief on her face was evident, and Jonah noticed her eyes were shining with tears. She pushed the chair onto the shuttle, and the door was closed behind her.

Jonah looked to see who had survived. In addition to Blutarsky, Guglielmo, Allroyd, Sanchez, Patel, and Dietrich, who had been on the shuttles, he learned that Commander Fung and Master Chief Bradshaw had made it, though Bradshaw was also in a hoverchair and had lost his left leg. He was also pleased to see that Fireman Bosco had endured the destruction of the ship. He had not been on duty in engineering when the cores were ejected. Neither of the two who were more severely wounded managed to live—one of whom was the hapless Lieutenant Kelley.

When he entered, Fireman Bosco jumped up immediately, barking, "Cap'n on deck!" while snapping a crisp salute.

The rest of the crewmen jumped to their feet and saluted. Halberd was touched by their gesture. He saluted them in return.

They pressed forward, hands outstretched. Bosco was first to give his captain a handshake, saying, "I told you, sir. The red shirt!"

Jonah smiled, then quickly shook the hands of the others until only Commander Fung was left. He noticed a tear rolling down her cheek. He meant to give her a handshake too, but she slipped past his outstretched arm, stooped down, and pulled him into a close hug, catching Jonah slightly by surprise.

She released him, stepping away and wiping a tear from her cheek. "I thought you were dead, sir," she murmured.

"Not yet," he chuckled. "Not yet."

"What happens now, sir?" she asked.

A message over the loudspeaker told them to strap in, as launch would be taking place in two minutes. Jonah nodded at the direction of the sound.

Renee made sure his hoverchair was anchored to a cleat then strapped herself in the nearest seat. The speaker announced a one-minute and then a thirty-second warning, then with a jolt, the shuttle left the battlecruiser.

The rest of the group began to talk amongst themselves. Fung took the opportunity to pull Halberd aside. "How is your eye?" she asked.

"Flight Surgeon Pavlishchev had to remove what was left of it," he explained. There is some damage to the nerves in the socket from radiation exposure and the cold, which will make regen or connecting a cybernetic difficult unless they can do the regen sequencing on the nerves soon."

Fung looked glum.

"I've already received excellent medical care," he assured her. "Pavlishchev did inject me with medical nanites to stop the bleeding and repair subsequent brain damage caused by the splinter that hit me. I really can't ask for anything more. Besides," he added, "I'll get them to give me a black patch to cover it up once the bandages come off. Maybe I'll get one with a skull-and-crossbones."

Jonah felt his strength fading. The last thing he remembered was the feel of Renee grasping his hand.

26

"Lieutenant commander?" Petty Officer Reed asked.

"Yes?"

"The comms monitor just spit something out I think you should look at, sir."

Lieutenant Commander Fred MacMurray looked at what the comms monitor had flagged. He read:

"Howdy, pardner—you know that bull done busted me up last rodeo, but the clowns done their job and got me to safety. Onliest problem, pard, is I'm stuck out where it all happened, and I was hopin' you'd give me and my compadres a lift. Ain't nobody here but us chickens. We'll be waitin' fer ya, pard, cuz we ain't goin' nowhere."

"Well, shee-it!" MacMurray exclaimed softly. "Petty officer, when did this here message get sent?"

"Time of transmission was 53 minutes ago, sir. It was sent in the clear, I think from the Rodinan ship that just transited in-system."

"Okey-dokey. Time to fire up the kewpie," he said. "Gotta call this one in."

MacMurray picked up the comm and selected the kewpie connection to the Admiralty. After identifying himself and informing the Admiralty that he had a priority one message for the sector commander, he was connected in a few minutes to Admiral Antonelli's yeoman.

The yeoman, hearing it was a priority one comm, said, "Please hold a moment, sir. I will go wake the admiral."

Less than a minute later, MacMurray heard, "Antonelli here. Go."

"Lieutenant Commander MacMurray, PB 410, sir. We're on station near the hyper exit in the Venera system. We just received the following message in the clear, sir. I believe strongly it's from Captain Halberd."

MacMurray had sent the text of the message to the admiral while he was speaking. He waited while the admiral read it.

"Lieutenant Commander," the admiral queried sharply, "how can you be sure this message is from Captain Halberd?"

"I served under him, sir," MacMurray explained. "He got to know me pretty well and learned my family is originally from Texas. I don't know if you're aware, but Texan culture is a little different."

"Go on."

"Well, sir, in the message, he talks about a rodeo. In a rodeo, riders called cowboys try to stay on the backs of either a wild horse or a wild bull. When I explained it to him, he equated it to combat. When the message references getting busted up by a bull, it means the wild bull threw him off its back, and he was injured. If we continue the analogy, that would be having your ship destroyed.

"In a rodeo, if a rider gets thrown off the horse or bull, special attendants dressed like clowns distract the animal and rescue the fallen rider. I would take that to mean that he was rescued. In addition, his mentioning the clowns I take as a different kind of joke, where he's calling the Rodinans clowns.

"The message clearly indicates that he is waiting to be picked up where it happened. That tells me he's in system H2813. The message was sent in the clear, we think from the Rodinan battlecruiser that just entered from H2813."

"Is this a trap? Do you think he would be sending this message under duress?" the admiral asked. "Quite frankly, there is no way he would have been able to send this message without the knowledge and assistance of the Rodinans. It just doesn't seem likely to me, lieutenant commander."

"I understand, sir," MacMurray acknowledged, "but from the way the message is worded, I don't think it's a trap, or at least he doesn't think it is. I agree that he would need some high-level help to make this happen."

"I'm going to turn this over to intelligence," the admiral stated. "They won't have answers for me immediately, but if you could position yourself near the entrance to the corridor, you'll be ready to move. Do you understand?"

"Yes, sir," MacMurray confirmed. "Thank you, sir. MacMurray out."

Jonah woke after a short rest. He guessed the *Pyotr Velikiy* had already transited into the Venera corridor. He turned to Commander Fung. "Commander, what's our status?"

"We're in our MAS, captain," she began. "There are 27 on board. The only systems that appear to be working are life-support, a very limited communications suite, very short-range navigation sensors, and thrusters. We're broadcasting a distress signal on every common frequency. We have enough supplies to last us two weeks—longer if we cut calories."

"Other than me, who is wounded and how badly?"

"Master Chief Bradshaw lost his left leg above the knee. It's currently in a stasis cap. Everyone who was on *Cumberland* was banged up to some degree—there are some broken bones, some sprains, and a dislocated shoulder, but nothing serious."

"Is anyone in pain? Do we have any medical supplies?"

"No one is in any pain, captain," she replied, "though Master Chief Bradshaw complains about his missing leg itching."

"You're goddamn right it itches," Bradshaw muttered.

"We have basic first aid supplies, including some pain meds, but shouldn't need more than that for some time."

"Very well," Jonah stated. "How were you all treated?"

"Better than I ever dared to hope," Renee admitted. "At first, they tried to find the officers bunks in a wardroom, but we insisted on staying with our people. They put us in part of the shuttle bays, with a number of the people from the cruiser we disabled. There was a little bit of tension at the beginning, but within a couple of hours, Bradshaw and Allroyd had somehow managed to strike up a conversation with the Rodinan senior noncoms. The next thing I knew, they got folks playing cards and the game went on until just before we left.

"Even though we were treated well, I have to admit it was a difficult time. On the one hand, I was grateful to survive, but on the other, I felt guilty because so many died. I was convinced we'd all be heading to the Federation as prisoners-of-war, and that was nothing to look forward to. On the fifth day, they took me to Captain Belyaev. I asked about you, and he wouldn't answer, so I thought the worst. He showed me what was left of *Cumberland*, sir. It's amazing that any of us survived."

Jonah nodded. "I was unconscious the first nine days, they told me, then I passed out again. How many days since the battle has it been?

"Today is the tenth day after."

"Ok. Then I wasn't out too long the second time. Anyway, when I woke up, I was in Captain Belyaev's quarters. He told me that Captain Kaun is his nephew."

"You're kidding?" she breathed. "Well, this makes more sense now."

Jonah continued. "He was going to release you and the others all along. He wanted to release me too but explained that there could be some substantial political backlash if he did. He was waiting for someone he called his mentor to run some sort of interference for him on that before he would let me go. As soon as he received assurance, they brought me to the MAS."

"That explains why he wouldn't give me any information about you," Renee mused.

"Probably so," Jonah shrugged. "He also allowed me to record a message that he could send in the clear to notify PB 410 that we're here if the boat is still in either this system or Venera. If Fred's still in the area, he'll come get us. Otherwise, we'll have to hope one of the rockrats does."

"The Commonwealth has always rewarded people well for returning stranded personnel," Renee commented, "and even their remains, so that's not an idle hope."

MacMurray had waited just under five hours when the comm lit up.

"Lieutenant Commander MacMurray, PB 410, reporting, admiral."

"Lieutenant commander, go get our people if they are there."

"Aye-aye, sir."

A little less than 24 hours later, MacMurray commed the admiral. When Antonelli's yeoman heard who it was, he put the admiral on the line immediately.

"Lieutenant commander," Antonelli answered, querying, "the mission?"

"Captain Jonah Halberd, late of HMS *Cumberland* also reporting, sir," Jonah interjected.

"Dear Gods," Antonelli breathed. "I'm extremely glad to hear from you, captain. How many of your people are on board?"

"There are 27 of us, sir," Halberd answered. "Though we do have an injured crewman who needs medical attention as soon as we get back to Commonwealth space."

"Twenty-seven?" the admiral asked. "Was anyone left behind?"

"No, sir," Halberd affirmed. "That's all there are of us."

"I've just seen what's left of your ship, captain. The scans are coming over the kewpie while we're talking. You're lucky to have had 27 survivors."

"Yes, sir," Jonah confirmed, "that's what they tell me. Commander Fung saw what was left of her. I haven't had the opportunity yet."

"I see," the admiral stated. "You were injured?"

"Yes, sir."

"Do you need medical attention, Jonah?"

"I will, sir," Halberd confirmed, "but I'm not in any danger at the moment."

"Besides you and the crewman you mentioned, are there any other significant injuries?"

"Yes, sir," Halberd responded. "The crewman is Master Chief Bradshaw. He lost his leg in the battle. The Rodinans put a stasis cap on it, and he's stuck in a hoverchair for now, but he should be fine until we get to Commonwealth space."

"I had HMS *Cleveland* put on alert yesterday. She's on her way to H2813 to rendezvous with you, lieutenant commander, and take on your guests. PB 422 will be assuming your station in the Venera system and will be enroute within a day. I'll want you both to proceed immediately to Aries."

"Understood, sir," MacMurray and Halberd answered, almost in unison.

"Once you transfer to *Cleveland*, please file your report as quickly as you can, Jonah," the admiral requested. "Ask Commander Fung to do the same."

"Yes, sir."

"Captain, I'm glad as hell we got you back. Lieutenant commander, well done."

"Thank you, sir," they answered again.

"In the meantime, try to get some rest. Antonelli out."

Jonah returned to the shuttle. Space was limited, and the life support systems had a difficult time keeping up. If everyone had not been in such high spirits, it would have been an uncomfortable time, but as it was, no one much minded, taking the lack of space and increasing odor with grace and good humor.

Four days later, they met HMS *Cleveland* and transferred aboard. The captain, Jake Rochford, went to the trouble of piping them over the side when they arrived. Jonah was touched by this honor. He felt a bit conspicuous, as he knew that after their time as prisoners and crammed into the patrol boat's shuttle, their appearance was a bit bedraggled, and they all needed a shower, plus his eye was still covered by bandages.

Captain Rochford gave Jonah and Renee access to his ready room and a tablet on which to compose their reports. The loss of the sensor logs on board *Cumberland* was a handicap in completing the reports, as neither had ever done a report without access to that detailed information. Jonah felt he had never used the words "roughly," "about," or "approximately" so many times in all the formal reports he had ever written. He also tried to write down as completely as he could the content of his conversations with Captain Belyaev. It took them the better part of two days to complete the reports.

The ship's surgeon examined Jonah's eye and Bradshaw's leg. The stasis cap on Bradshaw's leg would allow him to have a cybernetic prosthetic or regeneration of his leg which the surgeon estimated would take five months. The news was less encouraging for Jonah. The surgeon indicated that he thought the physical damage coupled with even the brief amount of time that had passed would make it unlikely that Jonah would be able to use a cybernetic eye. He did praise the Rodinan medical staff for injecting Halberd with nanites, telling Jonah that they had prevented him from suffering traumatic brain damage.

The rest of the trip was uneventful. The *Cumberland* survivors found themselves in the role of minor celebrities on board, and some of them relished it. Jonah found one letter from his mother. He wrote to tell her he was fine and had been through an exciting time but unfortunately could not tell her more. He had secretly hoped there might be a letter from Julia, but when there wasn't, he told himself that it was foolish to expect ever to hear from her again.

After they had entered the Aries system, Jonah gathered the survivors in the mess the night before they were due to arrive at the station. He stood in front of them and said, "Men and women of HMS *Cumberland*, I don't have a lengthy speech prepared—"

"Whew!" Bradshaw interjected loudly. Most of the crew laughed.

"On a more serious note," he continued, "I wanted to take this opportunity to thank you. Together we saved thousands of lives. I'd also like to take this opportunity for us to remember those shipmates who are not here with us by calling the roll one last time."

Command Master Chief Allroyd jumped to his feet and barked, "Atten-shun!"

Halberd turned to Fung and asked, "Commander, are you ready to call the roll?"

"Yes, sir," she responded crisply and began.

"Abingdon?"

"Here!" came a shout.

"Adams?"

"Here!"

She continued until she reached "Volkov!"

Jonah answered, "Here!"

Renee turned to him and saluted. "*Cumberland* present and accounted for, sir."

Allroyd began to read the roll of his men. Again, someone answered for every name called out. He turned to Halberd and saluted. "Yard crew present and accounted for, sir!"

"Crew dismissed!" Jonah ordered.

On his way out of the mess, Jonah made sure he spoke to every survivor, exchanging handshakes and even hugs. When he finished, he was emotionally drained.

27

They were due to dock at 10:30 the next morning. When he arrived, he pressed his palm over the entry plate, and the door hissed open. "Captain Halberd, reporting as ordered," he stated and saluted.

Rochford returned his salute and then said, "You're to video comm the vice admiral, Jonah."

Rochford left, closing the door behind him. Halberd sat at the console and keyed the link. Vice Admiral Antonelli appeared almost instantly.

"Captain Halberd reporting, sir."

"Good to see you, captain," the admiral replied. "You're due to dock in a couple of hours. You have an appointment with the hospital immediately upon your arrival. They want to run some scans on your eye and see if there's anything they can do. When you're finished there, please come to my office, and we'll begin debriefing."

"Yes, sir."

"A couple of things, captain," the admiral continued. "First, you need to be prepared. You and your surviving crew are heroes throughout the Commonwealth. There is likely to be a horde of media waiting."

Jonah groaned.

Antonelli chuckled at his reaction. "Don't worry, captain. There will be an Admiralty press officer there. You won't have to answer any questions. Just say, 'It's great to be back,' wave and smile for the cameras. We'll get you past them as quickly as we can.

"Before you face the press, though, you'll find two officers waiting for you inside the gangway—Lieutenants Lewis and Browning. One or both of them are to accompany you everywhere, and I mean everywhere, for the foreseeable future. If anyone asks, they are your adjutants. As much as you are a hero in the Commonwealth, you are Enemy No. 1 in the Rodinan Federation. We are concerned about the FSB."

A cold chill went down Jonah's spine. He didn't want to be in the media spotlight but being a possible target for the FSB was something to take seriously. "Yes, sir," he acknowledged.

When they arrived at the dock, as soon as the hatch opened to the airlock, two square-shouldered men dressed in lieutenant's uniforms were there, along with an Admiralty press officer, an attractive redheaded woman with the rank of captain. She introduced herself as Captain MacLeod and indicated that Jonah should exit first, followed by the surviving crew. As they walked down the gangway, Lewis and Browning fell in step just behind Jonah.

She asked, "Were you planning on saying anything to the press?"

"Uh, I was just going to say that it's great to be here, then wave and smile for the cameras."

"Perfect," she agreed. "I'll handle everything else."

They reached the end of the gangway. Before opening the door, she asked, "Are you ready?"

Jonah took a deep breath and nodded. She opened the door. Outside was a throng of people who started cheering as soon as they saw Jonah's face. Captain MacLeod steered him to a podium that had been set up. As the cheering began to die down, Jonah heard people yelling to him, trying to get his attention. Captain MacLeod took the podium and leaned into the microphone, holding her hand up for quiet. The shouting died down, and she said, "Captain Halberd has a very brief statement he'd like to make. We will *not* be taking any questions."

A groan came from the many reporters in the crowd. She indicated to Jonah that he should step to the mic.

Aware of his bandaged eye more than he had been up to this point and feeling very self-conscious, Jonah stepped behind the podium. "Thank all of you for coming," he said, at which the crowd began cheering again. Jonah shook his head slightly in disbelief at their reaction, then held up his hand. The crowd quieted.

"I just want to say it's great to be back."

The crowd erupted in cheers again. Jonah stepped away from the podium. Browning and Lewis steered him gently by his elbows in the direction of a path through the crowd that security personnel were keeping clear for him. Captain MacLeod accompanied him until they reached a wheeled car that was waiting. MacLeod opened the door for him, and he slid in. Browning went to the door on the other side and quickly got in, then Lewis slid in next to Jonah, shut the door, and the car began to move.

"That was nuts," Jonah breathed. He noticed Browning and Lewis smiling at that.

Fortunately, there was no one waiting at the entrance to the naval hospital. Jonah went to the receptionist's desk and was immediately escorted to an office three levels up, where he met with a team of doctors, led by Admiral

Mierzwinski. Over the next hour, he was examined and went through a variety of scans. Finally, he was left alone and told he could dress. A few minutes later, there was a knock on the door. Lieutenant Lewis opened the door to Mierzwinski.

"Captain," the doctor began, "I'm afraid I do not have good news. We will not be able to replace your eye. There is simply too much damage. The best we can do is some minor reconstructive surgery that will enable you to wear a glass eye because your socket took enough damage that it would not hold one right now."

"I appreciate your efforts, admiral. I'll probably take advantage of that at some point. How much longer do I need to wear the bandages?"

"There's no need to continue to wear a bandage, but I would recommend you keep it covered. The most important reason is to keep dirt and dust out of it."

Jonah smiled. "Can I have a black eye patch?"

Mierzwinski chuckled softly. "You can have any color you want."

"Black, then, with a skull-and-crossbones on it," Jonah requested.

"I don't know about that," she said.

Mierzwinski left and came back a moment later. He handed Jonah a black eye patch. Jonah went to the mirror and positioned the eye patch on his head. He tilted his face slightly and asked, "I think it makes me look perfectly disreputable. What do you think?"

28

Jonah reported to Vice Admiral Antonelli's office in the admiralty, flanked by Lieutenants Browning and Lewis. The yeoman commed to let the admiral know of his arrival and quickly waved him to the door.

Halberd entered and saluted. Antonelli sat down. "Congratulations," he said. "The plan you and your people came up with to stop the Rodinan task force worked as well as anyone could have hoped."

"Chief Allroyd and Lieutenant Blutarsky deserve the credit, sir. They came up with the idea, and Commander Fung was able to tweak the systems so it worked."

"It's amazing that anyone survived from *Cumberland*," the admiral added. He clicked a button on his comm unit, and photos were projected on the blank wall next to them. "These were taken by PB 410 as she was picking you up."

Jonah looked at the pictures. *Cumberland* was a scarred and blackened hulk, with huge scorch marks and three large ugly holes in her hull. The EM drives were shot away, making the rear of the ship look oddly truncated. The hole on the front quarter was particularly large.

Jonah winced and shook his head. "She was a tough ship, sir."

"If you don't mind, I'd like to talk to you about your conversations with Captain Belyaev."

"Yes, sir. What would you like to know?"

"In your report, you say that Belyaev alleged that there was a leak somewhere in the command of Third Fleet?"

"Yes, sir. As I recall, he said that he did not know for sure but that he thought it came from the command of Third Fleet."

"When he said, 'command,' did you get the impression he was speaking of Admiral Johanssen? Or was it perhaps someone on the admiral's staff?"

"I don't know, sir. As he said it, he put his finger aside his nose, like this,"

Jonah laid his finger next to his nose.

"Hmmmm. It's a pity he wasn't more specific," the admiral said. "Regardless, you are not to speak with anyone regarding your conversations with Captain Belyaev. As far as your rescue is concerned, the story we have released is that you managed to escape in pods, and Lieutenant Commander MacMurray made a daring dash through the system at incredible odds to rescue you and your people as soon as he saw *Pyotr Velikiy* re-entering the Venera system."

"I understand, sir," Jonah confirmed.

"For his actions, we are awarding him the Military Cross and promoting him to commander. He'll be assigned to *Essex* in a few weeks."

"Wow!" Jonah exclaimed, "That's wonderful news. I think he'll do a great job with her, sir."

"There's more," the admiral smiled. "You will be awarding him the Military Cross in a special ceremony at the court on Caerleon in two weeks. As a matter of fact, you'll be awarding the Distinguished Service Cross to every surviving member of your crew at that ceremony."

"I'll be honored to do that, sir."

"And King Edward will be awarding you the Victoria Cross," Antonelli added in an off-hand way.

Jonah wanted to say, "You're kidding!" but knew that would be inappropriate to say to the admiral. His mouth open, stunned, he struggled for the right words to say.

The admiral chuckled softly. "Your mother is invited, of course. I will leave it up to you to tell her. We've booked first-class accommodations on the liner that leaves York in five days. I'll send you the details in a few minutes. You'll be leaving tomorrow for Caerleon on a diplomatic service boat."

Jonah consulted his comm to see what the time difference was between his mother's location on York and Aries Station. The comm told him that his mother was ten hours ahead of him. If he waited a couple of hours, he would reach her early in their morning.

"This evening, you will be staying in an Admiralty apartment, along with Lewis and Browning," Antonelli continued. "As I mentioned in our discussion earlier, we think it is possible that the FSB might target you, so we're taking precautions to ensure your safety and that of your family. Lewis and Browning are not navy, by the way. They're members of the King's Own."

Jonah's eyebrow rose. He had thought his bodyguards were members of a naval security service. Learning that they were from the King's Own Guard was a surprise. The King's Own was the elite unit assigned to protect the King and the Royal Family. They had a fearsome reputation. Rumor had it their bodies were enhanced with advanced cybernetics.

"As for you," the admiral informed him, "after the ceremonies on Caerleon, the admiralty has decided that you will take the next six months to go on a publicity tour and visit all 31 planets of the Commonwealth, plus possibly the nonaligned planets of Bavaria, Lutetia, Rotterdam and Edo. The diplomatic service will be working out details on those visits."

Jonah's face fell. He hated the idea of a publicity tour. He thought quickly. "Sir, if there's a risk that the FSB might have me targeted, wouldn't that make it dangerous for me—"

Antonelli held up his hand, stopping Jonah mid-sentence. "Jonah," he admonished, "I know you don't want to do it, but there are important political considerations at play. Because of the failure of our attack on New Moscow, the Liberal Democrats are hollering that the government should open peace talks with the Federation. The impending marriage of Lord Chesterfield and Lady Hawthorne is a clear sign that the Liberal Democrats are gaining influence in the highest circles. The prime minister and the king feel that opening talks would be undesirable at the present time. Your tour of the Commonwealth will, we hope, renew support for the war effort and help re-establish confidence in the military.

"At the end of the tour, you will return to command. You have been assigned as captain of HMS *Indomitable*, one of the new *Dakota*-class battlecruisers nearing completion in the Caerleon yards. I'll send you her specs when we are finished here. She is due to begin trials in six months when your tour is scheduled to end.

"One last thing," the admiral said. "Would you do me the honor of joining me for dinner tonight in the mess?"

"Yes, sir," Jonah answered, "only I don't have a dress uniform."

"I took the liberty of ordering one from the shop here on station. Commander Fung told me you had bought yours there recently, and they still had your measurements. You'll find it in your quarters."

"Thank you, sir. What time?"

"Let's say at 19:00."

"Very well, sir. 19:00."

Lewis escorted the captain to one of the apartments in the admiralty. Waiting on the bed was not only the full-dress uniform that Antonelli had mentioned but four sets of undress uniforms, along with several sets of socks, underwear, and a pair of dress shoes. All the proper medals, ribbons, and citations that Halberd had won were already affixed to the dress uniform. When Halberd went to hang the clothes in the closet, he found a garment bag and full toiletries kit.

He took a moment to book a comm to his mother's house on the TelStar network, scheduling it for 22:00. He took a brief look at his orders and then began examining the specs and schematics of *Indomitable*. He noticed quickly that the designers had altered the original *Dakota*-class design to add rail guns to its point defense capabilities. There were five pairs of them along both the dorsal and ventral spine of the ship. He surmised that the feedback from their recent experience on *Cumberland*, plus whatever testing Advanced Warfare had done, showed the benefits of what the Germans had built into *Cumberland*.

Jonah was engrossed in looking at his new ship and didn't realize how much time passed. There was a quiet knock on the door, and Browning stuck his head in. "Sir, we're due at dinner in 20 minutes, and since I didn't hear the shower running, I thought I ought to remind you."

Jonah scrambled into and out of the shower and dressed quickly. He left the room and found Browning there, in full dress uniform also. Together the two of them went to the admirals' mess.

When they arrived in the salon, they found a small crowd waiting for them. Lieutenants Blutarsky, Patel, and Dietrich were there, along with Lieutenant Guglielmo in his marine dress uniform, Command Master Chief Allroyd, Master Chief Bradshaw, and Petty Officer Sanchez. Bradshaw was still in a hover chair, with a long tube now attached to the stump of his leg, the beginning of the regen process clearly underway.

Bradshaw looked glum. When Jonah asked him why, he told him, "Because I'm stuck with this for the next six months. And it itches and tingles and feels like I have ants crawling all over my leg that isn't even there. And they told me to get used to it because it won't stop until my leg is almost finished."

At 19:00 precisely, Vice Admiral Antonelli entered. They quickly settled into dinner. Laughs and jokes, and stories of each other's embarrassing moments were shared. Almost before he knew it, his comm chimed to warn him he had to make his call home. Jonah excused himself and said his farewells and left with Browning, and returned to his room just in time.

He quickly logged into the TelStar net and waited for the comm to connect. His mother appeared on the screen. She gasped when she saw him.

"Hi, mom!" Jonah said cheerily.

"Jonah!" she exclaimed. "Oh, honey! What happened to your eye, sweetie?"

"A big chunk of metal flew into it when my ship was attacked."

"Will it get better? Can you get a new eye?"

Jonah gave her a half-smile. "Afraid not, mom."

"Did you really do all that stuff they say you did?"

"I don't know what they say I did."

"Did you really stop the Rodinans from coming? And get your ship blown up? And then escape and everything? And what happened to your eye? That eye patch makes you look like a pirate."

"My crew and I stopped the Rodinans from coming, but my crew did most of the work," he explained. "And yes, my ship did get blown up. That's how I got this. A piece of the ship broke off and flew into my eye."

"A big piece?" his mother asked.

"About this big," Jonah answered, holding up his hands. "And I was lucky enough that someone came to rescue us."

"I'm just glad you're alive. I was worried to death about you."

"Mom, I wanted to let you know that I'm going to be getting a medal from the king. There's going to be a ceremony on Caerleon, and the navy has bought you a round-trip ticket on a liner that leaves in four days. I'm sending you the details now."

"You're kidding?" his mother gasped. "From the king?"

"That's what they tell me, mom."

"Oh god!" she exclaimed. "I don't have a thing to wear!"

Jonah laughed. "Don't worry about it, mom. We'll buy you an appropriate dress in Caerleon."

"Well, the shops on Caerleon are much more likely to know what's in fashion at the court these days. We'll have to find somewhere I can get my hair done, and new shoes, and—"

Jonah laughed and interrupted. "Mom, I promise. We'll take care of all those things. I'm looking forward to seeing you in a week or so and introducing you to some of the people I work with. I think you'll like them."

"Oh, Jonah, this is so exciting!"

"Yes, it is, mom. Yes, it is," Jonah agreed. "I hate to cut the comm short, but I've had a very long day, and it's late at night here. All the information you need is on the text I sent. I'll meet you when your liner arrives at Caerleon Station."

"Alright, honey. Goodnight!"

"Goodnight, mom."

29

The next morning Jonah boarded a boat belonging to the diplomatic service. Normally it was used to ferry ambassadors and high-ranking officials on missions outside the Commonwealth. Though its design was based on the navy's patrol boat, its interior was lushly appointed. Without the necessity of carrying a shuttle on board, the space had been given to spacious cabins, a small dining area with a bar, an exercise room and a common room that was also lushly appointed. The needs of the passengers were taken care of by a steward who also doubled as the cook and bartender. Jonah was the only passenger aboard, as Browning and Lewis did not accompany him. They told him that two of their comrades would meet the boat when it arrived.

It took nearly eight days to reach Caerleon Station. When he arrived, he was met at the gangway by two men who introduced themselves as Lieutenants Thompson and Winchester. They escorted him to a private shuttle berth that took him directly to the palace complex.

Caerleon was the seat of the Commonwealth government and the third most populous world in the Commonwealth. In the early 22nd century, an Anglo-American corporation, filling the void left when the American government had lost the will to explore space, had pioneered development of the first workable Alcubierre and EM drives along with the invention of plasma shielding to enable fusion reactors. The company then developed mass compensators and inertial dampeners, enabling advances in sub-light travel. The leading governments of earth leased spacecraft from this company to map out hyper-corridors free of dark matter through which the Alcubierre drives could travel.

Caerleon had been discovered by the British Interstellar Survey Service and claimed for the Crown. It was one of the first worlds discovered in the so-called "Goldilocks" zone: a planet similar to earth, with 98 percent of earth gravity and similar climate and atmosphere, a 23-hour and 48-minute day, a 358-day year, a mineral-rich asteroid belt, and two gas giants from which to mine and refine Helium-3 fuel for the fusion reactors.

To spur colonization, the British government offered individuals and corporations significant tax advantages if they moved to the new system. It also offered citizens of countries in the earth-bound British Commonwealth the same advantages if they moved to Caerleon. While this was not initially an important source of colonists, it became so later. In order to accelerate population growth, the colony employed widespread egg and sperm harvesting and ex utero gestation. Early colonists were expected to raise a family of at least six children, and tax incentives for large families continued until recently. Some corporations and entrepreneurs made fortunes quickly in the new solar system.

Colonization, which had been slow, accelerated after the Second Great Intifada. At this time, the Prince of Wales took up residence on Caerleon, primarily for security reasons, though officially the reason was that population of Caerleon had passed 50 million. A parliamentary form of government on the British model had already been established. A Caerleon House of Lords was established, with a new form of aristocracy established based on debt-free capital holdings of more than £500 million. The new Lords were required to reinvest a minimum of 50 percent of their annual income in small business incubators at fair terms arbitrated by the Crown and to pay a flat 35 percent tax rate on all income. Titles could be inherited, but the capital requirements still applied. If the debt-free value of their capital holdings dropped below the £500 million figure, they had to relinquish the title. This made the House of Lords important in the parliamentary procedure for the first time in centuries as they quickly realized they contributed over 90 percent of the tax revenue in the system. They re-established authority equal to the House of Commons.

Other planetary colonies were established by the leading world powers. Fueled by corporate investment, the most numerous were those which owed nominal allegiance to the United States of America. The Russians and Chinese also expanded aggressively. The Second Great Intifada had led to a "brain drain" among the leading nations of earth. The colonies founded by the western powers quickly surpassed their earthly progenitors in economic strength.

The Third Great Intifada severed almost completely the increasingly tenuous connections between the planetary settlements and earth. With the Royal family on earth killed during the nuclear attack on London, the Prince of Wales became King William VI or William of Caerleon. Since the British Isles on earth were almost completely uninhabitable due to radioactive fallout from the "dirty bombs" used by the terrorists, he was named king of the Commonwealth, which now included the planets of Avalon and Caledonia.

Earth was now an impoverished, radioactively polluted, and violent world. Leaders of the former first- and second-rank world powers had largely been killed by the initial attacks of the Third Great Intifada. Within months, residents of earth who had the ability to afford passage to one of the planetary colonies departed on whatever transport they could arrange, a migration called The Last Exodus. What remained of the governments of earth collapsed when they proved to be unable to feed the huge numbers of urban poor and refugees, let alone deal with the radiation sickness that grew worse as the clouds of fallout spread across the globe.

In space, the Russian and Chinese planets quickly established unified inter-planetary governments (in New Moscow and Yangtze). With much of their homeland on earth also covered in radioactive fallout, the inter-planetary Russian government changed its name to the Rodinan Federation of Planets. The nineteen American planets at the time had never established a unified governmental structure and had been governed as individual territories, often in rivalry with one another. An early attempt at forming a defensive alliance to protect one another against attacks from the aggressive Rodinan and Chinese governments was notable for its failures, despite the Americans' technological superiority. This resulted in the loss of the planets Roosevelt and Lincoln.

At this point, planetary leaders of three American-settled planets (New Boston, Carolina, and Alleghany) looked to the nearby planets of the British Commonwealth for assistance and signed the Treaty of Caerleon. Under the treaty, the three American planets put their fleets under the command of the Commonwealth Navy. When the Rodinan Navy attempted to invade the Carolina system, the combined Commonwealth/American navies managed to force them to withdraw. This led to the other American planets petitioning the Crown to be permitted to sign the treaty. With the 17 American planets adding their resources under Commonwealth command, the new force was the most powerful in space.

Two years later, the combined force successfully recaptured the planets of Roosevelt and Lincoln. The new planetary governments of the recaptured worlds then petitioned to join the Commonwealth. Debate in the Parliament over whether the new members would in some way be of lesser status than the three original planets was contentious. King William made a famous speech—The Inclusion Address—after which membership in the Commonwealth was extended to Roosevelt and Lincoln as full members. This also marked a turning point in the political structure of the Commonwealth. The role of the king grew from being ceremonial to that of a true constitutional monarch.

Within four decades, the economic strength of the Commonwealth, coupled with the "Offer of Inclusion" made by King William, convinced the other American planets to join the Commonwealth. In the hundreds of years since then, the Commonwealth had grown to include 31 planets. Of the different multi-system governments, it had the most robust economy and strongest military, though the Rodinan Federation and Chinese Republics were close rivals.

Availability of clean, almost-limitless and inexpensive energy from fusion reactors, establishment of mining and smelting operations in space (not to mention the metallurgical breakthroughs made possible by low-G smelting), and knowledge of the mistakes made during the industrial development of earth allowed the settlers of Caerleon and other planets to build cities in harmony with the natural surroundings. Caerleon was a beautiful world. Jonah had spent six years here while a student at the Royal Naval Academy and remembered the planet fondly. As a cadet, he had, of course, seen Caerleon Palace and taken the tour, but now he was going to stay on the grounds as a guest of the king.

Jonah rarely slowed down long enough to take stock of his life or count his blessings, but during the trip on the diplomatic boat, he had no other pressing duties or distractions. At the ripe old age of 33, he had accomplished more than he had hoped for in terms of his career as a naval officer at such a young age. Looking down on Caerleon on the shuttle's video feed as they flew down to the palace filled him with a sense of happy wonderment at how his life had unscrolled to this point.

Upon arriving on the palace grounds, Jonah was met by a member of the staff who showed him to the apartment where he would be staying. The magnificently appointed two-bedroom apartment almost took his breath away. Before the staff member left, he told the man of his mother's need to find a gown for the ceremony. The attendant gave him the name of one of Queen Celeste's ladies-in-waiting and told Jonah he would inform her of his needs. He indicated she would contact him soon.

He passed an uneventful evening, dining alone. The next day the liner his mother was on was due in. At breakfast, he asked one of the attendants to whom he should speak about whether the shuttle would be available. Shortly after, his comm buzzed, and he was told it was already reserved for his use. Accompanied by Thompson, he flew up to the station and was seated in a private room near the customs inspection area. Jonah's mother was escorted from the liner by a steward and was taken past customs to the room where he waited.

She threw her arms around Jonah and tut-tutted about his eye. Trying to field as many of her unstoppable questions as he could, he took her to the shuttle. They flew down to the palace, and her questions and commentary never slacked. She oooo-ed and aaah-ed over the apartment he had been given. Shortly after their arrival, the comm in the room buzzed. Upon answering it, an attractive woman who barely appeared middle-aged appeared on-screen. "May I please speak to Marian Halberd?"

The woman introduced herself as Laura and invited Jonah's mother to go shopping that afternoon. The two women chatted amiably and set a time. Marian ended the call and turned to Jonah, beaming. "Would you like to come?"

30

Jonah managed to beg off the shopping trip. Over the next several days, his comrades drifted in one or two at a time. He delighted in introducing his mother to Renee Fung, Tom Bradshaw, and the others. They met for dinner each night, and the wine and conversation flowed freely.

The day before the ceremony, everyone had arrived, and they were taken to the Throne Room where the ceremonies were to take place. The Royal Seneschal showed them how to process, where to stand, proper etiquette for addressing the king and queen, and other matters of protocol. There would be a receiving line afterward, and they were told the order in which they were to stand—or, in the case of the master chief, sit.

The Throne Room was enormous, with marble columns and a marble floor. The walls were faced with marble, and the only decorations were the portraits of the kings and queens, beginning with William of Caerleon, and the strip of red carpet leading from the entrance up the steps of the dais to the throne. The throne itself was a massive wooden chair, without ostentation, with an identical one next to it for the queen. The scale of the room and the person sitting on the throne were meant to inspire, not the decor.

Dinner that night was festive but a bit bittersweet. After the ceremony, they would go their separate ways. Fred MacMurray was taking over *Essex*. Renee Fung, promoted to captain, was assigned to command the light cruiser *Houston*. Lieutenant Blutarsky was promoted to lieutenant commander and would be executive officer on the frigate *Boxer*. All except Bradshaw received their assignments. Bradshaw's duty, it seemed, was to convalesce. He had received word that he was promoted to command master chief, and he delighted in the fact that his old buddy Doug Allroyd no longer outranked him. Jonah had the chance to meet the families of his remaining crew, which he enjoyed.

The next morning, they put on their formal dress uniforms and assembled as instructed. The most nervous of the group was the normally-cocksure Seaman Bosco. Seeing his obvious discomfort helped calm the butterflies in Jonah's own stomach. At the appointed time, they were ushered out of the anteroom and proceeded to the Throne Room. The enormous room was filled wall-to-wall with people. Their attire varied from full dress uniforms of the various branches of service to morning coats to elegant floor-length gowns.

The group advanced two by two, reaching the foot of the steps and either bowing or giving a curtsy as they had been instructed and peeling away to the side. Jonah and Renee were the last of the group. After Jonah had bowed, he joined the rank of people on his side of the aisle.

The king and queen stood. The king asked, "Captain Jonah Edwin Halberd, advance and be recognized."

As Jonah climbed the steps, the king said affably, "I don't get to give this one out very often, and even more seldom to someone who is able to stand and collect it."

The crowd laughed appreciatively, and the king read from a scroll:

It is our great pleasure to award the Victoria Cross for conspicuous gallantry in the face of overwhelming odds to Captain Jonah Edwin Halberd of His Majesty's Ship *Cumberland* of the Royal Navy of the Commonwealth. This man, with complete disregard for his personal safety, took actions that saved the lives of thousands when his ship stopped a force composed of a battlecruiser, a heavy cruiser and two light cruisers, destroying the two light cruisers, disabling the heavy cruiser and thereby causing the enemy to scuttle the ship to avoid its capture and causing enough damage to the enemy battlecruiser that it could not continue its planned invasion. His extraordinary heroism and gallantry in action were in keeping with the highest traditions of the Royal Navy of the Commonwealth and reflect great credit upon himself and his service and serve as an inspiration to us all.

The king took the medal from a flat wooden box and draped it around Jonah's neck. The king whispered in his ear, "How does it make you feel, knowing that there are several billion people watching this on video right now, secretly hoping someone trips and falls?"

Jonah straightened, trying to keep his face neutral as the king winked at him. Fighting to keep the smile off his face, he then saluted the king. As he dropped his salute, the entire crowd broke into cheers as he climbed backward down to the first step and turned to face the center. A series of pages came from the side and assembled behind him, each one holding a small wooden box. The first page gave Jonah a scroll.

His mouth had never been so dry; his throat had never felt so tight. Nevertheless, Jonah unfurled the scroll and began to read:

> By the command of King Edward XII and Queen Celeste of Caerleon, it is my great pleasure to award the Distinguished Service Cross for conspicuous gallantry in the face of overwhelming odds to the surviving men and women of His Majesty's Ship *Cumberland* of the Royal Navy of the Commonwealth. These men and women, with complete disregard for his personal safety, took actions that saved the lives of thousands when their ship stopped a force composed of a battlecruiser, a heavy cruiser, and two light cruisers, destroying the two light cruisers, disabling the heavy cruiser causing the enemy to scuttle the ship to avoid its capture and causing enough damage to the enemy battlecruiser that it could not continue its planned invasion. Their extraordinary heroism and gallantry in action were in keeping with the highest traditions of the Royal Navy of the Commonwealth and reflect great credit upon themselves and their service.

Jonah then called each surviving member of the crew by name. Each person came up one step, turned to him, and saluted. He returned the salute, took a wooden box from the page who stood just behind him, opened it, and took out the medal, and draped it around the crewman's neck. Each one then turned to face the king and queen, saluted, backed down a step, and returned to his place.

When Jonah finished with his shipmates, the crowd again broke into applause. He was handed another scroll. When the applause died down, he began to read again:

> By the command of King Edward XII and Queen Celeste of Caerleon, it is my great pleasure to award the Military Cross for conspicuous gallantry in the face of overwhelming odds to Commander Fred MacMurray, late of His Majesty's Ship PB 410 of the Royal Navy of the Commonwealth. This man, with complete disregard for his personal safety, undertook a mission of great daring to rescue the men and women who had survived the destruction of the Cumberland. His extraordinary heroism and gallantry in action were in keeping with the highest

traditions of the Royal Navy of the Commonwealth and reflect great credit upon himself and his service.

After draping the medal around Fred's neck and exchanging salutes, the crowd again applauded. At this point, the Royal Seneschal had told them that the ceremony would conclude, but the king had other ideas. He rose from the throne and held up his hand for silence.

"Captain Renee Ogden Fung and Command Master Chief Petty Officer Thomas Scott Bradshaw, front and center if you please."

The two moved to the center facing the king, Allroyd guiding Bradshaw's hoverchair. Both Fung and Bradshaw looked surprised and nervous. Two men dressed in crimson satin robes lined with taffeta came out of the crowd and stood next to the two.

The king spoke. "Captain Fung and Command Master Chief Bradshaw, we have selected you for inclusion in the Royal Order of the Bath. Are you willing to accept this honor?"

Renee, the most poised, spoke first. "Yes, Your Highness." Bradshaw quickly followed suit.

The king then said, "I will read you the oath. When I am finished, you will say, 'I solemnly swear so to do.'"

He then began:

> You shall honor God above all things; you shall be steadfast in your Faith; you shall love The King, your Sovereign, and The Queen, your Sovereign Lady, and them and their rights defend to your power; you shall defend maidens, widows, and orphans in their rights and shall suffer no extortion as far as you can prevent it; and of as great honor be this Order unto you as ever it was to any of your progenitors, or others.

The two then repeated, "I solemnly swear so to do."

The men in the crimson robes then produced swords from under their robes. Renee had her sword buckled around her waist; Bradshaw's was hung over his shoulder with a baldric. Then the men draped similar crimson robes on the shoulders of the two and affixed a golden collar with a cross hanging from it around their necks. While this was going on, a pair of similarly attired men and women had advanced from the crowd and stood behind them. When Fung and Bradshaw had been suitably garbed, the men with them whispered instructions into their ears. The man at Captain Fung's left then drew his sword about halfway from its scabbard with the hilt towards the king. All the others did the same, in unison with him. Fung and Bradshaw followed suit.

The king spoke:

> I exhort and admonish you to use your Sword to the Glory of God, the Defense of the Gospel, the maintenance of your Sovereign's Right and Honor, and of all Equity and Justice to the utmost of your Power.

The crowd erupted into applause. The members of the Order of the Bath retreated. The king waited for the applause to die down, then raised his hand again for quiet.

"Captain Jonah Edwin Halberd, in whom we are well pleased, advance to the throne and be recognized."

Jonah climbed the stairs, unsure of what to do. As he approached the top, the Royal Seneschal whispered to him from the side that he should kneel on his right knee in front of the queen. When Jonah had done so, the king spoke again, "Today is April 23 of the year 3024. When we chose the date for honoring these brave men and women, we did so with forethought. For today is Saint George's Day, and it is only on Saint George's Day that we may announce new members of the Royal Order of the Garter. Are you willing to accept this honor?"

"Yes, Your Highness." Jonah was stunned.

The king then stated:

> To the Honor of God Omnipotent, and in Memorial of the blessed Martyr St. George, tie about thy leg, for thy renown, this Most Noble Garter; wear it as the symbol of the Most Illustrious Order never to be forgotten or laid aside, that hereby thou mayest be admonished to be courageous, and having undertaken a just war, into which thou shalt be engaged, thou mayest stand firm, valiantly fight, courageously and successfully conquer.

The queen then bent down and tied the ribbon around Jonah's calf. The king then continued:

> Wear this Riband, adorned with the Image of the blessed Martyr and Soldier of God, St. George; by whose imitation provoked, thou mayest so overpass both prosperous and adverse encounters, that having stoutly vanquished thy enemies, both of body and soul, thou mayest not only receive the praise of this transient combat, but be crowned with the Palm of eternal Victory. Do you swear loyally to keep and observe the statutes of the said Order as far as

within your loyal ability you are able?"

Jonah responded, "I solemnly swear so to do."

Jonah was gestured to stand. Vice Admiral von Geisler came up the steps and fastened a sword around his waist, then retreated. The Royal Seneschal draped a dark blue mantle lined with taffeta on his shoulders. On the right shoulder were attached a dark red velvet hood and surcoat, and on the left breast was embroidered the heraldic shield of Saint George's Cross. A gold collar was placed on his neck and tied with white ribbons to his mantle. A Tudor cap with a feather was then placed on his head. The Seneschal whispered to him that he should thank the king and queen and then turn to the center.

Jonah looked at the king and queen. "Your majesties," he said softly, "thank you. This is far more than I ever expected."

"And far less than you deserve, captain," Queen Celeste chided gently.

"Thank you for your service," the king added. "We appreciate it more than you realize. It would be an honor for me, captain, to shake your hand." The king then stunned Jonah by reaching out his hand to shake.

They shook hands, then the king made a small gesture indicating that Jonah should now turn. He did, and the crowd erupted one last time in applause. When it died down, the Royal Seneschal guided Jonah as he backed down the stairs and established all the honorees in the receiving line.

Jonah stood next to Renee Fung, who managed to make even the medieval crimson mantle she had been given look elegant. Person after person came through the line. Most Jonah did not know. There were some were faces he recognized because they were famous people. A few were people he had met in the navy. Vice Admiral von Geisler came through.

"Thank you for the sword, sir. I haven't even had a chance to look at it yet, but I'm honored that you gave it to me."

"Wear it in good health, Jonah," the admiral replied, clasping his shoulders. "I am very proud of you."

Not long after that, First Space Lord Chesterfield appeared, accompanied by Lady Julia. Chesterfield uttered some comment that Jonah only half-heard as he was trying not to stare at her. Julia said only, "Congratulations, Captain Halberd." He wanted to think that perhaps her clasp of his hand lingered a shade longer than normal but decided it was wishful thinking. He tracked her from the corner of his eye while she gave Renee a hug and whispered something to her and then again when she bent to whisper to Tom Bradshaw.

"Probably telling them to keep an eye on me," he thought to himself.

Finally, the receiving line ended, and Jonah joined the others in the reception that followed in one of the grand halls in the palace. Just as he was wishing that someone would come and take away the heavy mantle and the strange floppy cap, the Seneschal appeared with a page and asked him if he would like to take them off. With a sigh of relief, he handed over the heavy garment and hat.

Jonah found his mother, as elegantly dressed as he had ever seen her, thick in conversation with a woman about her age. She introduced him to her new friend Laura who had helped her with her shopping. Jonah had gone to the trouble to find out who Laura was and could not resist the opportunity to tease his mother. He leaned in close to her ear and said softly, "You do realize, mom, that Laura's proper title is Lady Thorner?"

His mother leaned back quickly in surprise. "No way!" she exclaimed. She then gave a look to Jonah and mouthed, "Really?"

Jonah nodded with a smile. His mother burst out laughing. Laura, Lady Thorner, raised an eyebrow in curiosity. Jonah quickly explained, "Marian didn't know you were also Lady Thorner, ma'am."

Laura smiled and tucked her arm in Marian's and said, "Nope. As far as Marian is concerned, I'm just Laura. As a matter of fact, we have another date to go shopping and have lunch tomorrow, now that all the hullaballoo is finished. And by the way," she added, "now that you are a member of the Order of the Garter, your proper title is Sir Jonah Halberd. So there." She stuck her tongue out at Jonah in a most un-ladylike way.

Marian saw this and stuck her tongue out at Jonah as well and the two women laughed. Jonah laughed as well and raised his hands in defeat. The two women began chattering amongst themselves about their shopping trip, and Jonah took the opportunity to scan the crowd. His eye stopped on Julia, of course, and at just that moment, she turned her head and looked him right in the eye and smiled at him. Jonah quickly looked away, embarrassed.

He quickly searched out the members of his former crew to make sure he said goodbye and wished them well before the reception ended. He found the enlisted men and women near one of the bars where Bradshaw and Allroyd were holding forth. One by one, he said his goodbyes, saving Renee Fung for last. He caught up with her just as it became apparent the reception was drawing to a close. She held her arms out, inviting a hug. When Jonah tucked his head to the side, she pulled hers back and kissed him softly on the lips. Just to make sure he got the message, she did it again, holding the kiss longer—not so long as to convey any romantic intent, instead a gesture of sincere friendship.

"Jonah," she said, "though we've only known each other a few months, we've certainly done a lot. You are one of the best men I've ever known, and I hope our paths often cross in the future."

"Renee, it has been a pleasure and an honor to sail with you," he faltered, tears filling his eye. He gulped, trying to hold his emotions in check. She clasped him in a warm hug. "I shall miss you," he said in a strained voice.

31

When he returned to his apartment, he found Thompson waiting for him. He checked his comm. There were messages of congratulations from friends and acquaintances and new orders from the Admiralty requiring his presence at Berth 22A, Caerleon Station at 07:30 the next morning. The orders also stated that he was to spend the night on the station and to inform the Admiralty office on-station of his expected arrival.

He also found, laid out on his bed, a case for his sword and for the golden collar, a blue sash, and two short ribbons with a pin mechanism attached at one end. Written instructions had been left, indicating that he should remove the cross from the collar. He should attach the cross to the wider of the two red ribbons and store the collar in the box, leaving the box in his room as it would be collected and stored with his mantle and hat here in the palace. He was to remove the Victoria Cross from the ribbon around his neck and attach it to the smaller of the two red ribbons. The instructions also told him the correct manner of displaying the two medals and wearing the sash and informed him that, as a Knight of the Royal Order of the Garter, his sword was now considered part of his formal dress uniform.

He used the comm in his room to ask when he would be able to take a shuttle to Caerleon Station and was told there was one standing by waiting for him. He took off his sword and placed it in the handsome wooden box that was provided for it. He quickly changed from his formal dress uniform into a service uniform, moving his placket of service ribbons and other awards from one to the other and taking care to affix the Victoria Cross in its proper place. He packed his dress uniform carefully in his garment bag. He noticed all his clothes had been cleaned while he had been out and put away. Packing everything took little time.

He, Thompson, and Winchester boarded the shuttle which took them to Caerleon Station. During the brief trip, Jonah had the opportunity to examine his sword. The hilt and guard of the sword was gold with a lion's head on the pommel, and the grip was covered with shark skin. The blade had a single edge, extremely sharp, that tapered to a point. The sides of the blade were engraved. The scabbard was made of rawhide with gold mountings. As he examined it, he saw engraved on the inside of the guard:

Sir Jonah—Audentis Fortuna Iuvat—KVG

When the shuttle docked at Caerleon Station, he commed the Admiralty office. Thompson and Winchester accompanied him to the office, where he was shown to his quarters for the night. His comm buzzed shortly after he dropped his bags. Captain MacLeod, via text, requested a meeting at sixteen hundred, followed by dinner. As it was 15:40, he texted her back and said he would be there. He was not looking forward to this publicity tour.

He went to the conference room she had indicated and knocked. She opened the door. She really was arrestingly good-looking, he thought. About 175 centimeters tall, slender, with straight red hair that reached just to her shoulders and light blue eyes. Her face was dotted with freckles, indicating that her red hair was its natural tint. Since they were going to be together for six months, she asked if they could dispense a bit with formalities and suggested he call her by her first name, Elaine. He agreed and asked the same. She teased him slightly by asking, "Jonah, or 'Sir' Jonah?" He shook his head and said, "Just Jonah, please."

Once they sat down, however, she was all business. She activated the projector and displayed their planned itinerary. She brought up a holographic display of the Commonwealth planetary systems from the tabletop, and it showed their route mapped out. She began to explain. "The proposed itinerary has us visiting the other 30 planets of the Commonwealth, plus Bavaria, Lutetia, Rotterdam, and Edo." As she said this, links to the four non-Commonwealth systems appeared on the map. "Due to the layout of the hyper corridors, we will be visiting the nonaligned systems in the middle of our tour. With 34 stops in 183 days, we have an average of five and a half days between stops, so our opportunities for sight-seeing will be limited." She smiled; Jonah did not.

Picking up on his non-reaction, she put her hands on the table and leaned forward. "Look, Jonah," she said, "I get it. You don't want to do this. You're here because you're following orders. But let me ask you this. If you were back at the academy as a cadet and ordered to clean the head with a toothbrush, what sort of consequences would you face if you approached that task the way you're approaching this one?"

"Touché," he acknowledged. "You're absolutely right. I apologize."

"Accepted," she said briskly. "Now, the format of each of our visits to Commonwealth systems will be largely the same. We'll shuttle dirtside, you'll make a speech and answer some questions from reporters. Most of the questions should be pretty easy, but we'll work over the next two days to develop natural-sounding answers to some of the more difficult questions we can anticipate. If a question seems tricky and you aren't sure of the Admiralty's position, just defer by saying something like, 'I don't know the answer. I'll have to get back to you on that.' It's often a good idea in those circumstances to ask the reporter if he feels it is an important issue. Very often, they're just trying to be provocative to get ratings. It's nothing personal; it's just how they make their living."

"I understand, I think," Jonah agreed.

"Be prepared," she warned. "Some of the questions may seem hostile or the reporter's attitude might be aggressive. Stay on the high road and remember that any policy questions are potential landmines, so you're better off not attempting to answer them. Is there anything in your personal life that's off-limits?"

Jonah thought. His personal life was pretty boring. He had not been in a relationship for a few years. His last, with a fellow officer on another ship, had ended badly. Since then, except for his attraction to Julia, he had indulged in the occasional 'one-night stand' with old acquaintances but nothing serious. "No," he answered finally.

"It's bound to come up," MacLeod explained. "You're a handsome man, a hero, single, and your eye patch gives you a romantically dangerous look. The gutter press has already jumped all over that kiss you gave Captain Fung this morning."

"You're kidding!"

"Nope. Look at it from the public's point of view: two extremely attractive people, who've served together in close quarters the last few months, both war heroes who have braved danger and escaped, literally. It's extremely possible that the two of you would have forged a romantic relationship, regulations be damned."

Jonah was exasperated. "But—" he began.

She held up her hand. "I know. I know. It was a friendly kiss. You weren't snogging or anything close to it. Just keep in mind that people are always hoping that fairy tales do come true. Hmmmm—" she stopped.

"Hmmmmm—what?" Jonah demanded.

"Certainly an angle we can exploit," she said almost to herself.

"What?"

"Nothing. Don't worry about it. Just an idea I had. So how would you answer a reporter who asked you about your relationship with Captain Fung?"

"My first reaction would be to tell him that it's none of his business," snapped Jonah, but then he sighed, "but that would only make it worse, wouldn't it?"

"Definitely. Try again."

"How about, 'I'm flattered that you think so. Captain Fung is obviously an intelligent, capable, and attractive woman, and she's someone with whom I have been through a lot recently, but she's a good friend and a trusted comrade, nothing more.'"

"That's much better but use 'colleague' instead of 'comrade.' 'Comrade' belongs to the Rodinans. Let's work on your speech."

"Ugh. Okay. What do you want me to say?"

"Nope," she corrected, "start with what you want to say."

"But I don't want to say anything," he complained. "This isn't my idea."

She sighed heavily. "Pretend Vice Admiral von Geisler has given you an important mission. Support for the war effort on, uh—say, Armstrong, has dropped and he is sending you there to make a speech and have a photo op with the planetary executive to restore public enthusiasm. How are you going to accomplish your mission?"

"Well, before we landed dirtside, I'd check my files to see if there were any crewmen on *Cumberland* who were from Armstrong. Out of 225, the odds are decent that there's someone from every planet in the Commonwealth."

"I've already prepared a list," she said, nodding, "and you're right. So, take a look." She sent the file to Jonah's comm.

"Anne Ericson," he said, "somewhat heavyset woman, worked in engineering. Sebastian LaPointe, good-looking young man with a beautiful singing voice, a marine."

"So, what would you say?"

"I suppose I'd thank everyone for coming to listen to what I have to say. That I understood that they were listening because I was one of the few who survived and happened to be the guy in charge, but that I wanted to talk about heroes they might know, like Anne Ericson, an able seaman first class who worked in our engineering department, or Sebastian LaPointe, a marine lance corporal who had taken part in the mission that rescued Lady Hamilton."

"Go on."

"Everyone in our crew knew the odds we faced. We knew that most of us, probably all of us, would not survive the battle. We also knew that we had to do our best because if we failed, tens of thousands of people would die and the Rodinans would damage our military strength significantly.

"In spite of knowing we were all likely to die, the mood of our crew was unfailingly positive. We were going to do our duty to the best of our ability. We had to because we knew how much was depending on us.

"I was lucky enough to survive. Of the ten people on the bridge, Captain Fung and I were the only ones to live, though I lost my eye. Seaman Ericson died when a laser breached engineering, and the fusion cores were automatically ejected to prevent a catastrophic explosion. Everyone in the engineering department was ejected into space along with the cores. Ejecting the cores is similar to setting off a small explosion to prevent a much bigger one. Lance Corporal LaPointe was likely killed when a laser shot through the shuttle bay where his damage control station was.

"Courage, like that displayed by Ericson and LaPointe, and the entire crew of *Cumberland*, is rare. I would hope that the people of Armstrong would honor the sacrifice they made. No one knows the cost of this war more than I do. Of 265 men and women on my ship, only 27 survived. The other 238, all of whom I knew by name, did not. The Rodinans started this war with an unprovoked attack on us in the Franklin system. Thousands of brave men and women, like Seaman Ericson and Lance Corporal LaPointe, have given their lives to protect the rest of us. Will their sacrifice be in vain?"

MacLeod sat in stunned silence. She shook her head after a moment and said softly, "Wow. Just...wow. That was...exactly what I hoped for. Let's work on some of those unpleasant questions then."

They worked their way through several of the troublesome questions she expected would come up from reporters. At 18:30, she suggested they break for dinner. Jonah agreed. After they sat down in the restaurant, she smiled and said, "I don't want you to think I'm such a hard taskmaster. I planned a little treat for you tomorrow morning to start our time together."

"Really?" Jonah asked, "what sort of a 'treat' do you have planned for me? My orders told me to report at 07:30 to Berth 22A."

"Berth 22A is a shuttle berth," she informed him. "How would you like to visit the Caerleon Yard and see your new ship?"

Jonah grinned. "I'd like that very much," he admitted. "Let me guess, though, you'd like me to say a few words to the workers in the yard."

She gave him a sly smile. "I'm that transparent?" she asked coyly. "If you're wise to my tricks already, this could be a very dull six months."

32

At 07:30 the next morning, Jonah and Thompson met Elaine at Berth 22A. They boarded the shuttlecraft and took the short flight to the Caerleon Yard. Watching on the viewscreen as they approached, Jonah was awed at the size of the facility. From a distance, he could see what looked like ten ships under construction, varying in size from a superdreadnought to three frigates.

As they drew closer, the pilot slowed the craft and redirected the cameras to show a battlecruiser nearing completion. His voice came over the speakers, "Captain, here she is. HMS *Indomitable.*"

Without realizing it, Jonah had leaned forward in his seat towards the viewscreen, trying to take it all in. He could see constructor pods maneuvering the last few sections of armor onto the hull and welding them in place. He had reviewed the specs on his comm many times since learning it would be his new command after he finished the press tour, but there was simply no substitute to seeing for himself.

She was 753 meters long, 78 meters from dorsal to ventral spines, and 112 meters wide. She had 30 missile tubes and 12 155 mm photon cannons. There were three fusion reactors to power it all and four huge EM drives to provide thrust. She was rated to achieve 515 G of acceleration, as fast as a light cruiser. He drank in the sight with his eye as long as he could.

Too soon, they docked at the yard, not far from where *Indomitable* was being finished. They were met by a Captain Nehru, who offered to take them on a tour of the ship. He explained that most of the interior had atmosphere, though certain sections of engineering and the shuttle bay did not. He explained that there was quite a bit of work being done on the interior, so certain areas might be too congested.

Captain Nehru was a knowledgeable guide and gave them a thorough tour of the ship. He made sure Jonah saw what would be his quarters and ready room (unfinished), the bridge (tremendously busy with electronic consoles being installed), and also a representative sampling of the crew quarters, along with the messes, sickbay, magazines, and the secondary bridge. The tour took the better part of three hours. As they came back to the gangway, Nehru took them to the commissary, where the workers were gathering for their lunch break.

There was a podium with a microphone set up at one end of the huge room. Captain Nehru asked, "Sir, it would be a great honor if you would speak with the men and women working on your ship."

Jonah nodded and headed to the podium. As he walked across the room, whispers from the crowd of workers started as they recognized him, many having watched the videos of the ceremonies the day before. By the time he was halfway across, people had begun standing and applauding, which quickly grew to cheers and whistles and became a thunderous ovation by the time he reached the mic.

He held up his hand for quiet, and the roar of the crowd died down. "Golly," he said, "that's a way to make someone feel welcome!"

The crowd began to roar again, but he held up his hand and waited. When they quieted, he said, "I just took a tour of the ship, and, damn, she's a beauty."

Again, the crowd erupted, and again, Jonah waited for them to quiet. "I want to thank you for the hard work that you've done and the work you have yet to finish. While I'm here, I wanted to tell you about a group of yard dogs I had the pleasure to work with recently. Before my last mission, your colleagues at Aries Station worked their butts off to get my ship back in service. When our orders needed us to ship out, 30 of them came along to finish the job. They continued to do their jobs and finish the repairs, even after we learned that the ship was about to get blown to hell."

At this, the crowd of workers broke into applause, less raucous, almost, Jonah felt, respectful. He waited for it to die down and resumed speaking.

"On the eve of the battle, all thirty men and women volunteered to help us in whatever way they could. Everyone on board *Cumberland* knew what was coming and knew that our chances of survival were pretty much zero. Yet, as I toured the ship in the days and hours before battle, I saw the bravest men and women I have ever known face those odds with a positive outlook, confidence in their abilities and, a determination that we would make the enemy pay the greatest price possible.

"We succeeded in making the enemy turn back, but at a terrible cost. Of the thirty men and women—the yard dogs—who stayed on board from Aries Station, only two survived: Command Master Chief Doug Allroyd and Machinists' Mate Maura O'Leary. The determination of all those men and women, who were determined to do the job right, who volunteered to help in the darkest of hours, who were willing to give their own lives so that thousands more would not—I see that same determination here, with the yard dogs of Caerleon Station.

"Thank you for the excellent work you do. God bless the Commonwealth!"

The crowd erupted as Jonah stepped down. Elaine smiled at him, and Captain Nehru shook his hand vigorously. Jonah asked Elaine, "Do we have time to eat here with them? I'd like to if it's alright."

She nodded, so Jonah turned to Nehru and said, "Let's go grab a sandwich, captain."

Nehru led them through the crowd. A path parted for them, but all along the way, the workers offered their hands to shake. Jonah shook every one he saw on his way to the counter. When he arrived at the counter, he took a tray, ordered a sandwich and a drink, then turned to look for a table. A skinny bosun's mate saw him looking for a seat and waved him over to his table. Jonah went over, leaving Elaine and Nehru behind. The workers at the table scooted over on the benches to make room for him, and he sat.

They all introduced themselves. One said he had seen him on the video the day before. There were nods of agreement from most of the table. A purser's mate, a dark-skinned woman with close-cropped hair, asked. "Is it true about you and Captain Fung?"

Jonah, with a bite of sandwich in his mouth, spluttered in surprise. He quickly swallowed, wiped his mouth with his napkin, and smiled at his being surprised. "Ms. Jones," he said, reading her nameplate, "Any man who was romantically involved with Captain Fung would be a lucky man indeed. I'm afraid I used up all my luck just in living through the battle. I could have maybe used a little bit more," he said, pointing to his eyepatch.

Some at the table chuckled at this. Jones pressed on, "But we all saw her kiss ya. C'mon—"

Jonah asked her, "When you see one of your close friends, a friend who has stood by you even in the worst of times, do you greet that friend with a handshake, Ms. Jones, or something else?"

Jones reflected for a moment, and her face fell. "Dang," she said disappointedly. "I give 'em a kiss, just like Captain Fung gave you."

The bosun's mate who had invited him to sit asked, "Were you scared when your ship blew up?"

"No," Jonah answered with a straight face, "I was unconscious."

He waited for the laughter at the table to die down, then explained, "When their laser penetrated the bridge, a piece of metal about this long," he held up his hands, "got me right in the eye and went into my brain. I was unconscious for nine days after that."

"What about after?"

"After I woke up and was told what had happened, that we'd stopped them from being able to attack the Commonwealth," Jonah paused. "I was surprised, I guess, that any of us survived, but losing so many people that you know is…well, it's not a good feeling."

"Were you surprised when Commander MacMurray arrived to rescue you?"

"It took an awful lot of courage to pull that off," Jonah said. "He took a big chance guessing that the Rodinans couldn't fire on him. So, I guess you could say I was pretty damned happy Commander MacMurray showed up."

They laughed at this, but just then, all the workers' comms buzzed. "Time to go back to work," one of them explained. They all shook hands as they left. Jonah turned to find Elaine and saw her already walking towards him.

"Time to go?"

33

In a little over four months, they had visited 20 Commonwealth systems, plus the planets of Rotterdam (originally settled by the Dutch and several eastern European countries), Bavaria (one of three planets originally settled by German corporations, now one of two still under German control since the Rodinans had invaded and occupied New Bremen three and a half years earlier) and Edo (originally settled by a Japanese-Korean joint venture).

During the first three months, Jonah and Elaine had developed a good working relationship and got along well, traveling on the same diplomatic service vessel he had taken to Caerleon. His working relationship with Elaine had progressed to the point where they had developed a repertoire of 'in jokes' based on things that had happened and people they had met on the tour. After two months, Elaine had started teasing Jonah, dropping double entendres into her comments from time to time when they were alone. She had made it clear to him early on that she had a boyfriend back on Caerleon. Jonah realized it was just harmless flirting, so he began to tease her in return.

They had arrived on the ground on Lutetia, settled by the French. This was one of the few stops on their tour where they had the opportunity to stay overnight. After his speech, the French premier offered to show Jonah the bustling city of New Paris. Jonah accepted. He was led to the premier's groundcar and seated in the back next to a beautiful woman he had never seen before.

She spoke English with an endearing accent, and Jonah quickly learned her name was Manon Beart, that she was an actress and the current face of "Marianne"—the French symbol of liberty and the allegorical embodiment of the government. Jonah was puzzled by this, but she explained that the French government, for over a thousand years, had chosen a woman every generation to be 'Marianne.'

"Imagine," she explained, "one of the ancient Greek goddesses, such as Aphrodite. Now imagine that the government chooses a woman every twenty years or so who is to be the face of Aphrodite so that any paintings or sculpture of Aphrodite done during this time can use this woman as a model. I am not 'Marianne' just as I could not be Aphrodite. It's that the government has decided for the time being that 'Marianne' looks like me."

Jonah, once he understood the concept, could easily see why she had been chosen. She had a classic beauty, light brown hair tied back, and deep brown eyes that he found more and more captivating. Her dress, a summery print, while not revealing, clung to the curves of her lithe body and emphasized her femininity. Their conversation flowed easily, and she often emphasized her points with brief touches of his hand or arm. She was a charming companion and entertained Jonah with funny stories of her mishaps when she was getting started as an actress. He genuinely enjoyed spending time with her. The tour ended in the early evening, and she invited Jonah to have dinner.

Accompanied by Winchester, they went to a restaurant where she was well-known. Paparazzi photographers surrounded the entrance and shouted questions at them in French. She grasped Jonah's hand and strode to the entrance, trying to ignore them. The maître d' showed them to a secluded booth in a corner of the restaurant where they sat next to one another. At some point early in what was an exquisite meal, Jonah realized he was being seduced. He quickly decided that he didn't mind the idea. When she invited him to her apartment for a nightcap, he was not surprised and accepted.

They braved the paparazzi outside the restaurant and took a cab to her building. Upon reaching her apartment, Jonah suggested to Winchester that he would be occupied until morning, then shut the door. When he turned around, he saw her standing in the middle of the room with her dress on the floor and her hair let down across her shoulders.

After making love twice that night and again in the morning in the shower, Jonah dressed and contacted Thompson and Winchester. Thompson was waiting outside the building, so Jonah suggested he hail a cab and he would be down in a minute. His goodbyes with Manon were not awkward, and he took the lift down to the lobby in a cheerful mood. As the lift doors opened, he saw Thompson waiting for him. A man was coming through the entrance door from the street just as Jonah started to say hello to Thompson.

A lot of things started to happen at once, and time seemed to slow down. The man coming through the door had a coat draped over his right arm. As he raised his arm, a fléchette pistol appeared, and he fired. Thompson gave Jonah a hard shove to the left, and as he was falling, he felt the impact of three fléchettes from his left breast diagonally down to his right hip. He saw the man at the entrance stagger backward and fall back into the door, his chest turning red as he fell.

Jonah's head hit the floor sharply, stunning him. He flopped onto his back and saw Thompson, holding a fléchette pistol, moving his jaw as though murmuring to himself. Time returned to normal speed. Jonah was still trying to figure out exactly what had happened when Thompson knelt down and ripped Jonah's dress uniform jacket and shirt open with a single hard yank. He glanced quickly at Jonah's wounds then pressed his finger on a place on Jonah's left breast. "Does this hurt, sir?" he asked.

"Ugh," Jonah grunted. It hurt like hell.

Thompson quickly flipped the left side of Jonah's uniform coat over, then smiled. "Being a hero saved your life, sir," he said. "Your Victoria Cross stopped the first fléchette, or else it would have ripped your heart open." Thompson then poked his lowest rib on the right side.

"Does this hurt, sir?"

When Thompson poked it, a knife-sharp pain stabbed Jonah's side.

"Yes," he hissed.

"Looks like this one cracked a rib and spun off somewhere," Thompson commented. "Probably missed your lung because I don't hear any gurgling. This one just caught your side. In and out, no problem."

Winchester then burst through a side door, accompanied by four men in business clothes. "Sir," he explained, "there's an ambulance waiting for you at the side of the building. These men are DGSI—like our MI-5. Can you walk, or should we carry you?"

"Let me try to walk," Jonah requested.

Thompson helped him to his feet, and though his knees were a bit shaky on his first couple of steps, he was able to walk to the ambulance and climb inside. It was then that he noticed he had bled quite a bit all over his shirt and uniform jacket. They made him lie down on a gurney, and the ambulance attendant placed absorbent pads on his wounds. Jonah looked down at his chest and saw his Victoria Cross. It was bent diagonally across the middle at a 90-degree angle, with the right and lower sections of the cross sticking straight up.

Jonah finally had the presence of mind to ask Thompson, "Were you hit?"

Thompson smiled, opened his jacket, and showed Jonah a line of five fléchettes stitched through his shirt. "Body armor, sir," he explained. "It's heavy and hot and uncomfortable as hell."

"And totally worth it on the rare occasions when you need it," Winchester added.

At the hospital, they found the fléchette which had hit his rib. After breaking his rib, it had spun down into his liver. The other fléchette had gone completely through the edge of his lower torso but had hit nothing vital. The doctors put him under anesthetic and removed the fléchette from his liver, then fused his skin together over the wounds.

When he came to, the doctor explained that the liver damage would heal itself in a month or two but that he should get exposure to UV light to break down the excess of bilirubin that might build up in his bloodstream until then. Winchester checked the specs of the limited med facility on the diplomatic boat and found that they could do that on board. The doctor explained that his rib would knit quickly but would hurt quite a bit until it did. He then explained that Jonah was released.

As they rode in a groundcar back to the shuttle, Jonah checked his comm and saw messages from a wide variety of people, including Elaine and Manon. He texted Manon to let her know he would be fine. As the shuttle climbed through the atmosphere, Thompson looked at his comm. "Just received a message from our friends in DGSI, sir. Our assassin had false ID. His clothing could not be traced, and the pistol he used is a fairly common model. His fingerprints and dental records were not in the system, and none of the facial recognition systems could identify him."

"FSB," Winchester stated matter-of-factly. Thompson nodded in agreement.

"So," Jonah asked, "now what?"

"So," Thompson said, "no more dates, sir. You stay where we control who comes and goes."

"Understood," Jonah confirmed.

In the hospital, he had time to think and realized he was disappointed in himself. He had engaged in one-night stands before, but always with people he already knew—sort of 'friends with benefits.' On top of his embarrassment, he suspected that Elaine had arranged this liaison with Manon Beart as some sort of publicity stunt. Hell, he thought, she probably called the paparazzi to tell them which restaurant we were going to. He felt used.

He used his comm to query the tabloid press on Lutetia. Sure enough, he was headline news. The first article he saw was titled, "Romantic Date Ends Badly for Commonwealth Hero—Beart Devastated!" accompanied by pictures of him sightseeing, then entering and leaving the restaurant holding hands with Miss Beart, the two of them going into her apartment building, a picture of the dead assassin from the building lobby and a long-range picture of Jonah being wheeled into the hospital on the gurney.

After docking at the station, he stalked back to the diplomatic boat with Thompson and Winchester beside him, in as foul a mood as he could ever recall. When he entered the boat, Elaine jumped up and started to say, "Jonah, I'm so glad—"

He stopped her with a cold glare, and a finger pointed at her. "Captain MacLeod," he hissed, "Sit down. I know that you arranged for Miss Beart to join me on the premier's sightseeing tour. I know you did it to generate publicity. I hope you didn't go so far as to pay Miss Beart to have sex with me."

Elaine looked at him, clearly horrified that he would think such a thing.

"Good," he said. "I had hoped she was acting out of genuine attraction and interest: she seemed like a nice person. I would hate to think she was a cold and manipulative bitch too."

"Jonah," she protested, "I hoped she would go sightseeing with you. That's it. I swear!"

"Hmmph!" Jonah grunted as he sat down.

"Jonah, do you think I pimped you out?" she asked in disbelief. "That the only reason she would sleep with you is that I set it up?"

"Nooo," he said uncertainly.

"Well, I didn't," she said matter-of-factly. "Man, I'd like to meet her."

"Who? Miss Beart?"

"No. The woman who did such a number on you. You are an extremely attractive man and a hero. You've got the whole humble, 'aw shucks' thing down pat because that's who you are. You've got an eyepatch that makes you look dangerous in a romantic kind of way. You're a genuine person, a nice guy. Any woman, even one as famous on her world and many others and as beautiful as Miss Beart, would sleep with you given a chance."

"Mmmmmm," Jonah hummed noncommittally.

"Trust me," she said. "Whatever woman broke your heart really messed you up."

Jonah left and went to his quarters and filed a report to the Admiralty on what had happened. As he was sending it, he felt the ka-chunk of the ship undocking from Lutetia Station. Their next stop was Roosevelt, home of Third Fleet and Admiral Johannsen.

Jonah lay awake for hours thinking about what Elaine had said.

The next morning, he saw Elaine over breakfast. "I apologize," he said.

"You want to talk about it?" she asked.

"Not really," he answered, "but I'm thinking maybe I should. I've never talked about it—never had anyone I could talk to about it."

"Well, you've got me," Elaine offered, "and I think it sure couldn't hurt you to talk about it. It might help you figure things out."

"Oooookay," he said hesitantly.

"Start at the beginning."

"Her name is Beth Triscari. She was marine lieutenant. I met her on leave about six years ago. We had a mutual friend who suggested we look each other up. We did, and I have to say I was smitten. She's attractive and vivacious. We spent the day together, then the night, then the rest of our leaves."

"How was the sex?" Elaine asked.

"Ordinarily, I'd say none of your business," Jonah retorted, "but I'll admit it was fantastic. At least I thought so."

"Mhm. Go on."

"We matched up our leaves as often as we could over the next two years and met up whenever we were on the same station at the same time. Every time we were together was just as exciting as the first. We stayed in touch with frequent comms. I was head-over-heels in love, and I thought she was too. I had never been in love so hard.

"The last time I saw her, we had planned a leave together on Aries—two weeks in a bungalow on the beach. I had a ring in my pocket. I was planning to ask her to marry me at the end of the leave. I had it all planned out—it was going to be super-romantic.

"When I got to the bungalow on Aries, she was already there. I noticed she was a bit tipsy, maybe more than a bit. It wasn't long after that, and we fell into bed." Jonah blushed. "That wasn't unusual."

"And?" Elaine prompted.

"And a little later, when I… When we—"

"Um, started?" Elaine suggested

"So, just after we started, she started to cry. She asked me to stop. I asked what was wrong, and she said, 'I can't do this. I'm in love with someone else.'"

"Oh, wow," Elaine breathed.

"Yeah," Jonah agreed. "Yeah. Well, my heart broke right there. I didn't say a word. I got dressed and left. The next day she commed me and tried to tell me she was sorry. I ended the call. She's commed me a couple of times since when she was drunk. It makes me hurt just like it did then."

"I'm sorry," Elaine said sincerely. "And since?"

"The next few girls I dated," he explained, "I treated poorly. As soon as I knew they were invested in a relationship, I'd dump them, and not politely. Once I got through that stage, then the next few years, I tried to turn every girl I dated into a relationship. That didn't work out too well either."

"I'll bet," she commented.

"I've had a few one-night stands with old acquaintances, but that's been it."

"And the night with Miss Beart?"

"Was not real," Jonah snapped. "That was fantasy-land."

"What if I told you it was probably a fantasy come true for Miss Beart?"

Jonah snorted. "I'd wonder how much you'd had to drink."

"Jonah," she sighed. "For someone as smart as you are, you're awfully dumb."

"Gee, thanks," he said sarcastically.

"No, I mean it," she said, shaking her head. "D-U-M-B, dumb."

Seeing his puzzled expression, she started again. "Jonah. What that woman did to you?"

"Yes?"

"She's not a nice person. That's just not something that a nice person could do. A nice person wouldn't even be able to consider doing that to someone that she knew cared about her," she explained.

"Hmmm."

"Seriously," she stated flatly. "What you told me is one of the nastiest and most cruel things I've ever heard. Even worse, you've been thinking since then that there's something wrong with you. Good God! The only thing wrong with you is you fell in love with someone who is fickle and cold-hearted. The sooner you get it through your thick head that what she did was mean and nasty and that you didn't deserve to be treated that way, the sooner you'll get your head on straight again."

Jonah was speechless, thinking about what Elaine had said.

"You think about it," she told him. "We'll talk more after you have a chance to think."

Jonah left the table and went to his quarters, such as they were on the small ship. He lay on his bunk and stared at the ceiling, thinking. He emerged hours later when it was time for dinner. He and Elaine didn't talk anymore about his romantic travails but did discuss some details regarding the itinerary coming up. Afterward, he returned to his cabin.

34

He slept until morning when the aches from his injuries woke him. After showering, exposing his body to the UV lighting in the medical cubicle for the prescribed time, dressing, and eating breakfast, he read a message from Antonelli on his comm. The vice admiral informed him that the Admiralty was sending a courier ship to meet them at their next stop with a new Victoria Cross to replace the one bent by the fléchette. He also informed him that he had made some assignments to begin to fill out the commissioned and non-com ranks on *Indomitable* since she was due to begin trials in less than three months.

His new XO would be Commander Thornton 'Mel' Mellon. Though starting as an enlisted man, Mellon had been identified early as a young man of great promise. The navy had sent him to Caerleon University on an ROTC scholarship, where he finished as the command cadet, majoring in history and minoring in classics. Jonah thought that was an unusual combination. His most recent posting was as a lieutenant commander in command of PB 371, where he had an exciting time dealing with pirates who infested a three-corridor route between the Commonwealth Alleghany System and a Chinese system.

The new head of engineering would be Commander Genevieve Gessert. She had been a classmate of Jonah's at the naval academy. She had been more of an acquaintance than a friend, but he remembered she was in the top fifth of his class.

The senior non-com was Command Master Chief Tom Bradshaw. Jonah laughed out loud as he read this. Bradshaw had done it again, though, with the success the two of them had enjoyed, Jonah thought for the first time that maybe the Admiralty was reluctant to break up such a winning combination.

The commanding officer of the short company of Royal Marines on-board would be Nathan 'Nate' Taylor. Taylor's marine rank was captain, but on board *Indomitable,* he would be addressed as 'Major' Taylor since tradition dictated that there could only be one captain on a ship. He had distinguished himself during the Battle of New Delhi a little over a year earlier.

New Delhi was one of three planets that had been settled under the auspices of the United Nations following the Second Great Intifada. Of the three, New Delhi was the only one that could be termed successful. Patagonia was wracked by corruption, and Nyumbani had been wracked by political unrest and ethnic warfare for most of its history.

Taylor had led a successful effort to retake New Delhi Station after the Rodinans had captured it. Capturing an orbital station from an enemy without it being destroyed was one of the more difficult things to accomplish. Taylor had won the DSC for his efforts.

Jonah, after checking his schedule, sent a message to all four and set a time for a conference call when he reached Roosevelt Station. All but Taylor were already at Caerleon Yard, becoming familiar with *Indomitable* while she was still being finished. Jonah was slightly envious.

He finished up and noticed Elaine had not yet made an appearance. He thought about their conversation the evening before. Elaine had been the first person to see his heart had not healed and what she said the night before had given him a new perspective. He felt as though a weight had been removed from his soul. During the balance of the trip to Roosevelt, he thought more and more about it and finally felt as though he might be recovering.

As they docked at Roosevelt Station, Elaine's comm buzzed. She said, "I have to take this," and went to her quarters. A couple of hours later, she appeared after lunch. Jonah noticed her eyes and nose were red. She looked as though she had been crying. Jonah asked, "Are you alright?" She waved him off, indicating she did not want to talk about it.

The rest of their visit to Roosevelt was disturbing. Every other time they had visited a system that was HQ to a fleet, the fleet brass had shown up for Jonah's appearance. On Southhampton, Vice Admiral von Geisler had brought the Fifth Fleet staff. On Aries, Admiral Antonelli (recently promoted from Vice Admiral) had brought the staff of Second Fleet. On Avalon, Admiral DiGiovanni and the Fourth Fleet staff were part of an enthusiastic audience. Here on Roosevelt, Admiral Johannsen and the entire Third Fleet staff were notable in their absence. In fact, the only naval personnel present were some enlisted men and a handful of junior officers. Not only was that troubling, but the mood of the crowd was subdued, almost sullen. The crowd was by far the smallest they had seen. On the shuttle returning from the planet, Jonah, Elaine, and even Winchester and Thompson discussed how different the appearance on Roosevelt had been from all the others on the trip.

After they returned to Roosevelt Station, they were waiting for the courier boat to arrive that Admiral Antonelli had said was on the way. Elaine looked over at Jonah and said quietly, "He dumped me."

"Your boyfriend?" Jonah confirmed, kicking himself for asking such a dumb question.

She nodded.

Jonah thought quickly of what he should say, finally offering, "I'm sorry. He's an asshole."

"Yes," Elaine said smiling, "he is."

Jonah shook his head later at the irony. Elaine had helped him to find and begin repairing his emotional scars only to suffer her own heartbreak. He felt awful for her and wanted to offer some help to her, as she had helped him.

He had a flash of inspiration. He checked their itinerary to make sure it would work and smiled. Their next stop after Roosevelt was York. It was also one of the few stops where they had a little bit of time for sightseeing. Before they left Roosevelt Station, he made some calls.

35

The courier boat finally arrived and delivered a package for them. In the package were a new dress uniform and a new copy of the Victoria Cross for Jonah. There was also a paper envelope addressed to him. He waited to open it until after he returned to the ship.

Once aboard ship, he sat down and opened the envelope. It contained an invitation to Lady Hawthorne's wedding on Caerleon in a month. Jonah looked at it with lips pursed. Elaine asked him what it was.

"An invitation to Lady Hawthorne's wedding. It says I can bring a guest. Want to come?"

"What's the date? I'll see if I'm free," she said, smirking.

"October 22. And I'm serious."

"Hang on a sec. I think we're scheduled to be visiting Caerleon sometime close to that." She checked the schedule on her comm. "No. We'll be on Caerleon ten days before."

"So we can't go?"

"Hang on," she said, pulling up a holographic star map from the display unit. "Let's see how we can juggle things."

"You really want to go?"

"Sure," she said. "Why not? Who knows when I'll ever get a chance to go to a wedding this fancy. Besides, having you attend the wedding of First Space Lord Chesterfield makes it almost imperative that you go."

Together the two of them figured out a way to reconfigure their schedule so they could attend. It involved flip-flopping a couple of visits in the last month of the tour. Elaine sent a comm to her superiors at the Admiralty informing them of the opportunity and asking for their approval on the schedule changes.

She heard back before dinner. When she came to the table, she was grinning. "I'm guessing we're going to a wedding?" Jonah asked.

"Yup," she confirmed. "Now, let me see that invitation."

She looked at it. "Six-thirty p.m. So, formal. That means I have a decision to make."

"What do you mean?"

"Well, formal dress for you is easy," she shrugged. "You wear your dress uniform. For me, I can either wear my dress uniform or a gown. I'll probably stick with the uniform, though. Buying the right gown will be difficult and hideously expensive."

"Well, I'll send the RSVP regardless," Jonah said. "You can figure out what you're wearing later."

He went to his room and replied to the wedding invitation, indicating that he would be bringing a guest. He also filed a report with recently promoted Admiral Antonelli, informing him of both the strange reception on Roosevelt and their schedule changes due to the wedding. Finally, he sent another message ahead to his mother on York regarding his earlier flash of inspiration.

Four days later, they arrived on York. Before they left the ship, Jonah suggested that Elaine should bring a change of clothes for afterward, including comfortable shoes. Elaine wanted to know why, but Jonah told her not to ask too many questions, or she would ruin it. "What is *it?*" she demanded to know.

"Top secret," Jonah replied. "I could tell you, but then I'd have to kill you," he joked. "Or I'll have Winchester do it," he added. "He owes me for losing so badly at cribbage last night."

Jonah gave his speech in the main city of Leeds. The welcome they received was completely different from Roosevelt. Of course, Jonah had grown up in the suburbs of Leeds, so he was hoping for a warm response, but the huge, wildly enthusiastic crowd exceeded his expectations.

After the speech, they took a groundcar to the suburbs and the home where Jonah had grown up. It was in an affluent but not ostentatious neighborhood. Jonah's mother met them at the door and gushed over how pretty Elaine was and insisting that Elaine call her Marian. One of the first things Marian wanted to know was whether Jonah and Elaine were, as she put it, 'an item.'

"I hate to let you down, mom," Jonah said, "but no. We are going to a wedding in a few weeks, though."

Immediately Marian wanted to know all the details: who was getting married, where, the time and what Elaine would be wearing. When Elaine told her that she would likely wear her dress uniform, Marian barked, "Nonsense!"

"But—" Elaine tried to explain.

"Nonsense, I said. How many times in your life will you be invited to a high-society wedding like this?" she demanded. "Oh, I know you're a navy officer and proud of it, so if that's the way you feel, then wear your dress uniform. But if you ever wanted to play dress-up, this is one of the few times in your adult life when you'll be allowed. You're so pretty; why not let everyone see you?"

"Well," Elaine said, "we're traveling constantly between now and then, so I don't really have time to shop for the right dress. And the wedding is in Glastonbury Cathedral on Caerleon, and I don't know anywhere to get my hair done on the whole planet. Besides, a gown like this will be atrociously expensive. It's just too much—"

"Hush," Marian said. "Let me help. Thanks to Jonah, I have a new friend, Laura—"

At this, Jonah snorted. His mother continued on after glaring at him with mock ferocity. "Laura," she repeated, "on Caerleon, who knows all the top designers. They will probably fight each other for the chance to dress someone as lovely as you. I'm certain she can find someone in Glastonbury who will be able to give you a final fitting and someone to do your hair and anything else you need."

"But it will cost—"

"Pah!" Marian exclaimed. "Jonah will pay for it. You're his guest. Besides sweetie," she said conspiratorially, "he's worth millions. He'll never miss it."

Elaine looked quickly at Jonah. He shrugged. "Prize money," he said. "She's right. I never spend anything. This will be fun."

Marian asked, "Send me your measurement files right now and let me take some quick pictures of you. I'll send them off to Laura, and we'll get started on this right away. You won't have to worry about a thing!"

Jonah stepped away, telling them, "I'm going to go change. Elaine, when mom's done with you, you should change too."

After Jonah left, Elaine tried to find out what he had planned, but all Marian would say was, "It's a surprise. You wouldn't want me to spoil it."

Elaine went to change, and Jonah returned. His mother gave him a large wicker basket, and Jonah went outside to confer with Winchester. Moments later, a flitter touched down in the front yard of the house, with Thompson at the controls.

Elaine came out dressed in casual trousers and a blouse, with walking shoes on. Marian came to the front door with her and handed a smaller basket to Winchester, then told her, "Have a wonderful day, dear. Don't worry about a thing. This is going to be so much fun!"

Elaine walked out to the flitter where Jonah was stowing the basket he had. She cocked an eyebrow at him. "Where are we going?"

"On a picnic," he replied. "It's a gorgeous sunny day for one." After watching Winchester stow his basket, he opened to door of the flitter for her. Once they were all inside, Thompson eased the craft into the air.

"Where are we going?" Elaine asked again.

"Someplace special," Jonah replied.

Exasperated, Elaine asked, "Thompson, where are we going?"

"On a picnic, ma'am," he answered with a straight face.

"Winchester, where are we going?"

"Someplace special, ma'am," he answered, equally deadpan.

They flew for about 45 minutes. Jonah suggested, "If you can, Thompson, try to fly around it once before we have to land."

Under them was a large lake that ended in a small channel that led to the edge of the land they had been flying over. There was a steep drop of about 400 meters to a gorge about six kilometers wide. At the bottom of the gorge was a huge river. Thompson flew in an arc, descending to the level of the plain, turning the flitter so Elaine could see. The water from the lake gushed through the small channel and flew out away from the side of the gorge, falling into a pool at the bottom that then drained into the river.

"God," she breathed, "it's magnificent!"

Thompson landed the flitter in a parking area. Jonah retrieved his basket and Winchester the other. A sign indicated they were in the Minerva's Bath Planetary Park and admonished them to tread gently and leave no rubbish. The four of them set off along a path, passing two visitors who were returning to the parking area.

The path was rocky and led through a stand of tall trees. When they emerged from the trees, the path turned to the right sharply, and then Minerva's Bath could be seen. The falling water had carved a bowl into which the falls thundered. On either side of the bowl was a series of broad flat grass-covered steps, each roughly ten meters wide, that rose bit by bit, starting at the edge of the bowl and curving back to the side of the gorge.

Jonah led her to one where they could sit and watch the falling water. Thompson and Winchester chose a spot a little bit above them and just far enough away to be out of earshot. Jonah spread out the blanket that was covering the basket and indicated Elaine should sit.

There were only a handful of other visitors to the park, most closer to the falls or walking along the bridge that had been built along the edge of the gorge behind the falling water. Jonah and Elaine were far enough away that the roar of the cascade was not too loud to carry on a normal conversation but close enough that the breeze occasionally drifted some of the mist their way. It was a sunny day and would have been almost uncomfortably hot except for the cooling effect of the water.

Jonah sat down and began pulling items from the cooler, naming each as he did. "Some grapes. A bit of cheese. Some crackers. A knife for the cheese. Wineglasses. That's a good sign," he joked. "Mmmm—cold fried chicken. A couple of chocolates—must be for later. A bottle of wine, good. Two plates. Napkins. Ah, a corkscrew!"

"What is all this?" Elaine exclaimed delightedly.

"A picnic," Jonah answered. "Haven't you ever been on a picnic?"

"No," she shook her head. "I've only read about them. Never been on one."

"Well, you've been missing out."

Jonah opened the bottle of white wine and poured them each a glass. He unwrapped the cheese and put it on a small plate, then used the knife to cut some slices and placed some crackers on the plate, and set it down. He then picked up the bunch of grapes by the stem and offered them to her.

She plucked a grape from the stem and popped it in her mouth. "Am I doing it right?" she asked after she swallowed.

"Yup."

They sat and snacked on the cheese, crackers, and grapes, sipping on their wine, watching the cascade of water. After a while, he offered her a piece of fried chicken. She looked at it skeptically, took a small bite, decided she liked it, and ate the rest of the piece quickly.

They finished their lunch and sat in comfortable silence, watching the waterfall and sipping their wine until it was time to go. Jonah put everything away in the basket, and they walked back to the flitter. They returned to Jonah's childhood home and returned the baskets. Elaine, Thompson, and Winchester were all effusive in their praise of Marian's picnic lunch and thanked her profusely. Jonah kissed his mother goodbye. Marian then pulled Elaine aside and engaged her in quiet conversation.

Jonah and the others returned to the spaceport and climbed aboard the shuttle. Elaine took the seat next to Jonah and rested her head on his shoulder. This was a bit unexpected by Jonah, but he certainly didn't mind. He asked her what his mother had to say.

"Just that she's already been in touch with her friend, and she will be sending me drawings in a few days. Who is her friend?"

"Laura? You and I would know her as Lady Thorner, one of Queen Celeste's ladies-in-waiting."

"Oh, god!" Elaine sighed.

They reached the station and then the ship. Jonah sat on the couch in the lounge, hearing the ka-chunk as they disengaged from the station. Elaine flopped down next to him and put her hand on his arm.

When he turned to her, she said quietly, "Jonah, thank you for a wonderful day. It was exactly what I needed to restore my soul. But your job isn't finished yet."

"It's not?"

"No," she said, looking at him intently. "In order to finish the job, we should either get drunk and have wild monkey sex, or else you should take me to bed and hold me and wait and see what happens then."

Jonah quipped, "If I don't like what happens then, can I go back and choose the first one?"

She hit him on the arm. He bent down and kissed her. Without another word, they went to her quarters.

Later, she was tracing with her finger the red scars from his recent injuries. Her head was on his chest, her hair splayed out. He asked, "A penny for your thoughts?"

"Can I see it?" she asked.

"See what?"

"Your eye. Can I see it?"

Up to now, Jonah had not felt self-conscious about his injury, but this turned his attention to it. "Uh, I guess," he mumbled.

Elaine leaned over him and tipped up his eyepatch. He could hear her sharp intake of breath. "Ewwwww," she breathed.

"It's kind of gross," Jonah offered.

"It's not so bad," Elaine answered, still looking at his injury, "kind of cool." She kissed it and put his eyepatch back in place. "Thanks for showing me."

"You're welcome?" Jonah said uncertainly.

She sighed, turned her head, and looked him in the eye. "I don't want a relationship, Jonah."

"Mmm?"

"You are an incredible man. I feel affection for you. Hell, I admire you," she said. "I would trust you with my life. But I'm on the rebound right now. I'm not ready for another relationship, and if we tried to make it work, it would end badly, and I don't want that for either of us. I get the sense lately that you're on the rebound, too—finally.

"But this," she stroked his chest, moving her hand downwards, "was really nice. And I want more of it. Lots more. But," she stopped stroking and looked him in the eye, "when our tour is over, we go our separate ways. We think fond thoughts of one another, have happy memories, and consider ourselves good friends, but that's it. Can you do that?"

Jonah smiled and kissed her forehead. "Elaine, I didn't realize how damaged I still was until you pointed it out. So, in that sense, I am on the rebound. I think you're right. And I agree," he said, stroking his hand down her back to the curve of her hip, "this," he smacked her lightly, "was really nice. And I want more of it. In fact, now would be a good time," he said as he rolled over on top of her and kissed her.

36

Over the next month, Jonah found himself more and more occupied attending to *Indomitable* business. His officer corps was being filled out; Commander Gessert had brought the reactors online; there were files to review and reports to read. He and Elaine now slept together most nights. Whatever was happening with her gown, she kept secret from him. Marian and Laura had sent her some designs from which to choose, but she did not involve Jonah in this.

They arrived at Caerleon Station early in the morning of October 22. When Jonah arrived in Glastonbury to give his speech, he was surprised to see his mother waiting for him. With her was Lady Thorner. After Jonah gave his speech, the two older women took Elaine with them and gave instructions to Thompson on where and when he could come with Jonah to pick her up to take her to the wedding.

With nothing to do for most of the day, Jonah returned to the courier boat to get out of his dress uniform for a few hours. He spent the afternoon catching up on paperwork, then played a few hands of cribbage with Thompson. Finally, the time came to get dressed and go. He and Thompson flew down and obtained a groundcar. Thompson had the address, which was a stately home in the near suburbs of Glastonbury.

Jonah went to the front door and rang the bell. His mother opened it. "Oh, good, you're here just in time for the unveiling."

She turned and called to the upstairs of the house. "Jonah's here, Elaine. Are you ready to go?"

Jonah looked up the stairs and what he saw next took his breath away. Elaine came to the top of the stairs. She was dressed in a turquoise gown. The top was strapless and clung to her figure. The skirt, a lighter shade, billowed out in a cloud of organza. She wore white elbow-length gloves. Her hair was done up in plaits. As she climbed down the stairs, he could see jewels glimmering, tucked artfully in her hair at the junction of the braids. She wore earrings with diamonds dangling at different lengths, similar in size to the ones in her hair. She wore a diamond necklace with more jewels sprinkled across her chest, again similar to the ones in her hair. The diamonds in the necklace were connected by the thinnest platinum strands. Her makeup was understated but set off her beauty perfectly.

She looked down at him as she descended. "You like?"

"You look incredible!" Jonah breathed.

"Goodie!' she exclaimed. "I feel like Cinderella! I've had such a fun day. Your mom and Laura are a hoot! They've been so nice. Do you like the necklace and the earrings?" she tilted her head side to side so he could see better. "Laura is letting me borrow them. They're real, but the ones in my hair aren't. And do you like the back?"

She turned, and Jonah could see that her dress was not only strapless but backless, dipping all the way to where the skirt was. "How does it stay up?" Jonah wondered.

"It's a secret for now," she said with a coy smile, "but maybe I'll show you later, big boy."

Thompson coughed discretely, signaling that they needed to leave for the wedding. Jonah offered Elaine his arm, saying, "Thompson is telling us it's time to get in the pumpkin, Cinderella. Shall we?"

The wedding was lovely and brief. At the reception, they were seated with some of Julia's cousins. Elaine excelled at making small talk with them, and they were impressed to be seated with Jonah. After dinner, a band began to play, and Elaine asked Jonah to dance. Elaine was an accomplished dancer, and the two of them twirled around the floor gracefully. She complimented Jonah on his skill. "You dance well. Is there anything you can't do well?" she asked.

"Thank my mom for the dancing. Two years of torture, during second and third form," he quipped. "She insisted I learn. I hated her for it at the time, but you'll be pleased to know I just sent her a silent prayer of thanks."

As they danced, they chatted about some of the people they saw. Elaine was quite skilled at pointing out the leading politicians in the crowd of guests. At one point, she looked him in his eye and said, "People seem to be watching us, don't you think?"

Jonah had noticed they seemed to be attracting some attention as well. "It's because of you," he said, then raised his lip as though to indicate she had something stuck on her teeth.

"Oh god," she whispered. "Why didn't you tell me?"

"Just kidding," he admitted. She smacked him on the arm.

"It's because I'm dancing with the most beautiful woman here," he said, "and I haven't tripped and fallen yet."

"Flatterer," she admonished. "Keep that up, and you might just get lucky tonight," she teased.

"It doesn't hurt that you're a devilishly handsome war hero," she added a few turns later.

"Keep that up, and you might just get lucky tonight," he responded.

The song ended, and someone tapped him on the left shoulder, the signal that someone wanted to dance with his partner. He turned to face Lord Chesterfield.

"May I have the next dance?" Lord Chesterfield asked.

"Certainly, milord," Jonah said graciously. "Congratulations, sir," he offered.

"Thank you, Sir Jonah, though I must say you look like you're enjoying my wedding more than anyone. You two make quite a pair."

The music started again before Jonah could respond, and Elaine swept away with Lord Chesterfield. Jonah took a step back and was beginning to turn to leave when he felt a tap on his right shoulder and a voice asked, "May I have this dance?"

His right was his blind side, so he had to turn halfway around to see it was Julia, now Lady Chesterfield, who was asking. He smiled when he saw her. "Of course, milady. Congratulations on a beautiful wedding."

She stepped into his arms, and they began to dance. Her bridal dress was a sheath that highlighted her petite figure. She moved well, obviously a good dancer.

"I'm so glad you came. I was worried you wouldn't. Your date is the prettiest woman here," Julia commented after a few turns. "Are you two...?"

"Just friends," Jonah confirmed. "She's Captain Elaine MacLeod, from the Royal Navy's Office of Public Affairs."

"Oh," Julia realized, "she's the one who has been taking you all over the galaxy the last few months. Just friends?" she teased. "You seem so much more—happy isn't the right word. Self-assured isn't quite it either, but somewhere in there."

"She helped me figure out that I needed to get over something that happened a few years ago," he tried to explain.

"Well, whatever it is, it seems to have done you some good. Are you happy?"

"It depends on what we're talking about," Jonah qualified. "If we're talking about my career, I don't think I've ever been unhappy. I've been very blessed. If we're discussing my personal life, and particularly my love life, I can say I've regained hope in the last few weeks. Does that make sense?"

"I think that's what I was noticing," she replied. She looked down at his chest. "I'm sorry if I hurt you," she said softly.

"Julia," he sighed. "There is nothing to forgive. Fate has other plans for you and for me."

They danced in silence a few turns, then Jonah, to change the subject and the mood, asked, "Did everything go smoothly in planning the wedding? Or were there hiccups along the way?"

Julia grinned up at him. "Oh yes," she said, with a hint of nasty delight in her voice, "one of my bridesmaids couldn't fit in her dress yesterday. It seems she's gone and got herself preggers with the caddy master at her golf club. The matriarchs in my husband's family are simply in a swivet about it. The poor cow thinks she's in love and wants to carry the baby full term, which just isn't done these days, you know. The scumbag already has three children with three different lovers, but this stupid girl thinks she's different."

Jonah laughed. The music ended. Jonah looked at her and kissed her cheek. "Thank you, Julia," he whispered.

"Thank you, Jonah," she whispered back.

Lord Chesterfield reclaimed his bride. Elaine asked, "Can we get something to drink?"

As they walked to the bar, Elaine whispered, "Lady Chesterfield is going to have her hands full. Her new hubby got awfully handsy on the dance floor."

Jonah cocked his eyebrow at her questioningly. She nodded solemnly and put her hand on her butt, and simulated giving it a yank. Jonah looked at her with mock ferocity, flaring his nostrils and putting his hand on the hilt of his sword. "Where is he?" he hissed. "The cad! I'll run him through!"

Elaine giggled. "Don't do that!' she said with pretend seriousness. "They'd take you away in chains, and I'd have to find another dance partner. Though I have had my eye on Lord Burnham over there."

"Which one is he?"

"Over there," she nodded sideways. "About 160 centimeters, 150 kilos, that oh-so-sexy double chin—"

"I would hate to stand in your way," Jonah offered.

She hit him on the arm as she laughed. After a flute of champagne, they returned to the dance floor. A few other men cut in on him the rest of the night, but he didn't mind. Finally, the time came when the bride and groom departed, signaling an end to the reception.

When they returned to the ship, Elaine allowed Jonah to see how the bodice of her gown and been held up. Jonah swore it was magic. Tired and happy, they fell into bed.

The next morning, Elaine woke him with a poke to the ribs. She was naked except for the earrings and necklace. Her hair was tousled with the braiding all undone, and the jewels which had been in it were scattered throughout the bedclothes.

"Wha—" Jonah mumbled.

"Thank you," she said, giving him a quick kiss on his chin, "for one of the best nights of my life. I'm so glad I let your mom talk me into playing dress-up. It was literally a dream come true for me."

"You're welcome."

"I had a great time. You're a lovely dancer. I felt I was the prettiest girl there, with the most attractive man. But…" she paused.

"But…?" he prompted after a few seconds.

"But," she sighed, "I want to make sure this doesn't change anything between us. Weddings are romantic. Last night was a romantic fantasy come to life. It's easy to get caught up in it. There were times last night when I was getting caught up in it, but—"

"But in another month," he joined in, "we say goodbyes and go our separate ways, right?"

"Right," she agreed, exhaling.

"Okay, but that's another month away," he said, then with a sly smile, moved his hands under the sheet and down her sides. "Whatever will we do in the meantime?"

"I'm sure we'll figure out how to pass the time," she answered as she straddled him.

37

Their last month together passed in a hurry. After the last speech on the planet of Ilium, they held a small celebration with Thompson and Winchester. Jonah and Elaine continued to make love every night on the way back to Caerleon, but it took on a bittersweet quality. They talked and admitted to one another that neither of them felt they were "in love" with the other, but they had become dear friends and would miss one another. They agreed to stay in touch but made no commitments.

The morning they arrived, Jonah immediately took a shuttle to the Caerleon Yard, where *Indomitable* was waiting. He pondered how he felt about saying goodbye to Elaine. He knew he would miss her. She was easy company, and they had enjoyed a lot of their time together, but he'd known that there hadn't been that spark between them. He felt no sense of loss or regret and, though he was surprised to admit it to himself, felt more whole and emotionally healthy than he had since before he had met Beth Triscari.

As soon as he was aboard *Indomitable*, they could begin space trials. The commissioning was scheduled for January 23 in the new year. The first thing he did was to meet his new officers face-to-face. Even though they had spent many hours together on video conferences, Jonah felt there was no substitute for in-person contact.

Jonah boarded without ceremony and took his bags to his quarters. He had commed his staff while on the way to set up a meeting that would start at 13:00. That left him enough time to unpack and make a very brief tour of the ship.

When he reached his quarters, he found that someone had hung a framed black and white photograph of the original *Indomitable*. There was a note attached to the frame which read: "Jonah—this is a picture of the first ship named *Indomitable* in the Royal Navy. She was the first wet-navy battlecruiser in the fleet and served with great distinction in a great war that began six years after she was commissioned. All the best—Renee."

Jonah smiled at the kind gesture from Captain Fung then set off to tour the ship. At just over three-quarters of a kilometer long, he would not have time to visit every deck and department immediately but wanted to see engineering, propulsion, damage control, and the bridge. Even so abbreviated, his tour would take all the time he had before the meeting.

Along the way to his first stop, propulsion, at the rear of the ship, he noticed the ship was neat and tidy. All the confusion and jumble of construction he had seen six months before had been cleared away. In propulsion, he ran into Commander Gessert. He had not seen her in person since the academy, but they had spent many hours in video conferences in the last few weeks. She was short and plump, possessing a voice that cracked like a whip as she called to a tech doing something out of sight. With her was Captain Nehru from the yard. After exchanging greetings, she explained that a power relay in the 'C' drive had shown up on a diagnostic as having a fault, so she was supervising having it pulled and replaced. That job finished, she accompanied Jonah to engineering. Along the way, they discussed a few other faults that had popped up, which she felt were relatively minor and perhaps fewer than she expected in a ship just completed.

In engineering, he saw the consoles monitoring the three huge fusion reactors and the ship's systems all manned. He asked Genevieve if she were happy with her people and the ship. "She's a beauty, sir," she replied, "and I was able to pick and choose who I wanted. There were a lot of personnel requesting transfer to *Indomitable*."

He then headed to damage control. Command Master Chief Bradshaw was there and explained he was in the process of giving a tour to a group of petty officers who had just reported. Jonah was pleased to see Tom, as always, but even more to see his leg had now fully regrown. Bradshaw introduced him to Master Chief Lola Applegate from the yard, a short black woman with gray hair. He left Bradshaw and Applegate and headed to the bridge.

On the bridge, he met Commander Thornton Mellon. Mellon was Jonah's height but was stocky, outweighing Jonah by twenty kilos or more. Mellon was dark-skinned, with close-cropped black hair. Mellon introduced Jonah to two junior officers on the bridge, Lieutenants Vince Caputo and Kate McSpadden. He explained that the other junior officers were currently on a "scavenger hunt" he had assigned them to familiarize themselves with the ship. Caputo and McSpadden had been on board for over a week and had already completed Mellon's "hunt."

In the meeting that followed, Bradshaw and Mellon echoed Commander Gessert's comment about the quality of people they had been able to add to the crew. Though not all the crew had been able to report yet, they had enough to begin trials on schedule when they were supposed to depart early that evening from the yard. Mellon and Gessert had prepared a schedule for the next four weeks, covering comprehensive testing of all the ship's systems.

They would then return to the yard on December 23 for eight days, giving the yard a chance to fix any issues they uncovered. They would depart for trials again on January 1, by which time the entire crew, including the marines, would be aboard. Two more weeks of trials, followed by one last week in the yard, would see them to their commissioning ceremony.

Captain Nehru and Master Chief Applegate then went over status reports on various items. They would be joined by 53 workmen from the yard during this first phase of trials, with most of those needed to help tune the four massive EM drives once they began moving under their own power. The remainder were split between electricians and programmers to fix any problems they encountered. As with any machine of such complexity, they expected bugs to appear when they began trials.

The meeting concluded, giving everyone a chance to have dinner and make sure everyone was ready before their scheduled departure time. Jonah stopped by his quarters and sent a quick message to his mother, asking for her help in buying Elaine a suitable Christmas present. Marian understood the nature of his relationship with Elaine, and he trusted her judgment better than his own in selecting an appropriate gift.

As he was leaving his ready room, he literally bumped into his new steward, an enlisted man named Kowalchik. Kowalchik had a roly-poly figure, apple cheeks, and a cheerful disposition, very much unlike Jonah's former steward Ginepri. Like Ginepri, though, he tried to cover his balding head by combing his hair from the side over the bald areas.

He went to the officers' mess and there met the rest of the officers who had been on Mellon's "scavenger hunt." When he sat down to eat with them, the four ensigns in the group seemed particularly goggle-eyed to be sitting with him. He remembered how awestruck he had been as an ensign when first meeting Captain von Geisler who was now somewhat of a mentor to him. He hoped that perhaps someday he would have the same kind of relationship with one or more of these men and women.

They departed Caerleon Yard on schedule, with tugs nudging them clear of the construction gantries. They used their thrusters to move far enough away that the EM drives could be engaged. Almost as soon as they engaged the drives, they had to shut them down. There was a harmonic tremor in the drives, which was entirely expected.

Though each drive had been tested individually before being installed, this was the first time the four had been engaged at once. It was common for new sets of drives to have harmonic tremors due to the similarity of their construction. Unfortunately, harmonic tremors could literally crack a ship open if left unchecked. The schedule they had gone over devoted most of the first five days to tuning the drives.

As the fifth day came to a close, Captain Nehru and Commander Gessert finally pronounced themselves satisfied with the tuning of the drives. They had taken *Indomitable* up well beyond its rated maximum acceleration of 515 Gs with no hint of tremors. They spent the remaining part of the first set of trials testing the Alcubierre generators by traveling in hyperspace, adjusting the targeting of the photon cannons, the point defense lasers and the railguns, test-firing dummy missiles, and measuring the strength of the ship's plasma shielding to make sure there were no weak spots.

They returned to Caerleon Yard on schedule, and the officers and crew departed for a brief leave to enjoy Christmas. Jonah, however, was staying aboard ship. There was not enough time to travel home to York and make it back before the second set of trials, plus he had mountains of paperwork to do, with the balance of the crew due to arrive after the holiday.

He received an invitation that afternoon from Lady Thorner on his comm to come for dinner Christmas Eve. He thought briefly about declining but decided to attend. He responded that he would be coming and was told that the dress would be casual. Jonah didn't own any appropriate casual winter clothes, so figured he would head dirtside a little early to buy some. Remembering that he was not to leave the yard without an escort, he called Thompson to ask if someone would be able to accompany him tomorrow.

The next day he flew down to Caerleon and went shopping, meeting a young man who introduced himself as Remington in the lounge while waiting for the shuttle. He had already picked out a present for his mother and sent it to York, and she had helped him pick out a present for Elaine, so all he needed were some non-uniform clothes. Remington had a groundcar waiting, and Jonah asked him if he knew where he could buy some clothing.

They went to a fashionable shopping district, and Remington indicated a couple of stores where Jonah would find what he needed. The first store featured more formal clothing, but the second had what he wanted. He bought some flannel shirts with button-down collars, corduroy trousers, and comfortable shoes. He wore some of his new clothing out of the store, with his uniform in his garment bag. Remembering his mother's advice never to show up to someone's home as a guest without a gift in hand, he bought a couple of magnums of extremely expensive champagne since tomorrow was Christmas.

At the appointed time, Jonah arrived at Lady Thorner's door and rang the bell. A light snow was falling, making the scene look like something from an old storybook. Lady Thorner's maid answered the door and had Jonah come in. Lady Thorner came out and instructed Remington that he need not stay, that Jonah would be spending the next two nights with them. Jonah tried to protest that he couldn't impose when his mother came out and joined the conversation. Jonah was slightly surprised to see his mother, as she had told him she would be staying home for the holiday but was delighted she was here.

After Remington left, the two older women both began to talk, trying to explain how his mother had come to be there. Like good friends everywhere, the two were able to finish each other's sentences. They led him back into the house where Jonah met Lord Thorner, a balding man of medium height who always seemed to be in a good mood. There was a wood fire burning in a fireplace with a sofa and two comfortable armchairs arranged near it.

They sat and began talking. Lord Thorner ("call me 'Geoff'") began to update Jonah on the current state of Commonwealth politics. He praised Jonah's "goodwill tour," as he called it, reaffirming that it delayed the Liberal Democrat's plan to call for a no-confidence vote. He warned that the vote might be coming soon regardless, as Lord Hawthorne had been working diligently to woo certain members of the House of Lords to his side. He mentioned four names of people Jonah had only heard of vaguely, but the fifth caught his attention—Johannsen.

When Jonah tried to follow up to find out more, he was interrupted by one of the maids telling them that dinner was served. They rose and went into the dining room. There was a massive table that would easily seat 24 but had only four places set along the one end. On the sideboard was a small turkey with green beans, mashed potatoes, creamed onions, and stuffing. Once they had served themselves and sat, the two women immediately asked Jonah to describe the more interesting things he had seen during his trip through the Commonwealth. Geoff then interjected that all he wanted to hear about was Lutetia, which made the ladies giggle.

Jonah regaled them with stories of things he had seen and done on the trip. He did mention the trip to Lutetia but focused more on Thompson's quick reflexes saving his life instead of any lurid details. As dinner was nearing completion, he managed to bring up the strange reaction he had observed on Roosevelt, but Geoff cut him off politely, asking if they wanted an after-dinner drink or dessert by the fire. Waiting for the women to leave the room first, Geoff put his hand on Jonah's arm and whispered that the two of them could talk later.

Marian and Laura went off to talk about some design ideas Laura had seen and Geoff offered Jonah a glass of port and a cigar. Jonah accepted the port. Geoff busied himself lighting his cigar and, when he was satisfied, turned to Jonah and asked, "So, Johannsen—"

Jonah noticed that the jolly nature had departed from Geoff's eyes, and his face had taken on a harder appearance. It was a side of Lord Thorner that Jonah had not yet seen, but he understood that a man like Lord Thorner, influential and powerful enough to have his wife named as one of the Queen's ladies-in-waiting, would undoubtedly have depths not revealed in the social settings where Jonah had previously met him.

Geoff puffed on his cigar, then spoke. "You understand, Jonah, that what I'm about to tell you can't leave this room?"

Jonah nodded soberly.

"The Johannsens are opportunistic lightweights and have been for generations. They've probably already switched sides, but there hasn't been a critical enough vote in Parliament for them to show their colors. Hell, we bought 'em a few years back by promoting their idiot son to admiral, so we shouldn't be surprised to see them flop back. Anyone with half a brain knows the numbskull completely botched the attack on New Moscow, then required all our available reserves to bail him out. Hell, if it hadn't been for you, Jonah, the whole thing would have ended in a disaster.

"He claims, of course, that the reason the attack failed is that we didn't give him the resources he needed to be successful. Hell, we gave him everything we had and then some, and he signed off on the plan enthusiastically, but now he claims he never felt comfortable with any of it. Sadly, he's got Chesterfield convinced. The damn fool told the media today that he doubted whether the war was winnable.

"Even now, Johannsen is screaming at the admiralty to replace his lost ships. God alone knows what he's doing with them. Whatever sector we've assigned him to always seems to be the quietest in terms of navy activity, but Lloyd's always raises rates sharply wherever he goes, so you do the math."

Jonah knew that Lloyd's of Caerleon was the biggest insurer of merchant shipping in the Commonwealth. Their raising rates in an area was directly proportional to the amount of risk they judged to exist and was based entirely on cold, hard statistical computation with no regard for people or politics. That meant that ships in Johannsen's sector were suffering losses far more frequently than anywhere else. Coupled with a lack of reported naval activity, it showed that Third Fleet was not doing its job as far as protecting the trade routes.

Geoff could see from the tightening of Jonah's brow that he understood. After another puff on his cigar, he summed up, "So, the Johannsens are bought and paid for by the Liberal Democrats, most likely by them convincing Chesterfield to agree that the attack was flawed from the beginning. Shit, son, the only reason we haven't brought the moron up on charges of dereliction of duty is that we need his family's votes too. Well, that and we've lost Chesterfield's ear."

"So, what happens when they finally call a vote of no-confidence?"

"Well, if the Liberal Democrats win even a handful of seats in the Commons, they will have enough to form a coalition with one or two of the fringe parties to force us to begin negotiating with the Federation. That will be approved in the Lords with the people we think are switching. The Rodinans will drag things out as long as it suits them while they rebuild. On our side, the Liberal Democrats will immediately cancel all building programs and pull us back from wartime footing, so we will lose ground quickly. At some point, the Federation will force concessions from us because we won't be in any condition to oppose them."

"How do we prevent this from happening?" Jonah asked.

"Hah," Geoff snorted. "This would never have come up if we'd had a competent admiral in charge of the attack on New Moscow. We thought even a complete blockhead could make it work, but Johannsen defied our already low expectations. Things are too tight politically to risk another throw of the dice right now. But enough of politics. Tomorrow is Christmas. Let's find the ladies and get back in a holiday mood."

With that, Lord Thorner's genial nature returned. Jonah got up with him. They found Marian and Laura in the next room, looking at fabric samples. They convinced the women to bring the sample book back in front of the fire. They spent the rest of the evening talking about patterns and fabrics for a chair Laura wanted to recover.

In the middle of the night, Jonah woke, startled by a movement of his bed. His eye snapped open, and he started to sit up, but a soft hand on his chest and an accompanying giggle stopped him. In the darkness, he recognized Elaine's laugh. "Merry Christmas, Jonah," she whispered.

"What are you doing here?"

"I was invited. Laura and Marian called me tonight."

Jonah chuckled softly. "Merry Christmas, Elaine." He leaned over and kissed her. As he reached to hold her, his hands did not encounter any clothing. He swept them down and around to make sure.

"Mmmm," he hummed. "No clothes. Awfully confident I wouldn't kick you out of bed?"

"I hoped you'd be in the Christmas spirit," she teased. "And I think you have a package for me," she said, reaching below his waist.

All too soon, the holiday was over, and he returned to the ship. Elaine headed back to her family and her job, and his mother was on her way back to York. When he returned, he dove back into his paperwork. On New Year's Day, the entire crew of the ship returned, including the marines.

They set off on schedule for the last two weeks of trials. This set of trials was more of a familiarization period for the crew than a test of the ship and her systems. Watch rosters were made up, battle stations were assigned, and drills began. They returned on January 15, having encountered only some minor bugs and glitches. The crew continued to train, using simulation programs built into the ship's software, while they waited for the commissioning ceremony.

Jonah was ordered to report to the Admiralty on Caerleon, to the Admiral of the Fleet. She was the highest-ranking officer in the Navy and also commanded the Home Fleet—the ships surrounding Caerleon. He reached the office on time and was ushered inside. Admiral Wendy Lothes was a large woman—not fat, but tall and with broad shoulders. Her hair was gray, though she did not appear to be older than 40. After exchanging salutes, she indicated that he should sit.

"Welcome back, captain," she began. "It appears your trials have gone well."

"Yes, sir. We should be on schedule for the commissioning on January 23."

"Good. Following the ceremony, you will be heading to Roosevelt. You will report to Admiral Johannsen and join Third Fleet." She clicked her comm and Jonah's new orders arrived on his.

38

Upon entering the Roosevelt system, *Indomitable* received orders to establish a parking orbit around the planet and for her captain to report to Admiral Johannsen at his headquarters on the ground. Jonah thought this a bit unusual, as most admirals maintained their HQ operations on their flagships or on the orbital stations where their fleets were based.

The next day, as they approached the planet, Commander Mellon pointed out something else unusual. "Captain," he stated, "it appears as though the entirety of Third Fleet is in orbit."

"What?" Jonah was surprised.

"Sensors show 12 superdreadnoughts, 8 battlecruisers, 10 heavy cruisers, 17 light cruisers, and 20 frigates in orbit, sir. According to the Naval Register, that's all of Third Fleet."

"Perhaps an operation has been readied that would require the fleet to gather," Jonah offered. It was highly unusual for a fleet to be gathered like this under any other circumstances. With a whole sector to cover, with six inhabited planets and dozens of hyper corridors, usual practice was for the lighter ships of a fleet to be sent on picket or convoy duty and for the capital ships to be broken into two or three task forces that patrolled the systems.

Mellon added, "Even more strange, sir, but sensors show that almost all the capital ships and heavy cruisers are powered down to a maintenance level."

Jonah was now mystified. Going into maintenance mode meant powering down all but one reactor. That meant that four of the five reactors on each superdreadnought were cold at the moment. The single reactor provided plenty of power to maintain orbit and life support systems, but the ship could not power shields or weapons until the others were brought online. Restarting an inactive fusion reactor was complicated. Jonah had heard that it could theoretically be done in 45 minutes, but that had only been done in simulation. Usually, the process of bringing a reactor online took the better part of two hours for each one, and only a great fool would try to power up more than one reactor at a time.

They reached their assigned orbit and were instructed to adjust their clocks to Roosevelt Mean Time. This was only a two-hour change. Jonah was ordered to report to the admiral at 10:00, which gave him little time. He headed immediately to the shuttle. In the shuttle bay, he found 'Major' Taylor and two marines waiting for him. They exchanged salutes, and Taylor spoke. "If you don't mind, captain, these men will accompany you dirtside."

Jonah cocked an eyebrow at this. Taylor quickly explained, "Part of my orders from the commandant are to provide you with an escort anytime you go dirtside, captain."

Jonah nodded in understanding. Captains of capital ships rarely stepped foot on planets while on-station, so his bodyguards from the King's Own had not accompanied him. Naval Intelligence must feel there was still a threat to him, though, and had ordered the marines to fill in. "Thank you, major," he replied.

On the shuttle trip down, Jonah noticed the marines both wore a variety of badges indicating expertise in various fields. They were both rated as combat marksmen and skilled in hand-to-hand combat. One, Robinson, according to his name tag, was a black lance corporal. The other, a PFC named Mak, had an Asian cast to her features. Neither said a word, sitting stiffly and staring straight ahead.

When they arrived at the spaceport, they were directed to a groundcar with the admiral's pennant affixed to it. A warrant officer in full dress uniform saluted him and said, "This way, sir," while opening the rear door. Pfc. Mak moved to get in the vehicle, and the warrant officer said, "Not you, marine."

Mak stood up straight and looked right through the man. "Warrant officer, with all due respect, where the captain goes, we go. Orders."

The warrant officer frowned in distaste. "Very well," he sneered, then turned his back to them and entered the driver's seat.

Mak entered, then Jonah, finally Robinson. The warrant officer drove them into the suburbs of the city of Theodore, into a neighborhood populated with ostentatiously large houses with manicured and landscaped grounds. He stopped in front of one of them with the admiral's pennant flying from a flagpole. The warrant officer stayed behind the wheel and did not get out to open the door.

Jonah and the marines exited the car and walked to the front door. Since this was Johannsen's headquarters, Jonah thought he would enter and talk to a receptionist. He was mildly surprised to find the door locked. He rang the buzzer next to the door.

After a wait of more than a minute, the door was opened by a Lieutenant Malchoff in full dress uniform. He looked Jonah up and down, in seeming disapproval that Jonah was wearing a service uniform. He did not salute Jonah.

"Captain Halberd," he said finally in an oily voice, "the admiral is waiting for you."

Malchoff turned and strode down the hallway. Jonah followed, trying to wrap his head around the snubs and breaches of military etiquette he had observed since landing. He kept his thoughts to himself and followed Malchoff to a waiting room with a yeoman sitting behind a desk, typing on a console.

"Wait here," Malchoff said then, turning to the yeoman, instructed, "Tell the admiral that Halberd is here." With that, he turned on his heel and left.

Jonah waited nearly twenty minutes before the yeoman told him he could go in. Jonah entered, strode to three paces in front of the desk, and saluted. "Captain Halberd, reporting as ordered, sir."

Admiral Johannsen did not return the salute. He remained sitting. He looked like someone who would be cast as an admiral in a video. He had aristocratic features, with just enough lines in his tan face to give it character and white hair.

"So," Johannsen said finally, "the great Captain Sir Jonah Halberd, the hero of the hour," he sneered, sarcasm dripping from his mouth. "I'm surprised they sent you. We don't like you, you know."

"Sir," Jonah replied, staring at a spot just over Johannsen's head. "Orders, sir?"

Johannsen waved his hand dismissively. "Oh, go back to your ship. If I need you, I'll let you know. Don't get too comfortable, though. We're likely going home in a couple of weeks."

"Yes, sir," Jonah acknowledged. He continued to stand at attention.

"You can go now, Halberd," the admiral said, again waving his hand towards the door.

"Sir," Jonah replied. He snapped a crisp salute, performed an about-face, and strode to the door.

His marines were standing at attention in the waiting room. They followed him out of the house. The groundcar was waiting for them. The warrant officer did not get out of the car or acknowledge them in any way. When the doors shut, he drove them back to the spaceport.

Jonah was silent on the ride back to his ship. If what he saw was any indication, there was something wrong with Third Fleet. His comm buzzed, telling him he had messages waiting for him on his secure console back on the ship.

When he reached his ready room, he activated his console to find three messages. The first contained his orders which were to maintain station and await further instructions. The second was from his mother, and the third was from Captain Pierre Delhomme, HMS *Carnarvon*.

His mother's message was a text that read:

"Geoff asked me to let you know that they called for the vote today. He said to tell you that the people you discussed did what he thought they would, and elections are in six weeks. I have no idea what that means, but he suggested that you be careful. I hope you are well. Please do be careful. Love, Mom."

The message from Captain Delhomme was a video. Jonah pulled it up, and Delhomme's face appeared. "Captain Halberd," he said, "welcome. If you don't mind, I'd like to invite myself over for dinner so I can steal a look at *Indomitable*. Please let me know when you receive this, and I'll come right over. We have a lot to discuss."

Jonah recalled his conversation with Admiral von Geisler and realized Delhomme had been assigned to Third Fleet for over a year now. He had known Pierre since their days at the academy. They had served together as ensigns on board HMS *Hebrus* under the command of then-Captain von Geisler. The two of them had been friendly rivals almost from the time they met, though the rivalry was not as sharp as their friendship was deep.

Jonah sent a video message back. "Capitaine Delhomme," he said using a bad imitation of a French accent. "Since I understand you are my senior in rank by a few hours, I would be deeply honored and touched if you would deign to visit and grace my humble ship with your magnificence. Please come as soon as you wish."

Forty minutes later, Jonah's comm buzzed, telling him he was expected in the shuttle bay. When he arrived, Captain Delhomme was just disembarking. He strode up and snapped a salute. After Delhomme returned it, the two men grinned and shook hands. "Welcome aboard *Indomitable*, Pierre. Tour first or talk first?"

"Talk, I think. Your ready room?"

"Sounds good."

The two men set off, Jonah leading the way. Delhomme was within a centimeter of Jonah's height, with slightly broader shoulders but narrower hips. His hair and his eyes were dark brown. When they reached the ready room, Jonah asked if he would like anything to drink. Pierre shook his head and sat down.

"The eyepatch makes you look quite dashing. Now, tell me how you managed to blow up that nice German cruiser I captured for you and turn it into a battlecruiser."

Jonah described what had happened when *Cumberland* stopped the Rodinan advance. Pierre was most interested in how they had been able to deploy the missiles in advance. "Hell of a risk," he commented. "If the Rodinans had been a bit slower to arrive—"

"We didn't have a lot of good options," Jonah said dryly.

"True. I understand from my sources that you met our fearless leader this morning."

Jonah breathed out heavily. "Yes."

Pierre began to laugh. "Welcome to Third Fleet. Or as I like to call it, hell."

"Pierre, what is going on here?"

"The good admiral runs things his own way," Pierre started to explain. "Where would you like me to begin?"

Jonah thought for a moment. He had so many questions. He settled on, "It looks like all of Third Fleet is in parking orbit. Is it?"

"Yes."

"You're kidding!"

"No."

"But—"

"Who's on picket duty?" Pierre interjected, anticipating Jonah's questions. "Who's escorting convoys? Who's patrolling the sector?" He shook his head sadly. "No one."

Seeing Jonah's incredulous expression, Pierre continued, "Johannsen has deployed sensors at the hyper corridor entrances, believing they will provide adequate warning of enemy activity or encroachment in the sector."

"But what about merchant shipping?" Jonah asked. "There are dozens of unpopulated systems along the hyper routes. It's our job to police those!"

"Not according to our orders," Pierre said grimly. "One of the many rumors is that Johannsen has negotiated with the pirates surrounding the sector and that as long as they don't hit too many ships and give Johannsen a percentage of the take, he gives them freedom to operate."

"Is it true?"

Pierre shrugged his shoulders. "I don't know. It would be in character with the man."

Jonah took a moment to absorb this, then asked, "Why are most of the capital ships powered down?"

"Ah," Pierre sighed, "the Inner Circle." Seeing Jonah's lack of comprehension, he explained. "The most incompetent sons and daughters of the aristocracy to reach command rank all seem to be posted to Third Fleet. Those are their ships—all the superdreadnoughts, all but two of the battlecruisers, half of the heavy cruisers, and a handful of the light cruisers and frigates. The captains have relocated dirtside. They commandeered most of the neighborhood where Johannsen's HQ is located. They spend their time down there doing whatever young lords and ladies do—riding horses, playing golf, drinking, fucking, you name it. There is a dinner party every night, hosted by our beloved admiral, and they are all expected to attend."

"But why power down the ships?" Jonah asked

"Because the majority of their crews are dirtside on liberty," Pierre said flatly. "Where they have most assuredly worn out their welcome. They've been acting more like pirates than navy personnel. No surprise, as there's no punishment for them for committing any crime short of murder or rape. Their officers intervene with the local authorities. The residents are scared to death of them."

Jonah nodded, remembering the cold reception he had observed on his visit to Roosevelt during his tour with Elaine. He mentioned it to Pierre.

"We were forbidden to attend," Pierre said. "Any navy personnel you saw in the crowd had to sneak over to see you."

Jonah shook his head in wonderment, trying to grasp all Pierre had told him. "Wow," he muttered, then, "Tell me about New Moscow."

Pierre sighed heavily. "They knew we were coming," he began. "When we entered the system, we saw only half the ships we expected to see. Thinking this was a great opportunity, our brilliant commander ordered the entire fleet to pursue them down into the gravity well. Once we had been sucked into the system, the other half of their forces, which had been lying doggo near the corridor entrance, blocked us in. We were trapped like a fly in a bottle. If Antonelli and Second Fleet hadn't come and forced his way through the blocking force, we would have all been destroyed.

"It was such a debacle, Jonah," Pierre continued, "that I had hopes the Admiralty would finally relieve the incompetent boob. But I was disappointed in that again."

"Well, maybe I can shed some light on that," Jonah remarked. He passed along what he had heard from Lord Thorner, then added, "The Liberal Democrats passed a vote of no-confidence. Elections will be in six weeks."

"That's it then," Pierre said resignedly. "Damn."

"What do you do," Jonah asked, "to stay busy?"

"That's the worst part," Pierre explained. "Those of us who aren't part of Johannsen's little group just keep circling the planet, holding station. We've asked repeatedly if we could conduct maneuvers but have always been shot down. We still run drills and have set up a tac net to run multi-ship simulations, but when everyone knows we're still stuck in orbit, it's hard to maintain enthusiasm. No one even wants to go dirtside for liberty anymore since the locals have grown to resent and mistrust anyone in uniform. We do our best to keep spirits up, but it's a battle we're not winning."

39

Counter Admiral Fedosia Vasnetsova reviewed the latest status report with satisfaction. One of the patrol boats sent ahead of her task force reported that they had destroyed the Commonwealth sensor drones watching the hyper corridors in System F204. F204 was the fourth and final unpopulated system she would have to cross before entering the Roosevelt system.

Her task force of five *Gagarin*-class superdreadnoughts, three of the new *Makarov*-class battlecruisers, four *Putin*-class heavy cruisers, and eight *Kuznetsov*-class light cruisers was on course for the hyper corridor entrance leading to the Roosevelt system. They would enter the corridor in less than a half-hour at 0.23*c*. The corridor would normally be a seven-hour transit, but they would be exiting early to avoid detection by Commonwealth sensors.

The information she had received from FSB contacts indicated that the entire Commonwealth Third Fleet was still in orbit around the planet. Even better, they confirmed that all 12 Commonwealth superdreadnoughts and six of their nine battlecruisers continued to have most of their reactors shut down, meaning they would be helpless to defend themselves. The 506 missiles her task force could launch in a single salvo would completely overwhelm the point defense capability of the remaining ships and the orbital defense platforms.

After exiting the hyper corridor early, out of range of the Commonwealth sensors the FSB had been able to identify, her task force would coast into the system for roughly 52 hours on a ballistic trajectory and wait to flip into a deceleration burn until after they had launched their first salvo. They would circle around the primary of the system, launch additional salvos if needed, and boost for the hyper exit.

Her job was not to destroy every Commonwealth ship in the system. Twelve superdreadnoughts and six battlecruisers would be enough. Her task force had been assembled one and two ships at a time from different fleets to keep the Commonwealth's Office of Naval Intelligence from finding out about it. They rendezvoused in the unpopulated F172 system, two hyper corridors away from Roosevelt, and had been waiting for the order to proceed.

Earlier, they had positioned patrol boats in the F204 system to take out the Commonwealth's sensors. By the time the Commonwealth dispatched a ship from Roosevelt to replace the sensors, and it climbed out of the gravity well, her task force would already be in the Roosevelt system. Unless that ship happened to fly right into her force, they would pass undetected. Given the unprepared condition of the rest of Third Fleet, she hoped that the Commonwealth would be slow to respond.

Jonah was two hours into the forenoon watch on February 2 when he received an urgent message from Captain Delhomme requesting a secure transmission. He turned the ship over to the third officer and went back to his ready room. He sat down and activated his console, opening a secure transmission to Pierre.

"Jonah," Pierre opened, "something's up. I just heard from the commander of the frigate *Chesapeake* that she has been ordered to system F204 to replace sensors at the corridor entrance that went offline. We just switched those sensors five weeks ago, so something had to happen to them. The likelihood of all three sensors failing at the exact same time is nil."

Jonah quickly pulled up his system map that showed the location of the hyper corridors and transit times for each one. "How long ago did the sensors go offline?"

"A little over 21 hours ago. My understanding is they attempted to contact Admiral Johannsen yesterday afternoon, but he was 'unavailable.' They just reached him after 09:00."

Jonah shook his head in disbelief. "What do you think it is?"

"The Rodinans," Pierre answered flatly.

Jonah nodded in agreement. He entered some information on his console and checked the results. "If the sensors went down 21 hours ago, they're probably in-system already. Are the sensors on this side of the corridor still operational?"

"Yes, but—"

"But that doesn't mean they're not here. I know," Jonah confirmed. "They probably exited hyper early, outside of sensor range, and are coasting in ballistic. Wait a minute," he said, struck by a sudden thought. "Why am I hearing this from you? Shouldn't the fleet be going to at least orange alert status?"

"That's why I'm calling," Pierre explained. "There's been no communication from the admiral."

"Who is the senior captain of those of us up here right now?"

"That would be Captain Rosene of *Lion*," Pierre replied, "but in the absence of any sensor data on this side of the corridor, she is unwilling to contact the admiral."

"Crap!" Jonah spat. "Who else is there?"

"Captain Wagner of *Scorpion* has also expressed his strong reluctance to contact the admiral," Pierre replied grimly. "Jonah, you're the only other captain of a capital ship up here. There are some others who are senior to you in date of rank, but your command of a capital ship trumps that."

"Pierre, you know the whole Johannsen family hates me, right?"

"I've heard the rumors," Pierre answered with a sad smile.

"Fine," Jonah sighed. "I'll try."

They severed the connection, and Jonah looked at his console again, double-checking his figures and estimates. After checking, he made some notes. Then he commed Admiral Johannsen's office.

A receptionist answered. Jonah stated, "Captain Halberd, HMS *Indomitable*, to speak with Admiral Johannsen on a matter of some importance."

The receptionist replied, "Please hold."

After almost a minute, an oily voice spoke. "Captain Halberd, what do you want?"

"Who is this?"

"This is Flag Lieutenant Malchoff, Admiral Johannsen's chief of staff. I repeat, captain, what do you want?"

"Lieutenant," Jonah said icily, stressing the rank, "I must speak to Admiral Johannsen on a matter of some importance."

"I'm afraid, captain," Malchoff replied in his oily voice, "that the admiral cannot take your comm right now. You can leave a message with me, and I will see that he receives it at his earliest availability."

"Lieutenant," Jonah said in a steely voice, "are you aware that the sensors on the far side of the corridor to system F204 all went offline some 21 hours ago?"

"Yes, captain, I am aware," Malchoff replied. "May I ask how you came to be in possession of this knowledge?"

"That's unimportant!" Jonah retorted.

"On the contrary," Malchoff replied smoothly, "I'm sure the admiral would think it very important."

"Are you aware that it is highly improbable that three sensors would fail in the same place at the same time? That enemy action is the most likely explanation?"

"I am Admiral Johannsen's chief of staff, captain," Malchoff instructed as though to a child, "I manage his schedule. He does not confer with me on matters of strategy."

Jonah was close to losing his temper, which he knew would be counter-productive. He paused and took a deep breath. "Fine, lieutenant. Please tell the admiral that I believe the sensors went offline as a result of enemy action. That I further believe the enemy to already be in the Roosevelt system, following a ballistic course down the gravity well, and that I believe an attack is imminent. Please tell him that I suggest that he bring the fleet to orange alert status as quickly as possible."

"Is that all, captain?"

"Yes," Jonah said through clenched teeth. "Please see that he gets the message immediately."

"As I said, captain, I will deliver the message to him at his earliest availability."

"When might that be?" Jonah wanted to know.

"When he informs me that he is available," Malchoff said in a snide tone. "Will there be anything else?"

"No," Jonah growled.

"Thank you. Have a nice day, captain," Malchoff said as he cut the connection.

Jonah had rarely been so enraged as he was at present. By his best estimates, they had thirty hours or less before the Rodinans reached missile range of the fleet. It would take at least ten hours to bring the reactors of the superdreadnoughts online, though probably longer if many of the engineering personnel were dirtside. He toyed with the idea of contacting Admiral von Geisler or Admiral Lothes to intervene but quickly dismissed it. No admiral would want to interfere. He did send a message to Lord Thorner to let someone outside the system know what was happening, sending a copy of his recent conversation with Lieutenant Malchoff with it.

He would just have to wait. He sent a text message to Captain Delhomme to let him know what had transpired. He then returned to the bridge.

Counter Admiral Vasnetsova was pleased. They had entered the Roosevelt system just over 24 hours before and had 27 hours and a few minutes until they reached missile range. So far, the only activity from the Commonwealth fleet they had picked up on passive sensors was the departure of a single frigate heading their way.

They would pass the frigate in roughly 16 hours. It was unlikely the frigate would stumble into her task force. Space, after all, is very large, and unless the frigate happened to paint them at short range with active sensors, it would likely pass right on by.

The afternoon watch was coming to an end, and Jonah had not yet received a reply from Admiral Johannsen. He commed down to the planet again. The receptionist put him on hold as before. After a long wait, a familiar oily voice asked, "Captain Halberd, what do you want now?"

"Lieutenant, have you given my message to Admiral Johannsen?" Jonah demanded.

"Yes, captain," Malchoff said in a bored tone.

"And his response?"

"The admiral instructed me to remind you that your orders to remain on station with the rest of the fleet still stand and that you are not, and I quote 'to run off tilting at windmills like some goddamn Don Quixote' end quote," Malchoff said in a snotty tone. "Is there anything else, captain?"

Jonah swallowed his anger. "No," he said calmly and cut the connection. He made sure his conversations with Lieutenant Malchoff were copied to his official log. He checked his console and saw that his estimate of when the Rodinans would reach missile range was now just under 24 hours away. He sent a message to Captain Delhomme requesting a secure comm.

Within moments his console indicated Pierre was responding. Jonah quickly recapped his recent conversation with Malchoff. Pierre whistled through his teeth, shaking his head at the same time. "Gods," he sighed.

"Yeah," Jonah agreed. "So…what now?"

"Well," Pierre began, thinking out loud, "we don't have any idea how many ships are coming our way, do we?"

"No," Jonah agreed, "but I think we can guess that they'll be targeting the superdreadnoughts and battlecruisers that are powered down."

"Agreed," Pierre confirmed. "We'll have three battlecruisers, eight heavy cruisers, fifteen light cruisers, and sixteen frigates. If they can launch a salvo of over 250 missiles, it will overwhelm our point defense capability, no matter how carefully we try to position ourselves."

"Right," Jonah agreed. "Now, if you were planning an attack to take out these ships and knew that the superdreadnoughts and most of the battlecruisers couldn't contribute, what's the minimum throw weight you'd bring to the party?"

Pierre thought, then answered, "It depends on whether they're coming to wipe out the whole fleet or just doing a hit and run. If it's only a hit and run, I'd make sure I had a salvo weight of about double what I figured the point defense could handle. That way, I'd be sure to get all my targets on the first salvo, then could use any additional salvos to take out the smaller ships that were fighting back."

"That's what I'd do, too," Jonah nodded. "Now, our throw weight is 478 missiles, right?"

"I think so."

"Except we can tow frames," Jonah added.

"We've done it in simulation," Pierre informed him, "but haven't done it for real yet."

"If you can do it in the sims, you can do it for real," Jonah assured him. "Now, each battlecruiser can pull four frames, the *County*-classes two, and the *Town*-classes one. That should give us another 172 missiles in the first salvo, for a total of 650. So, we can guess they're coming with ships that can fire a salvo of about 500 missiles and probably a point defense net that can handle the same. So—"

"So," Pierre picked up, "whether they're coming on a hit and run or to wipe us out, they're going to be able to destroy our superdreadnoughts and the six battlecruisers with the first salvo no matter what we do. We should be able to cause some damage with our first salvo, but after that, our throw weight is a little less than theirs and our point defense probably a lot less, and that's in the best-case scenario." Pierre shook his head. "Jonah," he said calmly, "we're going to get tagged pretty good."

"Can you set up a comm with the other captains? We ought to discuss this with them. Maybe they'll have some ideas."

"I'll set it up," Pierre affirmed. "Until then?"

"Until then."

Counter Admiral Vasnetsova watched her console tick down the time until all her task force was within missile range of the furthest Commonwealth ships on the far side of the planet Roosevelt. She had set up the tactical net so that the first salvo of missiles would target only the superdreadnoughts and the battlecruisers that were powered down. After that, the system would seek targets of opportunity. She allowed herself a smile. This would be the most decisive blow against the Commonwealth since the opening attack of the war and, with any luck, would be the one that ended it.

She wondered if any of the Commonwealth ships were prepared. If she had caught them sleeping, her task force would likely escape unscathed. If they were prepared for her appearance, they might be able to cause some damage. Even in the extremely unlikely event that they somehow eliminated her entire task force, this battle would still be a resounding victory for the Federation.

She watched the counter reach zero, then entered the "execute" order. Within moments, the task force activated their targeting sensors. Once the sensors identified the targets, 506 missiles launched. The Rodinan ships then began to decelerate sharply as their missile tubes reloaded for another salvo.

"We just got lit up by targeting sensors, captain," called the petty officer on sensors. "Multiple launches…salvo of four hundred fif—check that— salvo of 506 inbound. System identifies five *Gagarins*, three *Makarovs*, four *Putins* and eight *Kuznetsovs*."

"Tactical?" Jonah asked.

"Tac net is green," Commander Mellon responded. This meant that the tactical net of the Commonwealth ships had registered the presence and make-up of the Rodinan ships. "Fire," Jonah said calmly.

The Commonwealth captains had held a video conference hours before. Captains Rosene and Wagner insisted that Captain Halberd command the force, and this proposal was quickly approved by the other captains. As a group, they discussed and had agreed on targeting priorities. Without knowing the makeup of the Rodinan force, they had to set parameters in the system. Now that the Rodinans had revealed themselves, the parameters chosen earlier aimed all 650 missiles of their first salvo exclusively at the five *Gagarin*-class Rodinan superdreadnoughts. Jonah hoped it would be enough.

Indomitable's railguns began firing hundreds of chaff cartridges as the other ships began releasing dozens of ECM drones. Their intent was not to protect the powered-down capital ships—after a lengthy discussion, as a group, they had determined that all their best efforts would not be able to save them. Instead, they hoped to create clouds of chaff behind which the smaller ships might hide and to deceive the targeting sensors of the missiles that would surely be sent their way in upcoming salvos.

An hour earlier, Jonah had finished his report of the entire situation and everything that had happened since he arrived in the Roosevelt system. He then took the unusual step of transmitting it to Admiral Lothes, the Fleet Admiral at Caerleon in addition to Admiral von Geisler. In the event that *Indomitable* was destroyed, he wanted to make sure there was something on record that would give the Admiralty a clear picture of what happened here. A number of the other captains had agreed to do the same.

The Commonwealth ships also began to maneuver as they had planned. The frigates changed course in an attempt to put the powered-down capital ships between themselves and Rodinans. The hope was that the inevitable wreckage of the capital ships would provide them some cover from the following missile salvos. The remaining cruisers clustered themselves around the three active battlecruisers to create a point-defense network.

The first salvo of Rodinan missiles reached their target distance, and the bomb-pumped x-ray lasers erupted from them. Thirty missiles were aimed at each unprotected superdreadnought and 23 at each unprotected battlecruiser. The lasers carved into the unshielded hulls. Huge chunks of the ships broke off. Eight of them ejected their fusion cores, but the fusion cores of the other ten exploded when hit, destroying the ships and creating clouds of debris.

The Commonwealth ECM drones then went active, generating false signatures of battlecruisers and heavy and light cruisers to distract upcoming Rodinan launches. The Commonwealth missiles reached their targets. Of the 650 missiles sent against the five Rodinan superdreadnoughts, 131 survived to detonate. The second superdreadnought of the Rodinan formation was targeted by 34 of the x-ray lasers. Overwhelming its plasma shielding in an instant, the lasers gouged deeply into the hull. The cores of the five fusion reactors ejected into space almost instantly, leaving the battered ship a drifting hulk. One of those cores unluckily crashed into the bow of a *Makarov* battlecruiser and blew up. The explosive force of a miniature star vaporized the front third of the ship while the shock of the explosion shattered the remainder.

The fifth of the Rodinan superdreadnoughts was hit by 29 Commonwealth lasers. Its shields failed, and the lasers carved into its core, penetrating a missile magazine. The fusion cores and warheads of the four missiles remaining in the magazine exploded, cracking the ship in two roughly equal halves. The remaining three Rodinan superdreadnoughts took lesser damage, suffering hull breaches and having point defense cannons and sensors literally boiled away from their hulls but survived to launch their second salvo of missiles.

Counter Admiral Vasnetsova had seconds to admire the destruction of the Commonwealth capital ships before her ships came under fire. Her ship suffered four hull breaches and lost two shield generators and three missile bays on the port side. The captain ordered the ship to roll to present its starboard side to the next salvo of Commonwealth missiles. The second Rodinan salvo launched, of only 362 missiles due to losses and damage, but the targeting computers aimed all of them at the three remaining Commonwealth battlecruisers.

Captain Halberd winced at the destruction of the Commonwealth capital ships. Even knowing there was nothing they could have done to save them, it still disturbed him. Commander Mellon updated him on the damage to the Rodinan force, and Jonah ordered him to concentrate their fire on the three remaining Rodinan superdreadnoughts in the next salvo and to target the remaining battlecruisers with whatever remained of their force for a third salvo.

The Rodinan missiles targeting *Lion*, *Scorpion*, and *Indomitable* came streaking in. Ninety-one of them were led astray by the ECM drones and chaff thrown out by *Indomitable*. The point defense networks eliminated 230 Rodinan missiles, but 16 survived to hit *Scorpion*, and 15 hit *Lion*. *Indomitable*, with its anti-missile railguns, was hit by only ten.

The missiles quickly penetrated the plasma shielding of the battlecruisers. The fusion reactors of *Scorpion* were hit, and the ship exploded. *Lion* managed to eject its reactors when its hull was breached, but the Rodinan lasers savaged the ship, breaching the hull and ripping deep within it. Within moments life pods began to eject from what was left of it.

The lasers breached the hull of *Indomitable* in seven different places and destroyed two of the ship's four EM drives. Five of the shield generators were destroyed, four of them on the starboard side. Two of the dorsal railgun emplacements were vaporized as well. The ship shuddered and bucked as the lasers did their damage. Without waiting for the damage control report, Jonah ordered the ship to roll to present the less-damaged side to the enemy.

Of the 478 missiles in the second Commonwealth salvo, 141 survived to attack their targets. Forty-five of them struck the ship of Counter Admiral Vasnetsova. Two of them bracketed the engineering section, causing one of the fusion reactors to explode. The other four reactors detonated in a chain reaction, and the ship disintegrated, pieces of it spinning in all directions. One of the chunks spun directly into the side of a Rodinan light cruiser. The damaged ship lurched and slowed, spewing atmosphere. Life pods began to eject from the ship. The leading Rodinan superdreadnought was the target of 40 of the laser warheads. Its fusion reactors ejected, but the x-ray lasers dug into the body of the ship. Life pods began to launch from the unpowered wreck. The last superdreadnought in the formation was hit by 33 missiles. Slicing down into the ship, one of the lasers hit the mass compensator. The superdreadnought shook itself apart. The first of the two remaining Rodinan battlecruisers received 13 powerful laser blasts. It ejected its fusion cores as the lasers hacked into the hull. Ten missiles hit the remaining Rodinan battlecruiser, the now-repaired *Pyotr Velikiy*. The bomb-pumped x-ray lasers tore the ship's rebuilt EM drives completely off the ship, leaving it powerless.

Despite the damage to *Indomitable*, Jonah realized they could destroy what was left of the Rodinan force. While a strong part of him hungered to do just that, instead, he ordered Commander Mellon, "Hold the third salvo. Transmit a demand to surrender."

First-rank Captain Vasili Yurchenko, commanding the now-repaired battlecruiser *Pyotr Velikiy*, was the senior officer in the task force now that Vasnetsova was dead. He heard the surrender demand moments after he had launched the third salvo of missiles. Realizing that the remainder of his force faced almost certain destruction and with their mission accomplished, he decided to capitulate. He ordered his executive officer to surrender. Self-destruct messages were sent to the just-launched missiles and the remaining Rodinan ships lowered their shields.

On the bridge of *Indomitable*, sensors reported, "They just blew up their missiles and lowered their shields, sir. They've surrendered."

The bridge crew started to cheer, but Jonah barked, "Belay that! They just wiped out 20 of the 21 capital ships in Third Fleet—everyone except us—at a cost of only eight of theirs. Stand down from general quarters. Initiate SAR immediately. Let's go find any survivors. Commander Mellon, you have the bridge."

40

In his ready room, he quickly wrote an account of the day's action and transmitted it immediately to Admiral Lothes on Caerleon via the kewpie. His steward, Kowalchik, knocked softly and asked if he wanted anything. Jonah thought, then asked for a cup of coffee.

Shortly after Kowalchik returned, Jonah turned his attention to the damage control reports and after-action updates on his console. Other than the damage sustained by *Indomitable*, *Scorpion*, and *Lion*, the remaining ships had escaped unscathed except for some minor damage caused by hitting debris. The four *Putin*-class heavy cruisers and seven *Kuznetsov*-class light cruisers had been ordered to establish stable orbit around the planet and to keep their shields and targeting sensors deactivated. The two heavily damaged *Makarov*-class battlecruisers were drifting: one without power, the other with no drives. First-rank Captain Yurchenko had requested to speak with him, offering to assist with SAR. Not feeling he was in the mood for polite conversation, Jonah forwarded that message to Mellon, instructing him to refuse the offer politely and to suggest instead that Captain Yurchenko begin to shuttle the survivors from the unpowered Rodinan battlecruiser to *Pyotr Velikiy*.

Without realizing it, nearly two hours had passed since he began reviewing the reports. His console beeped, indicating that Admiral Lothes was initiating a secure commlink. After rubbing his face with his hands, Jonah accessed the link. The admiral's face appeared immediately. She looked tired and grim. His console indicated that her local time on Caerleon was 04:20

"Captain, Admiral Johannsen has been relieved of command. He, and the officers on Roosevelt, have been ordered confined to house arrest until they are taken into custody by members of the Naval Investigative Service due to arrive in four and a half days. Separately, Marine Captain Taylor has been ordered to enforce that house arrest. Captain Taylor has also been ordered to supervise all marine personnel currently in orbit. Those not engaged in the house arrest will be assisting Roosevelt police forces in gathering and detaining all naval personnel currently on Roosevelt until they are removed in four and a half days.

"Your Rodinan prisoners will be removed in four and a half days by members of the ONI who, like the NIS, are currently en route. You, as captain of the lone remaining capital ship, will be in command of all Commonwealth naval forces in the sector until you are relieved in four and a half days by Vice Admiral Preston Sayyah. The vice admiral is leading a task force culled from Home Fleet to take over the sector. His commlink has been sent to you so you may coordinate proper and immediate deployment of the surviving Third Fleet forces.

"When you are relieved, you are to return to Caerleon. *Indomitable* will return to the yard for repairs, and you will report to the Admiralty for an extensive debrief involving NIS, ONI, and JAG. While on Caerleon, you will be sequestered at the Admiralty until your debriefing is complete. Written copies of these orders have just been transmitted to you."

She paused and took a deep breath. When she began speaking, her tone was less formal. "Sir Jonah, you have distinguished yourself and your service once again. I would like to offer my personal thanks for providing us with a ray of hope on what is otherwise one of the darkest days in the history of the service. That is all. Lothes out," and the connection was cut.

The next four and a half days were a whirlwind of activity. He sent the frigates and light cruisers out on long-neglected picket duty. Jonah visited every compartment of his ship, viewing the damage first hand. He visited sickbay and called upon the wounded. He composed letters home for the relatives of crew members who died during the attack. He met briefly with First-rank Captain Yurchenko. Jonah worked with Marine Captain Taylor, who had succeeded in rounding up all the naval personnel on Roosevelt, though it took nearly four days to do so. Some of them had tried to go into hiding, but all were turned in by Roosevelt natives. He met with Commander Gessert, who had her hands full repairing the damage from the attack. She had determined that it would be possible to make it back to Caerleon with the two remaining EM drives. She felt that was the better option since the shipyard at Roosevelt Station did not have EM drives that matched the remaining two. Gessert felt they either tried to make it back on the two, or she would need to replace all four with the different drives in stock in Roosevelt. As it was, she needed to retune the remaining two EM drives.

After meeting with Vice Admiral Sayyah upon his arrival in-system, Jonah was able to relax for the journey back to Caerleon. He received messages from his mother and Elaine. In responding, he told him he was well and that he was returning to Caerleon shortly. He apologized for not being able to tell them more than that.

Upon return to Caerleon, once *Indomitable* was docked at the yard, he was ordered to a shuttle and taken down to the planet. Upon landing, he was met by uniformed agents of the Naval Investigative Service who took him to the Admiralty. On the way, they instructed him not to discuss any of the events that took place in the Roosevelt system with anyone. They took his comm unit and gave him a very basic one that would allow him to be contacted but would not allow him any outside access.

The next day his debriefing began, conducted by ONI and NIS agents and always supervised by at least two lawyers from the JAG. He was instructed at the outset that he was under oath, that everything he said could be used as evidence in criminal proceedings and that the entire process was being recorded. They went over his logs and official reports in excruciating detail and asked him repeatedly to recount his conversations with Admiral Johannsen and Lieutenant Malchoff that had taken place on Roosevelt. This lasted for three days. On the morning of the fourth day, they revisited some of their questions but before 10:00 pronounced that they were satisfied.

They did not return his comm unit but did tell him he was to be picked up by a member of the government who would be taking him to stay somewhere else and that this person would give him a very short list of people with whom he could discuss the events on Roosevelt. He returned to his room and packed his garment bag, and sat to wait. In less than an hour, there was a knock at his door. When he opened it, he was surprised to see Lord Thorner and, just past his shoulder, Thompson.

"Lord Thorner!" Jonah blurted.

"Tsch," he replied. "I asked you to call me Geoff, Sir Jonah!"

"Yes, si—Geoff. Are you the one they said was coming to pick me up?" Jonah asked.

"Got it on the first try. We want you out of sight for a bit," he explained. "You'll be just as safe at my house as you would be here and a damn sight more comfortable. Just abide by the rules they've given you. Are you ready to go?"

Jonah picked up his bag and nodded, then followed Lord Thorner to a groundcar, followed by Thompson. He threw his bag in the trunk and got in beside Lord Thorner. Thompson got behind the wheel and drove them away.

As they were driving, Lord Thorner reached into the inside breast pocket of his suit jacket and pulled out a piece of paper, and handed it to Jonah. "This is the list of people with whom you'll be allowed to discuss what happened."

Jonah looked at the list. After a short paragraph reminding him he was not allowed to discuss the events of Roosevelt with anyone other than ONI, NIS, or JAG, the following four exceptions were named: King Edward XII, Prime Minister Gaius Anderson and Lord and Lady Thorner. Jonah cocked his eyebrow at Lord Thorner when he finished reading it.

"We're all having dinner tonight, by the way," Geoff informed him. Seeing a hint of worry cross Jonah's face, he added, "It's not fancy dress, so your service uniform will be fine."

41

At eighteen hundred, Geoff and Jonah left in a groundcar, again with Thompson driving. Geoff explained, "We're dining at the palace. It's a lot easier to sneak you in than to sneak him out."

They drove into the city and entered a parking garage. Thompson drove down to the lowest level and pressed a button on his comm unit. A set of service doors opened, just wide enough for the groundcar to fit through. Behind them was a long tunnel that lit as they proceeded. They drove for what seemed like a couple of kilometers before arriving in a garage with four other nondescript groundcars. Thompson parked, and they got out. Geoff led the way to an elevator. When he pressed the button to summon it, he held his thumb on the button for a longer than a normal time. Jonah guessed it was some form of biometric identification.

When they exited the elevator, they were in a hallway in what Jonah assumed was the king's private chambers. Geoff knew where he was going and led Jonah off to the right, down a short hall, and to a door on the left. He knocked, and they heard "Enter" called from within. Geoff and Jonah entered, while Thompson did not.

It was a small dining room, with wood-paneled walls and a fire burning in a small fireplace on one side. There was a table with six chairs upholstered with embroidered fabric. Places were set for four people with the two ends of the table empty. Seated facing one another were the king and the prime minister. They both rose to greet Jonah and Geoff.

Unsure of protocol, Jonah thought he might follow Lord Thorner's example. His plan fell apart when Geoff merely shook hands with them, saying "Gaius" and "Edward." Sensing Jonah's hesitancy and discomfort, the king stuck his hand out to shake and said, "Sir Jonah, no bowing and scraping or 'Your Majesty' this evening. You will call me Edward, him Gaius, and him Geoff. Just don't call me late to dinner."

Jonah smiled at the old joke and shook hands. "Edward," he said. "Gaius.

Please, just Jonah. I'm still not accustomed to the 'Sir Jonah' label."

The king smiled and indicated that Jonah should sit next to him. Quickly after they sat, the king poured a glass of red wine for Jonah and Geoff. A servant entered and placed a plate of salad in front of each of them. The other three men lifted their wine glasses and looked at Jonah expectantly. Jonah, remembering protocol, realized, as the most junior in rank in the room, he was expected to rise and toast the king. Jonah blushed with embarrassment, realizing he would be toasting the king while sitting next to him. He started to rise, and all of the other three men burst into laughter.

The king, still laughing, said, "That one never gets old." Taking pity on Jonah, he said gently, "You can offer a toast if you'd like, Jonah. Just don't toast me, okay?"

Acting as though he had planned it all along, Jonah lifted his glass and said, "Gentlemen, confusion to our enemies!"

The others smiled and repeated this, then Jonah sat down. "Well done," the prime minister offered.

Geoff apologized. "I'm sorry to put you on the spot like that, Jonah, but as Edward says, that one never gets old. Now, you've probably been wondering all afternoon why we wanted to have dinner with you and might be expecting that we'll pepper you with questions. Don't worry about the questions. We've all read the report of your debriefing. We've also read the debriefing reports from the officers who fought beside you and some preliminary interrogations of the officers who are currently in custody and awaiting court-martial."

The king added, "We asked you to dinner as a way of expressing our gratitude for being able to extract even a small amount of good out of the most horrible disaster in Royal Navy history."

"We also wanted," the prime minister chimed in, "to provide you with some additional information and maybe help fill in the missing pieces for you."

Geoff took over speaking. "Johannsen will be facing a court-martial. In addition to his utter incompetence, NIS has learned that he has bribed public officials on Roosevelt and bought off the local media outlets to keep what he was doing on Roosevelt quiet. He also took payment from different organized crime syndicates, which preyed on commercial shipping in the sector. After his court-martial, he will face criminal charges for some of his actions. Even better for us, the investigation has already uncovered ties to his father and his brother. We think the end result will be that the House of Lords will vote to remove them, enabling Edward here to strip them of their titles."

"More important to the welfare of the Commonwealth as a whole," the prime minister continued, "is that their recent switch to support the Liberal Democrats has tarnished their entire party. The media are having a field day with it. They are attacking this in ways we cannot."

"How?" Jonah asked.

"They are able to insinuate," Geoff explained, "things that we suspect but would never be able to prove. For instance, they are making a link between Lord Chesterfield's recent marriage to Julia Hawthorne and the Johannsen family's recently announced change of party allegiance. Originally the media praised the marriage of a high-ranking member of the Conservative government to the daughter of the leader of the Liberal Democrats as a type of 'bridge-building' between the parties. Now the media is casting the First Space Lord's marriage as a political payoff to get him to switch parties without resigning his office, and that the Johannsen family's change of allegiance is linked to an understanding that Chesterfield would protect the 'idiot admiral' as the media are now calling Johannsen."

"Chesterfield has been disgraced," the prime minister added. "The media are painting him as disloyal and dishonest. We're certain of the one, and but would substitute stupidity for the other," he snorted. "We expect his resignation any moment now and his divorce not long after."

Jonah was shocked to hear this. His mind raced. Julia might soon be free! Then the sobering realization that her association in all this would make it a form of career suicide for him to become involved with her. He realized someone had just asked him a question.

"Pardon me?" he said. "I'm just trying to absorb all this."

"You went to the wedding, didn't you?" the prime minister asked.

"Yes, I did. I believe she invited me because I was involved with her rescue from Venera."

"Oh yes, quite so," the prime minister said.

The king chuckled. "You didn't exactly keep a low profile at the wedding, Jonah. You and Captain MacLeod were talked about at court for weeks afterward. You made quite a dashing couple. Are you two—?"

Jonah blushed to be asked such a question by the king. "N-n-no," he stammered, "just good friends."

"Laura helped her find her gown," Geoff interjected to deflect the subject. "By the way, Jonah, you may not have noticed in your accounting statements, but the designer told Laura he decided not to charge you for it. Captain MacLeod's appearance that night generated so much business for him that he canceled his invoice."

Jonah smiled broadly. "I haven't checked my statements that closely," he admitted, "but it certainly was a beautiful dress."

Desperately wanting to change the subject, Jonah asked, "With all that's happened, how do you feel the elections will turn out?"

The prime minister answered. "As I mentioned, the Johannsen's recent switch to the Liberal Democrat side—"

"Coupled with the media's slant that there were dirty political deals made," added the king, "which there were—"

"Not to mention the disaster at Roosevelt—" Geoff tacked on.

"As well as a growing feeling that the Liberal Democrats are somehow in league with the Federation," the prime minister continued, "have combined to turn public opinion sharply against the Liberal Democrats. Public perception across the Commonwealth is that a Liberal Democrat government would have the same success in dealing with the Federation as Johannsen did at Roosevelt. Contrasted against this is, well, you, Jonah."

"I don't understand."

"You are a hero, whether you choose to see it or not," the king commented. "You were seen on video across the entire Commonwealth receiving our highest honor for gallantry and being knighted. You then embarked on a campaign to speak on behalf of the war effort on every planet. You are viewed by the Federation as such a thorn in their side that they tried to kill you on Lutetia. Then, in the worst disaster the fleet has ever suffered, a disaster caused by someone now firmly associated with the Liberal Democrats, you managed to destroy five Federation superdreadnoughts and a battlecruiser and damage and capture the rest of the invading force.

"I doubt you have ever done anything," the king continued, "motivated by political considerations. Regardless, you are the symbol of the Commonwealth war effort. The Conservatives have been the party that has supported the war effort. Your success is associated with the Conservatives' policy, even though I'm sure you never intended it. You were simply doing your duty to the best of your ability."

He paused, then added, "I know a little something about being used as a political pawn."

The others chuckled softly as Jonah thought about what the king had said. "Whose side do you support, Edward?"

"The Commonwealth's," the king replied easily. "Gaius and Geoff know that I do not agree with them on everything."

"So, if the Liberal Democrats were in power and supported the war effort?" Jonah asked.

"Then Bill Hawthorne and John Polk would be sitting here at dinner with you and Edward," Geoff stated.

Jonah nodded slowly in understanding.

The next day, as the men had predicted at dinner, First Space Lord Chesterfield tendered his resignation. That afternoon, two agents of the NIS, accompanied by Winchester, came to Lord Thorner's house. They returned Jonah's comm unit and told him he was allowed to return to his ship, again cautioning him not to discuss the events on Roosevelt with anyone.

Jonah quickly packed the few belongings he had brought off the ship, found Laura and thanked her for letting him stay the night, and asked her to pass along his thanks to Geoff. He and Winchester went to the groundcar, and the two agents drove them to the spaceport. After a brief wait, he and Winchester boarded a shuttle to the yard. Upon arrival, Winchester accompanied him to the dock where *Indomitable* had been berthed, stopping at the gangway.

Jonah was happy to be back aboard. The political maelstrom of which he found himself an integral part was alien and uncomfortable. He dropped his bag in his quarters and headed to the bridge. Commander Mellon quickly brought Jonah up to speed on the status of the various repairs needed. According to the estimates, *Indomitable* would be laid up for a minimum of six weeks, but more likely ten to twelve, followed by a minimum of two weeks of readiness trials.

Jonah busied himself as best he could during the time. He spent the weekends as the guest of the Thorners, and Elaine came and visited him there occasionally. He was fitted for a glass eye. He found it uncomfortable and didn't wear it, preferring his eyepatch.

As a result of his dinner with the king and prime minister, he paid close attention to the Parliamentary elections for the first time since he had been in prep school. Fueled by the media's attacks on the Liberal Democrats, Admiral Johannsen, and Lord Chesterfield, the Conservatives won the House of Commons by a healthy margin—slightly more than the 60 percent needed to overturn any attempt at a veto by the House of Lords.

One of the first measures put on the floor in the new Parliament was an aggressive ship-building campaign to more than replace the ships lost in Roosevelt. The construction was to be funded by the sale of a new issue of war bonds. The bill passed easily. Shortly after, he was invited to dinner during the week by Lord and Lady Thorner. When he arrived at their house and found that the other dinner guests were Elaine and the prime minister and his wife, he suspected something was up.

He was unsurprised when Geoff asked if he would allow himself to be recorded for some advertisements promoting the new war bonds. A month before, this request might have troubled him, but what the king had told him at dinner about being on neither the conservative nor liberal side but always on the side of the Commonwealth made his decision easy. It didn't hurt that Elaine had already been placed in charge of the campaign (that she spent the night with him that evening he considered a nice bonus).

As the repairs to *Indomitable* were being completed, the court-martial of Admiral Johannsen began. Jonah was called as a witness and spent a week attending the trial. Admirals Von Geisler, Antonelli, and Lothes were presiding as the tribunal. The amount of evidence the NIS had compiled against Johannsen in such a short time was impressive. Jonah was only called to the stand once and only asked two questions, verifying the accuracy of his logs.

The tribunal conferred for less than an hour following the lawyers' closing statements. They found Johannsen guilty of all charges, the most serious of which, Improper Hazarding of a Vessel or Vessels, could have resulted in Johannsen's execution, but the tribunal sentenced him to life imprisonment without possibility of parole and ordered as restitution the confiscation of all his personal property as of the date of the Rodinan attack on the system. Jonah thought that a clever move as the Johannsen family had probably been quick to try to shift assets to other family members. The government's forensic accountants would be busy for quite some time on that, he thought. The amount they recovered, however substantial Johannsen's holdings might be, would hardly begin to repay the government for the lost ships, though.

42

A week after repairs to *Indomitable* had been completed, while the ship was in the middle of readiness trials, Jonah was summoned to the office of Admiral Lothes to receive his new orders. Instead of being shown into her office, he was ushered into a conference room. In addition to Admiral Lothes, the Foreign Secretary, Brian Stewart-Crosland, and one of his aides were waiting for him.

After introductions, Admiral Lothes bid him sit and activated a holographic three-dimensional star map that was projected above the conference table. "Captain, after nearly five years, the Germans are launching a bid to retake the New Bremen system from the Rodinans. The German fleet will be reinforced with Edo, Lutetia, and Rotterdam all contributing task forces and ground troops."

The foreign secretary then added, "The Commonwealth has made repeated offers to assist the German government both before and after the capture of New Bremen. All our offers have been politely, but firmly, refused. Now the German High Command has finally asked us for assistance."

Admiral Lothes resumed, "They were very specific and very limited in their request. They asked if we would lend them the 43rd Battalion Royal Marine Force Recon and you."

"Naturally," the foreign secretary said, "we agreed, even though our naval assets are stretched thin following the debacle at Roosevelt. This is a long-sought opportunity for the Commonwealth to forge stronger ties with the most important nonaligned systems."

"Your role, captain, is to serve as an advisor and an observer," the admiral pointed out. "That was made clear in their invitation. Unlike the marines, who will be taking what we presume will be a lead role in the assault of the planet, *Indomitable* is not to take an active role in their attempt to recapture New Bremen, except as a last resort. There must be no misunderstanding of this point. Detailed rules of engagement have been worked out with the

German High Command and are included in your written orders. The Force Recon Marines will be traveling on the MT/AC HMS *Gawain*. *Indomitable* will retain its normal contingent of marines, but they are unlikely to take part in the fighting.

"The gathering of the different forces has been announced as joint maneuvers. This group of nonaligned systems has practiced joint maneuvers in the past, but not since New Bremen. The Commonwealth has not been invited to participate in any way for over one hundred years, so this is a diplomatic breakthrough of sorts.

"To assist you," the foreign secretary continued, "you will be accompanied by Miss Davidson here, who will be acting as a liaison in her role as chargé d'affaires. She speaks fluent German, French, and Japanese, and passable Polish in case you run into any difficulties. The High Command has informed us, though, that the *lingua franca* for all elements of the combined force is English."

"*Indomitable* is scheduled to depart one week from today," the admiral concluded. "Miss Davidson will be coming aboard in five days. I would suggest that you two should put your heads together before then, captain, after you have read your orders carefully. Do you have any questions?"

"Not at this time."

"Very well. The foreign secretary and I will leave you two to exchange contact information. Good luck, captain."

While the admiral and foreign secretary were leaving, Jonah took a moment to look more closely at Miss Davidson. She was an attractive woman, with light brown hair, blue eyes and appeared tanned from the sun. When she stood to say goodbye to the admiral and her boss, he noticed she was of moderate height, about 165 centimeters, and though she was wearing a business suit, she appeared to be fit and have an attractive figure. She appeared to be in her early 30s, though Jonah was a terrible judge of age. He remembered that when being introduced, she said her name was Amy.

"Do you mind if I call you Amy," he asked, "or would you prefer Miss Davidson?"

She smiled easily. "In public, probably Miss Davidson, but when it's just us, Amy is fine. Your title is trickier, though. Is it Captain Sir Jonah Halberd, Captain Halberd or—"

Jonah winced and said, "How about just plain captain when we're in public and Jonah when it's just us?"

"Done," she said and stuck out her hand to shake in agreement.

They shook. Her hand was warm, her fingers slender, and her grip strong. "My mother and my girlfriends are going to be very jealous of me," she said as she released his hand.

Jonah cocked his eyebrow over his remaining eye in response.

"They think you're a dreamboat."

"Well, please don't tell them how normal and boring I am in person. Let them enjoy their fantasies a little while longer," he said with a grin.

"I'll do that," she agreed, matching his grin. She pulled her comm out of her pocket and asked, "If you don't mind?"

Jonah retrieved his comm and pointed it at hers. The machines both buzzed to indicate they had exchanged information.

"I'll look over my orders tonight," he told her. "Should we set up a time for a meeting or a comm tomorrow?"

"You're heading back up to your ship now?" she asked. Jonah nodded.

"I have a number of things I have to wrap up here," she explained, "so it will have to be a comm." She checked her schedule on her comm unit. "Would 10:30 work?"

Jonah checked his own schedule and nodded. "Great," she said. "I'll talk to you then."

43

The repairs to *Indomitable* were finished after eleven weeks. One of the last things to be installed were kewpie nodes supplied by the members of the coalition to enable *Indomitable* to communicate in real-time with everyone else. Miss Davidson had come aboard. As a battlecruiser, *Indomitable* had been built with quarters for a flag officer in the event it was to be used as a flagship. They moved Miss Davidson into those. Unlike many civilians who brought too many clothes and personal belongings, then complained about the lack of space on a naval vessel, Davidson had packed economically.

They proceeded to an unpopulated system, K3610, to rendezvous with the task forces from Rotterdam, Lutetia, and Edo. Jonah and Amy had participated in video comms with the admirals of all four members of the coalition. So far, everything had gone smoothly. The different task forces were meeting in the unpopulated system to practice maneuvers and coordination between the different groups. While occasionally the unaligned systems had held joint military exercises in the past, this was the first time since the Rodinan capture of New Bremen that the governments had been willing to let any of their navies travel outside of their home systems.

Amy shared dossiers with Jonah, profiling the leaders of the different task forces. During these video comms she wore her "uniform" of a conservative business suit, but the rest of the time on ship, she wore undress khakis. Participating in these conferences felt a bit odd to Jonah. He was the only person not of flag rank, and the discussions about station-keeping practices and communications protocols they had engaged in were, quite frankly, boring. He understood the importance of them and the difficulty in meshing the four different navies into one force, but he had nothing of value to add to these discussions.

Amy, on the other hand, proved to be a valuable resource during these conferences. Her ability to speak to all the admirals in their native languages, her obvious intelligence, and her pleasant personality enabled the discussions to flow smoothly. He commented after the third video conference, "You're really good at this."

"Ha," she said, "make sure to tell my boss!"

"I'm quite serious," he reinforced. "I take all these details for granted because I've only ever had to know one way of doing things, and it was drilled into me. You manage to stay positive and cheerful and keep things moving forward. I would not have been able to do that."

"It helps that there is a refreshing lack of ego in this group," she replied. "I can't take all the credit. It's apparent that they are all committed to the success of this venture. Besides, they didn't ask you to come for your expertise in this stuff. When we start discussing the actual plans to retake New Bremen is where they are hoping you will contribute."

Jonah enjoyed the few opportunities he had to speak with her. He learned she had grown up on the planet Carolina on the coast of one of the planet's oceans. She explained the reason for her tanned skin when she told him that her two favorite hobbies were kiteboarding and racing small sailboats. Jonah had never tried kiteboarding but had enjoyed sailing quite a bit as a boy at summer camp. He learned that the boats she raced were the same class as what he had sailed as a boy.

He learned that while she had been in secondary school, she was selected for a prestigious King's Scholarship to the highly selective College of Interstellar Relations at the University of Caerleon. She had stayed in school long enough to earn her master's degree and had immediately joined the Foreign Service. Her first posting had been to the Commonwealth's consular office on New Bremen, and she had many fond memories of the planet and its people and was hoping this mission would be successful. She had then spent two years on Caerleon before being posted to a consular office on Edo. After that, she joined the embassy staff on Lutetia and had actually been there when Jonah had visited.

She teased him about being a ladies' man, telling him that spending the night with Manon Beart was something most of the men and many of the women on Lutetia dreamed about. Jonah turned red at this and tried to stammer out a response, but her laughter at his embarrassed reaction cut him short. She then teased him about his dashing appearance at Lord Chesterfield's wedding and asked if he were still involved with Captain MacLeod.

This time Jonah did not blush. He answered, "No, Captain MacLeod—Elaine—is a dear friend. I will selfishly admit that I think she was the most beautiful woman at the wedding, and her dress was simply amazing, but—just a friend. She helped me come to grips with a relationship problem I had from years before, and I'll be forever grateful to her for that."

Amy asked what the problem had been, and Jonah explained, "I was very seriously in love with a woman several years ago who broke my heart. It hurt me so much that I tried to ignore it rather than dealing with it. Elaine pointed out to me what I was doing, and ever since then, I've been able to put it behind me."

"Sounds familiar," Amy offered. "When I returned to Caerleon after New Bremen, I met a man, and we got married. When I received the posting to Edo, he stayed behind. I thought we were going to try to make it work despite our separation, but he had other ideas. Within two weeks, one of my friends told me she had seen him with another woman, and at the end of the month, he sent me divorce papers. My mother gave me some good advice: to go see a counselor. I did. It was a real test of my Japanese, trying to explain to my therapist what had happened and what I was feeling, but she helped me realize quickly that it was not my fault and that he was a wanker. Been fine ever since!"

By the time they all reached the K3610 system, ten days after she had boarded, Jonah had to admit to himself that he was powerfully attracted to Amy. In addition to her intelligence, she had a warm personality that made him feel as though he were the center of the universe when they spoke one-on-one after the video conferences. Seeing her in the physical training center confirmed his suspicion that she was fit. It took him a couple of days to notice that she seemed to have matched her workout schedule to his. He took that as a promising sign.

Since being knighted, Jonah had rekindled his interest in training in mixed martial arts, something he had been taught as a cadet at the academy but had neglected since then. In these days of fléchette guns, fighting hand-to-hand was completely impractical in the real world, but it was still valued as an endeavor that required physical fitness and mental dexterity. During the last two hundred years, it had enjoyed a resurgence of popularity and was often featured in video thrillers. Most capital ships in the Royal Navy had practice 'bots in their physical training centers for anyone who wished to practice.

While a cadet, Jonah had been trained to fight leading with either hand but was predominantly right-handed. Now that his right eye was missing, he was forced to use his left much more, making it more of a challenge. He had only been able to work his way up through the third level of the ten on the 'bot but was close to mastering the fourth. Though, as a cadet, he had reached the seventh level, he was not discouraged due to having to use his off-hand and having neglected practice for more than a decade.

One day when he came into the training center, he saw Amy working out against the 'bot, fighting quite competently on the fifth level. He watched her graceful movements for a few minutes. When she noticed him watching, she was momentarily distracted, and the 'bot slipped her guard and whacked her smartly on the ribs. A depressing low-pitched tone came from the 'bot, indicating it had won.

"I didn't know you practiced," Jonah commented.

es
Rubbing her side where the 'bot had hit her, Amy replied ruefully, "I saw you working with it the other day and thought I'd give it a try. Haven't done it since uni. I'd forgotten what a workout it is," she said, still trying to catch her breath.

"Well, you looked pretty smooth," he allowed, "especially compared to me."

"Thanks," she said. "Working against a 'bot is great for practicing the things you know, but I always found I learned more from sparring with people. Care to have a go?"

"Sure," Jonah shrugged.

He put on his gloves and headgear and stepped onto the mat. He bowed to Amy, following custom, and she returned his bow. They shuffled around. Jonah felt slightly awkward leading with his left but tried to put those feelings aside and concentrate.

Amy was the first to make a move, opening with a brief flurry of punches followed by a kick. Jonah countered them without difficulty. He decided he would try a combination and stepped forward. Amy blocked his first two jabs. Suddenly, Jonah found himself on the mat, stunned. Amy was kneeling next to him with a distressed look on her face.

"Oh, I'm so sorry!" she exclaimed.

It took Jonah a moment to focus his eye on her. "What happened?" he said with a tongue that felt thick and unresponsive.

"Um—" she began hesitantly, "well, you started a combination, and I countered with a kick, but um…I caught your blind side. I'm super sorry," she apologized.

"S'okay," Jonah mumbled in response.

"I'm calling the flight surgeon," she said.

"Good idea," Jonah murmured.

Shortly afterward, the flight surgeon arrived. Amy assisted a woozy Jonah in walking to the sickbay. After a comprehensive exam and some treatment to counter the effect of the blow to his head, Jonah was pronounced fit for duty and admonished that further training of this sort was not recommended.

44

During the journey to K3610, the details of meshing the different task forces into one coordinated unit had been worked out. The time had come to begin discussing the plan of attack. Jonah was invited to attend a conference aboard the German flagship, the superdreadnought *München*, at zero eight hundred the next morning. There he would meet with the German Admiral Herman Schwarzkopf, the Edoan Admiral Yoshiatsu Niimura, the Lutetian Admiral Valerie de Saint Phalle, and Rotterdam's Admiral Clarise Kuiper.

Though subsequent conferences would likely be held over commlinks, this was the first opportunity to meet one another face-to-face, and Jonah was looking forward to it. The leaders of the ground forces were conducting a similar meeting aboard the Lutetian flagship, the superdreadnought *Gaulois*. As he and Amy neared the German ship on the shuttle, she hurriedly asked, "Have you ever boarded a ship of another system as a guest?"

"No. Why?"

"Protocol," she answered. "When you first step onto the ship, you will see a German flag. You salute the flag before you salute any officers. Then you ask permission to come aboard."

"Ah. Thanks."

When they opened the hatch and stepped into the shuttle bay, Jonah saw the Germans greeting him with full side honors. Grateful for Amy's instruction, he marched over to where the honor guard was assembled, saluted the flag first, then turned crisply and saluted Admiral Schwarzkopf. The admiral introduced Jonah and Amy to his flag captain, who escorted them to the conference room.

Within fifteen minutes, they were joined by the French and Edoan admirals and their aides and a few minutes later by Schwarzkopf and Kuiper. When they all had taken their seats, Schwarzkopf activated the holographic star map showing the New Bremen system and the seven hyper corridors leading into it. Jonah had studied the map during the voyage and was familiar with it.

Of the seven hyper corridors that exited in the New Bremen system, two led to Rodinan space, one through two unpopulated systems, one that traversed three empty systems. Two corridors led to the German system of Bavaria, and one led to Saxony, with all three crossing a different single unpopulated system in between. One corridor led to the system where they were, K3610, with an unpopulated system in between. The last corridor led to a progression of empty systems, as far as survey crews had explored.

The K3610 system where they were was accessible to both Bavaria and Saxony, as well as Lutetia, Edo, and Rotterdam, and even the Commonwealth, though through multiple empty systems. At various times in the past, it had been a haven for pirates because of its accessibility to merchant shipping routes, but the nonaligned nations had long ago hammered out a treaty to share responsibility for patrolling the system to prevent pirate activity. As a result, Schwarzkopf, Niimura, de Saint Phalle, and Kuiper all had some familiarity with each other, though they had not worked this closely for several years.

Schwarzkopf began the discussion in English that betrayed only a trace of accent. "Welcome all. We have all spoken by conference several times leading up to this moment, but I wanted us to meet in person so that when the missiles start to fly, we have confidence and trust in one another. I insist that any of you speak up if you have any misgivings about our plans. We need to look at the challenges from every angle we can and to that end, we have invited Captain Sir Jonah Halberd to join us as an advisor and observer.

"Captain," Schwarzkopf said, addressing Jonah directly, "no one in this room has had as much direct experience against the Federation or as much success as you in recent years. I am told you are a humble man and like to credit your crews and luck, but the fact remains that you have fostered some innovative ideas and unusual approaches. We hope you can help us do the same."

Turning to the holographic display, Schwarzkopf returned to the mission. "We have two significant challenges. The first, of course, is to establish control of space in the New Bremen system. With our combined fleet, I am confident of our ability to do that. Our salvo weight is more than a third larger than that of the Rodinans in the system, and our point defense much stronger. The bigger challenge, I believe, will be to hold the system against their almost certain counterattack.

"The two are directly related. The fewer losses we suffer in retaking the system, the stronger our position to defend it. The Rodinans have a force of five superdreadnoughts, six battlecruisers—though of the older *Zhukov*-class, not the new *Makarov* class—six *Putin*-class heavy cruisers, eight *Kuznetsov*-class light cruisers and generally a minimum of eight and sometimes as many as a dozen frigates, most of which are on picket duty in the surrounding systems. Countering that, we have a force of ten superdreadnoughts, four battlecruisers, eight heavy cruisers, eleven light cruisers, and six frigates, though more frigates will be sent if we are successful in retaking the system.

"The Rodinans typically have frigates on picket duty in system K3612 between New Bremen and Bavaria, in system K3615 between New Bremen and Saxony, and in system K3617 between New Bremen and this system. In the last ten days, we have managed to insert stealthed sensor drones into those three systems and can confirm that there are two frigates in each system. One frigate in each system is located near the corridor to New Bremen, the other frigate near the corridor to either Bavaria, Saxony, or this system.

"Transit times for each of the three systems are just over three days. If our force is observed entering any of the three systems, the Rodinans will have ample time to position their ships in New Bremen to cause us the greatest amount of trouble. I have some ideas for how we might be able to counter that advantage but would like to hear from all of you first."

Kuiper spoke first. "I doubt there is anything we can do to avoid alerting them to our transit, no matter which system we choose."

Niimura offered, "Ideally, we should hit all three systems at the same time. But to split our forces between three systems, with three different exit points in New Bremen, that makes me nervous."

De Saint Phalle concurred. "I agree. It would be difficult to coordinate and would enable the Rodinans to position their force to annihilate one of our groups. The losses would jeopardize the entire effort."

Kuiper joined back in, "Even if we sent smaller forces, just to take out the first pickets, the pickets closer to New Bremen would have three and a half days to watch to see which system the main force chose."

Jonah spoke up. "How did the Rodinans solve this problem when they attacked the system?"

"They didn't have the same problem," Schwarzkopf explained. "Each of our systems has only one corridor that leads back to Rodinan space. All the corridors lead to at least one empty system before one can reach Rodinan territory. We had withdrawn our pickets on the far side of the nearest empty systems because our new government did not want to risk an 'incident' with the Federation. They snuck a heavy cruiser into each system and destroyed our remaining pickets, leaving us blind and needing to defend all three systems: Saxony, Bavaria, and New Bremen. We tried to guess which of the three systems they would attack and guessed wrong. When they entered New Bremen, we had no time to move reinforcements over from Saxony or Bavaria. They got into the system without a scratch. Their force had a 3:2 advantage in salvo weight. Our people did the best they could and managed to survive for three days, but the last ship was destroyed long before any reinforcements could arrive."

"Herman," Niimura asked, "could you show us the system geography for the picketed systems on our possible approaches to New Bremen?"

Schwarzkopf changed the display, and Niimura looked at the approach routes intently. "Can you project a ballistic course from the entrance corridor through each system at 0.23c?"

This took a bit longer as Schwarzkopf input the necessary information, but when he finished, red arcs appeared showing the ballistic trajectories. "Kuso!" Niimura swore softly.

De Saint Phalle nodded, guessing what Niimura had hoped to see. "None of them comes close to the exit corridor."

"You were hoping to ghost ships in that would take out the pickets nearest New Bremen?" Kuiper asked to confirm what she was thinking. Upon Niimura's nod, she asked, "Herman, can you delete the pickets closest to us and then project gravimetric sensor range of the remaining ones?"

They waited patiently while Schwarzkopf keyed in the data. Shimmering spheres of light purple appeared, showing the range at which the Rodinan frigates could detect emergence from hyperspace. In all cases, the sensor range overlapped the usual corridor exit. One showed an overlap of 30 light-minutes, the second about 55 light-minutes and the third at 80 light-minutes.

Kuiper explained what she was thinking. "If we send a second ship to destroy the pickets near New Bremen, they can sneak in if they leave the corridor early and make their course adjustments out of the pickets' sensor ranges."

"Too much time," de Saint Phalle responded. "The second ship couldn't emerge until the first picket was removed. Transit time for the second ship would be about five days. The fleet wouldn't be able to enter until the second picket was eliminated. That would make it just under ten days from the time we hit the first picket until the fleet could enter New Bremen." She turned to the German admiral. "Herman, can you show us an estimate of Federation reinforcements that could reach New Bremen in ten days?"

Schwarzkopf again busied himself inputting data. When he finished, he responded, "Seven superdreadnoughts, seven battle cru—"

"Never mind," de Saint Phalle interrupted.

"Admiral Schwarzkopf," Jonah asked, "what reinforcements can the Federation send to New Bremen in six days or less?"

The answer came much quicker this time. "Two battlecruisers, some lighter ships."

"Good," Jonah said. "What are the corridor transit times into New Bremen from the three systems?"

"Nineteen hours," Schwarzkopf replied, "sixteen and ten."

"Can you pull up the New Bremen system again and show the corridor exits with the transit times?"

Seeing the admirals' slightly puzzled expressions, Jonah explained. "We don't have the time to eliminate the second picket, but we could send the fleet through outside the range of gravimetric sensors, adjust course, then go ballistic to the exit. The pickets would likely pick us up when we are about three hours away from them, so from the time we were detected, the Rodinans in New Bremen would have roughly 22, 19, or 13 hours until we emerged in-system."

"Ah," Niimura acknowledged. "So, you want to see if they would be able to cover the exits one at a time?"

"Exactly," Jonah responded.

The system map of New Bremen showed the three exits connecting in a shallow angle. Schwarzkopf pointed out that the center point was the exit with the shortest transit time.

"Please show missile range from the exit points," Jonah asked.

Schwarzkopf keyed in the instructions, and spheres of light green appeared around the corridor exits.

"Now," Jonah asked, "expand the range from the center exit by 13 hours' acceleration at 500G, that one by 19 hours, and the last by 22."

None of the expanded spheres came close to intersecting. "Good," Jonah grunted. To recap his thinking, he said, "If we send a small force to each system to eliminate the first pickets, we can send the fleet through any of the systems. We'll want to drop out of hyper before we reach detection range, make course adjustments, and go ballistic as far as we can. The second pickets will pick us up about three hours away from the exit corridor when we would have to light up our drives to make course adjustments to hit the exit. The Rodinans will then know which corridor we'll be using, but they won't be able to set up an ambush for us. They'll need to hold back and wait for our arrival."

"They might guess," Niimura offered. "I can't see much disadvantage to them if they guess incorrectly. A bad guess on their part gives us a head start, but that gives us no advantage. After all, we're not likely to bombard New Bremen."

"If you were going to gamble," Schwarzkopf asked, "which corridor would you guard?"

"The center," Kuiper responded.

"The center," everyone else murmured in chorus.

"I guess we can eliminate that one," Schwarzkopf chuckled. "That's the corridor from K3615 and Saxony."

"Which is the corridor from this system?" de Saint Phalle asked.

"This one," Schwarzkopf pointed, "the 16-hour transit."

"How quickly can we position something in Bavaria and Saxony big enough to eliminate the pickets?" Niimura inquired.

"Not long," Schwarzkopf replied, "We can send ships currently in those systems, though I may be required to dispatch ships from our force to backfill. Are we in agreement that this is how we wish to proceed?"

Heads nodded. Schwarzkopf then said, "The last question is timing. At some point in the near future, I am sure the Rodinans will know that we are, at the very least, conducting joint exercises. In the past, joint exercises have typically lasted about two weeks. We should look at the feasibility of destroying the outlying pickets in the systems bordering New Bremen no later than June 16, which is twelve days from today. If we can advance that timetable, we should try to do so. Any objections?"

Schwarzkopf looked around the table. "I will draft our plan of attack and submit it to you for oversight and approval. Once that is done, we can each send copies to our admiralty offices and begin. Any further questions? Fine, consider this meeting concluded."

45

As the meeting concluded, Jonah was surprised when all four admirals wanted to chat with him. Admiral Niimura was the first to ask to take a picture with him, explaining that his children would be very excited to see it when this mission was over. The other admirals all agreed and enlisted Miss Davidson to use their comms to take pictures of themselves with Jonah.

All seemed very happy that he was there to advise them. Each of them invited him to tour his or her flagship before they had to depart the system. Though Jonah was most interested in touring only Niimura's flagship, due to the reputation Edo had for technological prowess, he did not feel he could say yes to one and not the others, so ended up accepting all the invitations. He asked if he could bring some of his people along, and that presented no problems. He left with tentative promises to tour Niimura's ship the next morning, de Saint Phalle's ship the next afternoon, and Kuiper's and Schwarzkopf's ships the next day.

On the shuttle back to *Indomitable,* Amy commented on how the admirals had acted. "It was almost as if you were a famous actor or star athlete," she remarked.

"It's uncomfortable," Jonah admitted. "If I were a famous actor or star athlete, maybe I'd feel that I deserved that kind of reaction from people more than I do now. I'm famous now for being extremely lucky, living when most of my crew didn't, and it doesn't sit well."

"I've always believed that people make their own luck, to a certain extent," she replied.

Jonah snorted softly. "My first captain, now admiral, Von Geisler, is fond of saying that. I don't know if I ever believed it," he said with a slight smile.

"Who will you take with you on the 'Grand Tour' tomorrow?" she asked.

"Commander Mellon, Commander Gessert, Mr. Bradshaw, and you."

"Me? Why me? I won't understand any of what we'll be seeing."

"To prevent a diplomatic incident," Jonah replied smugly.

"Oh," she grinned, "I get it now. Misery loves company."

"Something like that," he smiled in return.

"Do you think the plan they came up with will work?" she asked, changing the subject.

"We'll certainly be able to retake the system. Based on the force we're bringing with us, and what they have to oppose us, there really isn't any doubt about that," he explained. "The key is, as Admiral Schwarzkopf said, doing so with a minimum of losses so that they have a chance of holding it after the Federation counterattacks."

"Do you think they will?"

"I suppose it depends to a certain extent on that question—how much damage we sustain in taking the system. Based on the numbers, the Rodinans don't have enough to hold the system, but they do have enough to make it costly for us. If they're able to reduce our firepower by more than, say, thirty percent, it makes a counterattack likely. If they can reduce our firepower by as much as fifty percent, which is possible, it makes a counterattack inevitable and almost certainly successful."

"What do you think will happen?" she asked earnestly.

"It's going to be a near thing," Jonah admitted. "Closer than I would like. When we were in the meeting, I was hoping we could find a way to slip into New Bremen without giving the Rodinans days to prepare for our arrival. The way they've stationed the pickets prevents that. It's shaping up to be an old-fashioned dogfight, and that makes me nervous."

"Why?"

"I like to find opportunities where I can improve the odds," Jonah shrugged.

"Ha!" she said triumphantly. "What did I say about people making their own luck?"

"Hey now—"

"I could call it cheating," she teased, "except all's fair in love and war, right?"

Jonah did not respond, suddenly lost in thought. Amy was unsettled by his sudden silence and tried to wait it out. As they flew into the shuttle bay, she asked, "Was it something I said?"

"Huh? No—Yes. Not you." He smiled at her, he hoped reassuringly. "You made me think of something that might help us improve the odds. Come to my ready room. We need to comm back to Caerleon."

"About what?"

"About some information I'd like to share with the coalition that's classified," he said, striding towards his quarters, "but if we are allowed to share it, it might provide an edge."

They sat down, and Jonah initiated a call to Admiral Lothes. His console told him that it was still late afternoon where she was on Caerleon. He reached her yeoman, who recognized Halberd immediately and completed the connection.

"Yes, Captain Halberd, what is it?" Lothes inquired.

"Admiral," Jonah began, "I've contacted you because I believe the coalition would benefit tremendously if I were able to share our missile frame tactic with them."

Jonah continued and explained the situation the coalition faced, describing in detail the geographical and tactical hurdles. He apologized for not yet having filed his written report but explained that the meeting had just ended, and he wanted to get approval as soon as possible. He also described how the coalition's ability to withstand the expected counterattack from the Federation would be enhanced by the ability to deploy missiles remotely, as he had in *Cumberland's* final battle. Wrapping up, he mentioned that Miss Davidson would be contacting the foreign secretary to brief him.

"This is not something I can authorize immediately, captain," Admiral Lothes replied. "It might take a few hours. In the meantime, I urge you to file a written report quickly. Though I trust your judgment and agree with your assessment, other people will need to sign off on this."

"Understood, admiral," Jonah responded. "*Indomitable* out."

He turned to Amy. "Time to comm the foreign secretary."

Amy did just that and explained the situation as best she could. Since she did not understand the technology to which Jonah referred, she glossed over it, stressing instead his belief that sharing these developments would help ensure the coalition's success and paint the Commonwealth in a favorable light. She also pointed out that the coalition had not asked Jonah about these, rather that Jonah had thought of them himself and wanted to offer them voluntarily. The coalition was not aware that Jonah had made the request of the Admiralty, so refusal by the Admiralty would not carry any negative consequences in the diplomatic arena.

"True, but offering these enhancements freely," the foreign secretary responded, "certainly would give us some political capital to use. Captain Halberd, when will you file your report?"

"Within an hour."

"Very well. I'll give Admiral Lothes a chance to read it over and call her in 90 minutes," he said. "Is there anything else, Miss Davidson?"

"No, sir."

"Then I'll sign off. I'll contact you if I need any further clarification."

As the comm ended, Jonah ran his hands through his hair and said, "I have to jump on this report. I'll buzz you once it's been sent."

Jonah wrote up his report and analysis. At the end, he included his recommendation to share the missile frame technology and how it might help minimize losses to the nonaligned force in retaking New Bremen. He also pointed out that deploying remotely controlled missiles at the hyper entrances to the New Bremen system would enhance the coalition's ability to defeat an almost-inevitable Federation counterattack. When he finished, he noted it had taken him almost the full hour to write it. He sent the report and let Amy know it was finished.

"What now?" she asked.

"Now," he sighed, "we wait. I'm going to grab some lunch in the mess. Care to join me?"

Over lunch, they discussed the admirals they had met. Jonah was particularly interested in Amy's impressions of them to see if she had picked up anything he hadn't.

"Admiral Schwarzkopf," she related, "is clearly used to command. Working with a group of equals like this is not something in which he has a great deal of experience, I think. I picked up a number of instances where he betrayed his impatience with little tics, but he was very conscious of the need to work together, so he suppressed them."

"Now that you mention it," Jonah commented, "I remember early on he jerked his hand slightly at one point, as though he was going to make a gesture when Admiral Niimura mentioned splitting our forces into three groups. No one in their right mind would split a force between three different systems, so Niimura's comment was unnecessary."

"Well, it seemed to me that Admiral Niimura might have said that so he could gauge how the others reacted," Amy offered. "He seems more comfortable in a group setting, but he doesn't know this group very well."

"He's a quick thinker, though," Jonah added.

"He is," Amy agreed. "They all are."

"What about de Saint Phalle and Kuiper?"

"Most of what they had to say was focused on avoiding negative outcomes," Amy remarked. "Contrast what they had to say against Admiral Niimura, who was trying to offer ideas that would produce positive outcomes."

"Interesting," Jonah murmured. "I hadn't looked at it that way, but you're right."

"It's easy to understand why," Amy said. "Rotterdam and Lutetia have not been in a battle in over a hundred years."

"Neither has Edo," Jonah pointed out.

"True, but Admiral Niimura comes from a different culture, one that is a bit more martial in character originally. Though Edo has not had to fight battles with ships and missiles in many, many years, they are quite aggressive in their approach to trade. Lutetia and Rotterdam less so."

"Would it be a stretch to say Niimura would be more comfortable in offensive maneuvers and de Saint Phalle and Kuiper in planning a defensive strategy?"

"No," Amy shook her head thoughtfully, "it might turn out that way, but this is only one meeting."

Jonah later admitted to himself that he was quite smitten with Miss Davidson. She was intelligent, extremely competent, and physically attractive. He enjoyed her insight, as she made him consider things from different perspectives than he usually would have. He also enjoyed her sly sense of humor, something they shared. He even admired her for dropping him like a bag of wet cement on the practice mat, though they had not spoken of it since.

46

Jonah returned to the bridge to stand the afternoon watch. He busied himself in the normal routine. Moments after he was relieved by his third officer, Lieutenant Christie, his comm buzzed, indicating he was wanted by Admiral Lothes on a secure comm. He hurried to his ready room and connected via his console.

"Captain Halberd," she said, "after reviewing your report and analysis, we have decided to allow you to offer both the frames and the remote placement to the nonaligned nations. Admiral Antonelli, in particular, was pleased you brought this to our attention. We do insist on one condition. Miss Davidson will be asking through her channels that they share with us any enhancements they develop to the technology we will be sharing. She will also be letting them know that they will need to pay royalties on the frames as the design is covered by patents. As they are all signatories of the Interstellar Patent Law and Intellectual Property Treaty, this will be no hardship for them. I believe she is getting her instructions from the foreign secretary at this moment. We will leave the two of you to work out the details on how you want to present this to them."

"Understood, Admiral Lothes."

"Sadly, one reason that ONI agreed to this is their assessment that, by now, it is possible that the Rodinans have developed this capability. You need to share that with the admirals as well."

"Damnit!" Jonah sighed. "Well, it was bound to happen. They're not stupid."

"No," Lothes replied, "they're not. ONI does not have any hard intelligence that they have developed it but suggest we err on the side of caution. In your initial deployment of the capability in Venera and from the engagement in Roosevelt, they likely received extremely limited sensor data, if they received any at all. From the action in H2813, they have full sensor data, and ONI is basing their assessment on that. Since your sensor logs were destroyed with the *Cumberland*, we have no way of knowing what that data might look like but worry that it has given them enough of an idea that they would develop the capability."

"So, ONI believes it's possible," Jonah mused. "Well, I've always believed in preparing for the worst."

"Exactly!" Lothes agreed. "Regardless, good luck, captain. Lothes out."

Jonah waited for Amy to contact him, which only took a few minutes. She appeared in his ready room immediately afterward. "So," she began, "what do you think the next step is?"

"We're scheduled to visit Admiral Niimura's flagship, *Akagi,* in the morning. I would rather not wait until then to broach this subject. I'd prefer to communicate now and use tomorrow's meeting to cement our agreement," Jonah answered. "What are the things you need to accomplish?"

"Well, we need to make sure you and I agree on the way we present it. We need to get them to sign off on the royalty agreement, and we need to get them to agree to share any enhancements they develop. I've been given permission to share the royalty document with them. I don't think any of these will be a problem."

"Well," Jonah said, running his hand over his face, "I was thinking of just telling them that I wanted to share this new tech with them, tech that I'd used successfully in recent battles and that I feared the Rodinans might have developed since then and had just received approval from the Admiralty to do so. Is there anything more than that?"

"Just that we are doing so because we want this effort to be as successful as possible. It goes without saying that we are trying to generate some goodwill from this," Amy agreed. "I'll let you take the lead, and if you overlook anything, I'll jump in, if that's alright with you?"

"Sounds fine," Jonah concurred. "Now, who do we start with? Schwarzkopf? Or should we set up a video conference through him?"

"I think we contact him and ask him to set up a video conference as quickly as possible," Amy said. "They are the lead partner in this endeavor."

"I hoped we would get approval, so I pulled together the schematics of what we're sharing to send to them immediately. I can send it to Schwarzkopf as soon as we get him on the comm."

Amy nodded, so Jonah used his console to contact the German admiral. It took a minute, but then Schwarzkopf's face appeared. "What can I do for you, captain?" he asked.

Jonah smiled in response. "It's not what you can do for me, admiral, but what I can do for you."

Noticing the German's quizzical expression, Jonah continued quickly. "After our meeting today, I realized some technology we had recently developed might help the success of the effort to retake and hold New Bremen. Because this technology is so new, it's highly classified, so I contacted my Admiralty and was given permission to share it with you."

The German admiral thought for a moment, then asked, "Not to be too cynical, captain, but what does the Commonwealth hope to gain from this? I believe 'What's the catch?' is the expression you use."

"The Commonwealth benefits if the coalition is able to recover New Bremen. Beyond that, we would ask that you work out a licensing agreement with the patent holder and agree to share with us any enhancements you develop to this technology. I will send you schematics of what I'm talking about, and Miss Davidson will send you a copy of the licensing agreement between the Commonwealth and the patent holder. If you would then share this material with the other admirals and set up a time for a video conference, I would be grateful."

"When would you like to hold this conference?" Schwarzkopf asked.

"This evening, if possible," Jonah replied. "I am scheduled to tour the *Akagi* tomorrow. If we have any issues we cannot resolve this evening, we could follow up in person then if that's acceptable?"

"Send the schematics and the licensing agreement. I'll take a look and get back to you," the German said. "Anything else?"

"Yes, sir," Jonah added. "I just wanted to share with you that I have used this technology recently and am prepared to share with you the results of those battles. It is imperative that I share it because my Office of Naval Intelligence calculates that the Rodinans have possibly developed similar technology since we have used it against them three times now."

Schwarzkopf's eyebrow raised. "Very well, captain. I will be in contact soon, I'm sure."

The connection terminated, and Jonah let out a deep breath. He looked at Amy. "You're the diplomat. Did I do it right?"

She smiled. "Not bad, but it was hardly a tough test. If you were trying to work out an agreement to sell them agricultural equipment, I somehow think it wouldn't have gone so smoothly."

"True," Jonah admitted. "Now what?"

"We wait," she replied. "How long do you think it will take for them to respond?"

Jonah thought. "I'm hoping that it will be less than a couple of hours."

It was, in fact, only 23 minutes later when Admiral Schwarzkopf contacted Jonah. "Captain Halberd," he began, "with your permission, I have the other admirals on the line. May I bring them in?"

"Certainly," Jonah replied, cocking an eyebrow at Amy over the quick response.

One by one, the other admirals blinked in on Jonah's console. Once all were linked in, Schwarzkopf took over. "Captain, we are very intrigued with what you shared. The licensing agreement is no obstacle, and we will agree to share with the Commonwealth any enhancements we develop to this tech.

I will assume Miss Davidson will work through your embassies to forward whatever covenant you need. If you don't mind, we'd like to ask a few questions about how you deployed this technology."

"Please," Jonah answered, "go ahead."

The admirals took turns asking Jonah about his experience with the missile frames and then the remote deployment of them when he turned back the Rodinan force in H2813. He answered them based on his personal experience. During the conference, it was clear that the admirals were excited by this new development. Admiral Kuiper was the first to mention the possibility that the Rodinans had similar capability.

"In the attack on Roosevelt," Jonah explained, "they did not deploy anything like this. Roosevelt was the third time I used the missile frames. In the first engagement in Venera, we destroyed the Rodinan ships. In the most recent, at Roosevelt, we destroyed or captured their ships. How much sensor data made it back to the Federation from those two actions is a guess— possibly none, possibly enough for them to piece it together. They do have full sensor data from the engagement in H2813. In that battle, we did not tow the missile frames but had deployed them remotely."

"Like defense platforms," de Saint Phalle pointed out. "Which is tech we all have. So perhaps—"

Schwarzkopf interrupted, "If the Rodinans don't deploy them, so much the better for us, but we should be prepared in case they do."

Everyone agreed with that, which ended the debate. They ended the conference agreeing to have their tactical and munitions people meet the next day on *Akagi* with Bradshaw and Commander Mellon to go over particulars.

47

The next day, Jonah and his people, including Miss Davidson, flew to *Akagi*. Admiral Niimura met him with full side honors. Jonah saluted the flag when he arrived.

After exchanging salutes, Niimura apologized. "I'm sorry, captain, but your tour of my ship will have to wait for another time. We have all thought of many questions we would like to ask and also want to go over the latest assessments from our combined intelligence operations. If your tactical people would follow my flag lieutenant, she will conduct them to their meeting."

Niimura's flag lieutenant stepped forward. Jonah nodded at Commander Mellon, who stepped forward and saluted her, then introduced himself. She led Mellon and his group down a side corridor.

Niimura then indicated Jonah should follow him, saying, "This way, please, captain."

Jonah and Miss Davidson followed to a conference room where refreshments were waiting. Davidson helped herself to some tea. Within minutes they were joined by the other admirals. Once Niimura returned to the room, Schwarzkopf spoke first.

"We have had a busy night, Captain Halberd, considering the possibilities of the new capability you shared with us." Schwarzkopf activated a projector and displayed a table displaying missile launch capability. "Originally, we calculated our throw weight to be just over a third greater than the Rodinan force in-system." He then displayed a set of numbers that showed the effect of adding the towed missile frames. "If we implement this new capability, even in the worst case—that the Rodinans have developed it too—our throw weight in the initial salvo is 40 percent greater than what we would face in return."

Schwarzkopf keyed another display, adding point defense capability estimates. "From the standpoint of comparing throw weight against point defense, implementing the new capability provides an initial salvo that will be almost double what our intelligence feels the Rodinan force will be able to defend. If the Rodinans have also implemented this capability, their throw weight does not increase enough to overwhelm our point defense net."

Admiral de Saint Phalle jumped in, "Of course, we understand these are abstract and very general numbers, captain, and, depending on Rodinan targeting priorities, they will still be able to break through our point defense in places. What is most encouraging, though, is that our initial salvo should be able to overwhelm them. This reduces the chances of getting into a prolonged missile duel."

"On the negative side, though," Admiral Kuiper added, "are the ability of our tac net to handle the increased number of missiles and the logistics of resupply. Your Commander Mellon is working with our tactical officers right now. It has made it necessary for us to revise the design of our tac net. Originally, we planned on using *München* to host it, but now will be using *Akagi* instead. Edoan system architecture is much more easily expanded to be able to handle the increased number of missiles. The point defense net will continue to be run from *Gaulois*. Depending on what the tactical officers decide, we will need to work on programming. This has the potential to delay us."

"The other part of the problem is logistics," Admiral Niimura said. "Not so much for our assault on New Bremen, but for our defense of the system. We had not planned on planting remote defense platforms at the entrance to the corridor that leads to Rodinan space because they are expensive and of limited capability. Your method of pre-positioning frames of missiles, as you did in H2813, is a much more attractive strategy. We would like to position as many missiles near that entrance as possible, given the size of the counterattack we believe the Rodinans will mount. Accordingly, freighters are already being loaded in our home systems, but it will be a race to get them to New Bremen and get the missiles and frames deployed in time."

"What sort of forces do you think the Federation will be able to gather for a counterattack, and how quickly?" Jonah asked.

Schwarzkopf nodded to a German officer seated next to him. The man stood up, saying, "Captain Brandt, MAD."

Seeing that Jonah did not understand what MAD stood for, Amy whispered, "Military intelligence." Jonah nodded.

Captain Brandt had activated a holographic projection showing the New Bremen system and the nearest Rodinan systems, with icons representing the Rodinan ships in each system. "We estimate that the Federation would be able to mount a counterattack by the end of two weeks from the time they recognize that we are assaulting the system, probably when we take out the pickets on the near side of the bordering systems. Within that time period, they can assemble a force from different elements of their Home Fleet of ten superdreadnoughts, seven *Zhukov*-class battlecruisers, six heavy cruisers, five light cruisers, and as many as eight frigates. Because of Commonwealth losses at Roosevelt, they will be able to transfer ships from frontline systems back to their Home Fleet without jeopardy."

Jonah winced at the mention of how Commonwealth losses at Roosevelt would be felt even here.

Admiral de Saint Phalle took over. "Based on Captain Brandt's estimates, we would like to pre-position roughly 2,000 missiles to intercept the Rodinans."

Jonah whistled softly to himself.

"We are confident we can handle the programming challenges," Admiral Niimura said, "but we do not have the missiles. The most the coalition partners can deliver on short notice, based on available cargo capacity, is just under 1,400. Would the Commonwealth be willing to lend us freight capacity to carry 600 or more missiles? The ships would need to load our missile stocks and deliver them to us by June 16."

Jonah thought quickly, mentally reviewing what he remembered of system geography and transit times as Amy responded diplomatically, "Of course, we would be willing to consider this."

Jonah looked at her and shook his head slightly, then spoke to the group. "We couldn't do it."

Amy glared at him and hissed, "Captain!"

"Let me explain," Jonah said. "To hire available civilian freighters positioned close enough to meet the deadline just wouldn't be possible. We would waste time identifying the ships and negotiating the contracts, plus we would have to reveal that we would be sending them to the fringe of a war zone. Not only would that make it harder to hire the ships, it also puts information out that we don't want to spread."

"What about military transport, captain?" asked Schwarzkopf.

"Military transport would certainly help keep things quiet," Jonah responded, "and I'm pretty sure the Commonwealth would be happy to lend you the capacity, but it's based too far away to be able to make a trip to any of your planets or bases and then here by the jumping off date. May I suggest another solution?"

"By all means, captain."

"Would the coalition be willing to consider buying 600 or more Vulcan missiles from the Commonwealth? I don't know that my superiors will approve this or under what terms, but if they did, the transports could be loaded immediately and travel here by the most direct route. They would not need to stop in one of your systems to take on the cargo and then come here." He looked at Amy and gave her a sincere smile. "If our governments are able to come to an agreement, then we have a chance at getting the ordnance here in time."

"Under what terms, captain?" asked Schwarzkopf.

"I have no idea," Jonah admitted. "That is Miss Davidson's area of responsibility."

"I will need to contact the Foreign Office," Amy responded. "They will likely have questions for Captain Halberd and the Admiralty, so if we could adjourn this meeting for a few hours, Captain Halberd and I will contact our people."

Schwarzkopf looked around the table at the others. No one raised a protest, so he declared, "Agreed. Send me a comm when you have some more information."

"Admiral, the tactical meeting is likely to take a few more hours. Miss Davidson and I will return to *Indomitable* and send our shuttle back for Commander Mellon."

"No need, captain," Niimura replied easily. "We will send him back on one of ours."

"Thank you, sir." Jonah saluted, then asked, "If you would please ask someone to lead us back to the shuttle bay?"

Niimura called to a nearby member of the crew and issued him some brief orders. Jonah and Amy followed the crewman back to the shuttle. When they arrived, he told the shuttle pilot, "Change of plans. Miss Davidson and I need to return to the ship immediately."

They both waited until the hatch closed before speaking, but then both tried to talk at once. Jonah stopped and held his hand out, indicating she should speak first.

"I hope you weren't bullshitting them about transit times, Jonah!"

"I wasn't," he protested.

"Okay," Amy breathed a sigh of relief. "Then you might have opened the door to a huge opportunity for the Commonwealth if we can convince the Admiralty to go along."

"How so?"

"Well," Amy began, "my understanding of all the technology is limited, but if they're going to use our Vulcan missiles with their tac net, then we will have to share specs for what is undoubtedly some top-secret military hardware. Fair is fair, so we can certainly request that they share information on the tac net of similar scope."

"Okay," Jonah shrugged.

"You don't get it," Amy exclaimed excitedly. "This is huge. Technology-sharing agreements are the Holy Grail of inter-stellar diplomacy! Particularly with Edo! They have been the leading edge of technological implementation since forever."

"But they already agreed to share any enhancements they make to the missile frames."

"No offense, Jonah, but the missile frames are pretty simple tech. The idea itself is the breakthrough there. But a tac net and missile control systems are orders of magnitude more advanced and involved. The Edoan military and the Admiralty will need to work together to get everything to mesh properly. If it goes well, we can work to expand the agreement and broaden the scope later."

"If you say so. I still need to get the Admiralty to agree to do this," Jonah stated.

"Give me a few minutes to get the Foreign Minister up to speed," Amy asked. "Then he can help with the Admiralty."

"Just say when," Jonah quipped.

As soon as they returned to *Indomitable*, Amy went to her quarters, almost running. Jonah returned to his ready room at a more measured pace. He accessed navigational maps on his console to double-check his estimation that civilian freighters would not be able to meet the necessary deadline. He was pleased to see that his very rough calculations held up. He then determined whether military transport, leaving from the nearest Commonwealth military installations, could meet the deadline. He was about to access the Admiralty database to see where the transport assets were located when Amy burst in.

The door hadn't yet closed behind her when Jonah's console indicated he had a priority one comm from Admiral Lothes. He connected immediately. The admiral's yeoman asked him to hold, then Admiral Lothes and the foreign secretary appeared on a split-screen.

"Captain Halberd," Admiral Lothes began, "we are on a call with the foreign secretary regarding the opportunity you discussed with the coalition forces. I realize you have not yet prepared a written report, which we will require as soon as humanly possible, so please brief us as thoroughly and as quickly as you can."

Jonah took a deep breath and began a recap of the meeting, leading to the coalition's need for more missiles. He then reviewed his analysis of the impossibility of civilian vessels being able to meet the timetable and mentioned the security concerns. He then shared his preliminary analysis of whether military transport, leaving from Commonwealth bases, could meet the deadline. "Admiral," he explained, "I was just looking at the current disposition of transport assets when you commed."

Lothes replied, "My yeoman just pulled the list and we have the vessels in place and the missile stocks. We'll be a little short on the missile frames but can install a couple of fabricators on some of the transports and make up the difference by the time our ships arrive. We need to move on this immediately. I'll issue the orders to make it happen, but it will be up to the Foreign Office to get agreements in place before we can start sharing any sensitive information."

The foreign secretary spoke, "We'll start work on those agreements immediately and will keep you informed on their status. Captain, is Miss Davidson there with you?"

Amy stepped into the view of the camera. "Yes, sir."

"Miss Davidson, you need to contact the coalition admirals, particularly Admiral Niimura, and ask them to apply pressure on their end to make this happen."

"Will do, sir."

"Very well. Admiral? If you can get those transports on the way, the rest is up to my people and me."

"I will issue the orders as soon as we complete this comm," Admiral Lothes confirmed. "Captain Halberd, I will need your written report as soon as you can get it to me."

"I'll begin it immediately," Jonah promised.

"Then, foreign secretary? Miss Davidson? The ball is in your court. Lothes out."

The comm ended. Amy squealed in delight, spun Jonah around in his chair, grabbed his face with both hands and kissed him hard on the lips.

"Uh, you're welcome?" Jonah said uncertainly.

"Jonah, this is a career-changing opportunity. Thank you, thank you, thank you!" she said, punctuating each "thank you" with another quick kiss. When she finished, she released his head and ran out of the room.

48

Jonah contacted Admiral Schwarzkopf right away to let him know that the Commonwealth was already loading military transports and that Miss Davidson and the Foreign Office would hammer out the details of the transaction through diplomatic channels. After disconnecting, Jonah quickly wrote up his report and transmitted it to Admiral Lothes. Shortly after he finished, his comm buzzed as Commander Mellon let him know he had returned to *Indomitable*.

A minute later, there was a knock on the door. After Jonah called, "Enter," Mellon came in. "Grab a seat, Mel, and tell me about your meeting. Can I get you a cup of coffee?"

"No. Thanks," Mellon replied. Once he sat, he began, "Our meeting went well. The tac net will actually be run from *Akagi*, so we were able to get a lot done in a short time. I have to say, the Edoan computer systems are impressive as hell."

"How so?"

"Well, when we set up a tac net, we merely establish links between the computers on our ships. Each one is responsible for aiming, firing, and tracking its own missiles. The ships work in concert with one another, based on the instructions we've fed into them. It's a de-centralized approach. One problem you've already encountered is that each computer can only handle so many missiles, something that needed a work-around when you were in H2813."

"Right," Jonah concurred, "but we've beefed up our computers to handle larger numbers since then."

"Nothing like the Edoans," Mellon said, shaking his head. "Jonah, their systems are so robust they can run the entire tac net for a whole fleet from *Akagi*. The entire setup is capable of jumping to another one of their ships if anything were to happen to the original host. It gives their AI the ability to maintain control over the firing of every missile and to shift targeting based on a unified, overall view of the progress of combat. It ensures that the highest-threat targets are addressed, regardless of what happens to the firing capability of any ship in the fleet."

Mellon continued, "In both the Commonwealth and Edoan systems, the AI on the flagship uses the tac net to assign targeting priorities to the other ships based on damage assessments picked up by sensor readings. If something were to happen to *Indomitable* that prevented us from firing, our tac net would not change targeting for any of the missiles to be launched from other ships. It would, later, based on sensor readings of enemy damage. With the Edoan system, it would know that *Indomitable* could not fire and would instantly adjust targeting for every missile on every ship, reassigning targets."

Jonah nodded in understanding. "It wouldn't affect the initial salvo, but it sure would maximize the effectiveness of every salvo afterward."

"Exactly," Mellon confirmed. "Not only that, but the Edoan system theoretically can handle many times more missiles than any system of ours. The work-around you needed in H2813 would not have been necessary."

"Well, that ties in with what we discussed in my meeting," Jonah stated. He took a few minutes to recap the latest developments.

Mellon took a few moments to think and then stated, "Miss Davidson is right, Jonah. In order for them to use our Vulcans, even remotely fired, we'd have to allow them access to some really sensitive technology. We would also need to get a look inside their systems too. It could be a huge opportunity for technological exchange."

"That's what she said," Jonah remarked. "Who benefits the most, do you think, Mel? Long-term?"

"It depends on the scope of the agreement," Mellon mused. "For the Germans, French and Rotterdam, it could be a huge win. They could get access to more Commonwealth technology and they give up little in return—I don't get the sense they have much to offer us. For the Edoans and the Commonwealth, it's a 'give and take'."

"How so?"

"Without being too general," Mellon explained, "typically the Commonwealth is the leader in technological innovation. That would include the Rodinans and Chinese too. That would benefit the Edoans. But the Edoans are masters of implementation—they'll take our ideas and perfect them. For instance, from what I learned in my meeting today, the missiles that the coalition forces use are similar to the Rodinans' Sokol in terms of performance. The ECM on the coalition missiles is all supplied by Edo, though. And I caught a hint that the Edoans have special missiles that are entirely ECM and incredibly effective. I'd love to learn more about that capability."

"Sounds good, Mel," Jonah agreed.

Rising, Mellon said, "For now, I need to write my report. And if I'm not mistaken, you're on duty in about ten minutes."

49

For Jonah, the next few days were more or less routine. There were daily mission briefings with the other coalition leaders, and he was given tours of the four flagships. Miss Davidson was a whirlwind for the first two days, shuttling back and forth to *München*, *Gaulois*, *Akagi* and *Krakow*, Admiral Kuiper and Rotterdam's superdreadnought. Jonah didn't see much of her. On the third day, her eyes rimmed red from lack of sleep, she informed Jonah that agreement had been reached and the Foreign Office would be providing him a summary shortly.

When Jonah received the summary, he and Commander Mellon commed the Admiralty and went over in detail what could and could not be shared with the coalition members. The Vulcan missiles were on their way and Mellon had hosted several meetings where the details of working the missiles into the tac net were covered. *Indomitable*, as her role strictly limited to that of an observer, was not folded into the coalition tac net.

Admiral Schwarzkopf confirmed that the outer pickets in the three empty systems adjacent to New Bremen that lay between New Bremen and the rest of the coalition would be destroyed on the planned date of June 16. Detailed timetables for the entire task force were shared. The task force would enter the corridor to system K3617, emerging from the corridor one light-hour early to stay out of range of the gravimetric sensors on the Rodinan picket ship located near the corridor to New Bremen. The task force would coast in on a ballistic course until it neared the exit, at which point the coalition ships would need to activate their drives to change course and reach the corridor.

As soon as they closed within range, they would destroy the remaining picket ship (if it did not flee into the hyper corridor) and enter the corridor to New Bremen. If the Rodinans had guessed correctly that they were coming from K3617, they might be attacked immediately. If the Rodinans were waiting outside one of the other corridors, that gave the coalition time to assemble into formation. As a group, they went over detailed plans of engagement and tried to account for every possible Rodinan response to their entrance into the New Bremen system.

The two most problematic scenarios were if the Rodinans had guessed correctly which hyper corridor they were using or if the Rodinans had already begun a withdrawal from the system to preserve their naval assets for their counterattack. The intelligence services from all the coalition members felt strongly that the Rodinans would stay and fight—that the Politburo would dictate that response.

The escort ships would go first, followed by the capital ships. *Indomitable* would be the last capital ship to enter New Bremen. The military transports from the Commonwealth and the rest of the coalition supply train would wait until given the order to proceed into New Bremen.

Jonah did not see Amy until a few hours before they were scheduled to leave for the K3617 system. Once the initial cyclone of negotiations had ended, she admitted to him that she had slept for almost 20 hours because she had worked around the clock for two days. Since then, she had been busy working with the Foreign Office and the different coalition members, tightening up finer points of the agreement.

She asked Jonah for an update on the military situation, admitting she had not thought about it much for over a week. She had been in a couple of meetings with Thornton Mellon discussing aspects of the technology exchange, but they had not discussed the upcoming attack. Jonah was happy to take the time to explain.

He was in an unusual spot. It seemed odd to him to be heading into combat as an observer instead of as an active participant. He felt he had more time on his hands than he knew what to do with, so he was happy to take some of it to go over the coalition's plans with Amy. She was an attentive listener and had a way of looking into his eye that he found somewhat mesmerizing.

She asked intelligent questions. She agreed with the assessment of the intelligence services that the Rodinans would fight it out rather than retreat. "Politically unpalatable," she said, shaking her head. She seemed puzzled at first as to why the Rodinans would be waiting out near the entrances to the hyper corridors instead of taking a position in the middle of the system. When Jonah explained how increasing gravity reduced the ability of ships to maneuver, she grasped the concept quickly. "Gravity sucks," she quipped, "but it's the law."

Jonah had to return to the bridge for the scheduled transition to hyperspace, which ended their discussion. He felt *Indomitable* was prepared for anything.

The coalition force entered and crossed system K3617 on a ballistic course, virtually invisible to the Rodinan frigate that was on picket duty near the corridor to New Bremen. At the front of the coalition formation, two light cruisers were the first to engage their EM drives to adjust course and they headed directly for the Rodinan picket. The frigate immediately entered the hyperspace corridor and disappeared. As soon as it transited, Admiral Schwarzkopf sent orders to the rest of the ships to adjust their formation and proceed to the corridor.

As their transit time through K3617 had been more than three days, Jonah spent much of the time touring the ship. With a crew of 650, Jonah didn't feel as close to the crew as he had on the smaller ships he'd commanded. Touring the ship was difficult to accomplish in one day. He still made the effort but necessarily had to rely on his subordinates to a greater extent than in the past. He was blessed with good officers, both commissioned and non-coms. Tom Bradshaw told him *Indomitable* was a "happy" ship and Jonah had no reason to doubt.

Jonah was on the bridge for the transition to hyperspace but then went to the mess for dinner. Amy joined him a few minutes later. After a few minutes of small talk, she cut herself off mid-sentence, muttering to herself, "Screw it!"

Jonah cocked his eyebrow at her as she took a deep breath. "Look," she said, "I know we've done all sorts of planning and that the odds are in our favor in whatever action we face and that *Indomitable* is just supposed to be an observer and not really in the thick of things, but they're going to be shooting at us, right? And they could hit us, and all sorts of bad things could happen. I'm really scared and feel like I'm half about to barf and you're just sitting there chewing your green beans and making chit-chat like any other day."

Jonah smiled, finished chewing and took a sip of water. "I like green beans. What can I say?" he teased.

She glared at him. He held up his hand in apology. "You learn to focus on different things—more on things you can control and not so much on all the bad things that might happen. To tell you the truth, Amy, I'm more unsettled going into this action than I've been for some time."

"Oh baloney!" she exclaimed. "You're sitting there, calm as Buddha. Don't give me that!"

Jonah shook his head. "God's truth, Amy. I guess I've just learned not to let my fears control me, at least in battles. People—well, I've had some trouble with that. But for instance, the last action, in Roosevelt—we were out-numbered, out-gunned and most of the fleet was unprepared. We knew we were going to get the crap kicked out of us, and I was scared, no question. But I was also pretty powerfully pissed off that Johannsen put us in that position and was trying with the help of others to make the best out of an impossible situation. So, I focused on what I could do and on being pissed off and didn't dwell on being scared."

"What about that time on *Cumberland*? When you guys were all alone?"

she asked.

"Oh, I was pretty sure we were all going to die," Jonah smiled ruefully. "But again, for as long as I could, I focused on what we could do. When I couldn't do that anymore, I guess my main emotion was sadness."

"So, you're saying I should focus on something else? Like what?"

"Well, you've had a pretty busy time working on these agreements. Are all your reports up-to-date? All your files as well-documented as you would like them, in case anything did happen to you? Force yourself to take care of that, even though it's likely the least pleasant part of your job."

Amy snorted.

"Hey," Jonah protested, "I didn't say it would be easy. If you find that too distasteful, I find physical activity helps. Go to the health center, work out, fight the 'bot, find a way to burn off nervous energy."

She thought for a moment or two and replied, "Alright. I'll give it a try. But how can you eat when you feel sick to your stomach?"

"Can't help you there," Jonah shrugged. "That one took me years."

Amy gave up trying to eat, picked up her tray and left. Jonah finished his dinner then went to the bridge for a short spell of duty. His executive officer had tweaked the rotations so that he and the rest of the Alpha rotation would be on duty when they entered the New Bremen system. After his 90-minute shift, he returned to his cabin and went to bed.

No sooner had his head touched the pillow when he heard a soft knock on the door. He got up and opened it. Amy, wearing a robe, squirmed past him into the room. She dropped the robe, which was all she was wearing, and slid into his bed.

"You're the one who told me to do something physical to burn off nervous energy," she giggled. "I figured this would be better than kicking you in the head."

Jonah sat down on his bunk and ran his hand through his hair. "Wow," he breathed, then, "uh—Amy? I really like you—"

"Oh, shit," she exclaimed, sitting up, holding the sheet to her chest. "But you don't like me that way."

"No, No! That's not it!" he protested quickly. "I really, really like you and wanted to try to start something with you when we got back to the world, and I don't want to mess that up!"

"Oh…Sure…I'd like to start something with you too," she replied, wrapping her arms around his neck. "How about now instead?" She pulled him into a kiss.

Eight hours later, Jonah's comm chimed to wake him up. Amy was still in his bunk, her hair spread over the pillow, facing him. She cracked open her left eye. "Good morning," she mumbled. "Sorry if I messed up your plan to woo me."

Jonah chuckled in response.

She continued, "I know you wanted to wait, but I've been wanting to do that for a couple of weeks."

"Ever since you kicked me in the head?"

"Before," she admitted. "The bashing of your head was just a bonus."

50

Just under an hour before their emergence from the hyperspace corridor, Jonah took his seat on the bridge of *Indomitable*. Commander Mellon was at the tactical station. Jonah reviewed the logs and chatted with Mel and the other members of the bridge crew to pass the time.

Eventually, the warning of hyperspace emergence chimed. "Strap in everyone," Jonah ordered. As soon as he felt the flip in his stomach that marked the transition to normal space, he called, "Shields up! Sensors hot!"

"Contact!" Mellon called. "I've got Rodinans and the coalition. Coalition task force is reassembling formation. Rodinans are in transit from outside the Saxony corridor, range from their observed position is approximately 191 light-minutes. Sensors show them in formation, heading toward us. Assuming they continue, minimum time to intercept is just over five hours. Task force is heading to meet the Rodinans at 500G, captain."

"Navigation," Jonah called, "have us take our position at the rear of the formation if you would. Match course and speed."

The formation of the coalition task force was egg-shaped, with the more acute end pointing in the direction of the enemy. They would stay in this formation as long as possible before shifting into the final attack formation as late as possible. Which attack formation they used would depend on how the Rodinans arranged their ships. Admiral Schwarzkopf would issue that command.

Because of the distance, the information on the Rodinan fleet was three hours old by the time the coalition received it. The Rodinans, if they had positioned sensor drones with kewpie links outside the hyper corridors, would have no light-speed lag in seeing the coalition fleet when it entered. It was one of the disadvantages one faced when invading another system. As the two combatants neared one another, the light-speed lag would decrease until they reached maximum missile range, at which point the lag would be less than six seconds. In addition, the Rodinans had been tipped off by their picket ship, which is how they knew where the coalition would emerge from hyperspace.

Ordinarily, the Rodinans would expect the coalition force to decelerate as they drew nearer. In past fleet actions, the side which could launch more missiles would hope to maximize the amount of time both fleets were engaged since the numerical advantage would likely increase with each salvo while the side at a disadvantage would try to avoid a slugfest. The disadvantaged side would attempt to whittle down the stronger force in a series of hit and run attacks if possible.

The innovation of the towed missile frames had changed the coalition's thinking since they would be able to launch an initial salvo that was nearly double what they estimated the Rodinan defense net could handle. With the opposing forces approaching one another at as much as $0.3c$ and with missile reload times of as much as 90 seconds for some coalition ships, engaging in a high-speed pass would enable each side to fire only one salvo. The coalition hoped that they would be able to inflict significant damage in a single pass, then would return and deal with the Rodinan survivors.

Depending on the outcome of the initial engagement, the coalition would signal the troop carriers to enter the hyper corridor and head to New Bremen Station when they exited. The coalition greatly preferred to attempt to take the station instead of obliterating it. The escorts would have to eliminate the orbital defense platforms before the troop carriers could reach the station. Of particular importance was the shipyard attached to the station. Even though intelligence had indicated that the Rodinans had removed most of the equipment years ago, the physical structure itself represented an enormous capital investment.

For now, there was little to do but wait. Jonah turned the bridge over to Commander Mellon and went to his ready room to deal with some of the never-ending paperwork that plagued any commander of a Royal Navy vessel. After a couple of hours, he gave up and went to get a bite to eat before returning to the bridge. He sent Mellon to take a break, asking him to return a half-hour before the estimated time of intercept.

Jonah passed the time chatting with the bridge crew. The distance between the coalition and Rodinan forces continued to close. Mellon returned on schedule.

Shortly after his arrival Mellon reported, "Flagship has ordered formation Alpha-Delta, captain, and for all ships to tow frames."

Jonah had been expecting this. The Rodinans so far had not shifted out of their egg-shaped formation. He considered it unlikely that they would, as their current alignment maximized the effectiveness of an integrated point-defense network. The semi-spherical coalition formation would "cup" the approaching Rodinans and give the coalition their best chance of breaking through the Rodinan defense net.

At the center of the "cup" were *Gaulois* and *Normandie*, the French superdreadnoughts. This made sense since the point-defense network was being run from *Gaulois*. *Krakow*, Rotterdam's superdreadnought, was positioned above them, flanked by *Akagi* and *Hiru*. Flanking the center and positioned below were the five German superdreadnoughts, with *München* below the center of the formation.

Commander Mellon displayed a clock counting down to the time when both sides would be in missile range. *Indomitable* had not been integrated into the tactical net as the coalition insisted that they not take part in the attack. The compromise they had offered was to include *Indomitable* in the point-defense network. With both fleets closing so quickly, the time between missile launch and impact would be less than ten seconds. This battle would be extremely brief.

When the clock reached zero, Mellon confirmed, "Coalition missiles away." A moment later, "Rodinan launch detected." Then, "Holy shit! The point-defense net just crashed!"

Mellon's fingers flew over his console as he brought *Indomitable's* defenses back under the ship's own control.

"We're not being targeted, skipper, but—"

Within seconds, sensor blooms showed what happened. *Gaulois*, *Normandie* and *Krakow* exploded, ripping out the center of the coalition formation. The French battlecruiser *Glorieux* also disappeared.

The coalition attack had done even more damage to the Rodinans. Three of their superdreadnoughts had been destroyed, while the other two had lost power and were spewing atmosphere from multiple hull breaches as they drifted, powerless and ejecting life pods. The captains of those ships had already signaled their surrender by lowering their remaining shields. Five of the six Rodinan battlecruisers had been wiped out and the remaining one appeared to have taken serious damage. A heavy cruiser, two light cruisers and two frigates had also survived and appeared to be forming up on the damaged battlecruiser.

"Coalition flag has ordered full deceleration burn. Damage reports are flowing in, Skip," Mellon announced.

"Match deceleration with the fleet. What do you think happened, Mel?"

"Don't know, captain, but I'd guess sabotage," Mellon offered. "Systems just don't crash like that."

"Let's adjourn to my ready room and take a look at what happened on the projector," Jonah ordered. Looking around, he saw *Indomitable's* second officer. "Lieutenant Commander Radcliffe, take the bridge."

Jonah and Mellon went to the ready room and activated the holographic display. Mellon set it at the time of missile launch, advancing it slowly while consulting a tablet that provided information on different elements. He paused the display.

"Sensors indicate that the Rodinans launched 1,036 missiles, the coalition fired 1,458. ONI was correct about them being able to launch towed missiles. Now, here," he said, while keying the tablet, "we see the coalition point-defense net." A multi-formed green bubble surrounded the icons representing the coalition ships in the display.

Mellon allowed the display to advance slowly. The green bubble disappeared. He stopped the display. "That's when the defense net went down, skipper—about 1.8 seconds after launch."

Mellon resumed the display. Two new multi-formed bubbles popped into the display centered on *Akagi* and *Hiru*. "Wow," Mellon commented under his breath, "that was quick." Turning to Jonah, he added, "The Edoans restored a point-defense net on their own ships in less than a second."

"That is quick," Jonah agreed.

"If I were to guess," Mellon mused, "I'd reckon they had a fail-safe built into their system. To respond that quickly, it had to be an automated response. Based on what I've learned about their systems and capabilities, it makes sense."

"Okay, advance the display again," Jonah asked.

Mellon allowed the display to move forward, then glanced at his tablet and stopped it. He keyed in a couple of commands and had the display move backward. "Here," he pointed at some yellow dots. "It looks like the Rodinans lost guidance on some of their missiles."

"How many?" Jonah asked.

"Let me see," Mellon responded and advanced the display very slowly, then stopped it. "This is exactly four seconds after launch and the sensors indicate that 211 of their missiles lost guidance and went rogue. That's roughly two-thirds of the towed missiles they launched. Obviously, they have systems problems."

"Keep going," Jonah requested.

Mellon advanced the display and multi-formed green bubbles now started to appear, centered on the German superdreadnoughts, with one on *Indomitable*, trailing the rest of the formation. He paused the display. "Here, the Germans have begun to restore their point-defense, at almost the same time we did." He advanced the display and the bubbles around the German ships began to expand to include surrounding escorts. "It took the Germans and us almost three seconds to bring back point-defense—the difference between an automated fail-safe and human control."

Jonah's comm buzzed. "Mel, that's Schwarzkopf. Continue your analysis and write it up. I'll go find out how bad things are."

Jonah returned to the bridge and connected to the German admiral. Admiral Niimura was also on the comm. Both men looked grim.

Schwarzkopf spoke first. "We've lost *Gaulois*, *Normandie*, *Glorieux* and *Krakow*," he stated flatly. *München*, *Stuttgart* and *Köln* all took significant damage. *Frankfurt* and *Hamburg* took some minor damage."

Niimura added, "*Akagi* and *Hiru* suffered only minor damage, mostly cosmetic. We were able to restore point-defense more quickly."

"We don't know what happened aboard *Gaulois*," Schwarzkopf resumed, "to cause the defense net to collapse, and will likely never know now, but our people suspect the FSB played a part."

Both Jonah and Niimura nodded in agreement.

"Regardless, the damage is done." Schwarzkopf sighed. "With the loss of those ships and the damage we sustained, I don't see how we could hold the system. I'm going to contact my superiors and suggest you both do the same. I'm going to recommend that we withdraw. I will comm you both again in three hours. Schwarzkopf out."

The comm ended. Jonah buzzed Amy and asked her to come to his ready room. Jonah turned the bridge over to Radcliffe again and went to join her.

Commander Mellon was still there, working on his report. He looked up. "Bad news, Skip?"

"Yeah," Jonah said. "Let's wait for Miss Davidson and I'll tell you both."

Amy came in a few seconds later. "I heard it didn't go well," she offered.

"It didn't," Jonah confirmed. He and Mellon explained to Amy what had happened, with Mellon using the holographic display to provide detail. He then told them that Schwarzkopf was recommending that they withdraw and that he and Miss Davidson should comm Admiral Lothes and Foreign Secretary Stewart-Crosland.

All three were quiet for a moment. Mellon broke the silence. "Damn. That sucks." He pushed himself away from the table and rose. "I'll finish my report in my quarters, Skip."

Jonah nodded. "Thanks, Mel." He then suggested to Amy, "It will probably be best for us both to call the admiral and foreign secretary. I think we should probably start with Admiral Lothes. What do you think?"

"Yes," she agreed. "The military situation is dictating the diplomatic, so Admiral Lothes first."

51

Jonah initiated the comm to Admiral Lothes. A yeoman answered and asked him to hold. After roughly 30 seconds, Admiral Lothes appeared, looking sleep-disheveled. Jonah winced as he realized it was the middle of the night for her.

Jonah apologized but quickly began a summary of the battle that had just taken place. He informed her that Commander Mellon would be transmitting the after-action report shortly and finished by telling her that Admiral Schwarzkopf had indicated that the coalition would be pulling back. When he was done, Admiral Lothes rubbed her face with her hands and grimaced.

She took a deep breath then and responded, "Captain Halberd, when we're done, get on the horn and earnestly request Admiral Schwarzkopf to delay his decision for a few hours—the longer, the better, but try to get at least six hours from now."

"Yes, sir," Jonah responded.

"You and Miss Davidson have done a heckuva job, captain," Lothes commented, "and there are now a lot of things in motion on the diplomatic front with these nonaligned systems as a result. That's all I can say at the moment, so beg Schwarzkopf for more time before he pulls the plug. Have Commander Mellon transmit that report as soon as it's finished. Lothes out."

Amy and Jonah looked at one another. "What does that mean?" she asked.

"Heck if I know." Jonah answered.

He then initiated a comm to Admiral Schwarzkopf. The German Admiral's flag lieutenant, Hebborn, answered and informed Jonah that the admiral was currently unavailable. Jonah asked if he could hold and wait.

"Is this important, captain?" Lieutenant Hebborn inquired politely.

"Yes," Jonah replied. "I just spoke with my admiral, and she ordered me to beg Admiral Schwarzkopf not to make a decision to withdraw for at least six hours. I hate to ask you to do this, but would you be so kind as to write a note to the admiral and tell him that? That I've been ordered to beg him to delay issuing withdrawal orders?"

While he was speaking, Amy's comm buzzed. She looked at the screen. She caught Jonah's eye, pointed at her comm and left the room quickly.

Meanwhile, Lieutenant Hebborn commented, "This is unusual, but it has been an unusual time, no? Please hold."

The comm portion of Jonah's console went to a "hold" screen. The message scroll lit up with a text from Amy: "Fgn Secy. Big stuff."

While Jonah was waiting, someone knocked on the door of the ready room. When he called, "Enter," Commander Mellon came in.

Mellon noticed the "hold" screen, then said, "I just filed the after-action report."

Sure enough, the icon on Jonah's console indicated that the report had just entered his queue. Mellon nodded at the "hold" screen. "What's up, Skip?"

Quietly, Jonah explained, "Commed Lothes. She told me to beg Schwarzkopf not to withdraw yet. Waiting for him."

Mellon raised his eyebrows in mild surprise. Just then, Lieutenant Hebborn's face reappeared on the comm. "One moment, captain, and I'll connect you."

Admiral Schwarzkopf appeared on screen. "I was on the line with my admiralty, captain," he explained, "discussing what to do. During this, they received a comm from the chancellor's office. I now have new orders. I am to destroy or capture the Rodinan ships that remain in the system. I am to proceed with the assault on New Bremen Station and I am to delay issuing any withdrawal orders for at least 24 hours. Do you have anything to do with this or know why I received these orders?"

"I do not, admiral," Jonah responded truthfully. "I just commed my admiral to tell her what had happened, and she ordered me to beg you to delay issuing withdrawal orders for at least six hours."

"That's what the note said."

"That's all I know, admiral."

"Hmmmph. Very well, captain. I might have a job for you. Since my admiralty wants me to eliminate those six Rodinan ships, I asked them to contact your government to ask if we could change you from an observer to a combatant. I'd like you to go with *Takao*, the Edoan battlecruiser, two French light cruisers—*Marseillaise* and *Brest*—and two Rotterdamian frigates—*Tromp* and *Evertsen*—to destroy or capture the Rodinan ships. The Rodinans have set a course for the hyper corridor back to the Federation but are moving quite slowly. If you set off now, you should be able to intercept in less than a day. That should give the politicians plenty of time to change your orders, don't you think?"

"I hope so, sir," Jonah agreed.

"Good. I'm putting you in command, captain, and instructing the other ships as we speak. You'll need to exchange kewpie pairs with them, but I understand for now, you can contact them through the tac net. I will transmit your orders momentarily. Any questions?"

"No, sir. If my Admiralty confirms my change in status, there should be no problem."

"Good luck, then. Schwarzkopf out."

Mellon spoke up. "That's good news, I think."

"I agree." Jonah sent a text message to Admiral Lothes: "Admiral Schwarzkopf has requested that *Indomitable* change from observer to combatant, to eliminate six Rodinan ships remaining from engagement. Please advise."

Lothes responded immediately with a text: "Approved."

Mellon whistled softly. "Something *must* be up, Skip."

"How do I use the tac net to contact these guys?" Jonah asked.

"Let me take care of that, Skip," Mellon replied. "Give me five minutes and I'll set up a sub-net so we can get started. I'll work with the XOs to get the kewpie pairs sorted out."

"Sounds good, Mel. I'll grab a look at where the Rodinans are and figure out our intercept. Let's set up a joint comm for—" he looked at the clock, "20:00. That's a little less than 30 minutes from now."

Orders from Admiral Schwarzkopf had already arrived when Jonah used his console to show him the location of the Rodinan ships. Before Jonah could look at it carefully, his console and comm buzzed. The screen displayed a "Priority Override" message he had never seen before. He connected and a woman asked, "Captain Halberd?"

"Yes."

"Please hold for the Prime Minister."

ABOUT THE AUTHOR

John Spearman (Jake to his friends and colleagues) is a Latin teacher and coach at a prestigious New England boarding school. Before joining the world of academia, Spearman had been a sales and marketing executive for 25 years. In 2006, he walked away from an executive position with a Fortune 500 company to return to school. He earned his MA in Latin in a calendar year and began teaching thereafter. The Jonah Halberd series of books arose from his wife suggesting he find a hobby.

Dear Reader, if you enjoyed this book, please leave a positive review on amazon.com. Since sales of these books are in the tens, rather than tens of thousands, a positive review is what keeps me going. If you did not enjoy the book, I'm sorry.

Printed in Great Britain
by Amazon